Final Curtain

Final Curtain

An Edna Ferber Mystery

Ed Ifkovic

Poisoned Pen Press

Poisoned Pen Press
6962 E. First Ave., Ste. 103
Scottsdale, AZ 85251
www.poisonedpenpress.com
info@poisonedpenpress.com

Printed in the United States of America

for David Gillon,
thanks for friendship

Chapter One

The checkered cab slid to a smooth stop at the curb, and the doorman rushed to open the back door, a knightly gesture that unfortunately demanded he also shift the umbrella he held over my head, thus exposing me to the warm July drizzle. The hot sidewalk sizzled under the surprise rain shower.

"Mr. Kaufman," James purred, spotting the familiar face in the backseat. "A pleasure."

George leaned over and nodded at him. He was grinning widely, a dangerous sign, surely. "Edna, you're late."

"I am not." I glanced at my watch. "*You're* late."

"We've circled the block two times. It's maddening."

I smiled. "George, your inner clock is always set at…Pittsburgh."

"For God's sake, Edna, get in. James is getting wet."

I tucked myself into the backseat as the cab sped off—a little too Wild West for my taste. We slipped breezily across two jam-packed lanes, narrowly missing a lumbering city bus. I turned to George. "I really didn't expect you this afternoon, George. Your phone call took me by surprise." My tone purposely suggested that his presence was not only unexpected but unwanted.

But with that wide, feckless grin still plastered on his face, he drummed his fingers on the back of the driver's seat. "Edna dear, there are some events in life you don't want to miss: your wedding—mine, not yours, of course—a corned-beef-on-rye sandwich at the Carnegie Deli, and the redoubtable Edna Ferber making a fool of herself."

I bristled. "George, really. Have you ever seen me make a fool of myself?"

"Give me a day to think about it. Surely any human being on this Earth—"

I broke in. "I am not *any* human being. You should know that by now."

"But you have to admit, Edna, that this...this middle-aged adventure of yours is the stuff of Arthurian—or at least Broadway—legend."

I repeated the feeble rationale I'd rehearsed and meekly delivered for a month now. "It's just a lark, George. A lovely lark."

That quizzical smile persisted, though his words now betrayed an icy sharpness. "Your enemies are already sharpening their swords. Or should I say pencils?"

For a moment, quaking, I glanced out the window. Crowds shuffled along, lost under umbrellas. As the cab began moving through Central Park—purposely searching for puddles, it seemed—I felt a little dizzy. I turned back, faced him. "I have no enemies, George."

Now the smile broke into hearty laughter, uncontrolled. That was not like George S. Kaufman, esteemed American playwright and celebrated humorist. A knife-in-the-gut kind of wit, this writer, and never the rollicking barrel of laughs. Sardonic humor, sly innuendo, tricky phraseology, smart talk, outright sass—all his hallmarks, but rarely vaudevillian laugh-in-the-aisles guffaws. Until now—on this bizarre cab ride. And thus troublesome. When George approached the freedom of utter abandonment, he was at his most dangerous. Cruel, deliberate, hurtful, a man to be avoided. He was especially menacing around close friends. And I was a good and true friend, and one of his most successful collaborators on Broadway hits.

"Why didn't you stay at the farm in Pennsylvania?" I asked him.

"Well, I have a surprise, which you'll probably not welcome. I had a talk with Cheryl a few days ago, and we discussed your... folly. Ferber's Folly, I termed it. Then last night she called, one of her panicky calls, and I told her I'd be in the city today and would gather you from your expensive lair. I invited myself to visit with you and Cheryl."

I smiled. "So you've chosen to be the pesky fly that annoys innocent folks having coffee."

"Exactly." His eyes twinkled. "Edna Ferber the actress, the venerable Fanny Cavendish of *The Royal Family* in summer stock…in…good God! Oh no!…New Jersey."

"George, you know that I've always wanted to be onstage. I've bored enough dinner parties with that declaration. I've always seen myself as a blighted Bernhardt."

He stifled a laugh. "Edna, playwrights usually run for cover. We *hide* behind our typewriters."

I didn't like myself betraying such a weakness. "It's something I always wanted to do."

"Edna, I'd like to do a lot of things, but I resist the impulse."

I sucked in my cheeks. "That's the difference between us, George. I like the novelty of surprise. You are surprised by novelty."

"Lord, Edna, are we rewriting *The Royal Family* in the back-seat of a cab?"

Now I smiled. "George, behave yourself today."

"Why start now?'

He sat back, this string bean of a man, all angles, with his long quirky face hidden behind huge tortoise-shell glasses that exaggerated his huge nose. A high forehead under that Cliffs-of-Dover pompadour of uncombed pitch-black hair. Dressed in an expensive charcoal-gray suit with a wide burgundy tie, he pulled at the cuffs of his sleeves, a nervous gesture I'd become familiar with. That, and his constant tying and retying of his shoelaces. A fussbudget, nosy, abrupt, and acerbic, he looked the gangly nebbish, the butt of nickelodeon humor; but there was something else about the man. A first glance at him suggested an unattractive, bumbling sort, a sad sack; but when his face moved, when the long arms gesticulated like wild birds, there suddenly was a fierce beauty about him—an inner heat that drew you in. You saw it when he maneuvered his way around people, especially the fresh young backstage chorines he pursued feverishly. Those times revealed a magnetism that compelled, startled.

I saw it now, in the backseat of that jerky cab. His rollicking, uncharacteristic laughter made him dreadfully irritating—but oddly seductive.

It drove me mad, that warring mixture of personality. Aleck Woollcott, my sometime friend and chronic enemy, chided that I had a schoolgirl crush on the estimable George S. Kaufman. I suppose I did, but a slight, curable one. Of course, I'd never confess that to anyone. All my clandestine affairs of the heart migrated into the romantic lives of my feisty heroines.

The cab wove through the park, turned onto Columbus and over to Riverside, stopping in front of a weather-beaten building that fronted the Hudson River. Here producer Cheryl Crawford rented a furnished pied-à-terre on the top floor. Coffee, she'd said yesterday on the phone, just the two of us, an informal talk about my playing the matriarch Fanny Cavendish in her summer-stock production of *The Royal Family*, the hit play George and I wrote some thirteen years earlier, now to be resurrected in suburban New Jersey. Resurrected, I thought, with the end of tremendously amusing George and others of my friends. Edna gets to play actress, mouthing lines she wrote. Let's see her succumb to stage fright, to missed cues, to blathered, tangled dialogue. To abject panic, the deer in the headlights. Summer fun for the Manhattan cosmopolites. Something to do in the hot summer of 1940 as the world out there readied for another cataclysmic war.

"George," I mumbled as I stepped out of the cab, "just why are you here today?"

"I wouldn't miss this for the world." Then, a crooked smile. "And there are surprises in store for you."

Cheryl Crawford seemed thrilled to see George. He nodded at her—he felt shaking hands with folks spread Bubonic plague—and handed her a bouquet of roses I'd not noticed until he stepped out of the cab.

"Cheryl, dear, Edna insists I go everywhere with her. Such a damper on my social life."

Cheryl laughed but I smiled. "George trails me around like an old rheumatic dog."

"Ah, but one looking for new tricks."

Cheryl's small studio was stark in its decor: a glossy black leather Italian sofa set against a white wall, a huge Kandinsky-style painting behind it, illuminated. A long, dark-wood coffee table with an amorphous Brancusi statue plopped in the middle, too large and thus one of the objects in the room your eyes found—and not pleasantly. Cheryl saw me gaping at the ungainly statue. "I'm squatting here until the work on my apartment on Forty-ninth Street is ready." She smiled. "It's very…European, I think." She waved her arms around the sleek, expensive room and mentioned the name of some curator at the Metropolitan. "She's in London for the summer. She told me to safeguard the Kandinsky."

"It's real?"

"I suppose so." Cheryl glanced at it. "The sofa is a pull-out bed so I have to sleep under such…such lightning flashes of color." Kandinsky's swirling hiccoughs of vibrant color—all colliding and shrill—would drive me mad…and guarantee sleepless nights.

George was sitting in a side chair, eyeing a wedge of chocolate fudge. He'd poured himself a cup of coffee.

"There's a patisserie over on Amsterdam. Wonderful."

George swallowed. "This visit is already a success."

George was notoriously indifferent to food, save rich and creamy chocolate, which Cheryl obviously knew. I guessed the crisp apple strudel next to it was intended for me. I smiled. "George the avaricious gourmand," I grumbled, "with chocolate smears on his cadaverous cheek."

He nodded at Cheryl. "Edna likes to use big words. As a child in Appleton, she swallowed a dictionary. That explains her sudden digestive surprises."

Cheryl had invited me for coffee, a social invitation to review our final arrangements for my participation in her production of *The Royal Family* in the middle of August in Maplewood, New Jersey. Although our paths crossed around Broadway over the years, we'd never been friends. "Come for coffee," she'd told me. "A chat."

I knew she was close to George and his wife Bea—more so, his wife—and George often insisted she and I would like each other—two driven, single women, hard-nosed. I'd be the judge of that.

"You two look alike," he'd said.

Nonsense, of course. Cheryl was a tiny woman, slender, late thirties, with fits of restless energy. With her blue-gray eyes lost in a drab plain face, with curly close-cropped brown hair, she often seemed all business and purpose. She had to be—this vagrant woman producer in the exclusive man's-club world of Broadway. A "producer in skirts"—the dismissive phrase bandied about. She spoke in a clipped, forced voice with dry, hard-edged wit, and often reminded me of a character from a Damon Runyon story: hard-boiled, no-nonsense, and unblinking. A hard-drinking, chain-smoking woman. Like me, she sometimes wore mannish tailored suits, though I softened mine with obligatory strands of pearls and flowery brooches stolen from some Victorian treasure chest. George once insisted we were Siamese twins, joined at the hip.

"No," I countered, "joined at the intellect."

Now, idly but pleasantly, we chatted about the production of *The Royal Family*. Cheryl, a successful Broadway producer, had envisioned a summer stock with veteran Broadway actors in celebrated plays at the end of their New York run, with topnotch crews. She'd located a vast unused movie theater opposite the train station in bucolic Maplewood, a half-hour train commute from Penn Station, and was making a go of it—cheap tickets, short week runs, big names like Tallulah Bankhead and Paul Robeson and Luise Rainer. And me, Edna Ferber, writer and notoriously a non-actor who harbored delusions that…well…

Well, that was now reality. George and I had written *The Royal Family* back in 1927, a huge Broadway hit, then a splashy 1930 Hollywood movie called *The Royal Family of Broadway*, starring Frederic March, a veritable comedy-drama that everyone said was based on the Barrymore family—matriarch Mrs. Drew and her grandchildren, John and Ethel. But not Lionel, the boring brother. George and I protested. No, no, impossible, barely recognizable, though no one believed us. If anything, it was based on an earlier theatrical family, the Davenports. Who? folks questioned. Oh, really? Yeah, sure.

Infuriated, Ethel had threatened to sue us (and so, mockingly, did the frivolous Marx Brothers), and Ethel still cold-shouldered me at cocktail parties. She had a magnificent harrumph sound, very haughty, perfected through years of natural bile, that echoed off sleek Park Avenue walls. Robert Benchley once claimed she spoke in an Episcopalian voice, measured, deadly, each syllable heavy as iron. I found it amusing that she refused the celebrity that George and I inadvertently (yes, unintentionally) delivered to her. *The Royal Family* ran for 343 performances.

Now it would run for one week in New Jersey with me as Fanny Cavendish, the craggy, grumpy, but eminently elegant matriarch of the legendary Broadway family. My moment in the dramatic sun.

And I feared I'd misstepped. At the moment the nagging presence of George Kaufman at my elbow suggested I was right. Despite his satiric wit, George had the uncanny bad luck to be in places where disaster struck. He was the sort who mindlessly stumbled onto the platform just as two trains collided. Or the manhole cover exploded as his taxi zoomed over it. All of which thrilled him. Now, I supposed, I was providing the unnatural disaster he dared not miss. It had been Cheryl Crawford's idea that I play the part—admittedly she'd heard tales of me kvetching about my untapped dramaturgical genius. When George and I wrote the play, I suggested I play Julie, but George cast a jaundiced eye on me, and never answered. But now I suspected

George had put the bug in her ear. *Get Edna, Cheryl. Crowds will gladly pay a dollar-fifty for that three-ring circus.*

Cheryl was watching George closely now. I'd missed something being said.

Which was why I narrowed my eyes at him—he was blithely snapping up another piece of chocolate—and asked, in an exaggerated Southern belle inflection, "George, dear, are you coming to see me perform?"

Cheryl sputtered, looked confused. "George, you didn't…"

George never looked up. "Everyone is, Edna. We'll talk of this for years. You'll have to move to someplace no one goes to. Like…New Jersey."

"Please stay away, George."

"Not on your life."

Cheryl jumped in, nervous. "George, you told me you'd talked to Edna." A look of horror on her face, she turned to me. "Edna, George is up to no good. You see, our director Lawrence Burton is suddenly hospitalized and will be gone all summer, so I begged George to be the director of *The Royal Family*. A last-minute replacement. He said…"

"What?" I screamed. "George, when were you planning on telling me?"

"Just about now." His eyes got wide and shiny. "What fun we'll have, Edna."

George as director was legendary: authoritative, driven, but often horribly cruel. Dare I say…maniacal?

Cheryl sat back, flustered, but finally smiled. "All right, then, it's settled." A cautious pause. "More coffee, Edna?"

I glared at him. "So that's why you intruded on this afternoon chat."

"My dear, I wanted to see the pleasure in your face firsthand."

"Good." Cheryl looked content. "Edna dear, you're going early, you said?"

"Yes." My one-word response was glacial.

The one-week rehearsal didn't start for another week, but I'd be leaving in two days. I wanted to wander about the town—to collect myself, unhampered by busybody friends and a willful mother back in Connecticut. I'd be in the city for two more days, camping out with Peg Pulitzer, already having shipped a trunk on to Maplewood. Curiously, I'd have to memorize the lines I'd written myself. I'd forgotten so much as life moved on. In *The Royal Family*, Fanny's granddaughter Julie wants to leave the stage for a bizarre South American marriage. Grandson Tony (like pleasure-seeking and flamboyant John Barrymore, but don't tell anyone) has headed to Hollywood to lead a wild, dissolute life. The matriarch Fanny sees her beloved world crumbling. She insists there must always be a Cavendish headed out on the road or trodding the Broadway boards. Though she dies at the end—yes, this is still a comedy, though of manners—her resolve successfully holds the family to the age-old theatrical tradition. Success! Somehow I'd have to embody Fanny's venerable position—the steely-eyed, steel-ribbed woman who holds the play together. If I wrote the part, I could play the part. I told myself that over and over. Sometimes—early mornings—I actually believed it.

Earlier on the phone Cheryl told me she was hoping for a serene, uneventful summer. Last year actress Jane Wyatt, granting an interview to a giddy high-school student, announced that she was traveling shortly to Italy and hoped to meet Mussolini. "A firestorm, that indiscreet remark," she'd added. "She also mentioned the Pope, but the protest lingered."

I'd shivered. "That horrid man. Hitler's brutal sidekick."

Cheryl was now talking about a phone call earlier that week from Bea, George's wife. "I found myself saying yes, though I don't know why."

"What are we talking about?" I asked.

Cheryl looked irritated that I'd not been paying attention.

George was snickering. "Cheryl, Edna's already on that stage, taking a bow and accepting my bouquet of golden rod."

Cheryl leaned in. "George didn't tell you? Good God, George, what *do* you tell Edna?"

"Only what she doesn't want to hear."

I offered a sickly smile. "Obviously not always."

"Bea asked a favor," Cheryl went on. "It seems she has an old friend from her very short time at Wellesley, whose son is an actor. He asked to understudy the part of Tony, Louis Calhern's part. I told her we've been using another bit player, mostly unnecessary, but…" She breathed in. "Well, this Evan Street is now our understudy."

A bad feeling in my gut. "What do you know about him?"

"I checked, of course. A brief time in Hollywood where everyone spends a 'brief time,' a couple minor roles on Broadway, good-looking, eager."

George was staring at the Kandinsky. "And obviously a charmer, if he got Bea to pimp for him."

"Well, Bea rarely asks for favors."

"Which is why she is always granted them," George noted.

I added, "I doubt if we'll need him for one week's play-acting."

Cheryl shrugged. "Won't hurt."

"George, did you know about this?" I pointed a finger at him.

"Bea may have mentioned it."

"What do you know about this Evan Street?"

"I met him once or twice at some dinner his mother hosted. She's a schoolteacher in Scarsdale. We actually had to *go* there."

I smirked. "Lord, a pioneer into uncharted wilderness. You and Ponce de Leon."

"No Fountain of Youth, I'm afraid. It was Scarsdale, Edna. People believe in manicured lawns and manicured lives."

"You didn't like him," I concluded.

George's eyes were shiny. "Good for you, Edna. He's tall and athletic and dark and handsome—too handsome, really. Large cobalt-blue eyes. A real lady-killer. Ladies deny such men nothing."

"We'll see about that."

"Edna, I said…ladies." His mouth was filled with chocolate, so his words were mumbled.

Cheryl was trying to say something, finally cutting in. "You two. You're always writing dialogue you'll never use."

"Cheryl, you want to say something?" From me, all smiles.

"Well, this dashing hero, in fact, just called me. He thanked me for giving him a chance. He wanted Maplewood desperately, he said. He claims to know so much about my theater—a lie, of course. Yet he did seem to know Maplewood. The town. God knows why. That gave me pause."

"What's your point, Cheryl?"

"He flattered me mercilessly, even lowering his voice provocatively. I enjoyed every second of it, though I believed none of it."

"That's why you're different from Edna," George insisted. "She believes all of it, but enjoys none of it."

"Anyway," Cheryl went on, "he's rather a bold sort. Unapologetically brash. He may kill Louis Calhern to get his chance at playing lead."

The play starred veteran actors Louis Calhern and Irene Purcell, both solid Broadway troopers. Louis was inspired casting as Tony—dark and striking and muscular—and very charming. The compelling cosmopolite. He'd have to watch his back with that aggressive understudy.

George shrugged. "Frank Resnick is stage manager, right?" Cheryl nodded.

"Not Frank from *The Front Page*?" I asked. "I've met him." George nodded. "Exactly. Perfect for the job. The ideal stage manager. Taciturn, deliberate. A no-nonsense guy. A man whose pointed finger makes you jump hoops."

Cheryl added, "You know, he begged for the summer job, which surprised me. He's left the hit *The Fear Factor* at the Selwyn just to work summer stock with me. Unheard of, really. When I asked him why, he said he needed a change. Manhattan was getting to him, he said. Another lie, I figured. But he seemed hell-bent on being in New Jersey this summer. I found it a little odd."

"It is odd," I volunteered. "I've had only one short conversation with him—at some cocktail party. Like me, he didn't want to be there. You talk to the man for a few minutes and he looks as though he's fallen asleep. Then he'll mumble *yes* or *no* or *maybe*.

Then he turns his back on you." I frowned. "Quite the summer you've orchestrated for me, Cheryl."

"Only the best," she said without a smile.

"He'd best control this…this Evan Street." I sat back and sipped my coffee, watching Cheryl over the rim. She avoided looking at me.

"I wonder about that." Cheryl looked to the door.

"What?" From George.

"Well, when he called—earlier today, as I said—I mentioned Edna's visit for coffee and…"

"And he wants my autograph?"

"He invited himself over."

"For Lord's sake, Cheryl." I put down my cup a little too quickly.

"He has that way about him."

George was enjoying this. "Cheryl, I've never considered you subject to frivolous whims and idle flattery—surrendering to a man's charms."

Cheryl didn't seem pleased with that. She celebrated her own toughness, this feisty woman who'd made and sold bathtub gin during Prohibition and was a legendary hard-nosed poker player. Now she stood and moved dishes and plates into the kitchen, ignoring a look from George. She frowned at the Kandinsky, and I didn't blame her: it seemed a fourth presence in the room. Her back to us, Cheryl spoke firmly. "I kept saying no, no, no, and ended up giving him directions."

Of course, at that moment—with the exquisite timing of a Broadway melodrama—the doorbell chimed. Cheryl jumped, I flinched, and George simply shook his head. "Act one, scene one." His voice was laced with a mixture of amusement and, I thought, dread.

Evan Street, the unknown actor, strode into the apartment as though he'd recently conquered in battle, rushing into the center of the room, standing there ramrod straight, arms on hips, head tilted to one side, a dazzling smile directed at no one in particular. The behavior silenced all three of us. I thought suddenly of a Broadway curtain going up and the lead actor assuming the stage and expecting and obtaining the burst of rowdy applause from his loud and devoted claque. But no one applauded now. Evan Street laughed at something no one else heard, and half-bowed.

You saw a young man who seemed a refugee from a nineteenth-century melodrama, the swashbuckling hero—true, *sans* moustache or goatee—but with coal-black hair abundantly swept back from an imposing brow, a wide expansive face, darkly tanned, with a chiseled chin and riveting cobalt-blue eyes that seemed to purposely *not* blink. Tall, slender with a sinewy muscular frame, he stood there, a man used to being considered overwhelmingly attractive, and thus deferred to, willingly, happily. Now, after another rumbling laugh, he seemed to be waiting for an offstage cue to speak. George cleared his throat, and Evan Street spoke. "Hello." A velvet voice, a lover's smooth tenor, calculated, one that no one is born with.

He was still not looking at any of us, his greeting addressed to the Kandinsky on the wall.

It struck me that there was something wrong with his attire. Once you moved your gaze from the classical profile, eerily reminiscent of John Barrymore himself—once you allowed yourself to ignore the rich blueness of those eyes—you noticed the shabby pale blue dress shirt, frayed at the cuffs, the old-fashioned white linen sports jacket, the dark stain on one knee of his rumpled slacks, the cracked leather of his unpolished black-and-white tie shoes. A floppy derby hat, bent, protruded from a pocket of his jacket. The cultivated facial expression and the careful haircut clashed with the Hoover-village tramp. A poor boy, this one.

His was, it turned out, a gaudy cameo performance. He refused coffee, though he did eye the remaining apple strudel with a covetous eye. George had already devoured the remaining chocolate. Evan announced that he'd stay but a second, and began an apology about intruding that rang false. He spoke of the honor of being a part of our ensemble—of working with Cheryl, of working with George and me. "Miss Ferber, you and

Mr. Kaufman wrote those words." Something I already knew, thank you very much. To George in an old boy's-club chuckle, "You, too."

To which George grumbled, "Only the funny parts. Edna wrote the stage directions."

He stayed for perhaps fifteen minutes, doing virtually all the talking now, charming, laughing, flattering, twisting his body left and right, yet rarely looking any of us in the face. It was, perforce, Shakespearean monologue. A feckless Romeo in a West Side pied-à-terre, with nary a Juliet in sight. "I just wanted to say hello. I know I'll never be onstage in Maplewood, but to watch Louis Calhern doing Tony—an *honor* for me. I met Fredric March, you know. I understudied for him at a playhouse in Pasadena, in fact. He told me…" And off he went, lionizing, name-dropping. The fate of modern theater rested on his broad shoulders. Atlas in stage makeup. And Hollywood: that new theater for the world. Another horizon to conquer…someday… first to watch the master…New Jersey…Maplewood…

Maddening. Saccharine.

I interrupted him. "Have you been in Maplewood before?"

That stopped him. He hesitated. "No."

But that was a lie, I sensed—blatant, deliberate. A dark shadow in the eye corner, his head bowed. And for a moment I froze: I did not like this young man. True, I found most young men callous and vainglorious and…well, annoying. A cocksure and preening lot, most of them. The depth of oil cloth. Here, in Evan Street, was their unofficial leader. I understood how easily he could charm folks, particularly unsuspecting women—like, especially, Bea Kaufman, herself delirious around compelling and romantic bounders—but there was something else about this Evan Street: a streak of sly cunning that smacked of cruelty.

I shivered.

And just like that he was gone. Perfunctory handshakes, a curtain-call bow, servility that suggested its opposite—and still an avoidance of eye contact. Waving his hand in the air like a passenger setting sail for Europe from a Manhattan pier, he disappeared.

"Well," I said, "that's a show that'll close on Saturday."

Cheryl was biting a nail. "I may have made a colossal mistake listening to Bea."

"Get used to it." George grinned. "I have."

"But I have to act with him." I glanced toward the doorway.

"Only if Louis Calhern dies."

I shivered again.

Chapter Two

Two days later, two suitcases and a hatbox in hand, I boarded the Lackawanna train at Penn Station and traveled to Maplewood, watching Manhattan disappear. Automobile junkyards and filling stations speckled the landscape. As I stepped off the train, I felt a tug of emotion: the small village with its quiet, lazy-afternoon station, lines of automobiles parked in the shadow of the latticed two-story façade, brought me back to Stepney Depot, the train stop in Connecticut where I lived now, having built a massive fourteen-room Georgian stone house atop a thickly covered hill, just over a year ago. From my terrace I could see Long Island Sound. There, perhaps, the caretaker was now debating whether the old white birch had to be axed. There, now, most likely, my imperious mother was battling with Jason the gardener over the blackberry bushes she insisted were doomed to fail. Or she was sitting by the pool, shaded by a monstrous straw bonnet, writing me a cautionary note that reiterated how foolish my behavior was—once again. "Edna, I'm eating here alone with strangers." Yet I missed that country home because I'd worked for every piece of stone, every positioned fruit tree. Treasure Hill, I called it.

I glanced down the street. With Myer's General Store, Gruning's Ice Cream and Candy Shop, and the clapboard-sided Grange Hall, Maplewood seemed removed from the slick confection of *The Royal Family*, all that Upper East Side banter and privilege and opulence. Here was Norman Rockwell on a *Saturday Evening Post* cover. A placard in the train station announced: "Rosalie Gay and her Accordion," appearing at the Chi Am Chateau, a Chinese restaurant.

"Miss Ferber?"

I faced a smiling young man decked out in baggy white linen trousers and a periwinkle-blue tennis shirt, a happy-go-lucky blond kid with an unwieldy cowlick and an eager grin. I nodded as he scooped up my suitcases, half-bowed, and directed me to a cream-colored station wagon with faux-wood side paneling and a discreet lettered sign on the door: Jefferson Village Inn. "This way, please."

The inn was steps away—in fact, across from the train station and the grand Maplewood Theater, its welcoming sign visible above a line of Hawthorne trees that dotted the median strip down the center of the street. Very pastoral. The inn was tucked under ancient hemlocks and oaks, with a cobblestone pathway and an intimate gazebo too close to the sidewalk. A lovely three-story house, doubtless an old Victorian homestead with its wraparound porch, cluttered rows of weathered Adirondack chairs, and gingerbread ornamentation decorating the high eaves. Here was a whitewashed edifice that once catered to the Manhattan rich who summered in the town at the turn of the century.

At the front desk the clerk bowed and gushed and screamed approval of my stay. I learned that Sinclair Lewis had stayed there earlier that summer and had signed a menu, now framed and displayed in the dining room. "You are the second Pulitzer Prize novelist," he gushed. He directed the young chauffeur to carry my bags up to the second floor, and the boy, still grinning but awash now in sweat, beamed. I also learned that most summer theater folks chose to take the half-hour train ride back into the city each afternoon. The stars of *The Royal Family*—including Louis Calhern and Irene Purcell—would do so, to my consternation. They would only book rooms during the week's run. Cheryl Crawford, I learned, had rented a bungalow for the summer, though she scuttled back and forth to her Manhattan pied-à-terre. So, it seemed, for the moment I was the sole and lonesome grande dame from the Maplewood Theater in attendance in the venerable inn.

Of course, I'd come early on purpose—time to learn my lines, to relax, to walk, to feel the pulse of the town. Here was solitude. After all, this was my stage debut. In my nightmares I stood on the stage and opened my mouth: no sound escaped. And the audience, rolling in hysterics, pointed at me, tears coursing down their shiny cheeks. Some nights I startled myself awake, panicked, and I cringed.

Settled in, at leisure, I gazed down onto the avenue from my window, a gigantic tree nearby shimmering in the late-afternoon breeze. A rain shower was coming because the leaves of the sugar maple turned upright, and dust swirled in pocket eddies on the sidewalk.

I glimpsed a man hurrying by, then stepping behind a car and waiting. Then he ran, hunched over. Something about his posture…something familiar…but how would I know him? But something about the bowed head…

I shut the window and sat in a blue wing chair, my marked-up Samuel French copy of *The Royal Family* in my lap. Fanny Cavendish's lines. Too many of them, I realized. I had to memorize them now, and that stressed me. I practiced a line out loud, my voice sounding artificial and dull in the small room. Words echoed in my mind: pace, projection, cues. Disaster. Reading the script, I remembered—yes, George wrote that line. I wrote this one. We fought over that speech. I insisted…George glowering…me fiery.

The beginning of a slight headache. This was not going to end well, I realized—George had tried to warn me. Certainly his riotous laughter when I mentioned Cheryl's offer of the part should have tipped me off. Others had warned me. Neysa McMein's nervous titter. My sister Fannie's phlegmatic dismissal. My innate stubbornness, to be sure, bred in the blood. A vice I joyfully cultivated. And sheer Midwestern orneriness, hard-fought and decently come by.

The rains came, the drumbeat of heavy splatter against the panes.

At suppertime I strolled downstairs into the dining room where the waitress seated me at a small table by the back window. I could watch the rain splatter on the cobblestones as twilight settled in. The smallish room was sparsely populated. Two portly businessmen in wrinkled seersucker suits were laughing like schoolboys over some whispered joke; a moody mother eyed her squirming daughter of perhaps ten; three old women who could be sisters all talked over one another.

Quietly I ordered a simple sirloin steak with onions and mushrooms, expecting disaster, and a martini. The waitress, a chubby girl with her hair in Mary Pickford ringlets, winced at my order of a drink, her pencil frozen in the air. "Is Maplewood a dry county?" I babbled, but she had no idea what that meant. I gathered that a single middle-aged woman in a light rose-colored dress with three strands of sensible pearls should not be ordering firewater unless she was the local madam who'd taken a wrong turn from Newark.

The room featured heavy, ornate Edwardian curtains that festooned the floor-to-ceiling windows, dark burgundy with dusty gold tassels. Clumsy tables with legs the size of elephant trunks looked permanently in place—you'd need a waterfront crew to shift that furniture. Old faded white damask tablecloths reminded me of an ancient relative in Chicago—the persistent finery of those who insist anything one hundred years old is religiously worthy. A mausoleum, this petrified chamber, though the gum-clacking young waitress had been dropped, willy nilly, from a time capsule.

I expected drab, uneventful food, and was not disappointed. A steak so tough and fatty I judiciously ignored it, potatoes so gray I flattened them into a corner of the dish but they refused to disappear. I ate bread and butter, surprisingly tasty and crusty, obviously an accident of the kitchen, and managed to savor the martini, which was decent. I had two, in fact. The waitress wasn't happy. Perhaps she thought I'd arrived in town to star in

Ten Nights in a Barroom. But, of course, I doubted she'd heard of that venerable melodrama.

"Everything all right?" the waitress asked, staring at my untouched meal.

"Do you really expect an answer?"

She blinked wildly and turned away, disappearing into the kitchen. I expected an irate chef, cleaver wielded above a blood-red face, to sail through those swinging doors—and do me in.

Ready to leave, I heard a loud, booming voice. I recognized it—and suddenly realized whom I'd spotted running earlier in the street. A few feet from my table, through a wide archway, was the cocktail lounge. I observed a long mahogany bar, behind which a gigantic mirror reflected rows of liquor bottles arranged in tiers on glass shelves. The voice roared again, angry, metallic. Standing up and sitting back down in a chair on the other side of my table—at that moment the waitress emerged from the kitchen and regarded my version of musical chairs as an act of certifiable madness—I now had a direct view into the lounge.

Evan Street was thundering about something. Leaning against the bar, one elbow resting on it, he waved his other hand at someone, punctuating his words with a beer bottle. His presence startled me, though perhaps it shouldn't have. After all, he was the new understudy in town. But it did bother me because his boisterous manner was ugly and mean—a spine-chilling rawness to his fury. He demonstrated nothing of the obsequious blather he'd displayed at Cheryl's apartment.

He stepped forward, grunted, at one point pushing his index finger into the shoulder of the young man facing him. Dressed in a wrinkled summer suit, shopworn and faded at the elbows, Evan struck me as a blustery itinerant drummer who hadn't made a sale in days and thus took out his frustrations on hapless waiters. I had no idea what the altercation was about, though the mumbled words of the other man seemed to precipitate another volley of thunder and fire from Evan.

The young man, dark and slender with a long melancholy face under a shaggy haircut, drew his lips into a thin line. He backed up against the bar but Evan pushed closer, jabbing the man in the chest, and calling him by name: Dak. Or at least it sounded like that, the name momentarily lost in the tinkle of glasses and a long laugh from some unseen drinker somewhere else in the lounge. Then, to my horror, the young man struck out his fist, connecting with Evan's shoulder. Surprised, Evan jabbed at Dak's chest and then a fist grazed his cheek. Another solid punch to Dak's shoulder. Evan spat out, "Damn you." I heard the bartender yell something, and, like that, they separated. Dak's voice shook. "Damn you, Evan. You'll pay."

Dak turned to go but collided with a third man, suddenly in my line of sight: a smallish bull of a man, thickset, young but balding, his blond hair close-cropped and spotty. This new man flicked a stubby finger against Dak's chest, dismissive, nasty. Dak maneuvered around this interloper, who now purposely blocked Dak's path. Sweating, anxious, Dak twisted around him and disappeared from my sight.

An ugly scene, stunning. My hand gripped the edge of the table.

Evan arched his back and whistled triumphantly, but at that moment he looked into the dining room where he spotted me. Our eyes locked. An awful moment, truly, for I saw iciness there, a hard agate stare, unfriendly. The man scared me.

But then, shaking his head, he attempted an ah-shucks grin, a little-boy twist of his head as he bit his lip, and he moved away. Over his shoulder he said to an unseen Dak, "The drinks are on you, buddy. You got the bucks. I'm a parasite in this one-hoss town." His fireplug friend let out a false laugh, but didn't move.

In a cavalier, jaunty stride, Evan sailed into the dining room and paused at my table. "Miss Ferber, you do show up in strange places." He chuckled. "But obviously so do I." He looked back at Dak and the other man, both standing in the doorway watching him. Dak was absently rubbing a bruised shoulder, his eyes dark with anger. Evan leaned into me confidentially and said through clenched teeth, "No one believes that someday I'll return to Hollywood and be the biggest star." This bizarre remark, apropos of nothing I'd just heard, hung in the air like a threat.

I had no time to answer him because he tapped his finger on my table, a Morse code rat-a-tat-tat, and left the room.

When I looked back into the lounge, the other two men had gone. The bartender was dragging a rag across the surface but he was looking at me.

Back in my rooms, unsettled, unable to focus on my script, I glanced at the front page of the morning's *New York Times* I'd carried with me on the train. A pit in the deep of my stomach: the grim news from Europe. Every day the same raw story, the bleak headlines. The horror of Hitler as that madman now readied an assault and possible invasion of England. The Luftwaffe over precious storied England? The brutal air strikes in Gibraltar. France, gone now, the wishy-washy Vichy government cracking down on Jews. Madness, all of it. Mussolini in North Africa. Buffoons and hucksters, now in control.

Frantic, I phoned George at his country home in Bucks County, Pennsylvania, the retreat—a mansion of twelve rooms, with guesthouse and stagnant pond—he glibly called "cherchez La Farm." Crickets on the hearth.

Bea answered the phone. "Edna, is there anything wrong?"

I hesitated. "No, I…" I had no idea why I was calling except for the queasiness inside me.

"An exciting time for you," she went on.

I sucked in my breath. "Bea, dear, I watched your young friend Evan Street slug another man in a bar fight." I suddenly found myself at a loss for words. Silence, my mind racing, then I went on. "You know him well?"

"Well, not *well*. But, Edna, he's a rambunctious young man, filled with spirit. Dashing, wouldn't you say?"

My silence was too long. "Is George there?"

I could hear him talking in the background. Bea said nothing more but obviously handed him the phone.

"Edna, what's the matter?"

"George, tell me about Evan."

The question surprised him. "Why?"

"I don't like him."

I could hear Bea in the background mumbling to him about Evan's barroom brawl.

"Maybe he had too much to drink." George was speaking to her.

The sound of her walking away, her faraway voice saying, "Tell Edna he's all right. Just…pushy."

"Edna, Edna. Perhaps he'll grow on you—like a barnacle." But George deliberated, lowering his voice. "I don't like him either."

"Then why…?"

"Talk to my wife who is standing in the kitchen doorway, frowning at me. Or, perhaps, at *you*. Evan's her friend's son. He flatters and charms women. Not *you*, of course. Loyalty to college friends and all that."

"I don't like him," I repeated.

"I know, I know." A deep sigh. "What little I know…I asked Bea about him after we met him at Cheryl's…well…he loses every job he gets. That I know. He makes enemies. He's too cocksure. Trouble follows him. I'm paraphrasing Bea's laudatory description of him, or, better said, I'm reading between the lines."

"Wonderful." Now I sighed. "And he'll ruin my week here."

"Edna, I'll be there in a couple days. I don't think he'll ruin anything. He won't bother *you*. The worst he'll do is give you some bad memories."

George was the most notorious pessimist I knew—superstitious, a man who believed each new play or venture was doomed. So this burst of good cheer alarmed me. This wasn't the George Kaufman I knew.

"Is he dangerous?" The question seemed appropriate, if odd.

Another long pause. "All men are in danger when they near your rocky shores, Edna. Men are…"

The line went dead because I'd hung up on George. Not for the first time, true, and doubtless not the last.

Chapter Three

No one paid me any attention as I strolled down the street the next morning, not the usual clipped, purposeful walk I always did in New York—my military stride up Park and down Lexington, one mile, brisk and steady. No, in the growing heat of nine o'clock Maplewood, I sauntered past the shops and homes in the Village, enjoying the laziness of it all, the occasional passing car, a few briefcase-toting businessmen tipping their fedoras to me as they scurried to the train station for a late commute into the city.

But already the day was becoming blistering, the temperature edging upward, perhaps ninety by noon, and the thermometer outside Pietz's Deli already registered eighty-one. Perspiring, I stopped for a cherry soda at the Full Moon Café, just down from Foster's Five and Dime, which also wooed me with a special on banana splits. Alone in the café, refreshed, I was served with aplomb by a wiry old woman in a hairnet who stood close to my table, arms folded.

"You're Edna Ferber." A tickle in her voice.

"I am."

"You're *Show Boat*."

I nodded.

She walked away, though she glanced back over her shoulder, a sliver of a smile on her face.

When I went to pay, she shrugged my coins away. "A treat for me, ma'am." Then she laughed. "When you come back for lunch later on—my tuna casserole is the special today, you'll love it—I'll charge you double." She extended her hand. "Name's Mamie Trout, owner." She laughed at her own joke, and I joined in. A stringy old woman in a homemade embroidered apron, she moved with small, cat-like shuffling steps.

Of course, tempted, I did return later that afternoon, after the lunch crowd was gone, opening the front door so the overhead bell clanged. Only a couple of tables were occupied by single diners. I settled myself into a rickety wrought-iron ice-cream parlor chair by the window. A quiet room now, with Mamie Trout leaning against one of the dull gray walls under an old copper ceiling. Currier and Ives prints, much faded, in old wooden frames. "Knew you'd be back," Mamie chortled. "I refused Rufus Griswold, himself the mayor, the last portion of my casserole. For you. The man was fit to be tied."

She didn't wait for my response but hurried into her kitchen, emerging with a heaping dish of her daily special, served with a generous chunk of warm pumpernickel bread. She stood over me, arms folded into her bony chest, eyes bright, as I tasted the food. Before I could say anything, she flicked her head and turned away. Of course, she'd sized up my expression: utter joy. For, indeed, the tuna casserole—that redundant church supper staple and never a favorite of mine—was a savory dish, a wonderful amalgam of chunky tuna, celery, onions, carrots, and raisins, a bit of mayonnaise—but something more, some aromatic spice, undefined, that gave it a vaguely Moroccan touch. I knew now where I'd be eating lunch during my stay in Maplewood.

"Good, wouldn't you say?"

A voice from across the room. It was a line that should have been part of a conspiratorial smile or laugh, the desultory conversation of strangers in a restaurant who have made a culinary discovery. When I glanced over, the young woman repeated it—the same mechanical inflection, deadpan, the matter-of-fact rhythm of an announcer in a Pathé newsreel at the movies.

"Indeed."

"You're Edna Ferber."

"Indeed, I am. So you've heard of me?"

"I'm Annika Tuttle. You haven't heard of me."

"I'm afraid I haven't."

"You would have if you lived here."

"And why's that?"

Now a smile, smug, large, a mouth full of perfect teeth.

"I preach at the Assembly of God over on Tuscan Road. I work with the celebrated evangelist, Clorinda Roberts Tyler. You've heard of *her*, of course."

I hesitated. "I'm afraid I haven't."

That startled her, and for a moment she was silent, sipping her drink.

A small woman, given to girlish plumpness, with apple-red cheeks on a round, wide face that was somehow closed up. Long, puffy honey-blonde hair cascaded over her shoulders, neatly combed but with none of the shellacked coiffure so many young girls effected these days. Her eyes were a faded hazel, set too close together so that she probably always looked puzzled. Perhaps early twenties, she looked…matronly, in fact, yet still pretty, a farm girl. Wholesome with a kind of laundry-day brightness. This look was also the result of her dress: a checkered pale blue-and-white smock, gingham most likely, and utterly decorous, with a ruff of lace around her neck, her long sleeves cuffed with lace. The merest hint of lipstick on her lips, so faint perhaps I imagined it. A Mennonite lass, transported into Jersey.

Now she announced, a little haughtily, "Clorinda Roberts Tyler was a disciple of Aimee Semple McPherson in California. The legendary Sister Aimee herself. We are God's emissaries here. She is my teacher. I'm her lieutenant in God's army. I—"

I held up my hand, impatient. "You talk as if we're in a war."

She stared at me, unblinking. "Well, we *are*. With Satan. With *this*." Her hand pointed out the window as a rattletrap Ford jalopy sped by, horn blaring and tires squealing. Some hell-to-play Johnny out on the town, peals of laughter carrying into the café.

"Perfect timing." I was grinning widely.

"There are worlds to conquer for Christ." She half-rose from her seat, as though preparing to pontificate—or, worse, join me at my table.

"I wish you luck," I said a little too snidely.

But she wasn't listening to me. "You must come to hear Clorinda preach. Each week the crowds get larger and larger."

"And you preach there at…at the Assembly?"

A rapid nod. "I'm an acolyte. In training. I love God…"

I smiled again. "And, I gather, Mamie Trout's scrumptious tuna casserole."

Still no smile. "True, I suppose. Food being…food. But I'm meeting my intended here, if he finishes his work early. Clorinda's son, Dakota."

"Dakota?" I squirmed. "Dak?"

She looked surprised and unhappy. "Everyone calls him that. I don't. But you *know* him? How in the world?"

"Of course not. I happened to hear the name spoken last night…"

The bell over the door clanged. Evan Street shuffled in, spotted Annika immediately, and waved at her, saying her name loudly. She frowned as she dipped her head into her chest. Then, surveying the room, he spotted me, the ubiquitous bystander, sitting nearby. "Lord, Miss Ferber, we meet again."

"Evan," I said slowly. "You *are* a presence." I looked away.

He chuckled and tried to catch my eye: the persistent charmer unused to disregard from the fair sex. Yet I detected a hint of nervousness in his words. He'd rather I not be there.

"Annika." He turned back to the young woman, "Is Dak around?"

Annika was still frowning as she looked up. "No." A pause. "He'll be here in a bit. Maybe." Her voice was brittle and shaky.

He grinned at her. "Hey, you still mad at me?" He puffed up his chest. "Dak tell you about our squabble last night? We actually pushed each other around."

"No, we don't talk about you."

He grabbed a chair from her table, swiveled it around and straddled it, his long arms dropping over the back as he leaned into her. His mouth twisted into a sly grin.

"You're cute when you try to be mean to me." He glanced back at me, that grin still plastered across his handsome face. "Annika doesn't like people telling her she's pretty."

She rolled her tongue into a flushed cheek. "Evan, Dakota already told you he don't want you talking to me like that."

"Like what?"

"Flattering…you know, flirting."

"What's he gonna do? Beat me up? He's a little too scrawny for that. I used to knock him around when we were out in Hollywood. Did he tell you about that? One magnificent fistfight on Sunset Boulevard. Real Wild West stuff. I gave him a black eye. He cried like a baby." A calculated pause. "He almost cried last night."

Annika looked toward the doorway, as though fearful Dak would come in and find Evan at her table. She half-rose from her chair, deliberately, then settled back, circled her glass of iced tea with both hands. Suddenly, resolutely, she stared into Evan's arrogant face and betrayed a cool dislike so fierce it would have withered a less cocky man. Yet she also looked as if she could crack at any moment because the corners of her mouth twitched. "You have to have every woman look at you with longing, don't you, Evan?" Each word slowly spaced out, lethal. At the end she took a sip from her glass, her eyes still on him. "But it's not even that, is it, Evan? Clorinda was right. She told me about men like you. It's not even the…women. You just want to make all the men jealous. Or angry. Or fight you." She bit her lip. "Satan has a place reserved for lost souls like you, Evan Street."

Evan slapped the table, and roared. "Hear that, Miss Ferber? I got the attention of the big Evil One himself. Little Evan Street, heartthrob-in-training for the silver screen."

"Your charms obviously don't spread into the spiritual realm," I told him.

Annika smiled at me, and I realized how pretty she was once she abandoned the severity she demanded of herself. Yes, a farm girl's robust beauty, rosy and innocent. Her voice got stronger, more assured, fire at the edges. Like Evan, she was looking at me. "Evan's a foolish man, made happy by the throwaway smile from any passing girl or the hostile clip on the shoulder by a cuckolded boyfriend." She sat back, pleased with herself.

Evan pursed his brow. "What nonsense are you yammering about now?"

But Annika slipped back into her puritanical mask: tight lines around her mouth, the steely eyes, the jutting chin. She folded her arms across her chest. Evan started to say something but she pointed a finger at him. "Your name is in the Doomsday Book."

He stood and faced me. "I guess the only woman in this room who I can charm is you, Miss Ferber."

I locked eyes with him. "I don't find you charming, Evan."

"Of course, you do."

"If anything, I find you...alarming."

"What?" A puzzled look on his face, not happy.

"You're a fire that throws no heat, sir."

Annika snickered. "Satan's fire, dark and cold."

"Well, that's not exactly what I was thinking," I told her. "More like a Casanova spelling out one-syllable words from an old primer."

Though our banter confused him, Evan seemed flattered by the attention. "I'm in the room, ladies. I can *hear* you."

"So can Jesus." Said by Annika, not by me.

The door opened and Dak stood there, shadowy, framed by a wash of afternoon sunlight. His eyes darted from Evan to Annika. "What's going on here?" His voice cracked, nervous.

"Dakota," Annika whispered as he approached her. "You're late."

He was staring at Evan. "Seems to me I'm just in time."

Evan extended his hand. "Dak, my friend, sorry about that little send-up last night. No blood spilt, right? A little misunderstanding. I don't like scuffling with old buddies."

Dak watched him carefully, one hand gripping the back of a chair. Of average height and with a slight build, he seemed the boy here, the ragtag neighborhood lad who trembled before the swaggering town bully. A good-looking face with glistening blue-gray eyes set off by a warm olive skin, he nervously drew his hand through his messy black hair, an unconscious gesture that was very appealing. Color rose up his neck, his eyes suddenly sad. "It's all right," he mumbled.

Annika fumed. "No, it isn't, Dakota. For Lord's sake, listen to you. This…this Hollywood degenerate appears in town and tries to…to…you know…flatter me and ask me…" She stopped, lacking the vocabulary of questionable seduction.

"Harmless," Evan protested, though he winked.

"Let's go." Annika thundered, standing and looping her arm into Dakota's. "This meeting of the Maplewood Boys' Club is adjourned." She nudged him along as he stumbled, sheepish, red-faced. She paused by my table, the proper Victorian girl. "Miss Ferber, this is Dakota. Dakota, Miss Ferber, the famous writer." Dakota was nodding at me, confused by the serendipitous introduction. Annika went on. "Miss Ferber, please visit the Assembly of God."

Dak looked into my eyes. His embarrassed smile disappeared when Annika pushed him.

Before I could answer, she opened the door of the café. A step behind her now, Dak glanced over his shoulder and I caught his eye: confusion there, true, but something else—anger. At Annika? Perhaps. Or was it dislike? Or at Evan? I had no idea what his scattered glance meant.

Evan waited a moment and then left the restaurant. But he never stared my way. Mamie Trout began clearing dishes from the tables. "That girl got her hooks into that poor boy. Nothing good'll come of that. Mark my words. Trust me."

"You know them?"

"His mama's Clorinda Roberts Tyler, of course. You gotta know who that is, no? Hellfire and brimstone and salvation and redemption and Hollywood tap dance, all rolled into one hell's-a-poppin' spectacle. I never miss a sermon—it's better'n amateur night at Pal's Cabin over to West Orange. And that girl's the daughter she never had. Joan of Arc with eyes ablazing. She comes in here and scares the bejesus outta some folks."

"And Dak? This Dakota?"

She glanced toward the street. "Ah, that boy, the prodigal son, returned from wandering around America like a boxcar hobo. Some folks born not to know where to lay their heads down. I knew him as a boy, of course, always up to mischief in those days. Nothing mean or downright evil—just well…'Look at me! Look at me!' He was named for a one-reel William S. Hart movie, so I hear. Real stupid, that name. Lord, you'd think we was in Wyoming, galloping into the sunset." She grinned. "But I'll tell you a secret. I was always soft on that boy. A sweetheart. Harmless. You can spot a good heart, you know. You can hear it beating. He come back just in time to begin training to become tomorrow's new Billy Sunday."

"So you're a follower of his mother's religion, Mamie? The Assembly of God?"

She shook her head vigorously. "A little too damnation and hellfire for me, but, as I say, I don't miss a sermon. A little religion is all I got—born and bred Baptist—and it's enough to make me decent and law-abiding and God-fearing. Too much religion"—she pointed out the window at the departed Annika—"and you forget that folks got other things to worry about when they wakes in the morning."

"Dak seems a quiet young man. But troubled…"

"As I said, I known him for years. His trouble is that he listens to other people."

"And you don't?"

"Most times other people got nothing you need to hear." She paused. "Too many people talking to that boy—*at* that boy. He don't know what to believe."

Outside, hit by a blast of August heat, I deliberated walking to the nearby park, then changed my mind. A cool bath in the deep Victorian claw-foot tub, a glass of iced lemonade delivered from the kitchen, an hour with my Fanny Cavendish lines, and perhaps a welcomed nap.

As I stepped onto the sidewalk I spotted Evan Street across the way. He'd paused before a rooming house, glancing up and down the street as though looking for someone—or perhaps to avoid being seen—but he finally walked up the steps and disappeared inside. A decrepit place, this rooming house, the old clapboard Victorian with peeling yellow paint, sagging green shutters, and a faded sign hanging loose off one hook. ROOMS TO LET. MRS. SIMPSON'S. GENTLEMEN ONLY. The block lettering was fast disappearing. Respectable, certainly—the house had an aura of old musty gentility—but a painted lady down on her luck. An old man sat rocking on a chair by the front door. Dressed in a denim shirt and a railroad cap, a pipe stuck between his lips, he'd nodded at Evan, who ignored him, purposely stepping wide of the man. A residence, I considered, for itinerant workers, for drifters, fugitives from shabby Hoover villages, two bits for a night's lodging and a lumpy mattress and mouse droppings in the shared toilet. I knew such places…and so, lamentably, did Evan Street.

◇◇◇

That evening, near dark, I walked up the street to the Marlborough House, a restaurant recommended by a woman I met in the lobby of the Jefferson Village Inn. "A lovely inn, this place," she whispered, "but if you want good food try the Marlborough House." She glanced over her shoulder as though regretting her betrayal of the inn's kitchen, then rushed off to her room. She looked trustworthy: a schoolmarmish woman my age in sensible shoes, a silk shawl for a chilly night, with a bit of mischief in her brown eyes, a woman carrying a black patent-leather purse big enough to secret silverware service for twelve and perhaps a gravy bowl or two.

I imagined a blessing for her as I dipped into my savory pot roast and rosemary-slathered potatoes, toothsome and perfect. In the crowded dining room—perhaps that culinary spy had alerted others?—I devoted my energy to the meal. On the hot August night I'd donned a simple polka-dot summer dress, sleeveless, with my obligatory pearls, to be sure; and the modest clutch I carried could accommodate one sterling silver soup spoon, should larceny be my inclination.

I started when a voice whispered in my ear, "Women who dine alone are looking for vagabond heroes."

George Kaufman slipped into a chair opposite me.

"But usually we find ne'er-do-well scalawags, themselves one step ahead of the law." I breathed in. "George, you weren't supposed to arrive for a couple days. Why are you here?"

Wide-eyed, he waved his hand around the dining room. "My spies told me I'd find the best supper in Maplewood here. Therefore, using my powers of deduction, I knew I'd find you here, food fetishist that you are." He squinted his eyes. "And I'm not in the least."

"I highly recommend it." I smiled. "But that's not an answer to my question."

He sat back, his familiar slouch, and waved the waiter away. "It was Bea's idea, Edna love. 'You need to be there for Edna in her acting debut,' she said, or some words to that effect. Or maybe she said, 'Her hour of need.' Or maybe: 'She went there early. You leave her alone in that dull village that isn't Manhattan. You know she'll be at a loss for company, and she'll probably have stage fright when she's onstage.'" He paused. "All right, I made that last part. Some of the first part, too. But I thought, why not come early? What else is there for me to do? How many laps can a soul do in his lovely pond? After all, we did write the infernal play together and…"

"And you got tired of puttering around your summer garden."

"So here I am."

"Tell the truth, George. This directing job—it's not like you. Summers you stare into space, slack-jawed. You spend August imaging new illnesses that will kill you by September. Tell the truth—you want to see me make a fool of myself."

"I've already seen *that*, Edna. Over *me*."

"George!" I said through clenched teeth. "Enough of *that*!"

"I figure it will all be an adventure. Whenever we've traveled together, you and I, at some tryout or other misadventure… well, things happen."

"Nothing will happen, George. It's New Jersey."

"So when it does, we'll be surprised."

I sat back, and smiled. George's sudden appearance pleased me. Feeling a tad lonesome by myself, I knew George would, despite his sardonic commentary and occasional cruel jibe, be the loudest cheerleader for my adventure on the stage. There were times I rued his being nearby—times I suggested that he was wrong about something that I actually knew he was right about. Or those times he viciously dressed down an inept waiter or bellhop. Unpleasant, skin-crawling times. And George could be dreadfully nosy, the pesky snoop, and the hypochondriac who insisted I diagnose a low-grade fever or a heart murmur—all preparatory to a deathbed scene. He hated that I often interrupted him—which I had to. Most people, I'd discovered, are in need of being interrupted. I consider it an act of mercy. But I knew I got on his nerves, and he on mine. But…I was glad he'd come. With his carnival nose and gigantic hair, he sat there in his red bow tie and a white-linen summer sports jacket, and looked like a character from a Marx Brothers review.

"Frank Resnick is here." He pointed across the room. "Didn't you spot him here?"

I shook my head. "I only remember meeting him once, George. He didn't make an impression on me."

"No one ever remembers poor Frank."

"I do remember that he's Cheryl's stage manager for the summer. For reasons that bewildered her." A pause. "And he's your old buddy."

"No, I know him slightly, but I do like him. A strange bird, that one. Efficient as all get out, but distant, moody. Not one to blather like lots of show folks, present company included."

"George, most folks can't get a word in when you're in the room. You enter a room talking."

"I'm a sly fellow, Edna, as you know, but I always figure I'd better forestall the dullards waiting to share their dullness with me."

"Tell me about Frank. He's sitting with a very pretty girl."

Frank spotted the two of us looking at him, and nodded. He leaned in to say something to the young woman, but she looked tense, one hand nervously touching her hair.

A man probably in his early fifties, Frank reminded me of a silent movie actor—John Garfield maybe, a pencil-thin man, wiry, with a pencil-thin whisper of a Continental moustache, smartly clipped. A dapper Dan haircut, oily black and slicked back from his forehead, the part so painfully executed it seemed etched in the scalp. Dark-complected—or was it a summer tan? He sported a slightly out-of-style suit with a checkered pattern that, while not a zoot suit, was at least a distant cousin.

As he looked at us, his eyes got cloudy and wary—confused, as though our presence was something of an intrusion. Again, the quick aside to his companion. Perhaps it *was* an intrusion, at least his friend George's presence, as George cast his own covetous eyes on the slight but sultry girl at the table. She wore too much makeup for New Jersey, I thought, a crimson lipstick and accented eyes that made her seem an Erté figurine. Both were smoking cigarettes, both with arms extended as though in a scene from a Lubitsch German film, both mannered and a little preposterous. I was enjoying every bit of it.

"Our stage manager seems to be managing just fine," George commented.

"George," I seethed, "you have a leering gleam in your eye. A little unseemly, no?"

George was peeved. "Unseemly, Edna? A lovely girl, that one. I take an interest in young people."

I groaned. "A lovely euphemism, that line."

Frank now left his table and, with obvious reluctance, was maneuvering his way to us. "George," he began, "a surprise."

"Well, you *do* know that I've taken over as director?" Frank nodded. "And Edna needs all the help she can get. Edna, this is

Frank. Edna says she met you once, but can't remember anything you said because she fell asleep. Frank, this is…well, you've heard of her. You know, I wrote all of the Fanny Cavendish lines in our play and without me she's helpless."

I said nothing. Frank stood stiff and tense, his head bobbing. Now and then, he lifted a hand to touch his shellacked hair, and I feared his fingers might get stuck in the oily slick that passed for tonsorial splendor.

He also kept glancing back at the lovely young woman at his table who never took her eyes off us, her cigarette smoke wreathing her face.

"Miss Ferber," Frank addressed me, making eye contact for a second. Again, the unnecessary wariness. Why? "I look forward to working with you."

But he was already edging away.

George reached out to touch his sleeve. "Tell me, Frank, who is your dinner guest? So pretty."

Frank's eyes suddenly got hooded, dull black, and he actually turned, as though he had no idea someone had joined his solitary table. Flustered, he gave out a harsh phony laugh. "Oh, God, no. It's not what you think. George, really! That's Nadine Novack." A pause. "An actress. She's the understudy Cheryl hired for the summer. Beautiful, no? She'll be understudying Julie in *The Royal Family* and Talullah Bankhead in *The Second Mrs. Tanqueray*. She's already done Louise Rainer in *A Kiss for Cinderella*." He paused again, then stuttered, "An actress."

"You've established her profession already." My tone was icy.
"She doesn't know anyone in town."
"She knows you," George concluded. "She's very pretty."
Again, the fumbling words. "She's an…" His voice trailed off.
"An actress," I finished for him.
He was backing away. "Yes, she is." He looked unhappy, his final words brusque. "It's never what you think, George."
"That's true, it never is."
When he was gone, I looked at George. "I really don't understand the mating rituals of the aging American male. I

followed so little of that inane conversation. The two of you are like fifteen-year-old boys reaching puberty at the soda fountain at Woolworth's. I expected magnificent peacock plumage to appear, Hollywood-style, from somewhere beneath both your sports jackets."

"Edna, what are you talking about?"

"She's just an actress, George. This Nadine Novack. A preposterous name stolen from a silent movie plot. Yes, gorgeous, admittedly. But an understudy."

He was playing with me. "She'll have a long career."

"Yes," I insisted, "after Maplewood...the flood." I rose to leave.

Glancing back at them, I spotted Frank, silent now, watching us. Nadine was fixing her makeup, looking at her face in a compact mirror, mending her lipstick. Frank said something and she looked toward the door. Frowning, she shook her head. Then she looked back at her mirror and bit her lip. What she saw didn't make her happy.

Outside, George and I walked slowly in the warm stillness of the night. Not wanting to return to our hot rooms—"I've booked a room down the hall from you, Edna. No one will get past me, I promise you"—we lingered on a sidewalk bench, sheltered by a grove of trees at the edge of the park. A boy and girl walked past, ice cream cones in hand, giggling, in love. Fresh scrubbed, the boy in billowing trousers and the girl in white bobby socks. They glanced at George and me, and the boy nodded, deferential, sweet. I found it charming. George, however, cleared his throat and informed the lad, "We're not as happy as we look, young man. She's leaving me for a circus clown."

"Don't believe him," I countered. "I wouldn't make that mistake a *second* time."

The boy and girl, baffled by the nonsensical blather from the strange couple who could be their parents—and thus should be at home—scurried away, still giggling. The boy glanced back at the skinny man with the pompadour and the Barney Google eyeglasses and the beaky nose, sitting with the tiny lady with the three strands of pearls and expensive shoes from Saks.

"George, must you engage everyone in your silliness?"

"I'm a plagiarist. I steal everybody's happy moments."

I laughed. "God knows what they…" I stopped.

Frank and Nadine had left the restaurant, standing in front of the entrance, taking leave of each other. Leaning into her neck, Frank said something that made her laugh. She threw back her head and gently touched his arm. Then Frank turned away, headed up the street, walking at a brisk clip. Nadine watched him walk away and then headed in the other direction, pausing in front of a small rooming house. THE HARWINTON. FOR WOMEN. GOOD EATS. She fumbled in her purse for a key, dropped it, then lit a cigarette. She looked back up the street, but Frank was already out of sight.

She turned into the walkway and climbed the front steps. For a moment, enjoying the night, she leaned against the balustrade, breezily smoking. I sensed movement from across the street. A clump of small trees, a line of trimmed hedges, a garden trellis covered in purple wisteria. A confusion of night shadows under a faint moonlit sky. A figure shifted in the darkness. A solitary man stepped onto the sidewalk. Even from where I sat I could tell he was monitoring Nadine's movements so intently that he tripped on a stone, swore under his breath. He stood there, watching, frozen, while Nadine, unaware, snubbed out her cigarette, flicked it into the bushes, and walked inside.

The figure unfroze and in the still night I heard a heavy sigh, lone and plaintive and awful.

The slight graceful body rocked back and forth.

I recognized who it was. Dakota. Dak.

Chapter Four

We began our rehearsals. By the second day I'd learned my lines, though I had trouble with my onstage movements. I felt awkward and clumsy, aware that each step was being watched—and judged. George, to his credit, whispered encouraging advice, and was only cruel now and then. His "You can embody the character, Edna, and quite well" was immediately balanced by his grumbled remark, "Edna dear, you move like a wobbly bowling pin." George rarely complimented. "You're supposed to be good," he once famously quipped. "I'll tell you when you're not." But, ultimately, I came around. Yes, I could survive a week of performance without undue embarrassment and fatal mistake.

Nervous, I chain-smoked Lucky Strikes during our breaks, and George purposely avoided me. He detested smoking, especially by women. "Really, Edna, it makes you look like a fishwife."

I ignored him.

I looked out into the vast theater and trembled as I envisioned it filled with over a thousand eager theatergoers. A beautiful space, the Maplewood, with its large oval dome, its cut-glass chandeliers, the walls painted in shades of carnival red and sky blue, the proscenium arch a light green with a hint of red. An old-style theater, reminiscent of Manhattan's movie palaces of the Twenties. Here, Cheryl had told us, the first movie shown had been Valentino's *The Four Horsemen of the Apocalypse*. A Wurlitzer organ punctuated the silent frames.

Here, in a few days, I'd take the stage—not so silently.

Louis Calhern and Irene Purcell, who played Tony and Julie Cavendish, my feckless, impulsive grandchildren, were troopers, though both seemed hell-bent on catching the late-afternoon Lackawanna train back into Manhattan after each rehearsal. George and I shared a cup of coffee with both, a hasty lunch, and all was shoptalk. "You're staying in Maplewood?" Louis stammered when I mentioned my rooms at the Jefferson Village Inn. He looked as though I'd signed in at a leper colony for a lark.

"Ambience," I told him.

"There is none," Louis insisted.

Irene nodded. "How many oak trees can one sit under, Edna?"

George interjected, "Edna, the peripatetic novelist, is only happy on location. In fact, by the end of the week's run—when we close on Sunday to huzzahs and bouquets of roses at my feet—she will have sat under all those oak trees. As well as a few sycamores, for good measure."

During those first two days, as I polished my lines and wandered around town, George was right: I did like to soak in the atmosphere of the locales I visited. I relaxed, enjoying myself, lighting a cigarette when I wanted George to disappear. No gardeners worried me about insidious grubs, no poultry men battled over the building of the coops, and no mother was there to guide me, as they used to say in the Victorian novels by The Duchess. Here I was, a fiftyish spinster always apologizing to a mother I could never please. Yes, Mother. No. Yes. In frightening moments of reflection I believed I would always be that skittish little girl rushing home from school in Ottumwa, Iowa, or in Appleton, Wisconsin. Yes, Mama. Was it any wonder I sought out the far reaches of America's hinterland for plot lines? Eventually I'd take shelter in an igloo up in the Arctic Circle. I'd freeze to death as the aurora borealis painted the night sky. I was sure of it.

"If I lived with my mother, Edna," George told me whenever we discussed Julia Ferber's hold on me, "I'd be up on charges."

During those two days of hard work, incredible novelty, and moments of unexpected joy, I had little time to consider Evan

Street, who, despite being an anonymous understudy, managed to insinuate his annoying presence into the company. Even if you did not spot him lurking in the wings, script in hand, as though waiting for Louis Calhern to mysteriously disappear or at least stumble into the orchestra pit, even then you heard his thundering voice somewhere—that raucous look-at-me laugh, the loose-cannon rumble of his flattery, and the overtly dry cough from the back of the theater as George as director admonished Louis for a poorly delivered line. He was the understudy who filled the corners of the theater. The handsome man who'd always assumed the innate authority of those God-given looks, the lover with the cobalt-blue eyes, the Leyendecker chin, and the Richard Harding Davis exoticism. The privilege of accidental birth, that boy…blessed by a foolhardy God.

By the end of the second day, exhausted, the troupe gathered outside under the shade trees on green slatted benches, fed lemonade and cookies from Mamie Trout's café. We were all pleased with ourselves. The veteran actors were less wary of me, the rich and presumptuous interloper, now that I'd proven I could say a line without stumbling—and that I, the imperious playwright, refused to lord it over folks. They bantered easily with me—which I relished. In fact, I was still in awe of *them*, these hardy souls who lived in front of footlights and never knew when they'd work again.

During our lazy afternoon, I leaned against an oak trunk, my eyes tired. Suddenly I heard Evan's voice calling out: "Gus, hey, Gus."

I stepped a few feet toward the sidewalk. A short, stocky man paused in front of me, turned with his hands on his hips, and swore under his breath. Evan rushed up to him and clamped a hand on the shorter man's shoulder, but Gus, his face bright red and his chin rigid, shook it off.

"Evan, you're a goddamn fool, you know."

"We gotta talk, Gus. Sooner or later."

Gus stepped away. Dressed in workman's clothing, a worn denim shirt and faded dungarees, Gus glared at Evan. For a second, puzzled, he scratched his head, messing up the few strains of pale, wispy blond hair that circled a prominent bald spot.

"I don't like what you said to Meaka, Evan. You're a mean bastard."

A mock shrugging of his shoulders. "I was joking with her."

"You called her a tub of butter."

Evan roared. "Well, she is a bit…round."

Gus poked his finger in Evan's chest. "She's my girl, Evan. How do you think it makes her feel?"

Evan bit his lip. "Christ, Gus, I didn't think she had any feelings at all. She's like, you know, a…a machine. And that political crap she lays on you…"

Gus flared up, hot. "It ain't right."

Evan lowered his voice. "Hey, why'd you have to follow me to this dumb town? A master electrician, my foot." A phony laugh. "I didn't even know you knew how to string two wires together."

"I know plenty." He moved closer, and I almost missed his words, shielded as I was by some hedges. "And you know I know plenty. You thought I wouldn't show up? I'm on to you, Evan. I ain't a fool."

"You got no business butting in."

"Yeah, sure."

Evan laughed nervously. "All right, all right. Just keep out of my way. Friends, right? Hey, we go way back."

"Hollywood for a couple months don't count for 'way back,' Evan. We ain't never been friends."

"I don't want trouble. You know, I gotta trust you now."

"And you ain't gonna have trouble, but I won't let this one go. I *know* things."

Evan hissed, "Stop saying that." Then he went on in a tinny voice, "I didn't know you'd show up with Meaka. Why do you two got to be so…you know, that scary political crap."

"Where I go, she goes."

"Christ, Gus, you're talking nonsense."

"Just remember—you do something—I get mine. You hear?"

"Don't worry." A long pause. "You tell Meaka?"

"I ain't a fool." He started to walk away, but swung back. "Leave off the rotten comments, Evan. Meaka doesn't like you to begin with."

"Hey, it's mutual."

"If she was a chorus girl, you'd be after her with smooth talk…"

Evan broke in. "So you got no worries when I'm around."

"Never mind. Just be careful."

Evan walked away. Gus leaned against the entrance to Strubbe's Ice Cream Parlor, reaching for a cigarette and lighting it. When a schoolboy tried to walk in, Gus took his time moving. Alone, he glanced toward the departing Evan and muttered, "Burn in hell."

From where I stood, still unseen, I could see his profile: fierce, stony, his lips razor thin, his skin ashy and cold. There was something frightening about him, a man who could menace, or destroy, without conscience. He looked…dangerous.

Suddenly he yelled, "Here! Here! Hey, Meaka!" He sucked in on the cigarette, blew smoke out, and then spat to the side as a young woman tottered from across the street. He flicked the lit cigarette away, and it bounced off the plate-glass window.

"I saw you talking to that ass." Her first words, biting and raspy.

As blond as Gus, Meaka was also short, barely five feet. But while he was muscular and thick, a sinew-bound workman, she was wide and soft, the pale yellow dress hugging her bones and hips. She looked as if she'd fallen into a dress tailored for someone else, but decided she didn't care. It rode up on one side, bunched around her waist.

I walked from behind the hedges and strolled past the couple, both of whom got quiet. Meaka was whining about Evan's rudeness and cruelty—"You sure know how to pick them, Gus"—but clammed up as I neared. Both glared at me, and I shivered all of a sudden, involuntarily, surprising myself. There was something about the raw harshness of their mutual stares—frankly, I felt to my marrow that they *knew* me. And that knowing—whatever did that mean? —guaranteed they hated me. The *idea* of me. Irrational, that intuitive moment—but I trusted it.

I could never abide such cavalier dismissal, especially from louts, so I stepped back, feigned a smile, and addressed the gaping Gus. "I am Edna Ferber. Haven't I seen you working at the theater?"

Silence, heavy and ugly. I realized that Gus was the third man I'd spotted that first night during the confrontation in the bar lounge—with Evan and Dak exchanging words, pushing, shoving. Now, perturbed by my interruption, he bit his lower lip, raised his chin arrogantly, and answered, "Yeah."

"And you, my dear?" To the smoldering Meaka then biting the nail of her stubby index finger, where a thin line of dried blood had collected.

A hoarse grunt. "Meaka Snow."

"What a lovely name. You work at the theater?"

"No."

"Then…"

But I got no further because Meaka clumsily grabbed Gus' elbow, poked him in the side, and the two stepped off the sidewalk into the street so precipitously that a passing car narrowly missed clipping both. Meaka, to my horror, raised her fist at the disappearing car, and screamed, "Damn you!"

I headed to the Full Moon Café for some iced cherry soda. Mamie Trout, smiling broadly, welcomed me back and directed me to a seat by the front window. "Got some chocolate cake with your name on it, Miss Ferber."

"Every piece of chocolate cake comes with my name on it, Mamie."

She had a hearty laugh, long and throaty, and absolutely infectious. She pointed to a young woman sitting by herself at one of the back tables. "Another fugitive from your theater." She pronounced it *thee-eh-ter*.

Nadine Novack, Frank Resnick's dinner companion from last night, was sitting quietly, nursing a lemon phosphate, her face bowed close to the straw. The actress with the self-consciously alliterative stage name. Of course, I'd noticed her when I walked in, especially her eagerness when the bell clanged—and her disappointed look when she spotted the tiny frumpy lady with the three strands of pearls. Real pearls, in fact.

Nosy, I decided to join her. She fidgeted as she watched me approach her table, hastily looking beyond me toward the door. "Hello," I began, "I'm Edna Ferber."

A whispered, uncertain voice, girlish. "I know." Then a weak smile. "I saw you come in."

"You're the understudy for the part of Julie?"

She nodded. "And everyone else this summer—Gloria Swanson, even—though I'll probably never be onstage."

"You are…"

"Nadine Novack. I'm sorry. I'm rude."

"Not at all. May I sit down?"

A slight titter. "I guess I really am rude, Miss Ferber. Please." She motioned to a seat and I sat down. She glanced quickly toward the door.

"You're a very pretty young girl."

She flushed a faded pink and closed her eyes. "That's very sweet of you." She looked toward the door again.

"I'm interrupting. You're expecting someone."

"Oh, no. I mean…sometimes other actors come…crew… or…This is a popular place." A deep intake of breath. "I'm sorry. I'm babbling."

"No matter, really, Nadine. I find it oddly comforting after some of the bluster and noisome breast-beating I've witnessed these past few days."

"Well, you know, actors…showing off."

"I imagine you're not a show-off."

Her eyes got wide. "Someday maybe I'll *have* something to… yes, you know…show off."

I liked her. Such a petite girl, gamin faced, with wavy auburn hair and brilliant round hazel eyes with a hint of burnished gold in them, charming, lustrous, inviting. A wraith, this girl, a frail woman who nevertheless seemed to have an inner glow, a spirit. A Clara Bow face, but without the doll-like vacuity. Pretty, yes, but a bit mousy under the unnecessary layers of glossy lipstick and red rouge. Yet I imagined her—this neophyte actress—as an unassuming woman who could erupt into dynamic life and character and brio when she walked onstage. It was the intelligence in those eyes—and the real warmth in that upturned face.

"I saw you having dinner last night with Frank Resnick."

A hesitation. "Yes, he's very fatherly to me. He feels he has to protect me." She giggled. "The dark alleys and squalid corners of Maplewood."

"Why *are* you here…in Maplewood?"

The question startled her. She fumbled. "I…well…a job. Hollywood failed me…and Broadway, so I interviewed with Miss Crawford and…well, I wanted to come here."

"Maplewood?"

"I mean…well, yes."

"But why?"

Her face closed up, dreaminess clouding her eyes, as though suddenly she realized she'd said too much. She looked down at her trembling hands and immediately, dramatically, buried them in her lap.

The door opened and Dak entered, rushing in and out of breath. But he stopped short in the entrance, mouth open, staring directly at our table. Nadine emitted a faint gasp, almost a warning, and Dak twisted around, ready to flee. The screen door slammed against his back. Nadine looked down.

I whispered. "That good-looking young man has an interesting name. Dakota. I've briefly met him. He's…"

"I have to go." She stood so quickly she knocked her empty glass onto the floor, where it smashed into pieces. "Oh, Lord," she cried and reached for her purse and scattered a few coins onto the table. A meaningless nod at me and she rushed out of the restaurant, brushing by a startled Dak who was doing his best not to look at her—or, I supposed, reach out to stop her, hold her, put a calming palm against her trembling face.

Even when she was gone, he still didn't move, as though he'd forgotten his destination, and Mamie Trout, walking in from the kitchen, waved at him. "Posing for animal crackers, Dak?"

He slid into a chair.

When Mamie approached him, he waved her away, but not brusquely, a mere gesture that suggested fatigue. She frowned at the shattered glass on the floor and went back into the kitchen.

I waited, nursing my cherry soda, trying not to stare at the appealing young man. So ethereal his looks, so wistful, the long swan's neck and the puppy-dog eyes. An unintended sigh escaped his throat as he closed his eyes. Then, slowly, he reached into an over-the-shoulder bag he'd dropped onto the floor, extracted a pad and pen, and furiously began to sketch. From where I sat I could discern a hastily delineated table and chair against a backdrop of a lunch counter.

"You're an artist?" I raised my voice.

He looked up, offered a thin smile, but didn't answer. He looked nervous, suddenly laying his palm over the sketch, as if I'd discovered him in some compromising vice. He laid down his pencil on the table but then grabbed it, his fingers gripping it tightly. Nervous, he stared away from me.

"We've met. Briefly. Do you remember? In here, in fact. You were with a young girl…Your name is Dakota."

His mooncalf eyes got wide. "You remember that?" A long pause. "Of course. Yes, Annika."

"Well, I've seen you around a bit. Not only with your girl-friend but also at the bar at the inn with Evan Street…"

He looked scared. "That's right—I saw you. That wasn't pretty. The shoving. The punching." A crooked grin. "Not my best moment."

"No one looks good fighting."

He kept grinning. "It only feels good." Then a heartbeat. "But it didn't even feel good, I'm afraid."

"Your girlfriend Annika is very protective…"

That same thin, sweet smile, broken at the edge. "Yeah, I guess. Right now she's searching the town for me as we speak." Sadness in his voice, a tired man.

"I understand your mother is Clorinda Roberts Tyler, the famous evangelist. I'm afraid I don't follow—"

He broke in. "Yeah, the messenger of God." Said too quickly, sarcastically, but immediately he looked sheepish. "I'm sorry. I don't mean to sound so...so sharp. My mother is a good woman, a savior of souls for Jesus." But the sarcasm returned. "I'm the heir apparent to that celestial throne."

"You don't sound happy about it."

"People tell me when to be happy. It's an emotion I have trouble inventing for myself." He looked toward the door.

"When you were sketching a second ago, you looked happy. For a moment. A short one. A spark of life in you. Your face was animated."

That surprised him. "You saw all that? Well, that's because I lose myself there." He tapped the pencil on the pad. "I forget everything else."

"Then you're a real artist."

A pause. "Well, thank you, but I don't think so."

"But I sense no one believes that about you...probably few people."

A long pause. "Do you believe in predestination, Miss Ferber? A life charted eons ago in heaven by a resolute and infallible God? My mother and stepfather have built a kingdom that mimics a dark heaven like that. My mother, when she preaches, goes to that heaven—and lives are changed for the better. I understand that. I truly believe it. And it's all right, that life—that spiritual life—except that my mother insists God has chosen me as her successor. Me, the prodigal son, the mischief-maker growing up in Maplewood who ran away to California but has come back home, haggard maybe, who doesn't want..." He stopped. "Like my mother, I talk too much...or not at all. This is the way I talk to *myself.* I'm sorry—I don't know why I just said all that...I tell strangers..."

"I'm not a stranger. We have met."

A crooked smile. "I know, I know. But I knew you before we met. You're in *The Royal Family.* I mean, you're real famous."

"So, I gather, is your mother." I smiled. "You know, you don't *have* to do what people tell you to do."

He chuckled. "That's easy for you to say. During my wandering days, my hobo journeys, my stays in one-hoss-town jails, my mother was busy planning my life, filling in the blanks in my biography. The legend of the boy preacher grew in my absence. As a boy, I got on that stage—I preached. The boy Jesus at the temple. She knew all along I'd crawl back home. She even chose a bride for me."

"Annika?"

He nodded. "She even talks like my mother, Annika does. When she preaches, she *becomes* my mother."

"And you're to marry her?"

"I suppose so. This fall. I actually do *like* her." He squinted at his own troubled words.

"Dak, I like a lot of people but I'd never marry them."

He laughed. "You don't have Clorinda Roberts Tyler as your mother."

"No, I have a mother who has devoted her life to keeping me unmarried."

"That seems unfair...to you."

"After a while it became the life I wanted myself."

"And you believe that?"

That gave me pause. This quiet, unassuming man, so faint of voice, had me trembling in the small café. How had that happened?

Slowly, almost sadly, "I have to. Now."

"Well, maybe that's my life. A marriage this fall to Annika and years to follow in which I come to convince myself that it's what I wanted all along. Just call me Dakota Cotton Mather Roberts."

We lapsed into silence, paradoxically both comfortable and disconcerting. I empathized with this smart young man, though I sensed the rawness of his spoken feelings could be contagious—one of those souls who gives you pause. A mirror that reveals the darkness we want hidden. A *Sorrows of Young Werther* temperament, a little world-weary, housed now in a lost generation. Sitting there, eyes on him, I understood him. Yes, truly. I knew so little about him—a collection of moments watching him *react* to folks around him—and yet I *knew* him. I liked him. Here was a decent man. But I quaked because everything about him suggested doom and disaster. I couldn't shake my worry.

A voice screeched from outside the café. "Dakota, for heaven's sake."

Annika, arms cradling a stack of leaflets, barged into the café, nearly spilling the sheets onto the tiled floor. "Why do you wander away? You're supposed to help me hand out the flyers." Her words ran together. "Your mother is frantic. She almost called the constable. She threatened to dredge a river for your body." She laughed at her own unfunny exaggeration.

Dak glanced at me, then at Annika. "She knows I put in a couple afternoons at the theater." He turned back toward me. "Frank Resnick, the stage manager, hired me to do some handyman work. They didn't really need me but he insisted I be there. I mean, he *insisted*. I welcomed the job..."

"You don't need money." Annika spoke over his words.

"It's not for the money. It's...you know, different. All day at the Assembly of God makes me restless."

"So you need to hammer nails into boards?"

Dak's eyes got wide, alert. "Well, yeah."

"Let's go."

He stood and addressed me. "Goodbye, Miss Ferber." A slight, boyish wave in my direction.

Annika looked at me for the first time. "We meet again." There was nothing pleasant about her brittle tone. Suddenly, she rushed to my table and thrust one of the flyers into my hand. She scurried back to Dak and tugged at his sleeve. They walked out of the café, Annika muttering something into his ear.

From the kitchen, unseen, Mamie Trout spoke to herself. "That lass needs a truck of Bibles to bury her sins."

I scanned the flyer, not the flimsy throwaway paper I expected but thick, creamy stationery, rife with Biblical quotation and admonishment. An invitation to Wednesday afternoon's twilight service at the Assembly of God, Clorinda Roberts Tyler, preacher. *Do you have a soul that needs saving? Is the wrath of God Almighty at your doorstep?* Then, to my amazement, this unexpected line: *If you think New Jersey is paradise, you're in for a big surprise.*

Back at the Jefferson Village Inn, George sat alone in the lobby, his face buried in Mark Twain's *Innocents Abroad*. He pointed to the volume. "I thought it was written about your venturing into New Jersey, Edna." Then, closing the book, he manufactured a fatherly tone. "Just where have you been, young lady? Gallivanting around town with riffraff."

"No," I countered, "I assumed you already gathered all the suspect denizens of this town."

He put the book on the table. "Edna, have you been snooping into peoples' lives?"

"Of course." I slid into a chair opposite him.

He stared over my shoulder, his eyeglasses slipping down his nose. "Anyway, I have news. I have good news. I have bad news."

"Oh God, George, I think I need a nap before I hear this."

"No, you don't." He shrugged his shoulders and tilted his head to the side. "Bea called. She's driving up tonight, so we can have dinner together. She's spending the night."

"Now for the good news?"

"Very funny, Edna. The other news is that she's asked Evan Street to join us for dinner."

I squirmed. "Good heavens. Why? Was that necessary? A meager acquaintance with that lout is enough to last a lifetime."

"Well, he's Bea's good friend's son. Obligations, et cetera, et cetera. He called to thank her, I guess. He's good-looking and he's a sweet talker…"

I held up my hand. "Enough. Bea's weaknesses mirror yours, dear George."

"But men have province where women and angels fear to tread."

I grunted. "Tell that to Bea."

A little tiresome, the bizarre liaisons of some of my friends. Back to the now-disappeared years of the Algonquin Round Table, George—like Dorothy Parker and her dipsomaniac husband—gleefully fell into what I believe the French term a *mariage blanc*. Not surprisingly, the French would have a name for this errant social lapse. To be sure, they invented dalliance and misalliance, as well as the ingesting of snails. Of course. George dearly loved Bea, as she loved him—and they happily entertained on their farm in Pennsylvania. But each sought romance—let me be euphemistic for the moment—outside the orthodox license of wedlock, George pursuing the pitiful, monosyllabic chorus girls of Broadway, all tinsel and rhinestone—and recently Hollywood, if I could believe the awful scandal with Mary Astor—and Bea entertaining the bronzed stage-door johnnies with the lascivious wink and the deep empty pockets. Prettiness was the coin of the realm. For both of them.

"Dear George, I do hope Bea isn't involved with this annoying lad."

"We don't discuss dalliance, just household expenses." He locked eyes with me. "Ah, Edna, you and I don't want to have these conversations."

"Thank God."

So that night the four of us sat down at dinner at the Marlborough House, three of us spectators to a young man's stupendous gluttony and unfettered chatter. I kept trying to catch George's eye, which he avoided because he knew exactly what my censorious look conveyed. He looked unhappy, constantly pushing his glasses up his nose, twitching, bobbing his head, examining the silverware for dried food and poisonous bacteria, and slowly sipping lemonade. Bea, to be sure, ignored her husband's aberrant behavior and seemed surprised to see me sitting there, though of course my presence in Maplewood was the reason we were all assembled in that lovely room. I suppose she read my obvious dislike of Evan, but she smiled at Evan's blatant flattery and his dipping and swaying in her direction, the tall man's calculated movements reaching his intended audience. Admittedly too good-looking for a mortal man, this pathetic Adonis doubtless assumed his easy birthright from childhood. He obviously never had to learn humility or suffer insecurity or doubt—the way the rest of us did. Thus I should have pitied him, but his sweeping attention to a fluttery Bea grated on my nerves. I'm not used to being witness or captive to kindergarten behavior.

Bea was a presentable woman, an adjective I use with great care. In certain lights she would be attractive, the slightly plump Manhattan socialite with the well-tailored summer dress, the discreet ruby earrings and necklace, and the Vivian Leigh hairdo that made her look as though she were one step ahead of marauding Yankee troops approaching Atlanta. Signaling to the waiter for a second martini, she ignored the mumbled hiss from her teetotaler husband.

Evan was thanking her for calling Cheryl Crawford. "I don't know why I'm having trouble getting parts."

"Perhaps because you project an image of not needing one," I offered.

He squirmed. "Meaning?"

"Directors, on Broadway and in Hollywood, tend to be fearful of unwarranted cockiness."

"I'm not cocky." An edge to his voice.

"I mean no offense. I'm just saying…"

Bea broke in. "Edna, look at him. Handsome and smart, the matinee idol, a natural."

"A heartthrob, indeed." My robotic voice suggested an epitaph.

Bea hurled a sidelong glance my way, her eyes flashing anger, and she shook her head.

George spoke up. "Young man, why *did* you leave Hollywood? I would have thought you'd be in demand out there."

"George, be nice." From Bea.

"I am. Bea, not every syllable from my mouth is ironic."

I smiled. "The other ones, I guess, just register disbelief."

Evan sat back, sated from the copious meal and his third martini. His eyes gleamed like shiny marbles. A sloppy grin covered his face. "I'm going back there. To Hollywood. I just thought I'd try my luck back on Broadway, where I started. Hollywood…I didn't give it a chance."

"Maplewood is hardly Forty-second Street," George noted.

"Hey, it's summer, and I happen to know people here." He sat up and glanced around the room. He slurred his words. "I have reasons for coming here." He narrowed his eyes. "Reasons."

"Who you do know here?" Bea asked.

"Dakota Roberts," he said slowly. "Not really a friend, but…yeah…I suppose a friend. You know, his mother's one holier-than-thou preacher."

"How do you know him?" I asked.

"Hollywood." The word was stretched out, each syllable clipped.

"You were arguing with Dak the other night at the inn."

That stopped him. "I know. We put on a show for you. I regret that, Miss Ferber. Entertainment for your dinner. He thought I was flirting with Annika, his girl. Silliest thing. A little too much to drink, him and me. It got…physical. But we're buddies. From Hollywood days."

"How so?" From George.

Evan suddenly looked uncomfortable, fiddling with the napkin, balling it up. "I bumped into him out there a few years ago. I was doing bit parts in some Universal movies, nothing big, and he was working scenery on a back lot. As it turned out, we boarded in the same rooming house. So he became a drinking buddy, sometimes. A few games of pool. He's a wanderer, somehow ended up in L.A. We were two guys who didn't know a lot of people, you know, bumping into…you know…" He clicked his tongue. "Unlikely friends, the two of us, but when you're alone in a strange land…you know…Not my sort of buddy, really…but…but then he drifted back East. Nothing good happened to him in Hollywood. I remembered he told me he was raised in Maplewood, so when I got the job here, I looked him up." He shrugged his shoulders. "No big deal. He's a little too…soft for me."

"He didn't look happy to see you." I watched him closely.

"I don't think he's happy to see anyone. That Annika's got him chained to the cross. I'll tell you…at first he was surprised I showed up, seemed all right with it, but I'm…well…always the one people want to be with." He half-bowed, and I hoped he was as ironic as George usually is—but I doubted it.

"That night in the lounge you were with a small, short stocky man, harsh-looking, a man…"

"Gus Schnelling. Christ, that rabble-rouser. Yeah, well, he was in Hollywood with us, too. The three misfits. Three drinking buddies. Dak hated him. I mean…they barely *talked*." A chuckle. "I don't much like him myself—a bulldog. In your face, nasty. But he was the electrician who kept getting fired. He's got this new woman…"

"Meaka?"

He squinted. "Miss Ferber, you know everything."

"I like to."

"Meaka Snow. Aryan priestess. I don't know where he found her, but he's turned her into this…this firebrand. Hard as nails, let me tell you. I mean, Gus has got weird politics, but she's bonkers. I bumped into him by chance in New York—he was looking for a job in the theater district—and stupidly I mentioned this job in Maplewood. " A grin. "I talk too much, and I was sorry the minute I opened my mouth. So he needed a job and ended up here. I don't like it—I like to keep my distance from him. I don't want him around."

The lines sounded rehearsed, his words spaced out, precise. Why? I wondered.

"Gus scares me," I announced. "He looks like he's always sporting for a fight. The two of them, actually. Meaka has that penetrating stare."

Evan laughed. "Gus scares everyone. He scares *me*. And she's like a machine, hammering at you. Girls should be pretty—and quiet. She's always…*on* you. The reason Gus came to New York—maybe that's where he met Meaka, I don't know—was because of the rally last year at Madison Square Garden."

Confused, I leaned in. "Rally?"

"They're Nazis, Miss Ferber. Crazy as can be, handing out leaflets on street corners. Hitlerites. Last year the Pro-America Rally in February—on Washington's birthday, no less. The

German Bund. *Achtung* on Broadway. Like unformed storm troopers."

I froze. "My God!"

"My God!" George echoed me.

"I mean, he's okay with a couple beers in him. But I think he'd slit your throat if you crossed him." He laughed. "I'm joking. C'mon, folks. You all look so serious." Another pause. "He's proud that he's met this Fritz Kuhn, the high Bund muck-a-muck. The guy waves those swastikas at you. But, hey—Gus'll go away sooner or later."

That made no sense to me. Chilled, I recalled the much-publicized rally at Madison Square Garden with over twenty-thousand Bund members roaring and clapping. German flags. Swastikas. Kuhn mocking "President Frank D. Rosenfeld" and his "Jew Deal." I shivered. The news accounts had sickened me.

"I can't imagine Dak was happy to see him in Maplewood." I looked from Bea to George. "Gus is a menace. And Dak strikes me as a sensitive, troubled…"

"Gus hates him." Evan enjoyed sharing that information. "Dak hates him more."

"I'm not surprised."

"Gus just shows up here and somebody somehow hires him. Suddenly he greets me on the sidewalk. I'm not happy, let me tell you. But when Dak saw him, sparks flew. First me—then Gus." He smirked. "All his nightmares coming true. They had words during set construction. Dak was carrying a backdrop and Gus stood in his way, arms folded over his chest. It was great to watch. In Hollywood they stopped talking to each other. So Gus cursed Dak out, everyone froze, and Frank comes running, defending Dak. Gus yelled—he's a weakling and a sissy. Pitiful. Gotta have people save him. Frank spotted me standing there laughing at it all. You know, I can size up any guy's weakness. Almighty Gus, Hitler youth himself. That's *his* weakness—blind faith in authority. It comes in handy, you know, my sizing folks up. Dak is weak and Gus thinks he's strong. I got both their numbers. It gives you an edge over folks."

I raised my voice. "Not the building block of lasting friendship."

He shook his head. "You know, later on, I heard Dak telling Frank how much he hates *me*. Not Gus. *Me!*"

"You seem to enjoy being hated, Evan," George noted.

Bea looked nervous. "Evan, you're having fun with us, right?"

George shot her a look. It was like a cold knife stuck into the ribs.

"Sooner or later, everyone hates me." Evan interlaced his fingers behind his head.

"And that's an enviable state?" George's voice was chilly.

"Of course. It just tells me that I've won yet again."

Chapter Five

Two days later, returning to the inn after a lengthy and tiring morning rehearsal, I slowly climbed the flight of stairs to my room. Pausing in the hallway as I searched for my key, I heard a loud burst of chatter below in the lobby. I stepped back to the landing in time to see Evan leaning on the reception desk. Crazily, he was banging the reception bell, the *ding ding ding* punctuating his performance. His booming voice echoed off the old wood panels, up the stairs. Leaning over the banister, I saw him adjust a cuff, so mannered a gesture it seemed some stage business. He whistled. Finally, perhaps because there was no one left to annoy, he exclaimed to no one in particular, "A new home, and in style."

At that, he rushed up the stairs, and I wasn't fast enough to escape him. I backed up, fumbled for my key, as he planted himself at the top of the stairs. "Ah, Miss Ferber, we're neighbors."

"Lucky me."

"They told me you're in room 21. Lucky 21. Mr. Kaufman is in 23. Well, I'm lucky 27, at the end of the hall."

"I thought your finances, sir, were…how should I say this?—meager?" I found my key and turned away.

He let out a fierce, booming roar. He stepped close to me, leaning in, his face beaming, and I smelled onions on his breath. I backed off. "Please, Evan. This is a quiet inn." Down the hall a door cracked open for a second, then was quietly shut.

He was carrying some parcels wrapped in brown paper and tied with a white cord. Now, shifting his stance, one toppled to the floor and rested on the exquisite oriental carpet. Amused, he kicked it with his boot, as though maneuvering a football down the hall toward room 27. "New shirts. Blue and tan and... No holes in the elbows. When I take you and Mr. Kaufman out to dinner tonight, my treat, I'll look as stylish as you two." The kicked parcel banged into a wall. The paper ripped. Then, insanely, he dropped his other packages and kicked them down the hall.

"One, I have other plans for dinner." Though, of course, I didn't. I fixed him in my stare. "And two, you'll never be more than a new shirt, sir."

He ignored the slight—I doubted that he heard me. "How about a pearl tie-pin? Real gold-plated. Like a nineteenth-century gambler on your showboat?" He tapped a small package in a breast pocket.

"Pearls?" I questioned. "Accompanying swine?"

He didn't care, laughing so hard I thought he'd double over. "Now, now, Miss Ferber. You are a kidder."

Then, in a garish display worthy of, say, my own dandy Gaylord Ravenal leaping onto a showboat from a Mississippi levee, he withdrew a generous wad of cash from a pocket, fanned the bundle before me, and backed off, still kicking the parcels strewn before him.

I called after him. "Good fortune, Evan?"

"I've been waiting for this for a month now. An uncle I never met—the first Evan, conveniently—died and the money was delivered this morning. Didn't you see me skipping out of the Maplewood Bank & Trust?" A grin plastered to his face. "You probably missed me at rehearsal. I had a bit of shopping to do."

"You're a lucky man."

"Luck ain't got nothing to do with it." His own words sounded puzzling to him because he paused, furrowed his brow, and then announced, "Well, yeah, I guess so. I mean, it pays to have rich relatives, even if you don't know them." He grinned stupidly. "It's like my hard work has paid off."

With that, he scooped up his packages and disappeared into his new room. As I stood there, pondering his last puzzling line, the door to George's room opened, and a fuzzy head popped out.

"Edna, really, making a scene in the hallway."

"You didn't hear *my* boisterous voice."

"But you seem to attract a rag-tag element to perform for you."

"Did you hear Evan? He's awash in cash." I lowered my voice. "A dead uncle or…"

"Edna, you're so gullible."

"I didn't say I believed it. I'm just reporting…"

"There is no dead uncle. You forget I *know* the family. There's a struggling widowed mother who bothers Bea with long, weepy letters and mournful phone calls. She was an only child."

"Then…"

"A fabrication, Edna."

"But why?" I glanced in the direction of Evan's closed door. I could hear bureau drawers opening and closing.

"You should ask him. He seems to follow you around." A pause. "Or is it the other way around? You're one of those giddy swooners after matinee idols? Did you weep at Valentino's casket? I thought I recognized your prostate body in the news photos." He closed his door behind him and buttoned his sports jacket. "Lunch, Edna? My treat. You can tell me why you missed a cue this morning at rehearsal."

"George, I'm an actress now."

He laughed. "Keep telling yourself that, my dear."

Moments later, standing on the sidewalk, we watched Evan run around a parked Studebaker roadster, gleaming metallic blue and white, top down. He circled it as though it were elusive prey, just out of reach, but painfully tantalizing.

His voice bubbly, he yelled to us. "The car'll take me back to Hollywood." He danced around it, a little drunk.

I walked by, but George deliberated, bending to look at a fender. Now George never drove—didn't believe in driving.

Automobiles alarmed him. He would gladly be driven places, but the idea of his getting behind the wheel of a car was ludicrous and unacceptable. Bea drove, and poorly. George kept his eyes closed. He had to be dragged onto airplanes. Boats sickened him, yet he worshiped taxicabs because they had backseats. I drove lumbering town cars at my Connecticut estate, usually with the seats crammed with egg cartons or pool equipment—or, sometimes, my carping mother.

"Get in," Evan roared, opening a passenger door.

To my surprise, George slipped into the car, and Evan motioned for me to occupy a backseat. Reluctantly, offering George a disapproving look, I sat in back, and Evan, whooping like a back-lot Indian in a two-reel oater, sped off, the wheels of the car spitting pebbles and dust into the air. George had rested his arm on the back of the driver's seat and I tapped it, leaning forward. "We'll be killed, of course."

"Really, Edna!"

"I'd rather die a different death. Or, at least, with a companion less annoying."

George laughed. "Sit back, Edna."

Evan spun around town, passing cars, blowing through stop signs and lights, waving at strangers. A child, really, and not a very bright one. Yet a child propelling two tons of metal toward some dark abyss. We'd crash and I'd be strangled by my three strands of pearls, or, worse, be impaled on a gearshift. He pulled into the parking lot of a White Castle hamburger stand, just off Springfield, and pointed. "Anybody hungry?" But he didn't linger, throwing the car into gear and speeding off.

We sailed by the Assembly of God temple, where Evan slowed down near the massive front doors and pointed. "Sinners in the hands of an angry God."

He put the car in park, revved the engine noisily, and blew the horn. Dak and Annika stepped from the front entrance, squinted into the sun at the shiny blue convertible. I noted Annika gripping Dak's arm, and he whispered something to her. She stepped back, pulling at him, but Dak moved toward us, a puzzled look on his face. Annika reluctantly followed him, her face grim. Dak's look took in Evan and George, but rested, baffled, on me, the kidnapped spinster in the backseat. Evan waited until he was near and then leaned on the horn, a discordant *bah-bah-bah* that nearly drove me to distraction.

"Mine." Evan raised his body in the seat and waved his hand around the car.

Annika stood behind Dak but her hand gripped his elbow. Then, brazenly, she moved toward the car. "Could you show some respect for the house of God?"

"Mine." Evan was looking at Annika.

"Where'd you get the money?" Dak asked suddenly.

"Ask Miss Ferber." Evan pointed over his shoulder but did not turn around.

"A dead uncle." My voice flat, dull. "A conveniently dead uncle. From the pages of a novel only Evan has read."

"Dakota, let's get out of here." Now Annika sounded panicky. Her grip on Dak's elbow tightened. "Please don't go with him."

"Wanna jump in, Annika? We'll leave Dakota in the dust."

But at that moment Evan gunned the engine and the car flew off, jerking back and forth for a second, tossing me around the backseat. At the next corner he slowed to a crawl and said to George, who looked pale and nauseous, his eyes shut, "Dak doesn't love that horrible harpy."

"What?" From George, in a faraway voice.

"Dak doesn't want to be God's missionary. Or married to that witch from Salem."

"What?" George repeated.

Evan said through clenched teeth, "Those two pray to the wrong God. My God put cash in my pocket. God loves rascals and ne'er-do-wells. Everybody knows that. Ain't that a riot? God holds the note for this car. So I guess it does a soul good to…to believe."

Then he lapsed into silence and turned the car around. It was as though he'd made a point, and that moment ended. He dropped us off at the Jefferson Village Inn and sped off.

"Edna, you're so pale."

"George, this is all your fault."

An hour later, finishing lunch, I left George and headed back to the theater for an appointment with wardrobe. One of my costumes needed adjustment. I'd scheduled a short meeting with the wardrobe mistress who'd tactfully insinuated that I'd put on a few extra pounds since my fitting in New York a month back. My task completed, I opened the front door to leave, and I saw Evan's shiny convertible parked alongside the train station, but he was nowhere to be seen. The rear seat was heaped high with cardboard boxes.

But then I spotted him. He was in deep conversation with Nadine Novack, both partially sheltered by a panel truck. She stepped away from him, angry, knocking his hand away, and he threw back his head, laughing. I watched her closely: her body tense, her arms held out in front of her as though demanding distance. Even from across the street I could see her shaking her head and mouthing a word over and over: *no no no*. She backed away, turned, and suddenly, in a brazen move, he grabbed both of her shoulders, swung her back to face him, and held her. She pushed against him but couldn't free herself. He was laughing, but there was no pleasure in it: a cruelty there, a maniac's raw howl. Finally, desperate, she kicked his foot, broke free and wildly slapped him in the face.

She ran toward the theater and I stepped back, hidden by the half-shut door.

He came after her and yelled, "I can tell them, you know."

She shifted back. "And what good would that do? It doesn't matter anymore. Nothing matters now…you…you…"

"Is that why you're in Maplewood? I *knew* it. That's why you came to this hole-in-a-wall in the boondocks."

Pleading in her voice. "I got a job."

"I'll tell Annika. How about that? Did Dak mention you to her?" A dark laugh. "I bet he didn't, that sissy. Are you his forbidden secret? Nadine Novack, my foot. What name will you use next? She won't be happy to know you're in town."

"It doesn't matter anymore. It just doesn't."

"Oh, but it does."

"Just leave Dak alone now."

"He's a weak, pathetic ass, that Dak. 'Leave me alone, Evan!' Yeah, his mommy wants him to be tomorrow's Billy Sunday. It ain't gonna happen. He's a milquetoast, a namby-pamby, drawing those pictures. A sissy artist."

"Leave him alone. Leave Annika alone. They got to be married. They…"

"Over my dead body. Or, I should say, over *your* dead body."

"Leave me alone."

Suddenly, there in the middle of the street, Nadine broke down sobbing. Evan, startled, looked bewildered and jumped into his car. What he did next was bizarre. He drove around her, a complete loop, at one point coming so close she could have touched a fender. She froze there, watching. He circled her, mocking.

And I watched, too, stepping out onto the landing, peering into Evan's car. As Evan circled her, his eyes hidden behind sunglasses, defiant, his hands gripped the wheel so tightly they seemed blocks of dark stone.

When he was gone, I approached Nadine, taking her hand. She looked into my face and tried to smile. "He's crazy, you know."

"Why does he scare you so?"

She shook her head wildly. "He doesn't."

"He hates Dak."

"He wants to hurt Dak."

"But why?"

"Because he can." She hurried past me into the theater.

George and I sat on the Adirondack deck chairs late in the afternoon, and I discussed Evan's nasty behavior with Nadine. "Help me understand what's going on?"

"I have a confession, Edna," George finally said.

"Oh Lord, no, George. I'm not good with confessions. Especially yours. They always disarm me."

He sighed. "I suspected Evan was trouble all along. I mean, I hinted my dislike—my distress with him being here." A sly smile. "Or, at least, I expected you to pick up on my offhand observations. But over the years I've heard Bea and his mother chatting—not to me, of course, because I don't abide gossip, but the two talking in soft, hidden voices. Evan has a cruel streak, I learned. He's done some horrible things to his mother—stealing, for one. Another time he shoved her aside. Just the two of them—the father long dead. She keeps hoping he'll…well, you get the picture. He gets pleasure from manipulating people. People tell things to good-looking people because they believe good-looking people are moral and trustworthy and decent. It's a common character flaw of humanity. Evan stores the information."

"Just what are you saying?"

"When Bea mentioned how she got Cheryl to hire Evan—I mean, she *begged*, that woman—I got nervous. I think Bea lied to Cheryl. At Cheryl's apartment, when he showed up, I didn't like it. I should have stopped it. Then and there."

"Your silence punishes me."

"Ridiculous, Edna. Of course not. He'll keep his distance from *you*." A sickly smile. "He knows what battles he'd lose." A pause. "Someone is always hurt when he shows up. Bea *knew* that."

"I won't allow this. Perhaps a few choice words with Cheryl." I'd seen her cruising around town hours before in her secondhand Mercer.

"Somebody is gonna get hurt."

"Stop saying that, George. You're giving me the willies."

We lapsed into an uncomfortable silence, lazy in the hot afternoon, watching the quiet street. I expected Evan to blaze by, toot-tooting in the shiny convertible or carrying his *nouveau riche* trappings up to his new room, but that did not happen.

What did happen was more unsettling. A rinky-dink pickup sputtered to a stop by the train station, and we watched Gus

Schnelling and Meaka Snow get out. They had been arguing about something, both yelling at each other. But then, as though a switch were pulled, they stopped and embraced quickly, mechanically, all was forgiven.

For fifteen minutes they assailed souls stepping away from the train station, handing out leaflets, their faces grim. Most folks rebuffed them, some loudly, an old man actually shoving aside Gus' arm. George and I stared at them, this squat, ungainly young couple. Gus had a kind of fierce bulldog masculinity, all those abrupt movements and preening struts. His gruff voice alarmed passersby. Meaka said nothing the whole time, though I noticed she shot occasional glances at him, and none too happy ones. The taskmaster checking in. From across the street she appeared a cold, emotionless person, the termagant with her rotund body and the severe haircut. Both automatons, I realized, expressionless characters from some European avant-garde drama. Capek's futuristic robots. Meaka the mechanical doll, the robotic inamorata. Gus had supposedly wooed her to his demonic cause, and now, the fervent convert, she outpaced him in her fire and drive. The human being devoid of personality, infused, rather, with ice and vinegar.

At one point Meaka spotted George and me observing them, and she nudged Gus. They'd exhausted their armfuls of leaflets, and Gus kept pointing to a wristwatch—he even opened the door of the old Ford pickup and started to step in, a man in a hurry—but Meaka kept pointing at us.

"I think we are cynosures of local amusement," George observed.

"Lord, the Katzenjammer Kids of the body politic."

Reluctantly, Gus followed a determined Meaka across the street, both stopping at the foot of the stairs.

"Here." Meaka took a folded leaflet from the purse slung over her shoulder and thrust it into my outreached hand. A quirky, unfriendly smile on her lips, she made a hard, guttural rasp, and turned away. Gus, eyes narrowed, watched her with a curious mixture of adoration and dread.

My hands trembled on the sheet, this foolscap with the poorly printed message. A bold headline: RALLY THIS SATURDAY! AMERICAN NAZI PARTY! SPRING VALLEY PARK SOUTH ORANGE. NOON. These lines were followed by a mishmash of chaotic sentences—references to German might, Aryan presence, degenerate artists, capitalist vainglory, Hitler Youth, political fury, and…well, the rambling words went on and on. In block letters, crooked, the last brutal line: "International Jews control America's banks. The world's scourge."

I looked up to watch the retreating backs of the superior race, these two purposeful, lost souls opening the doors of the battered pickup. Gus struggled to start the vehicle which resisted—sputtering, gasping, but finally popping on. They sailed away, and through the open windows Meaka's throaty laugh punctuated the quiet of the street. A death rattle, that, I thought: personification of all my recent fears about the way the world was sliding into chaos and disaster.

Just that morning, in the local paper, I'd read that anti-Jewish laws had been enacted in Romania. German artists, dazed, walked off ships in the New York harbor. O my America, my newfound land! And not far away from Maplewood, at Camp Nordland in Sussex County, New Jersey, a Nazi training camp practiced survival skills, and only a few souls, alarmed, voiced their protest.

I handed the sheet to George, who shook his head. "Perhaps we shouldn't tell them that we're Jewish."

I fumed. "Ah, but I have every intention of doing so."

That unexpected moment on the front porch cast a pall over the rest of the day. The incendiary broadside, propped up against the mirror in my room, kept catching my eye. Truth be told, I wanted it to jar me. I needed to be reminded of the wholesale—and, to me, illogical—hatred that was growing in America, corrupting, eating into the decent fabric of so many towns. Small towns like Maplewood. Gus and Meaka, Americans in the service of evil. Zealots drawn to subversive lives, into causes that defied reason. Idly my thoughts slipped to Clorinda Roberts Tyler and her Assembly of God. Her deadly serious acolyte Annika Tuttle spotted Satan behind every bush. Well, they were looking in the wrong place. Satan walked among us, true, but he wore a Charlie Chaplin moustache and looked out at the world through a madman's eyes. And, horribly, he was now planning on invading England.

George watched me carefully as we sat for dinner at the Marlborough House. "Edna, you can't let that get to you."

"Too late."

He tried to make a joke of it. "And Gus is one of the electricians at the Maplewood Theater? Who the hell hired him? If I were you, my dear, I'd be careful with props you pick up."

"You're not funny, George."

"I don't try to be, Edna."

I ignored that. "You know, I see it on the streets of New York these days. You do, too. Everywhere, especially after last year's huge rally at Madison Square Garden, that rollicking meeting of the American Nazi Party. American flags hanging alongside German ones. All the roaring and crowing—and threats. There are training camps everywhere. America is sliding into fascism."

Then I recalled my most recent—and oft-told—story of burgeoning Nazism in my own backyard. He'd heard it at my dinner parties, so he was hearing it again now. I didn't care. When I was scouting for land in Connecticut for my new home—this, mind you, with the Depression still horrible on the land—I'd located a virginal hill with breathless views at Stepney Depot, in Easton, Connecticut, just off the Merritt Parkway. Manhattan would be a scant hour's drive away. Options taken, lawyers contacted. Deals agreed to—but the craggy old Yankee owner reneged. Over and over the closings were aborted, as the old man dug in his heels. Finally, in desperation, I assailed him. Why, for God's sake? Why? Reluctantly, he told us he feared I was buying the land to set up a Nazi training ground. We all gasped, of course, me especially, the skittish Jewish lady in the room. It seemed a Nazi camp was then active up Southbury way—you could hear the *Heil Hitlers* and spy the bayonet-waving folks. The man—this silent, stubborn, and totally decent, old guard American—feared Nazi infiltration on land he loved. Well, disavowed of my use of his property—"You? Jewish? Really?" A wide smile on his face—the land was deeded over to me. No goose-stepping on my territory. No swastikas in my windows. Take that, Herr Schicklgruber.

In the short time I'd lived there I found a curious comfort knowing the old man lived at the bottom of the hill. My ancient sentry sat in an old rocker on a decrepit porch, pipe smoke circling his head. My hero.

"I know the story, Edna." George sounded tired.

"Yes, but it bears repeating."

"But not with me."

That irritated me, his dismissal of my words, so I sat there silently.

"Edna…"

"Quiet, George. Your indifference indicts you."

"And your imperiousness frightens me."

Not a jolly dinner, sadly. I kept flashing to that leaflet stuck on my mirror. George looked ready to apologize, and I should have encouraged it, knowing he shared my dread of the nascent Nazi movement, especially in his beloved Manhattan. After all, he and Bea still kept an apartment on East Ninety-fourth Street. George protected Manhattan—his *idea* of Manhattan—as much as I did, seeing it as the epicenter of sophistication and culture—and outright fun. He was so obsessed that he hated traveling anywhere that would not allow him to return safely to Forty-second Street in under one hour. A touchstone of his security. Broadway and Park Avenue and Central Park and Grand Central and even the Bronx Zoo as stepping stones to his wholeness. So I knew he was bothered by proliferating Nazis, especially in nearby neighborhoods like the German Yorkville, steps from his apartment.

But I decided to be still now. The mood was too raw. Gus and Meaka, loutish souls, were afoot in the land.

Back at the inn, sticky from the lingering August heat, we sat on the front porch and watched the daylight begin to fade, darkness seeping across the lazy street. From the bushes, crickets chirped, and cicadas sang out in the hemlocks. I closed my eyes.

A horn blared, a squeal of tires, and I expected Evan's sparkling chariot to cruise by, behind the wheel Maplewood's new Ben Hur in a slicked-back haircut. Instead, a black Buick drew to a stop, a cardboard placard on the dashboard announcing: Constable. The driver stepped out. He stood there, momentarily disoriented, his face drawn. He stared up at us blankly, eyes puzzled. I was tempted to say something. Within seconds two more black cars and a squeaky dump truck pulled up behind the first, a gaggle of men in overalls and denim caps tumbling out, approaching the constable. The constable, emboldened, withdrew his gun and looked at it.

George leaned toward me. "If they rush the porch, Edna, I expect you to shield me. I have plays to write."

The constable was a burly shock of a man. His salt-and-pepper hair was shaggy under a uniform hat, and a bushy moustache was so gigantic it touched the edges of his Burnside sideburns, a look I'd assumed had disappeared with Grover Cleveland. He was dressed for backyard leaf-raking, not for law enforcement, but now, swaggering, he yelled up to us. "This here where Evan Street is staying?"

"Yes." From me.

The constable stepped onto the porch and identified himself as Horace Biggers, "head constable of this here town." He pointed to the restless men behind him, men who looked like farmers fresh from harvesting cucumbers in the lower forty. "Deputies."

"Evan's not here," I told him. "He's sailing around town in a new car like…"

He shook his head. "No, he ain't." He glanced back at the men, then back at me. "Someone put a bullet into his chest back in DeHart Park."

I stood. "Oh my God. When?"

"Car still running, the driver's door wide open. Parked there like he just stepped out. Some kids from town hiking through seen the car, jazzy one, a convertible, and then seen him lying nearby in the bushes. He was shot right in the heart, it seems. They let up a howl, them boys, crying and bellowing. His wallet says Evan Street and Lon there"—he pointed to a white-bearded man nodding furiously—"says Street was an actor and staying here." Constable Biggers tucked his gun back into his holster and looked a little embarrassed.

I nodded. "His room is...27."

The constable didn't seem to know what to do next. "If you'll excuse me, folks." He walked by us into the inn, tipping his hat. Just inside the front door he called out for the proprietor. Meanwhile stranglers sensing the commotion out front drifted from nearby stores and homes, a gathering of townsfolk who buzzed and whispered.

Evan Street, the garrulous romantic actor, shot dead in a park. Outside of his car, the driver's door open, the engine still running. Was he alone in his car? Or had he stepped out to meet someone, fully expecting the visit to be short? An assignation? But not one he was looking forward to, most likely. He was ready to run away. But he never got the chance...surprised, shot in the chest as he faced his murderer. No suspense there. A brief but explosive confrontation in a park, perhaps hidden behind trees and bushes, yet a public park. But Evan Street now lay dead in that park, a hole in his chest. The understudy now starred in a murder.

The men trailed into the inn after Constable Biggers, but the street was filled with the curious. I felt a tad foolish sitting on that porch, George and I gaping out at the growing crowd. We sat there, the two of us, while people watched us. "Act one," George announced. "Two cosmopolites silently view the town *hoi polloi*, expecting disaster. First character speaks..."

"George, really."

"Not a good opening line, Edna."

"I feel the need to say something."

"Don't you always?"

"Your timing is off, George. A man is dead."

"I didn't do it, Edna."

At that moment someone pushed through the twittering crowd and rushed up the stairs. Suddenly Frank Resnick stood there, trembling, out of breath. The quiet man was quivering and babbling, his face sweaty, his eyes darting wildly from George to me. The usually neat, debonair man looked disheveled, his dress shirt half out of his pants, his pants cuffs dusty.

"Frank." George reached out a hand and grabbed hold of the distraught man. "What?"

"You heard about…"

"Evan Street?" My own voice cracked. "The constable, Horace Biggers, is inside now…Evan's room, I guess."

He was paying me no mind, sputtering something that made no sense.

"What?" From me.

"Dak." The word was a plaintive cry, thick with fear. "Dak." Repeated, louder now. "Where is Dak? I have to find Dak."

Chapter Six

"The fat is in the fire."

The following morning, despite the static and panic in the air, George insisted we run through our scheduled rehearsal, which we did, mechanically, though lines were missed, cues ignored, and a distracted stagehand carelessly walked across the stage just as I was dying in the last act. Someone giggled a little too hysterically, and the stagehand toppled over a chair, nearly tipping me from my final sofa.

George sat in the first row, a notepad in his hand, and I hoped he'd not take this moment to critique my wooden delivery.

But when I joined him at break, I noticed he'd merely doodled nonsense.

"This rehearsal is foolish," I told him.

"We're days from opening, Edna. Nothing has come together yet."

"But it always does, magically, the first night."

Calling us back onstage for another go at two of the scenes, George finally threw up his hands, and dismissed us.

Few people, it turned out, really knew Evan Street, the anonymous understudy for Louis Calhern—lately he'd spent more time in the streets of Maplewood than in the wings of the theater—but the presence of Constable Biggers was disturbing. Folks didn't know where to look.

Last night as George and I sat on the porch and watched Constable Biggers and his Falstaffian posse leave the inn after sealing off Evan's room, George had observed, quietly, "The fat is in the fire, Edna."

"What?"

"I told you that Evan brought disaster with him. It begins now."

Minutes after the caravan of black cars sped off, an agitated Gus Schnelling arrived in his old pickup, one wheel up on the sidewalk, and rushed by us into the inn. The proprietor, Garret Smith, had been standing on the porch, watching the departing cars. Stunned, he trailed Gus inside, the door slamming behind him. Immediately his harried voice carried out to us. "Are you crazy?"

Gus had rushed up the stairs, banging into a wall and knocking a photograph down the stairs, the glass shattering into pieces. He jiggled the door of Evan's room, pushed against it with his thick shoulder, only to be grabbed by Garret who told him Constable Biggers had forbidden entry to anyone. Gus ignored him, again fiddling with the lock, damning the proprietor, and fleeing only when a frantic Garret hurried to call the police. Gus tumbled down the stairs, taking two or three at a time, and, red-faced and belligerent, stumbled onto the porch, banging his fist against the railing. George and I watched him, but he ignored us, jumping into his pickup, slamming the door so loudly I jumped, too.

"The fat is in the fire," George repeated.

Now, sitting with George in the orchestra after everyone else had left the stage, relief in their faces, he said it again. "The fat is in the fire."

"Please, George," I pleaded. "Enough of that line. Have you no other words? You sound like a…a spinster in a British mystery."

"That's *your* role, my dear." A trace of cruelty in his voice. But then he relented. "Act two. The plot thickens." He leaned back in his seat, staring up at the empty stage.

Cheryl Crawford, her usual implacable self, nodded at the two of us as she and Louis Calhern walked from the wings. "Stay out of trouble," Louis said to both of us.

"You two are not staying around?" I asked.

Both looked surprised. "Why?" Cheryl asked. And they headed out, Louis probably for the train station and Cheryl for the solitude of her bungalow.

"Well, Constable Biggers got Evan's personal information from her," George told me. "And Louis had nothing to tell him. I contacted Evan's mother."

"Did you call Bea?"

He squinted and waited a heartbeat. "You know, I was surprised at her coolness—I expected sobbing. Instead Bea just said, 'He was a boy doomed to die young.'"

"That's nonsense."

George agreed. "In fact, I used those very words, and added, 'You assume all good-looking young men, to whom you attribute sensitivity and angst, will die young. It's the liability of attractiveness.'"

"A sentimentalist, your wife."

"To which, she said to me in her blunt fashion, 'You'll live forever.' And I told her, 'It only seems that way, Bea.'"

"Did she hang up on you?"

"She started to, but decided to linger, practicing her lines for Evan's mother."

◇◇◇

Late that afternoon, sitting in the Full Moon Café with Mamie Trout hovering nearby, George and I said very little. The shadow of Evan's horrible death covered us. When Constable Biggers walked in, he spotted us and drew up a chair. The look on his face suggested he'd been looking for us. Mamie Trout—who, I discovered, was an eager gossip and had peppered us with questions about the murder, none of which we answered—sidled her way to a perfectly clean table, rag suspended in hand. But Biggers, eyeballing her with stern look, pointed to the kitchen. Reluctantly, she disappeared. No one else was in the café.

"Yes?" From me.

"A minute of your time, folks?"

"Of course."

A bulky man, Biggers settled in, his flesh bulging out of the too-tight murky gray uniform shirt, his yellow-stained fingertips fiddling with a cigar that he now placed in the corner of his mouth. It bobbed there precariously, and ashes drifted onto his shirt. "State police fellow coming over to run the case, I thought I'd tell you. But I'm doing some talking to folks. After all, I seen the victim in town—seemed to be everywhere he wasn't sup-posed to be. I figured theater people who knew this Evan Street might tell me a thing or two." He withdrew a small pad from a breast pocket, found the stub of a pencil that was shorter than his fingers, and waited.

"What do you want to know?" I asked.

"From what I hear, this Evan fellow made quite a few enemies, what with his charming the pants off the ladies and punching out the boys. Kind of fellow who's got murder written on his forehead. Tell me what you know."

So we did, George and I both summarizing what little we knew about Evan—his struggling mother, his acquaintances, the little we knew of his acting life. The sudden windfall of cash. Biggers never jotted down a word we said, seemingly interested only in watching the tip of his cigar as though he feared it would fizzle out. He thanked us, snapped shut the notebook, and stood, but I motioned him back down. He looked puzzled, but he dropped back into his seat.

"Constable Biggers, Evan was shot in the heart?"

"That's true. At close range. Someone talking to him, taking him unawares."

"So he knew his murderer?"

He waited a bit. "Looks like it. He hadn't planned on getting shot." A dry chuckle. "But then, who does, no?"

"No leads?" I asked.

George was tapping his finger on the table, his eyes on me—he was not happy with me. At one point he grunted and Constable Biggers eyed him suspiciously. "Edna!"

"Yes, George?"

Biggers squinted, uncomfortable. "Tell me what you know about this"—he flipped open his pad again and his finger ran down the sheet—"this Gus Schnelling. The two of them boys being friends with Dakota Roberts. I mean, I know Dakota a long time, yeah, but I guess they all knew each other, it seems and…" He shrugged, helpless.

"They all knew one another from the Coast," I told him. "Hollywood. I'm not certain when."

"Shoulda stayed there, the lot of them. Well, this Gus is a rabble-rouser, let me tell you. He didn't like being questioned. In fact, he stood there with his arms crossed and spouted some mumble-jumble nonsense in German. A Nazi, he told me—proud of it. Sickness when folks is proud of being crazy."

"Does he have an alibi?"

Again, the furrowed brow, as though my question startled—the family pet suddenly with an unnatural vocabulary. He hesitated. "What little I got from him is that he was over to Newark with this cold fish named Meaka Snow." He checked his pad again. "She's a piece of goods, that one. 'You don't gotta say nothing to him, Gus. He's browbeating you.' And all I'd said was, 'Where were you yesterday afternoon?' A federal offense, they make it. I been hearing that this Gus was none too happy with Evan who's made fun of this Meaka broad. Christ, I felt like mocking her myself." His eyes got wide with mischief. "Some folks naturally built to be make fun of."

"So she's his alibi?"

He let out a phony laugh. "Imagine that. One dirty hand slapping the other." His gigantic moustache twitched.

George was watching me closely, the tapping on the table getting louder. He cleared his throat, but I went on. "I don't have much to tell you, Constable. You did hear that Gus tried to get into Evan's room right after you left?"

"Sure thing. It's a small town. Half the citizens were witness to that."

"Well, did you ask him why?"

"He says Evan owed him money and he was afraid he won't get it now that his buddy was shot. 'I ain't done it,' he yelled, and then clammed up. Backed off. That Meaka woman grunts and stands in front of him, like she's a human shield. 'Hey,' I said, 'I ain't gonna shoot your boyfriend.' And she spits out, 'Anything is possible in a time of war.' A time of war? Jesus Christ! I got away from the two of them. My mother always warned me to step away from the crazies."

George grumbled under his breath. "That must be hard for you to do."

I shot him a look. "What about Dak?"

"Yeah, that one's up to something. You can bet on that. Everyone tells me about his argument with Evan in the lounge at the inn. The two shoving each other around like it's the Wild West. Punching, swearing. The bartender says Dak was red-faced and blubbering. He *hit* Evan. Evan, I guess, flirted with"—again he glanced at his pad—"Annika Tuttle."

"Do they have alibis for yesterday afternoon? I mean, Dak and…this Annika?"

Again George glared at me. *Tap tap tap.* Morse code I had little difficulty translating.

"Nope. Dak says he was driving around by himself, spent time at the stone bridge in Maplewood Park with his sketchpad. Lord, he said he drove near to DeHart Park, where the body was. He told me that flat out. Like he went by the entrance—but kept going. It turns out he was supposed to be working at the Assembly of God, and Annika went looking for him. He turns up and says he forgot about the time. Said he was here, said he was there. I guess he was everywhere." A sickly grin. "The Holy Ghost, maybe. Hiding something, that boy. I know him a lifetime, almost. Always an odd boy, mumbling to hisself on the sidewalk. I ran him in a few times when he was a boy. Mischief."

I got defensive. "I found him a charming young man. A little brooding, perhaps, and a dreamer…"

George broke in as the man watched us closely, steel-eyed. "Isn't he someone you've written about, Edna?"

"George, please. Not now."

Constable Biggers frowned at the interruption. "He's made it clear he was no fan of Evan Street. Lots of different folks told me that. Some rivalry going back some time. I'll get to the bottom of it—or, maybe, the state trooper will. Murder in Maplewood—it never happens." He stared off, bewildered. "But it did. You know, right now Dakota Roberts is suspect number one."

Hotly, protesting, "A little premature, no, officer?" I tried to smile.

"Ma'am, as I said, I've known Dakota since he was a young boy in the town, cared for by his aunt and grandfather. A bundle of trouble, that boy, vandalism and insolence and sassiness and pinching stuff from the Rowe's Five and Dime. Always angry, a troublemaker…"

"That doesn't sound like the sweet boy who sits by himself and draws…"

"Ma'am, a wild one. You don't know the half of it. A loner, that one. He runs off to California when he was seventeen or so, and I thought, good riddance to bad rubbish. But then, tail between his legs, he's back. Ten years back or so his wandering mother—another strange one, a woman preacher—moves back to town after her father died. She marries this Tobias Tyler, the fellow who set her up in this hell-raising tent revival church, the Assembly of God. And nothing in Maplewood's been the same."

"You don't like her church?"

"Look, Miss Ferber, I ain't got nothing against churches that are Methodist or Lutheran. But this holy-roller nuisance brings carloads of whoop-it-up folks, and when they get to going, you can hear 'Praise be to God' ten mile away. I like me a nice quiet town. So Clorinda Roberts Tyler is preaching and screaming and hysterical, and people are fainting. Then the buses filled with pilgrims come in and the old ladies wailing to God…Meanwhile Dak is like fourteen years old and running wild. Then he comes back from no good in Hollywood, and Clorinda announces he's the prodigal son, returned to find the fatted calf, or some such nonsense. Everywhere in town you go you see him arm in arm with this Annika girl. Turning him holy, his mother says. God's plan. The voice of the turtle, she says. Hallelujah. More like the hounds of hell baying at the moon. Mumbo jumbo."

Constable Biggers extracted a large stained handkerchief and wiped his brow.

"I still don't see why you suspect Dak of murder."

"Ma'am." He leaned in, and I watched a line of sweat trickle down his chin. "The sons of holier-than-thou preachers are always your killer."

"That's ridiculous." My voice rose, strident.

"Edna," George began, "why are you so angry with the man? You don't know Dak."

"Of course I do." I paused. "Well, at least I don't believe a young man like that is capable of such a horrible murder. I've observed him, spoken with him for a while—and I trust my instincts. Always. He's not a murderer. A gunshot to the chest. Brutal, deliberate, vicious. Never!"

Constable Biggers was talking to himself. "Nothing good ever comes out of these evangelical screamers, hands up in the air, swaying, crying." Suddenly his eyes caught mine. "Nothing good. And when that Crawford woman opened the Maplewood Theater and put on those live shows, I says to myself here we go again. Folks getting excited, clapping and whooping it up. Cars lined up in front of the train station. All these women in furs—in July, mind you—stepping off the train from Manhattan with their la-di-dah makeup, and wondering where the cocktail lounge is. Theater folks. This used to be a quiet town. Nobody—" he sucked in his breath and snarled—

I finished for him. "Got murdered?"

"You said it, sister."

When the constable left us, George said nothing but his whole manner suggested disapproval. The long narrow face was stiff, the eyes behind those huge eyeglasses were unblinking, and his lips were drawn into a razor-thin line.

"What is it, George?"

"Edna, don't do this." He waved his hand toward the street.

"George!"

"You want answers and you don't trust the town sheriff."

"He wants to railroad Dak."

"Edna, there's a murderer is in town. He's killed someone we knew, if faintly. There is no basis for your trumpeting of this…this poorly named Dak other than he's one of your under-dogs—romantic, doubtless handsome, and woefully flawed. Your nosiness has been annoying in the past, I must admit, but now it could be dangerous."

"I'm doing nothing of the sort."

He spoke in a small, fierce voice. "I heard it in the way you grilled that bumbling constable. Edna as Spanish Inquisition. Torquemado in pearls. The Chinese water torture, Ferber-style."

"George, a little over the top."

He sat back and sighed, "All right, I give up, Edna." A hint of a smile. "Please don't ask me to speak at your funeral."

I smiled and sat back. "The white flag of surrender always pleases me."

"Just a warning, my dear. There is someone out there with a gun. Now, personally, I know at least a dozen people who'd like to shoot you, but your absence would be…conspicuous. An oxymoron."

"I'm a big girl."

"I'm going to be watching from the wings, Edna. This bleak tragedy is Elizabethan. In three acts."

When I answered the knock on my door later that afternoon, I was surprised to see Nadine Novack standing there. For a moment she stared at me, as though she'd knocked on the wrong door, but then, breathing in so deeply she made a raspy sound, she tried to say my name, stammered, had to begin again. She shook her head back and forth, angry with herself. "Miss Ferber, I'm sorry. You must think I'm a fool. I rehearsed what I want to tell you and now my mind's a blank." Clumsily, she backed off and looked up and down the empty hallway as if she'd lost her sense of direction. I reached out and touched the sleeve of her dress. She was wearing a breezy pale-yellow summer smock, baggy, unattractive, a size too large for her, but I could feel her twig-like forearm under the cloth. My gesture rattled her but she stopped moving. Some of the bright crimson lipstick she wore had smeared a front tooth. It made her look vulnerable.

"Nadine," I began, "tell me." When she said nothing, simply batting her eyes wildly as though I'd shone a bright light into them, I insisted she come in, but she shook her head vigorously: no, no, no. "All right, then, let's go downstairs. A cup of coffee. The two of us." She nodded.

Not speaking, with too much space between us, we walked to the Full Moon Café and found a table at the back, away from the few customers who sat clustered by the front window. Nadine wanted hot coffee, though the room was close and sticky. She drank it black, in tiny squirrel-like sips, staring into the cup as though it held prophetic tea leaves.

"Tell me," I said again, this time gripping her hand. The coffee cup rattled when she put it down.

"Dak Roberts." Two words, both explosive with feeling.

A heartbeat. "What about him?"

She found her voice, even and cool. "They're gonna arrest him for murdering Evan Street. He *told* me." Her face trembled.

"That seems a little hasty, no?"

Pleading in her voice, a quiver. "Miss Ferber, he has no alibi. None. Worse, he was *there*."

That stopped me. "Where?"

"In the park. He keeps changing his story—like he doesn't know what to say. He confessed to Constable Biggers and the state police that he was driving around and spotted Evan's car cruise by. Stupidly he *followed* him to DeHart Park and saw Evan pull up and get out." A helpless shrug. "Why would he *tell* them that?"

I felt my heart racing. "Perhaps because it's true. The truth counts now, Nadine." I waited a second. "Was there anyone else there?"

She shook her head. "Dak says Evan headed off in a hurry, running even, disappearing behind a bank of bushes."

"Did Dak stop?"

"No, he kept going. He thought maybe Evan was meeting some girl…or something."

"I know—he told this to Constable Biggers."

Nadine smiled thinly. "You got to know Dak, Miss Ferber. He can't lie to anybody. I mean"—she blushed—"he sometimes avoids saying something he shouldn't, but he won't lie outright. He was driving around, sketching."

"So Biggers now suspects him."

"He confessed to *following* him—seeing him *there*. It's not good. No one goes to that park. I've heard it's deserted most of the time. Dak was foolish. And the constable knows him from years back—his wild days in town. Biggers never liked him. I mean, Dak as a boy then—he did…dumb stuff…but this is murder. He said Biggers told him not to leave town." She locked eyes with me. "It was like a line from the movies."

"But this is not imminent arrest, Nadine."

"Dak is convinced. You know that he fought with Evan. More than once. They even came to blows. Dak isn't a fighter but Evan always made him furious. He *hit* Evan. He told people how unhappy he was that Evan came here to perform."

I waited a second. "Tell me. Did Evan come here *because* of Dak?"

That perplexed her. "I can't imagine why."

"What do you want from me, Nadine?" I sipped my iced lemon soda slowly, trying to make sense of this.

She waited, looked over my shoulder. "Dak trusts you. He says he talked to you, and he thought, well, you trusted *him*."

I interrupted. "I do like him, but there is a murder to be dealt with."

At my use of the word *murder*, her hand rose to her mouth and she closed her eyes. "My God, Dak had nothing to do with that. Of course."

"How do you know?"

"I *know* Dak."

"Tell me, Nadine, how *do* you know Dak? I've sensed something I can't put my finger on. He seems to be interested in you."

She swallowed and whispered. "We know each other from years ago. Briefly. In Hollywood, as a matter of fact. I was a bit player." She shrugged her shoulders and dipped her finger into the coffee, stirred it mechanically. "It's not important. That's over with. When I got the job at the theater, I remembered that he lived here...grew up here. I didn't know if he still lived here. Really, I didn't."

As she spoke, her tone became hollow, faraway, and I suspected she wasn't being truthful. Some part of the story was missing. Dak had watched her from the shadows, and now she sought me out on his behalf. A puzzle, this one, and it came with missing pieces.

I repeated, "What do you want from me?"

"He wants to talk to you tonight. The two of you. He asked me to ask you. He doesn't want to come to the inn—get away from...from..."

I grimaced. "Will Annika be at his side?"

She shivered. "God, no. But Annika is worried about him. I know that. His parents, too. His mother's like a brooding mother hen, and Annika copies her. Annika is leery around me. I don't see him at the theater. He works afternoons, mostly. He *avoids* me there—purposely. I mean, he knows me from...from Hollywood. I thought we'd...you know...reconnect. But when I learned about Annika, I...backed off. One time she caught us talking and flew into a rage. She went crazy, yelling at me. We were in the middle of the Avenue. She was horrible, calling me a tool of Satan. 'Leave Dak alone—he's being used' and 'theater people are evil.' She went on and on. 'Life on the stage corrupts.' So we try to avoid each other. But today Dak slipped away and caught me as I left the dressing rooms. He mouthed the two words: Miss Ferber. I said—what? He told me to come here. See you. He hoped to see you alone, but you...you were always with Mr. Kaufman." She ran her fingers through her hair and smiled. "End of a long monologue. So here I am."

"I will meet with Dak."

"He's working with Frank on sets tonight. You'll find him backstage."

"Nadine, tell me the truth. You came to Maplewood knowing Dak was living here."

"Of course not." But she spoke too quickly, regretting the obvious lie, and retreated. "I mean, I thought we might bump into each other and…" She turned her head away, flushed.

"Did he know you were coming? Tell me the truth."

She shook her head vigorously, and then smiled. "Not really. He was surprised. I'm using my old stage name. Nadine Novack. In Hollywood—my brief moment in one bad movie—I used my real name. Nadine Chappelle. That's how he knew me. So short a time I knew him"—a wistful moment, teary-eyed—"that sometimes I think I dreamed it all."

She started to stand but I reached out to touch her wrist. "One last thing, Nadine."

She bit her lip, uncertain. "What?"

"Did you know Evan Street before you came here?"

A long silence, painful, but then her face sagged, her eyes dark, heavy. "Yes."

"And?"

A sob in her voice. "I couldn't believe it when he showed up here. I hoped I'd never see him again. An understudy. I remember thinking—Can God be that cruel to me again?"

"Again?"

"Miss Ferber, I hated Evan Street. I hated the sight of him." She gave out a laugh, a little hysterical. "I am so happy he's dead."

Then she started to cry.

◇◇◇

Frank Resnick wasn't happy when I asked to spend a half-hour talking to Dak, though he nodded. "He's a little frenzied," he told me. "I've come to like the boy, Miss Ferber. He's running scared, I think. I *made* him come to work tonight. Last night, when I heard Evan was murdered, I remembered how Evan treated him. Dak's stories about him. I guess I overreacted. I…" He was ready to blather on, defensively, but I held up my hand.

"A half-hour at most," I repeated.

Frank's head shifted nervously. "I didn't sleep last night." Then a smile I couldn't interpret. "Dak," he called out.

Dak was waiting backstage. "Thank you," he whispered. He led me down into the theater seats, walking slowly ahead of me up the aisle.

"Frank is very protective of you," I said to his back.

He paused a second and smiled. "He's like a father to me, you know. I like him a lot. My real father died before I was born. And my stepfather, Tobias Tyler, is a decent man but he's not good with children."

A strange remark, I thought.

"You're not a child."

"Well, he's not good with *me*. That's what I should have said."

"Why?"

We stopped walking, the two of us standing in the empty aisle. Dak's face was lost in shadows. "Tobias has only two things he loves unconditionally: the evangelical church he founded with—actually *for*—my mother and…well, my mother herself. His devotion to her borders on rapturous. That kind of love takes up all the air in the room, so he resents what little I inhale."

"What does he think of Annika?"

No smile now—weariness in his voice. "For him, Annika is a tool to bring me back to the church. I know I sound cynical, and he does encourage a loving marriage, maybe children, but Tobias wants me to keep the church going after he and my mother are gone. His legacy. His ticket to heaven."

"Then I'd think he'd want you around, no?"

"Around, yes. But not in sight."

We sat in the back of the empty theater, the last row, under a dim light, his handsome face indistinct and stark: a negative of a grainy photograph. Only those deep-set pale blue eyes shone, and disarmed. He'd slipped into the seat next to me, so close I could detect his cologne: woody, rich, with a hint of new-mown hay.

"I don't know what you think I can do for you," I began.

He looked exasperated. "I debated asking Nadine to go to you, and maybe I shouldn't have. Sometimes my behavior is foolish. But I panicked. Talking to Frank made me panic. And Constable Biggers. I just felt that you understood. I mean, our brief talk at the Full Moon…well…I heard your heartbeat." He shook his head. "A dumb line, I know. But I need someone who believes in me, I suppose. I know that sometimes I'm… naïve maybe…but I got no one level-headed to talk to. I look over my shoulder and expect to be arrested. My mother cowers, frightened her little boy is gonna be hanged. Tobias turns away, disgusted. Annika watches me warily, ready to pronounce sentence, expecting…I don't know what. The people who love me don't know me, and so they…well, can believe me a murderer." A harsh laugh. "I think Annika'd rather have me arrested for murder than spend time with Nadine."

"Tell me about Nadine."

A long pause. "I knew her in Hollywood. Briefly. So brief it almost didn't happen."

I rolled my tongue into my cheek. "You know, she says much the same thing. Almost the same words." I forced him to look at me. "Tell me, Dak, did you love her? *Do* you love her?"

He stammered, and then smiled. "I got a lot of people in my past, Miss Ferber."

"That's not answering my question."

Helpless, a shrug. "I can't answer it."

"And Annika?"

"I'm really not comfortable here, Miss Ferber. Annika has seen me talking to Nadine one time, and she exploded. Not pretty. She got…like out of control. No one knows about Nadine… and Hollywood. I don't talk about it. It's just that Annika is afraid of anything not spiritual. You know, people got my life planned for me. Christ, a whole church depends on me—on my coming home to it. When I was thirteen or fourteen, the early days, traveling with my mother, I'd get up there and preach. I was shy but I got into it. My mother was ecstatic. Like a sign from God. She *wept.* Everyone wept. She saw the future, and I was the blessed one."

"But…"

"But it was a a game for me. A lark. I was showing off back then. I was a wise-guy prankster. That's all. That's not me."

"And Annika?"

Dak waited a moment. Then he spoke as though reading a script. "She was created in my mother's image. An orphan girl from Newark. A devout congregant who insinuated her way inside the inner circle, adores my mother, and was chosen to marry me." A heartbeat. "She's actually very sweet."

I bristled. "No, I don't think that she is."

That surprised him. "You gotta get beyond the preachy shell."

"I'd rather not. Sometimes when you crack open a nut, there's nothing inside."

"Are you calling…"

I broke in, impatient. "You do have free will, Dak."

A shrug. "Yes, I like to believe that. But the Assembly of God is an evangelical church that mixes talking in tongues and salvation and forgiveness—all the trappings of tent-city Christianity—with my stepfather's ironbound Calvinism and boilerplate predestination. Free will is just four-letter words strung together. The wrath of an Old Testament God. The mighty hand of God on my trembling shoulders. Always with the whisper of a benign blessing from Jesus, the lamb of God."

"Why do you put up with it?"

He got a twinkle in his eyes. "Who says that I do?"

"Well, the evidence, really. You're still in Maplewood. You're in the church. You live in town. Lord, you are going to marry Annika." I smiled. "Or are you?"

"I don't know what to do. I keep nodding my head at everyone. You know, I had a talk with Annika and I think she might believe that I killed Evan. Imagine that! 'Where were you?' she asked me."

"Did she know Evan?"

"Only as a fool who dared to flirt with her."

"Why would he do that?"

Dak laughed out loud. "Because she's a girl. Some men are like that." He clicked his tongue. "Any girl. He has—had—to have every girl love him."

"But I gather he mocked Gus Schnelling's girlfriend, Meaka Snow."

Dak grimaced. "Lord, the ice maiden. A chilly day of winter, that block of ice. Evan called her an igloo, you know…she's squat and wide and…"

"So Gus hated him, too?"

"Yes, Gus hated him." A pause. "And, well, Meaka, too. I know that Evan was stunned to see Gus show up in Maplewood. Picking up that job as electrician. Gus is up to something. Well, so was Evan. They were often together, Gus and Evan, but it was like…like they each didn't dare let the other guy out of their sight. You gotta know where your enemy is, right?"

"What did Annika say about Gus?"

"She didn't want him coming around. Either guy, really. Not that he did, but we'd bump into him in town. I mean, Annika has refused to come near the theater—she thinks it's corrupting. But Gus would be handing out leaflets and, well, he'd strut his manly strut, all that tough-guy nonsense. He'd mutter about the master race or some such nonsense—and we'd keep going. Gus and I don't talk."

"You knew him in Hollywood?"

He looked away. "We all knew one another out there. A brief moment…"

I had little patience with that. "Everyone says…'a brief moment.' Folderol. Dak, you're not telling me something. It has to do with Hollywood. Something *started* there. I feel it. And it led to murder. You and Gus and Evan…even Nadine."

A downcast evasion. "No." Then he summarized, "We all ran away from California."

"And, oddly, you all end up in Maplewood, New Jersey?"

"Funny, no?"

I reached out to touch his wrist and he jerked back. "Actually, no, Dak. There's a reason all of you came here. And it has nothing to do with the Maplewood Theater. Evan could care less about being Louis Calhern's understudy in *The Royal Family*. Nadine came here using her old stage name. In disguise, as it were. Gus, Hitler's vagrant and mindless follower, does not fit into any group photograph of Maplewood, New Jersey. He belongs in a beer garden in Germantown with a stein in one hand, his other arm outstretched in awful salute."

"I want you to be my friend," Dak said suddenly. "I want you to believe I didn't kill that bastard, Evan."

We locked eyes for a moment. "I know you didn't kill him."

He grinned. "Thank you."

I noticed Frank stepping out onto the stage, searching across the dim-lit seats, looking for us. "Yes, I do believe you, but you're not telling me everything."

A sigh. "I will." He stood. "Not yet."

"Dak!" I shook my head.

A broad smile covered his face. "Come with me. Quick. Before Frank yells at me. I *am* working tonight. Come. It's my discovery."

He escorted me out the back door, through the unlighted lobby, and, switching on a hallway light, up the stairs and into a lounge that was someone's office. "There." He pointed as he switched on a lamp.

"What?"

"That painting." He drew me closer and I was staring at a tiny exquisite landscape of a splashy waterfall and ancient weeping willows and spotty moonlight: delicate, luminous, compelling. "I can't believe it's here. It's an Asher B. Durand." He did a quick two-step, a vaudeville routine, and went, "Ta-da! Look!"

"I have no idea…"

"The great Hudson River Valley landscape painter. He was born in Maplewood when it was Jefferson Village. He died in 1886. He loved landscapes, painted the wild scenery of Orange

Mountain. Maplewood is in a valley, you know, and he loved the mountains, wandering through forests of black walnut and pine and…My hero. I just came upon it hanging there, valuable, a museum piece. He's forgotten now. No one cares. You know, when I was a boy, doodling, drawing, a teacher told me that Durand was a distant relative of my mother, way back when. He's what made me want to paint and draw."

"It's gorgeous," I agreed.

"I started wandering in the woods, a boy hunting for grasshoppers, but I ended up sketching them. I wandered the same paths, Miss Ferber. You know, there's an old milestone marker in Maplewood Park beyond Tuscan Road—Five Miles to Newark. Old Indian trails, I imagine. The South Mountain Reservation."

While we were talking, his face underwent a magical transformation, the dark droopy gloom of his features transmogrifying into a vibrant, mobile boy's face, electric. His body rolled and twisted, backing up, his face peering closely at the painting, staring into my face, desperately wanting me to understand the awesome beauty of this personal discovery. So alive, so transported, this young man: the artist lost in his own pure world. For a moment, the two of us standing there, quiet, quiet, Evan's murder did not matter, nor the prosaic machinations of the church he was yoked to, nor the workaday job he had at the theater. And for a moment I forgot about the world out there: Nazi tanks lumbering through Alpine landscapes as beautiful as that of this Durand oil on canvas. No, here was a young man who had found a moment of joy that held him, and, wonderfully, took me with him.

The spell was broken by the sudden appearance of Frank who bustled in, his face scarlet. "Dak. Miss Ferber. What's going on? This is a private office."

I simply pointed to the Durand landscape, but Frank refused to look.

"I wanted to…" Dak began.

Frank cut him off. "You need to get back to work, Dak."

Dak bowed to me, smiled weakly, and sheepishly left the room.

"I'm sorry, Frank."

"It's not your fault, Miss Ferber. He's a troubled boy. An innocent, that one. A decent boy." He looked toward the empty doorway. "I'm worried about him. I like him. I'm like his father…"

"But you're not his father."

He stammered, "I know, I know. It's just that I don't like the way people treat him. His family. Evan murdered, and I'm afraid for Dak who is…"

"Who is innocent," I finished.

Frank breathed out and seemed to lose energy. "Thank God someone else understands that. Thank God." Then, a pained look. "But why was he following Evan that afternoon? It wasn't by accident that he spotted Evan. He told me today that he went looking for him. Why can't he keep his mouth shut?"

Chapter Seven

The voice on the telephone was creaky, yet authoritative. No hello—just "Miss Ferber. Tobias Tyler here." For a moment I had no idea who the man was. Then Tobias Tyler repeated his name, louder this time, and added, "From the Assembly of God." Another pause. "Dakota's parents."

I could hear irritation in his tone. This was a man who expected you to know him.

"Good afternoon, Mr. Tyler. This is unexpected." I'd been sitting in a rocking chair in my room, the *New York Times* in my lap, unread.

"It shouldn't be unexpected—it's just overdue. You see, ever since you and George Kaufman came to town—I don't attend theater so I was the last to know—I've wanted to speak with you. You don't remember me, but we've met, though many, many years back, and only one time. I was a younger man…"

"Tobias Tyler." My mind wrestled with the name. "Your mother was Maris Bradford Tyler?"

A soft chuckle. "Of course. I'm her only son."

"You stepped into her apartment…"

"Yes, a brief encounter. My mother liked to gather famous people to her home."

I cut him off. "I do remember the afternoon." My voice was cold now. "Not a pleasant memory, I'm afraid."

He cleared his throat. "I guess she had her biases."

"And then some." My words were snarled, purposely.

Again the soft chuckle. "All behind us." I heard him breathe in. "And I'm not my mother. Her prejudices were unfortunate and…"

"These days transferred onto a world stage, no?" I finished for him.

That confused him. "What?"

"No matter."

When I'd published *So Big* to great success and garnered a Pulitzer Prize for Best Novel, the bejeweled grande dames of Park Avenue issued invitations to lunch or tea, a habit of lionizing I soon tired of. George Kaufman referred to it as "artists being fed to the lions." I'd allowed myself, at George's suspicious request, to be feted by Mrs. Winthrop Bradford Tyler, an especially rubicund and enormously wealthy widow in her sky-high penthouse. A tiresome woman. "Maris" to her intimates, of which I was not one. Dripping in diamonds and black velvet at midday, Maris Bradford Tyler blathered on and on about her love of the arts, of artists, of *So Big* (which she heard was wonderful), on and on, dreadful, an eternity, a sinkhole of inanity. At one point George mentioned reading G. B. Stern's *The Matriarch*, a wonderful best-selling saga of generations. Mrs. Bradford Tyler heaved her tremendous bosom and roared, "A book about Jews. I tossed it into the fire."

Silence, long and heavy, as awful as it gets. In my most brutal tone, "And yet you fed me lunch today."

"You? Jewish?"

George quipped as he threw down his napkin. "Oh my God, Edna. You never told me."

At which point George and I both stood and stormed out of the apartment.

"Yes," I told Tobias now, "I remember your mother fondly."

He wasn't listening. "I must have been—what?—forty-five? I'm sixty now. An old man."

"What can I do for you?"

"An invitation to dinner, you and Mr. Kaufman."

"I don't think so. We've…"

Suddenly a diffident tone colored his words, an urgency, a little desperate. "Please. We need to talk about Dakota and the… the murder. His mother and I…"

Rarely one to forgive the sins of the parent, I nevertheless relented. "I like Dak."

"You'll come then?"

"I'll check with George."

A pause. "I've already spoken with him. He said he'll come if you do." That news rankled, truly. What game was this? But now his voice grew strange. "I'll send a car at seven. One of the trusted churchwardens who drives for me. A fine fellow name of Alexander. A safe driver."

"I'm more leery of what happens *after* I arrive, sir."

But he'd already hung up the phone.

Tobias Tyler was rich, heir to a fortune built on gas boilers and turbines, a magnificent pile of money that mostly remained intact after the Crash of 1929, though I remembered hearing that he holed up in the Park Avenue penthouse after his mother's death and was afraid to leave. Well, obviously he had ventured far from that crystal tower. And here he now resided. While waiting for the car to pick us up, George had shared other tidbits of the man's scant and lucky biography: Tobias, the notorious skinflint—legend had it he'd battled a homeless street bum for a dropped penny—was now spreading his fortune in the name of Christ. The perennial bachelor had been born-again and had fallen madly in love at middle age. "There's hope for you yet, dear Edna," George had sniped.

I ignored him. "A strange story."

"Well, he found God."

"In Maplewood?" I raised my eyebrows.

"A life with the renowned evangelist, Clorinda Roberts Tyler."

"Everyone talks about her as if she's famous. I never heard of her."

"You need to read the trashy tabloids. The *Post* loves her."

"Don't your letters count as pulp fiction?"

"Wisdom, Edna. I send you bits of wisdom."

At that moment Alexander pulled up in the town car, and George and I were ceremoniously bowed into the backseat. We didn't speak for the short ride.

Tobias and Clorinda Tyler lived in a sprawling stone mansion out beyond ritzy Burnett Terrace, an imposing home of excessive gables and medieval stone turrets and heavy leaded glass, stolid and dark, a burgher's paradisiacal trophy appropriated from an earlier century. An extension, I supposed, of the opulence of Tobias' genteel Park Avenue upbringing. There was a crew of gardeners in sight, all short and dark, all climbing into the back of a pickup as they ended their day's work. Italianate lawn statues and Baroque fountains dotted the pathways. Beyond the circular driveway, visible when the car turned, was a two-story Victorian guesthouse set back among towering oak trees, painted a harlot's red with black shutters and a jazzy white porch, an incongruous ladybug plopped down in the shadow of the sober mansion. Banks of Hawthorne trees lined the rolling fields—and I supposed there was no chance you might ever glimpse a neighbor. Even should you want to.

As the car pulled into the driveway of the mansion, I spotted a tiny man standing in the open doorway. It had to be Tobias—he looked as if he'd toppled from a Mayflower gangplank. Dressed in a severe black suit with black tie, arms folded across his chest, he looked the undertaker at a viewing. Or one of the Salem judges.

A compact little man, wizened, with a drab oval face, he blinked his eyes nervously, glanced back and forth from George to me, as though uncertain where to focus. This squirrel of a man stepped back, grinned foolishly, showing stained yellow teeth, and led us into a drawing room.

Massive mahogany furniture from another century, dark and forbidding, filled the large space so that walking a straight line was impossible. I wove my uncertain way around clunky claw-footed tables and brocaded sofas, past overstuffed ottomans and knickknack-cluttered bookshelves, my fingers grazing old-fashioned, yellowed antimacassars draped over the backs of chairs. A provincial museum, I considered, a room that stopped in time when Victoria died and Edward stumbled onto the royal throne. That was it, I realized: It was all so…British. Colonial. Imperial. Fussy. Here was Prince Albert's specter, the puritanical consort, bowing us in.

"Clorinda is tied up at the Assembly temple," he informed us. "Regrettable, I'm afraid. But she'll be here shortly. Being the preeminent spiritual leader on the East Coast has its liabilities."

I glanced at George. He was staring, open-mouthed, at a stuffed wolverine placed, lifelike, on a mantel. A taxidermist's catastrophe, to be sure, its fur matted and faded. Worse, its glass eyes had shifted in the sockets so that the poor animal looked wall-eyed, one eye facing the Atlantic Ocean and the other the Pacific. Keeping an eye on all of America. George kept nodding his head at me like a dizzy schoolboy, compelling me to look at the monstrosity, but I'd already taken in the hideous décor, this anachronistic space that stunned conversation.

George and I sat on a lumpy sofa, opposite the little man.

"We've looked forward to meeting the famous Clorinda," George said without a trace of sarcasm, still not diverting his eyes from that sad animal.

An old woman plodded in, dressed in a frumpy black-and-white maid's uniform, and clumsily placed a tray of biscuits and cookies before us. A pitcher of iced lemonade rested next to them, slivers of bright yellow lemon floating on the surface.

"This is Hilda." Tobias indicated the matronly woman who merely grunted. She maneuvered her ancient self around the cluttered room with admirable dexterity.

"She's wonderful." Tobias watched her retreating back. "We inherited her from a woman in Newark, where she'd been a faithful domestic since coming from Sweden ages ago. Clorinda's a loving spiritual woman, but she can be a demanding taskmaster. She demands a smoothly run household. Hilda can read our minds. I simply sit in my study and work on my book."

"Your book?" George said too loudly.

"A study of all the foods and herbs mentioned in the Bible and their symbolic implications…"

Neither George nor I said anything.

"Will Dak be joining us for dinner?" I broke in.

He shook his head vigorously. "No, his mother thought it best if he *not* be here. Just us, discussing this…this unpleasant development. That horrendous murder that, I fear, might tarnish the good work of our Assembly of God." He looked toward the window as though expecting a stone to be tossed through the glass. "So she's sent them—Dakota and Annika—off to visit parishioners over to South Orange."

I struggled to create a sentence. For a minute we sat in silence. George kept making a clicking noise, unhappy. Finally, I sputtered, "Tell me about your Assembly of God."

"You've heard of it, of course."

"Of course." I hadn't, to be sure, but thought it best to agree. There was a reason for this summons and I needed to hear it.

His voice got low, solemn. "When I found Jesus, I realized how I'd best spend the vast monies I didn't do anything to earn. In my middle age, wandering, a lost soul, I sought an answer from God. A pilgrim adrift in America listening to street-corner prophets." A sweet smile. "It took a long time coming, let me tell you."

George was smiling. "I'd have thought God would send messages more quickly. He seems to control the phone lines."

Tobias narrowed his eyes, disapproving. "You're having fun with me, Mr. Kaufman. That's quite all right. That's your *job*."

George sat back, amused.

Tobias went on. "A number of years back I had to be in California and I chanced upon Aimee Semple McPherson's Angelus Temple. A magnificent woman, that one, inspired." He breathed in and bowed his head. "That changed my life. A year later, hunting down a revival service in Buffalo, the night of a raging snowstorm, I chanced upon Clorinda's service. Here it was, a dark night with impassable roads, Buffalo as a howling wilderness out of the Old Testament, and yet this ramshackle rented Sons of Pythias hall was jam-packed with devout souls—farmers, mechanics, soldiers, housewives, all breathing the ethereal air of Jesus Christ. And Clorinda, magnificent in rainbow-colored robes and with a voice tinkling like crystal, took us all up to God's kingdom." He half-rose from his seat and grabbed his heart. "A year later I begged her to marry me."

"And you moved here?" From George, with only the mildest tinge of disbelief.

"It's Clorinda's childhood home. Maplewood, and her long-held dream of bringing Jesus back with her. The foundation of an empire would start here. Since her early days as an itinerant preacher traveling the hinterland in a broken-down bus, begging for quarters to print her devout messages, at one point with little Dakota tucked at her side and saying her prayers, she'd longed for permanence."

"The Assembly of God," I said.

"Exactly. A magnificent shrine to God, patterned after Aimee Semple McPherson's Angelus Temple. So here we are. Jesus comes to Jersey. Since I built Clorinda's temple, her reputation has swelled. Like high tide. Massive, massive. A sanctuary, my friends. A place of old-fashioned morality and rectitude. Look out the window at the world. What do you see? Sin and frivolity and orgies and drinking and smoking and profane love. And now the ugly specter of war in Europe. This is because we've stepped away from Christ. The Bible burned. Lost lives. Jonathan Edwards, who thundered at sinners in the hands of an angry God, dangled them over the pits of hell, once traveled from New England to New Jersey, and died with his message. Fire and brimstone—the true meaning of the Bible. Not the namby-pamby soft-center close-your-eyes-to-sin that passes for religion in some quarters these days. Oh no! Here, again, there is a live revival in Maplewood. The Old Testament lives and breathes."

George grunted. "Alexandria, Athens, Rome, London, Maplewood."

"Indeed!" Tobias beamed. "Clorinda is the world's most loving woman, charity itself, a blessing. A beautiful creature.

I never married until my fifties because God had me wait for perfection."

George choked on a cookie.

He went on. "The church and Clorinda are one. A rich legacy." His face then scrunched up, worried. "Do you see why I invited you?"

That jarred. "Ah, Tobias, I don't see…"

"Dakota is like a son to me, Miss Ferber. A fitful, wayward teenage boy when I met him, hell-bent, rebellious, a dreamer. But I knew—Clorinda convinced me—that God's master plan meant he'd be prodigal, a temporary wastrel, a gifted lad who would finally extend the power and the glory of the Assembly of God. We'd branch out from Maplewood—to Newark, to New York, New England—to the West."

"Does Dak *want* this path?" I tried to make eye contact.

He squinted at me. "It's not his choice. Would you defy God, Miss Ferber?"

George rocked in his chair. "Edna likes a good challenge. She'd take on God if He insulted her."

"That's why this murder nonsense must be squelched. Dakota told me that you"—he stared into my eyes—"favor him, trust him, understand his innocence. You can be his advocate."

"Well, I do think he's incapable of murder, but…"

He spoke over my words. "I'm not a worldly man, Miss Ferber. Nor is Clorinda. Though we surround ourselves with grand worldly trappings, possessions do keep so many from touching God. We're sheltered from so much. There is so much I do not understand. I invited you because we wanted to voice our *approval* of your friendship with Dakota. Your comforting support. I know you have no power to stem the inquiries of that foolish Constable Biggers, who lingers outside the temple with a pad in hand, watching, though I don't know what for. But I suspect he has *chosen* Dakota as murderer. So Annika tells us. Preposterous. And dangerous to our church. All I'm asking is that you"—he faltered, struggled—"I don't know…"

"Find the real murderer?" George tossed in.

A beautiful glow covered the tiny man. "That would be nice."

"I'll befriend Dakota, but…"

My voice broke off as the door opened and his wife rushed in.

Clorinda Roberts Tyler made an entrance that reminded me of an imperious Ethel Barrymore stepping before the footlights, pausing, expecting the roar of spontaneous applause. A moment purposely out of sync with the script—but did it matter? She was the blazing star in the night firmament. So, too, Clorinda paused, a quixotic smile on her lips, her hand fluttering in the air as though warding off pesky mosquitoes.

You saw a slight, slender woman, a willowy reed, whose velvety olive complexion and large stunning eyes immediately reminded me of her son, Dakota. A youthful woman, graceful, with her long dark hair flowing over her shoulders, covered with a black lace mantilla. As she moved, the diaphanous pink dress she wore flowed like gossamer. Eye-catching, mesmerizing, haunting—a woman in full possession. No makeup, not a trace of lipstick or rouge or powder, but the effect of that mobile face was one of utter glamour and appeal. Yet, when she passed under the overhead light, the actress understanding her spot, you caught the reflection of brilliant diamonds on her earlobes and gracing her neck: an angel in jewels, the sylvan sprite accented with top-drawer Tiffany jewels. Astounding!

She nodded to George and then to me, fluttering, gushing, inordinately pleased that we would visit, thrilled to meet such luminaries, renowned cosmopolites so far removed from her humdrum spiritual hideaway.

"I have fame but I don't have genius," she told us.

Tobias begged to differ. "Clorinda, your genius is the voice of God within you."

I wondered how long this nincompoopism would last and whether I'd survive a full evening of their simplistic rapture. Already George was tapping a finger nervously on the arm of his chair and making gurgling noises.

"Dakota has mentioned you, my dear Edna. I must tell you he *protested*—yes, indeed—our invitation to you and George here, saying it would *embarrass* him, but I pooh-poohed that. An innocent boy, my Dakota."

Hilda stood in the doorway and broke into the middle of Clorinda's endless speech. "Dinner is ready." Blunt, a little contemptuous. I supposed she tired of living in such rarefied atmosphere where the air got too thin and made breathing difficult. She turned away slowly, plodding back to the kitchen, one hand rubbing a hip.

"Come, come," Clorinda cooed, and obediently we rose and followed her into the dining room where, under a blazing mother-of-pearl chandelier, the table was set for five.

"Another guest?" I asked.

Clorinda looked over her shoulder and dropped her voice. "My sister Ilona lives with us." She pursed her lips. "She may or may not join us. Perhaps for dessert. She's somewhat shy of folks, and *unhappy*."

Unhappy: This last word was pronounced so deeply, melo-dramatically, that even Tobias smiled.

Glancing at Tobias through the rambling, uneventful dinner of overdone roast and soggy potatoes and anemic salad, I made one observation: Tobias sat quietly most of the meal while Clorinda rattled on about her Assembly of God and her destiny and her love of animals (though none was in evidence), and her love of literature (though not a book was in sight). I realized that what Dak had told me was true: There were two things—only two, emphatically two—that constituted Tobias' world, a love of God and a love of Clorinda. Both seemed to have coalesced into one entity so his obsession was somehow monomaniacal. He stared at her with such rapt absorption that, at times, he held a fork in midair, entranced by a platitude he'd doubtless heard sail a hundred times from her lips. A little scary, this scene, for I suspected the battle of dual allegiances created some restless nights for the devout puritan. Or maybe not. The eternal feminine with the glow of God within. All very baffling to me, the secular Jewish nun of the Upper East Side. The Jewish slave girl on the ancient Nile, as I often referred to myself.

"Tobias has such a strong faith," Clorinda was going on. "It fairly stuns. I am not worthy."

"My dear, please." He sighed. "But we must *focus* on solving our worldly dilemma now."

I interrupted. "I appreciate your invitation, but I must tell you—I don't know what I can do to help Dak."

Both stopped, gobsmacked. Perhaps my tone was a little too cutting.

"Dakota," Clorinda whispered.

"I know, I know." I was frustrated. "But I've already said that I…"

Tobias looked at me closely. "Scandal." His voice hummed the word, trembling. "Scandal. Awful scandal. Our church—my whole adult life, Miss Ferber—is predicated on what I deem one hundred percent morality. The ethical life. How else to lead our parishioners? The lost and saddened, the lonely, the misfits. Ours is a church of salvation after rigorous denial." He glanced at his wife. "Since Dakota has returned from that…that sad sojourn in Hollywood and other wanderings throughout America, well, we, Clorinda and I, have embraced him as savior. When Clorinda and I are gone to our reward, Dakota and Annika must lead…"

"That's an awful weight to thrust on one man."

I sensed George nodding his head.

"He wants it."

"Are you sure?" George asked.

"This Annika…" I began but stopped. The temperature in the sweltering room had become arctic.

"Murder will kill us." Tobias spoke slowly, spacing out the words.

George smirked, then apologized. "I'm sorry," he mumbled, "but it's a…a wonderful line."

Tobias' face got scarlet and his voice trembled. "You mock us in a house of God's servants."

Clorinda was the pacifier. "Now, now, Tobias." A dry chuckle. "Forget it. George is the jokester—that's how he sees the world. His bread and butter. We see it differently. Ours is the bread of life."

Tobias nodded and leaned toward me. "I believe the real murderer must be caught. And it will not be Dakota."

Clorinda fussed, running her hand through her hair. "They should be looking at this Gus fellow. An evil man. Annika tells me he's a godless Nazi."

Tobias smiled and lovingly touched Clorinda's hand. "That is why I wanted Miss Ferber here tonight. She agrees with us."

Kindergarten exercises, I told myself: contentment found in throwaway words, answers grasped at as though they were golden rings on a child's merry-go-round. Conversation that looped back around until every line was an echo of something said moments before.

George, having none of this, addressed Clorinda, smiling at her in an expression I recognized as preamble to a cruel jibe. He never cared what folks thought of him. "How did you get into this God business?"

She ignored the slight, laughing uproariously. "I have to remember to take your statements with a grain of sand, dear George. People like us are sent to test the waters of absolute belief. Anyway, Tobias and I sometimes call our church the Church of the Wild Oats. Redemption on the road out of Sodom and Gomorrah. Tobias searched the desert, a lost man. And so did I, a bumbling sinner on the West Coast, where sin is commonplace." She narrowed her eyes a second. "And expected and oddly celebrated. Dakota comes by his roving days honestly—a son of his mother."

"The long trek to sainthood." I was looking at George.

Clorinda reached across the table and patted my hand. "Exactly. How true!"

Irony and sarcasm, I guessed, were George's province, while mine was the glib truism.

"I left Maplewood for Hollywood just around the time the Great War began. I wanted to be in the silents. You know, I'd seen a Cecil B. DeMille movie in downtown Newark, and that's all it took. *Birth of a Nation*—I think it was. I was young, pretty, flamboyant, felt stifled by Maplewood and the Congregational

Church we attended. My mother had died when I was ten, and my father raised me and my younger sister, Ilona. Sadly, but perhaps providentially, my father was a stern, demanding country doctor, much respected, if severe. He trucked no disobedience. This furniture"—she pointed around the cluttered room—"came from the old house on Tuscan Road."

Tobias smiled. "When I first visited that house, I felt at peace. The glitzy Park Avenue was gone forever. This was serenity."

Clorinda hadn't stopped talking, and never looked at Tobias. "I fought my dear father, headed to Hollywood, acting in some forgotten silent two-reelers. The distressed maiden with the goo-goo eyes. Absurd. 'Oh sir! I'm just a motherless lass!' That stuff. Finally, hungry for something, I married another actor, the dashingly handsome Philip Roberts, who swept me off my feet. He'd just appeared in a William S. Hart western—he was the swashbuckling type, you know, dark, handsome, with a captivating moustache." Her voice fell. "Then my world crashed. I was carrying our child—Philip chose the name Dakota if it was a boy, proud of his love of westerns, would you believe?—and one afternoon a streetcar jumped its tracks and struck Philip. He died weeks before Dakota was born."

"I'm so sorry," I told her.

"I floundered, lost interest in movies, and one afternoon, distraught, I wandered into Aimee Semple McPherson's church. It was as though I'd been led there—driven like the Magi toward Bethlehem, following a star in the sky. I devoted the next few years to her crusade until, well, I began to distrust her…her authority. Her sincerity. She forgave sins too easily, especially her own. I went out on my own, traveling, preaching, and eventually met Tobias in Buffalo. Destiny."

"And Dakota?" I asked. "I gather he was on the road with you."

A long silence, uncomfortable. A ragged sound from deep in her throat. "Not at first. Well, he was a baby. A little boy. Later on I took him with me—taught him to preach. You have to understand my father, Edna. An old man, rigid, bitter. He thought kindness a dangerous trait. When Dakota was born, I was still an…an actress. Whatever that means. He insisted I bring Dakota back East, where he had Ilona care for him in this small town, quiet, decent, away from the nonsense of Hollywood. I had to agree. My sister had to agree, though she resisted. She refused at first, and still insists the heavenly charity crippled her life. I was still grieving over Philip's sudden death. So his first days were here—in my sister's care."

"And a lot of thanks I get for it, let me tell you."

We all jumped. I actually screamed, which I regretted—too much the showboat ingénue feeling menaced.

In the doorway stood a shriveled woman dressed in a charcoal gray dress that sagged below her knees, a gigantic rhinestone brooch stuck onto her chest like a bug splattered on a car windshield.

"Ilona, you sneak in like a cat." Clorinda wasn't happy.

"I live here. I told you I'd come down for dessert. Maybe. Then I'm startled to hear how I raised that brat of yours, for no credit. None. A delinquent, that boy, sassy, angry all the time, messing up in school when he drew pictures of dead winter trees. He never fit in."

Clorinda's voice broke. "Ilona, meet Edna Ferber and George Kaufman."

A sickly smile, humorless. "I'm charmed."

Ilona had been described as the younger sister of Clorinda, but looked much older, haggard even, wrinkled, a woman beaten down. She leaned on the doorjamb, insolent, observing us harshly.

"Join us?" Tobias stood and pulled out a chair.

Ilona cleared her throat. "Oh, I don't think so. I'm a bit under the weather. The heat God sends us this time of year." She chuckled. "I suppose—to prepare us for hell. He's doing a good job. Clorinda, I heard your nonsense about father's didactic authority. Does anyone recall anyone asking me if I wanted to deal with a squawking baby while you partied the night away in California? No, I don't think so. I made him a God-fearing boy, and you sent letters telling him to explore the beauty of life, to seek adventure, to sing from the treetops—or some such crap. And off he goes. Mama's boy. Then one day you're back, religion now seeping out of your pores, and you take him to your bosom. Turn him against me. And I'm left alone, the shunted spinster in a mausoleum. A vicious father dead. The house I lived in all my life given to you, the mother of the family heir."

Tobias was glowering. "This is no time for such revelation, Ilona. We have guests. We all do what we have to do in life."

She grimaced. "Oh, please. Spare me! And now you look for ways to protect the church from the sheriff's knock on the door. Dakota the murderer!"

Clorinda screamed. "Enough." She turned to me. "Ilona sees herself as the church mouse, the ignored, the…"

"The woman begging for crumbs at your"—she pointed at Tobias—"abundant table. Good night." She turned on her heels and left the room. A voice from the hallway. "A murderer!"

"Well," George began, folding his napkin and placing it on the table. "We must be going. It's been…"

"I'm so sorry," Clorinda jumped in. "Ilona is so unhappy." She squinted. "Yes, *unhappy*. She has refused to accept Jesus into her life and…"

"Well," echoed George, standing up.

"Dakota is our future," Tobias whispered.

Clorinda pleaded with me. "Edna, we don't know where to turn. I don't like Dakota spending so much time at the theater. I know the evils of the stage. I also wanted to talk to you about that. I begged him not to take that unnecessary job there. The theater can be so corrupting."

"Well, thank you!" George smiled broadly.

"No, not *you* two. But people like…Evan Street, a man born to plague and be murdered."

"Did you ever meet him?"

"Of course. Here. He visited Dakota. One unpleasant visit, unexpected. He ignored me. Too good-looking, trading his looks for evil. He came with the other…Gus…the Nazi. As frightening a man as I've ever met. That fisheye look of his. Why are those characters hired by your producer? Why? Tobias and I won't step into that theater."

George was standing, stretching out his arms, preparing thanks.

I wasn't ready to leave. "Dak knows them from California, I gather. A brief moment, I'm told. Whatever happened there came East with them—and to Maplewood."

Clorinda looked puzzled. "How can that be? A few months in Hollywood and this is what happens? Dakota never talks of Hollywood, Edna."

I suddenly thought of something. "Another player at the theater, too. I think Dak knew the understudy Nadine Novack out there."

Clorinda's voice got raspy. "Nadine Novack. An actress?"

"Yes, but in Hollywood she acted under her real name. Nadine Chappelle."

Clorinda stood, gripped the edge of the table. She screamed at the top of her voice, her body rocking back and forth, and fled the room. I could hear her slamming a door, the sound of her footsteps running up the stairs, still screaming.

"What?" I asked Tobias.

He shook his head.

George mopped his forehead with a handkerchief. "Well, thank you again…"

Chapter Eight

Constable Biggers stood outside the Full Moon Café, planted on the sidewalk, pad and pencil in hand. He was staring through the plate-glass window. Beads of sweat dotted his flushed face.

"Good afternoon, Constable." I marched by him, headed into the café.

He said nothing and didn't move a muscle.

Inside, greeted by Mamie Trout who announced fresh blueberry pie with homemade whipped cream, I watched Gus Schnelling and Meaka Snow, both positioned by the front window, staring back out at the constable.

"He's still there." Meaka Snow pointed out the window, looking directly into the impassive face of Constable Biggers, who stared back, unmoving.

"He's an ass." Gus jerked his head toward the constable. Then a mocking laugh, ugly, his voice carrying through the empty cafe. "I suppose he wants me to confess to killing Evan. A lunchtime confession. Indigestion at this greasy spoon making me confess." He stretched back, the prominent Adam's apple in a surprisingly scrawny neck jutting out. For a short, stocky man, he had a long, skinny neck that made his large head seem balloon-like. Casually, he lit a Camel and blew the smoke toward the front window. Meaka laughed derisively.

So Constable Biggers was obviously surveilling both Gus and Dak, Evan's two casual friends who had minor-league run-ins with the murdered man.

Meaka leaned forward, smug. "Ain't it clear that Dak did it?"

Gus said nothing, but glanced my way, his eyes hooded and wary. A slight grin appeared, a little sardonic, I thought. Nodding at Meaka, he stopped watching Biggers and focused on me. All morning long, in fact, as George rehearsed *The Royal Family* and kept carping about Irene Purcell's difficulty with a scene in Act Two, I would turn to find Gus in the wings watching me. A furtive glance, then a hasty turning away as he buried his head in some electric board. At one point, distracted by his shadow from a catwalk above us, I forgot my place, and George, already piqued by Irene's off-kilter performance, snapped at me. "Edna, you *wrote* that line."

I snapped back. "I wrote *most* of the lines, dear George."

He harrumphed, and called for a break.

Now, again in a staring contest with the errant electrician, I opened my mouth, "Gus, you seem to want to tell me something."

Meaka had been making faces out the window, but she swung around, annoyed. Her hard, dull eyes accused me.

"Nothing." Gus glanced at Meaka. "Seen you with Dak, that's all. And the grapevine tells us"—he suggested Meaka as part of the *us*—"you're pointing the finger at me."

Stunned, I sat up. "I *never* did so, young man. True, I'm certain of Dak's innocence…"

He spat out the words. "That's not what I heard."

"From whom?"

He glanced at Meaka, and I wondered whether she'd concocted such malarkey.

Meaka spoke up. "You were seen with him."

"I'm seen with lots of folks."

Gus bit his lip. "Evan was my friend." Said, the line hung in the air, false and strained. Even Meaka looked puzzled.

"And yet you did battle."

His blond eyebrows rose and his dark gray eyes got round and glassy. "Friends disagree. Yeah, we had a little spat. Shoving matches ain't much. Evan was a cad, Miss Ferber. I didn't like the way he treated Meaka."

Meaka stiffened, spine erect, fury in her face. You saw a chubby young woman, a cotton-candy moon face, and a hairdo doubtless chopped with sewing scissors in her bathroom. In a drab white linen blouse and black skirt, she looked the deadened schoolmarm, much feared by her youngsters.

I stood. "Might I join you both for a minute?"

I didn't wait for them to refuse, as both certainly looked prepared to do—Meaka putting a hand on the top of the free chair at their table and Gus turning his body away from me—and, cavalierly, I sat down.

Well," Meaka snorted. An unlovely girl, I thought, one used to dismissal and snide comment.

"I'm curious about something." A heartbeat. "Who do *you* think murdered Evan?"

Both spoke at once, loudly. "Dak." And Gus added, "I *told* you."

"Why?"

Gus sucked in his cheeks. "It ain't your business, Miss Ferber."

"Oh, but it is. I like Dak. He's one of the few people I've met in Maplewood I do like. He's not a murderer."

"That means you…you got to point the finger at someone else."

Meaka added, "Like right here at this table."

"No, I'll leave that to the sheriff."

All of us now peered out the window at the stoic Constable Biggers, still there, pad at the ready, pencil stub in hand.

"Hah," Meaka scoffed. "That two-bit yokel. What passes for justice in this fleabag berg."

"You don't like it here?"

She narrowed her eyes. "That's none of your business."

I tilted up my chin. I leaned in. "Why would Dak kill Evan?"

"Evan knew things."

That stopped me cold. "What things?"

"This conversation is over," Gus answered.

"But just tell me this." I shifted focus purposely. "I read the smudged juvenile leaflet you handed me the other day." Meaka sat back, grinning. "You two seem to have a foolhardy attraction toward Nazism. This love of Hitler. The master race and…"

Gus interrupted me. "The savior of Europe."

"Not everyone believes that."

"You'll see." Meaka added, "The world needs a powerful charismatic leader who is uniting…"

"Charlie Chaplin with a gun."

"I'm sorry you feel that way." He sneered. "America is in the hands of the international Jewish bankers who…"

"Poppycock," I sputtered.

Gus was taken aback by my outburst and seemed to soften a bit. "Is that a word?"

"Yes, and a particularly good one with louts."

His laugh was icy. "A difference in point of view. That's all."

I was furious. "Oh, I don't think so. Some points of view are destructive. Frankly, I feel in my bones that we're headed for a worldwide cataclysmic nightmare. Surely you can see that. Hitler's tanks across France. Scandinavia. The new assault on Britain. Ever since the Depression—all the breadlines, apple sellers, and crazy all-night dance marathons—a world has been shaken free of its moorings. And young folks like you, Americans, I trust, have been duped into believing some German buffoon is the answer."

"Well…" Gus hedged.

I spoke now with authority, my words spaced and cold. "I live in New York. Last year the Nazi rally at Madison Square Garden filled the rafters with pro-German sentiment. I've been told you were there. Shame on you, Gus. Some fake blather about George Washington and America. In my own backyard. In the morning I stroll down Lexington Avenue, and sometimes, late afternoons, I used to go to Yorkville for pastry at a German confectionary. A German neighborhood, that, and now in the window are pictures of Hitler, German Bund placards, Jewish businesses boycotted, worse—swastikas emblazoned on doorways. In my own backyard."

"Well…" Gus said again, wanting the conversation over, sitting there, this blunt man with his Aryan arrogance, dumb as butter.

"You're Jewish?" Meaka's voice hissed, lips rolling over the words.

"On my mother's side. On my father's side. And my mother's family came from Germany where, these days, they fear walking in the streets. I've managed to get four children and three adults out of Berlin, my mother's cousins. Just ahead of the madness." I stopped, out of breath.

"Leeches." Meaka thundered the word.

Looking at her, I realized she'd assumed the role of crusader. Gus was a simpleton, a knee-jerk follower, a lumbering ox. He'd brought Meaka into the fold, and, like many religious converts, she'd embraced the cause in a kind of maddened frenzy. Meaka was a roly-poly zealot filled with ill-defined bile. Doubtless an unloved child, mocked—and now, lamentably, a seeker of revenge. A dangerous woman, and ready now to pounce. Gus squirmed, uncomfortable with my presence and eager to leave. Paradoxically, Meaka thrived on it, relishing my uneasiness.

Gus pushed away his plate and was reaching into his pocket for cash. But Meaka, her face purplish, was not through. "You're gonna pin Evan's murder on us." Gus put out his hand to stop her. "Gus wouldn't waste his time on that…that playboy, that pretty lump of emptiness. A superficial man with get-rich quick schemes that went nowhere."

"Stop." Gus shot her a look.

"No, I won't. Dak is a weak sissy-boy, the kind who stabs you in the back in a fit of anger. The kind who's scared of guns but finds himself pulling a trigger. 'Oh oh oh. Now look what I did.' The little time I spent with him—all of us sucking beers at a tavern—he whined about his…his obligations. The demands of his mother. The Assembly of God. Tomorrow's preacher. The next Billy Sunday. God, it was tiring. And sickening. 'I can't do it. I can't. I don't want to do it. I want to paint.' It made me want to throw up."

Gus stood, annoyed. "Meaka, enough. Miss Ferber's not gonna believe *you*. Nothing can change her mind about Dak."

"Well, convince me."

Meaka ignored me. "Another time he brung along the chosen bride—Annika Something-or-Other—she stayed a few minutes and grabbed at him. 'These are not good people,' she actually said about us. And about Evan. Like we weren't even there in the room. 'Can't you see they're godless? You can't be around such...offal.' She actually used that goddamn word. Offal. Me! She got him the hell out of there fast enough. Never again."

"What did Evan say?"

"He laughed at the whole thing. Told her she was only pretty when she got angry."

"What did she do?"

Meaka threw back her head. "She slapped his face." She grinned. "The only moment I ever respected her."

Gus was nervous, jingling the coins in his pants pocket. "Dak kept apologizing for her."

"Because he's weak. There is no room for the weak in the world of the future."

"Does that include me? A Jewish woman?"

She waited a bit. A sickly smile. "Of course." Meaka started to walk away, pushing her fist into Gus' lower back. "I'm just surprised Annika doesn't kill Nadine."

That stopped me. "What?"

"The way Dak is mooning around her, following her around town."

"What does Annika know about that?"

"She ain't stupid, lady. Dak is pretty transparent."

"All right, yes, Dak has a crush on Nadine, it seems. Unfortunate, seeing that he's engaged to Annika. But I don't understand *that* relationship. Still and all, why would Annika kill her?"

Gus grunted. "He doesn't know what to do about Annika."

Meaka glanced at Gus. "I guess Miss Ferber doesn't know about Dak and Nadine."

Suddenly I flashed to Clorinda screaming at the mention of Nadine's name at dinner. "Tell me."

Gus looked triumphant, twisting that round head on that skinny neck, the Adam's apple bobbing. "God, the secrets some people got around here. Miss Ferber, Dakota and Nadine were married in California. A brief marriage annulled by the powers of Mommy with Daddy's big money and influence. Nadine has a soft spot for Dak still—why else is she here in Maplewood? But ask her about her *first* marriage, about the suicide of *that* husband. Christ, ask her about Evan."

"Married?" My head was reeling. "Evan? Suicide?"

"Yeah, ask Evan about that. Oh, you can't. He got murdered. Suddenly Nadine is in Maplewood for the summer. And Evan, too." He smiled. "And even me. All the Hollywood players assembling for the final curtain."

Back in my room, I lay on the bed, exhausted. The conversation in the Full Moon Café had been unsettling, more than I realized. George knocked on my door, bidding me to dinner with him and Cheryl Crawford and Louis Calhern—both actors staying the evening, but I refused, croaking out a *no* that left him puzzled. I ate soda crackers and sipped water, then fell into a deep sleep. Nightmares flooded me: chain-link fences, barbed wire, broken glass, overturned tables, smashed windows. Rumbling tanks. Airplanes showered fire down on screaming children. I woke with a start, and Gus' face floated in front of me: a Heil Hitler grin with blackened teeth and bloodshot eyes. I cried out. I flashed back to my young days. Ottumwa, Iowa. The little girl who brought lunch to her father daily and was taunted by the dirty street boys: *hey sheeny, kike, hey hey hey…*

Nazis in my old neighborhood, swastikas on the windows of the shops where I bought succulent strudel.

Suddenly I began weeping, out of control, and I couldn't stop.

Late that night, darkness outside my window, I heard a ruckus down the hall. I cracked my door to see Constable Biggers and two deputies wrestling with a belligerent Gus Schnelling. I stepped into the hallway as the men handcuffed him and pushed him past me. Red faced, spittle at the corners of his mouth, Gus was wild-eyed. "I ain't done nothing. He owed me money. It's my money in there."

Gus had slipped through the lobby and sneaked up the stairs, though Garret Smith spotted him. By the time Gus used a screwdriver to snap open the door and was rummaging in the room, an alerted Biggers intervened, dragging him out and down the stairs.

"I gotta right to my cash."

In the quiet hallway I stood with the proprietor observing the smashed lock. Garret *tsk*ed. "Gotta get that fixed tomorrow." He shut the door, which wouldn't latch now, and shook his head. "I don't suppose that fool'll be back tonight. They'll cool him off in a cell." He went downstairs.

George returned from dinner while I stood there. "Edna, what are you up to?"

I pointed to the broken door, describing the scene he'd missed.

"Edna, don't."

"What?"

"Edna, I know you."

"Good night, George."

He passed by me and entered his room. Waiting a second, listening, I quietly pushed open Evan's door and slipped in, switching on the light and closing the door behind me. I shoved a chair against it so it wouldn't swing open, though the door would not fully close. Light from the hallway streamed in. I was breathing hard and feeling like a lawbreaker. Of course, I *was* a lawbreaker. I didn't care.

So little in the room, considering Evan's short time there, his last-gasp spending spree. Some new clothes still wrapped in packages, pushed into a corner of the desk. A room that seemed alien to the flashy man, with quaint, country inn trappings: heavy damask draperies with the frilly borders, a dull burgundy. A sleigh bed with a flowered counterpane. A centennial Windsor chair. A walnut bureau with a matching nightstand. A large cedar armoire, the doors flung open. A few shirts and pants, still tagged, and a pair of shiny new shoes on the floor, also unworn. A suitcase, opened, stuffed with unpacked clothing and expensive toiletries. A brand-new leather satchel, empty, hanging off a wrought-iron hook. A piddling display of opulence, unrealized.

What drew me, however, was the small knotty-pine desk. On top lay a pristine copy of Samuel French's acting edition of *The Royal Family*. Hastily I leafed through it—unmarked, even his own part. I opened the top drawer and discovered it crammed with magazines and clipped articles and torn scraps of paper. A slick, glossy copy of *Motion Picture World* slipped out onto the floor—an old issue, decades old. Mabel Normand on the cover looking madcap and gullible. Quickly, I scanned the ungainly pile and realized that Evan had been a collector of Hollywood memorabilia. Some old programs, dog-eared. A lobby card. *Photoplay. Screenland. Motion Picture.* Hollywood intrigue and scandal. Yellowing pulp tabloids with headlines followed by multiple exclamation points. *Hollywood Folly!! Mae West Sex Romp!!!* A few clippings about recent movies. *Gone with the Wind. The Wizard of Oz. The Grapes of Wrath.* Last year's magnificent hits. I spotted a notation on the spread for *The Grapes of Wrath.* He'd scribbled in bold black ink: "A part made for *me*." An arrow pointed to Henry Fonda's name. On *Gone with the Wind*, an arrow pointed to Clark Gable. Just one word circling the name: *Me*. Well, not *you*, sadly. Never to be. *The Wizard of Oz*—no arrow pointing to Dorothy or Toto or even the Tin Man. The jottings gave me pause. What was the matter with Evan? Was he just one more Hollywood dreamer waiting for the big role but eventually abandoning that glitter land, a failure, and heading back East…to Maplewood?

Yet Evan had made it clear he was headed back to Hollywood. A star would be born. His name illuminated in lights. A sparkling fantasy carried in the soul. Unrealized.

A boyhood probably intoxicated with that dream machine. Dream street. Photographs torn from magazines and taped to a mirror he spent too much time looking into.

As I fumbled through the meager sheets, my hand touched something stuffed at the back. A wad of cash, thick as a fist, buried under a folded handkerchief. Lots of money. Twenties and tens. Fresh, new, crinkly to the touch.

The dead uncle he crowed about?

A piece of paper, ripped from a schoolboy's tablet, was bound with the cash. I unfolded it. A few cryptic lines in crooked sloppy letters:

Remember that I know. We'll talk. Cash. Heil Hitler.

No signature, but the author was obvious. So what did this mean? What did Gus *know*? Was this his wad of cash? Or was Evan giving it to him? For the German Bund? Unlikely. Evan did not strike me as one of the Führer's robotic underlings. Perhaps the Hitler reference meant nothing more than Gus' devious identification—no name save the tag he clearly embodied.

Was the money the reason Gus was trying to break into the room? *His* money, he'd insisted.

I stood still, contemplating, though I finally pushed the note and money back into the desk. Had Constable Biggers and the state police examined the room yet? It seemed unlikely, but how was I to know? Could this be why the constable was keeping an eye on Gus—when he wasn't banging on the doors of the Assembly of God and asking for Dak's whereabouts?

"Edna!"

I screamed and knocked a lamp onto the carpet.

George was peering through the opening in the doorway.

"George, really!"

"I knock on your door but discover you rattling around a dead man's things."

"You're so nosy, George."

He bellowed, "You…you accuse me of…"

"Well, of course."

"Edna, they have a police force in Maplewood."

"I know. But since the door was open, I thought…"

He cut me off. "I'm worried about you, my dear. Curiosity is all well and good, but we're talking murder here."

"I'm fully aware of that, George."

George's voice was a whisper. "Edna, I'm afraid something is going to happen to you."

"Nonsense."

But my hand trembled as I gripped the edge of the desk.

George waved a hand at me, helpless. "Oh, dear Edna. Will you be the body on the stage just as the curtain falls?"

Chapter Nine

"Nadine."

The young woman heard me call her name but turned away.

The morning's rehearsal was like a well-oiled machine, George strutting and stomping us into a polished, believable adventure. He preened, happy with the results, and we all glowed. Opening night was days away. Throughout my delivery, I was aware of Nadine sitting in the orchestra, the script resting in her lap, following lines as Irene Purcell played the role of Julie. She looked deadly serious, and at one point I caught her mouthing the lines she'd probably never get to recite the coming week. When George told us we were done for the day and folks rushed to catch the 2:11 into Manhattan, I walked to the apron and called to her. "Nadine."

She'd been backing up, headed toward the exit, but now waited, her arms dangling at her side, as I walked down and toward her. "Nadine, wait. Can we have lunch?"

"Lunch?" she echoed.

My voice was cool and deliberate. "Nadine, I like you. I believe you're a good young woman. And my instincts are rarely wrong. But you lied to me."

She fluttered about, a wispy butterfly unable to settle, her hands drifting up to her ears, her eyes downcast. "I'm sorry, Miss Ferber. I didn't *lie* to you. Well, I just didn't *tell* you something. I *couldn't*."

"Then you need to explain it to me."

"I…" She turned away.

I stepped closer. "Of course, you do. Would you have me revise my good opinion of you? I hate it when my first impressions are proven wrong." I smiled, attempting to be less intimidating. "Do I have to revamp my own self-image? Most folks would rather die than change their hard-fought sense of self."

A flicker of a smile. She looked into my face. "I *am* a good person."

"Well, we'll talk about that at lunch. I'll even treat. Back to Mamie Trout's. Sooner or later everyone ends up there."

We walked the block to the Full Moon Café, though, interestingly, she trailed a half step behind me, a little bit deferential but probably wary of my next words.

Seated, she looked ready to sob.

Mamie, approaching, started to say something but simply put a cup of black coffee in front of Nadine and a cherry soda in front of me. I nodded at her as she backed off. Once back in the kitchen she started humming as she wrestled with some pans. I swear it sounded like a discordant take on a ditty from *The Wizard of Oz*.

"Tell me." I spoke so sharply Nadine's head jerked up, her eyes locking with mine.

A deep sigh, melancholic. "I've been stupid, Miss Ferber. I've made some awful choices over and over."

"Tell me." I softened my voice.

Her fingers fiddled with the menu though she never looked at it. "Everything goes back to Hollywood. I headed there from Michigan, where I was born. Outside of Detroit, in Warren. You know the routine. High school actress, cheerleader, pretty—'You should be in the movies!' So I took a bus. My parents went nuts. You've heard the story a hundred times. Then nothing. A job in a doughnut shop. I got a small-time agent who renamed me Nadine Novack, which I hated and then sort of liked. I was an extra in a Clark Gable movie, but I disappeared on the cutting room floor. Old story, new girl. I changed agents, went back to using my real name." She smiled thinly. "I loved the sound of it. Nadine Chappelle. Then, a whirlwind romance, I married this assistant director, though I don't know why. It wasn't love—it was, well, something to fill in the pain inside me. So lonely out there."

"It never worked out?"

She blinked wildly. "Six months later he divorced me. For another woman, or so I heard. Then he killed himself a month later. I mean, he was into drugs—I hadn't a clue—and he'd just got fired from Universal. Out on a binge one night, he'd got picked up by the cops and, overnight in jail, he hanged himself." She looked me in the face. "Why would they let him keep his belt? I thought…never mind."

"I'm so sorry, my dear."

Her eyes were wet and she used a napkin to touch the edges. Her makeup was smudged and she looked like a damaged doll. "I blamed myself but I don't know why. And suddenly Dakota was there. The wanderer with the sketchpad who drew my portrait in the park one afternoon. He was working on a movie. He actually had an agent who promised him parts, the sensitive young poet—I don't know. That's how they described him. Something like that. Meanwhile he was chauffeuring stars to back lots. That sort of thing. We fell in love. He was so gentle and sweet…It really knocked me off my feet, that…that attraction. And there I was, getting married again. And it was good this time. We both sort of looked at each other—and relaxed. It was like… like coming home, being with him."

"But something happened."

A sliver of raw anger. "His mother happened."

"She knew?"

"Dak told her—joyous, thrilled, anxious to bring me back to Maplewood."

"But if he was happy…"

She was shaking her head. "Well, it seems Clorinda and Tobias *hate* Hollywood. She'd been there during the silent era—had her fill of it. Before she found God and those rainbow chiffon robes and her imaginary halo. She tried to stop Dak from going out there. So when she heard about the marriage, she went crazy. And Dak blabbed everything—how I'd suffered, the suicide of my ex-husband, the drugs. Especially the quick divorce. The scandal. The Assembly of God does *not* believe in divorce—and certainly not suicide. Two no-nos on their commandments of evil. Or, I suppose, budding actors. Make that three no-nos then."

"But Dak was a grown man."

Nadine took a sip of hot coffee.

"But always a confused one. You would be too—if you had that childhood. Tyrant grandfather, bitter aunt, wandering mother, no father. Think about it. For years his mother and Tobias hammered home that he had to be the next prophet, the prodigal preacher, up there in the pulpit, redeemed and saved. They sent him pictures of when *he* preached—this little boy up there. Cute as a button in those white robes, a mass of black curls and those…those eyes. But it turns out he can't be married to a divorcee, especially one like me who drove a husband to cocaine and death. That wouldn't go over well with the congregants who already hold Hollywood suspect. Folks in New Jersey see Hollywood as a…cesspool." She smiled. "Have they even *smelled* their own state?" A dry chuckle. "Suddenly, one day, she arrives by train from the East. The arguments, the pleading. She leaves. She comes back with a battalion of lawyers and maneuvered Dak and me through an annulment. Over and done. I was dazed. Dak hid in a park. A marriage that never happened. Dak headed back East."

"You're not telling me something, Nadine. All right, I admit Dak is easily intimidated, maybe a little weak. But he loved you. He would not cave in so…"

She held up a hand. "Smart lady, you are. You see, Evan Street and this Gus character were living there then, casual friends of Dak. At least they lived in the same rooming house for a while. Drinking buddies. They met in some bar or at a studio. I never really knew."

I pursed my lips. "Evan."

"Exactly. Romeo—the hound off the leash. Dak fought his mother, refused to listen to her, but one night when I was alone, Evan showed up, started flattering me, romancing me, and foolishly...I don't know why...I let him. I was so beaten down—sorry for myself. Maybe I was mad at Dak because he didn't fight hard enough, but of course Evan crowed about his sleazy conquest to Dak."

I sat back. "So Dak agreed to the annulment."

Her tone got sharp. "I swear, Miss Ferber, Clorinda was behind that...that foolish seduction."

"How?"

"I have no proof, but Evan's attitude was like he'd been sent on a mission." She shrugged. "Maybe I was imagining it. I hated him so much."

"And here you all are in Maplewood."

She smiled. "I never stopped loving Dak, Miss Ferber. I knew he lived here, of course. I read articles about the Assembly of God in the newspapers. And so when the understudy job opened up here—a small notice in *Variety*—I rushed to get it. I *wanted* to be here. Near him."

"Was he surprised?"

She chuckled. "Stunned is the word. I turned around and he was *working* at the theater. I never expected that." Then she lowered her voice. "But he was also pleased to see me. He... melted. But I knew I'd made a mistake."

"Because of Annika?"

She nodded. "That marriage was already planned, and Dak seemed resigned to it. I was only complicating his life, something he didn't need."

I bristled. "Why not let a grown man make up his own mind?"

She scoffed. "Not if your life belongs to Jesus Christ."

I waited a moment. "You know, sometimes I want to shake some sense into Dak. Shake the haze off him."

"There are too many people coming at him."

"Annika, for one. Suddenly she knew you were in town?"

"She didn't know who or what I was to Dak, our past, but she caught him mooning around me. That's all it took. We did battle, the two of us, out in the street like gunslingers in *The Virginian*."

"And now Clorinda and Tobias know that Dak's former wife is at the theater."

She started. "What?" Her hand trembled on the coffee cup.

"Well, when I had dinner with them last night, I mentioned your name. I'm afraid I stoked the fire, dear. You're here with your stage name, but I told them you were Nadine Chappelle in Hollywood. Your real name."

A mixture of horror and wonder flashed in her face. "Oh my God. What did she do?"

"She screamed like the hound of hell was ripping at her heels."

Involuntarily, Nadine burst out laughing, and I joined her, the two of us rolling in our seats, tears streaming down our cheeks. When we stopped, we smiled at each other like old friends with a new and delicious secret.

"What now?" I asked her.

"Evan's murder changed everything."

"Any ideas?"

Her voice got sharp. "Not Dak. Of course not Dak. Impossible. Though he hated Evan. I hated Evan. He'd seen me at the theater, of course, and whispered, 'I've got a secret. What's it worth to you? I'm gonna tell.' On and on, taunting. But it didn't work with me. He couldn't touch me anymore. I just want this summer to end and I'll leave Dak to his new life. But Evan's murder is somehow in the way. I don't understand exactly how."

"Any ideas?" I repeated.

"I keep thinking it was Gus."

"Why?"

"Every time Gus approached Evan—that I saw—Evan looked angry. Like…'Leave me alone!' Once I heard Evan say, 'I told you I'll take care of it.' Gus always stormed away. Once Evan said, 'You shouldn't have followed me here.' Gus said, 'I *know*. That's what matters.' Nonsense, all of it. Miss Ferber, nobody liked Evan."

"Except Evan. He was his own favorite love story."

"Yeah, but maybe that lopsided love affair got him shot to death."

Back in the hallways of the Jefferson Village Inn, reaching for my key, I stood outside Evan's room. Earlier, I'd learned from Garret that the constable and the state police had been in the room, making a quick inventory of the contents, probing, delving into Evan's life as represented there. Nothing removed, supposedly. Garret Smith, I noticed, had neglected to fix the broken latch, though the door was shut, a cord tied from the doorknob to the splintered jamb. I considered my cursory walk through the room after Gus was taken away, and realized I'd focused on that suspicious wad of cash and the strange note from Gus, wrapped around it. Gus wanted something in the room. He claimed it was money. Probably true, given Evan's sudden flashing of easy cash. Somehow Gus was connected to that sudden windfall. But how? But it had to be more than that. Perhaps he wanted that mysterious note. Incriminating, perhaps, embarrassing. Enough to warrant even more suspicion heaped upon him. Given what I now knew about the Hollywood years, I suspected I might uncover something missed by law enforcement.

Something in particular bothered me. That desk drawer with magazines and clippings, bulging, spilling out. Evan's suitcase was unpacked, yet he'd jammed in all that accumulated material inside the drawer. Stacks of it, purposely chosen. Why was the collection so important to him? What secrets did it hold?

Sighing, resigned to criminal trespass, I undid the cord, and the door swung open with an unfortunate creak.

George, I knew, was still at the theater, giving notes to Cheryl Crawford. They'd been having some disagreement, which I'd ignored. Cheryl—nicknamed Miss Poker Face—had found fault with George in a deadpan, dismissive voice. George, usually shy and soft spoken and one who despised spats, had walked back and forth, talking loudly to himself, nervously.

I slipped into Evan's room, shut the door behind me and pushed a chair against it so it would not swing open. This time I made certain there was no gap for a nosy George to discover me. I switched on a lamp. Standing in that room, so very much like mine down the hall with the antique trappings and quaint rustic atmosphere, I telescoped to Evan's moving in: his social arrival, of sorts. A move from the shabby rooming house to this upscale abode. A room with a view of what he imagined to be a glorious—if ill-gotten—future. An elegant tomb for the lost actor.

This time I was more methodical in my investigation, extracting the magazines and clippings from the drawer and piling them on top, evening out the sagging pile. I ignored the recent clippings—the *Gone with the Wind* articles and the other movies, all of which he believed he should have starred in—and delved into the other pieces. A couple of issues of *Moving Picture World* and *The Motion Picture News* and *Hollywood Time*. Leafing through them, I found nothing, not even a scribbled notation.

Evan was fascinated with Hollywood, its inelegant history, its evolution from the creaky one-reel silents through the talkies and the epic films of recent years. Intoxicated with celebrity, drunk on studio deals, caught by the minutia of this star's marriage, that star's divorce. It seemed harmless, if a little maddened. But how different was it from the early days of Hollywood when obsessed young girls in Keokuk, Iowa, plastered glossy fan-magazine photos of Alla Nazimova or Ronald Coleman or Francis X. Bushman on their bedroom walls?

But no: something *was* different, and aberrant. Evan had a decided fascination with the dark underbelly of Hollywood, its worm-white scandals, its raw sensationalism, its gnawing criminal inclinations, and its pervasive tawdriness.

There were articles on the Olive Thomas scandal, the actress famous for her wide-screen innocence who was found dead in a Paris hotel in 1920—suicide by poisoning. Her husband Jack Pickford, Mary's scattered younger brother, dead months later from a cocaine overdose. An article on Wallace Reid, that handsome leading man, hurt on a shoot in the Sierras and pumped full of morphine by the studio—only to become a ravaged addict, eventually committed to a sanitarium. Will Hays, the Czar of the Movies, brought in to clean up Hollywood. For many, Hollywood was parties, orgies, sex, liquor, drugs. Dance the night away until you topple, comatose, into the screening room floor abyss.

There were articles on the notorious Fatty Arbuckle debacle, the fat riotous comic arrested for the sensational murder of a young ingénue. Evan owned a dog-eared paperback thriller on the ugly end of Fatty's career—Hollywood titillation and juicy tidbit. The dark side of the Hollywood moon. But Evan had speckled the margins with editorial punctuation: an exclamation point, a question mark. Odd, indeed. And a few blotchy notations: *Sick people. Sad girl, dead. Rich bastard.* Even: *Nice car*, alongside a shot of Fatty Arbuckle's new Pierce Arrow, a car fitted with a toilet in the back and solid gold accessories. Idle doodling, most likely, but curious. Fatty Arbuckle, who on Labor Day weekend, 1921, rented three rooms at the St. Francis Hotel in San Francisco for a long party, only to see it end in trumped-up manslaughter charges. Fatty's career over, three trials. The richest man in Hollywood done for. Evan circled a mention of Fatty's five-reel movie *The Life of the Party*, and noted: *Not so lively now, buster. Got you, didn't they?*

I stuffed the clippings back into the top drawer. There were too many—I had little time to digest them, one by one. No help, these papers. A side drawer, stuck, finally yielded, though once again with an unnecessary creaking noise. Inside there was a manila folder that contained shots of Evan. Publicity photos. Evan smiling into the camera, looking roguish. Evan in a tuxedo, leaning on a Cadillac town car, the debonair man on the town. Evan in polo attire, mallet at the ready. Evan on a diving board, showing his toned physique. Evan, Evan, Evan. A handsome man, decidedly, but always about that face a hint of malice and cunning. Or did I imagine that?

In the folder were signed contracts, purchase papers for the new car, a bank statement that registered only small deposits—and another note from Gus. It had been crumpled up, as though Evan had chosen to discard it but then smoothed it out to save it. A note probably written before arrival in Maplewood—or just about the time he arrived. The same *Heil Hitler* penmanship, and still unsigned, but revealing: *So Dak will be surprised to see you. Let him wonder. He got nothing to do with us anymore. But on the other matter, hey Evan, one thing. Cut me in. Or else.*

I reread the words. What did they mean?

The note was clipped to a photograph. When I lifted the note, I discovered a publicity shot of—Nadine Novack. An eight-by-ten glossy of the young girl in her Rebecca of Sunnybrook Farm pose.

Nadine? Why?

I heard raised voices from the street so I moved to the window and looked down onto the sidewalk. Annika Tuttle was wagging a finger at Frank Resnick. I cracked the window and heard Annika yell, "You have no right to tell him what to do."

Annika was standing by her car, the door open, as though she'd just jumped from the driver's seat to confront Frank, probably strolling by.

Frank eyed her stonily, and then stepped back.

"Don't walk away from me." Annika jabbed him in the chest with a finger. "You mess with God's plans."

Frank spoke through clenched teeth. "And you, I suppose, know the inner workings of God?"

"A godless thing for a heathen to say."

Frank's voice was filled with amusement. "I'm always fascinated by the…the surety you religion folks have about God's work. Do you ever think you might be listening to the addled voices in your head?"

She screamed, "How dare you! Enough of this. Just leave Dak alone. Do you hear me? He tells me what you say to him…you promise a life in the theater…away from God…degenerates."

"Dak can choose…"

"You leave Dak alone."

Hurriedly, I shut the window, rushed out of the room, and clumsily retied the cord around the doorknob. I galloped down the stairs and through the lobby. The desk clerk greeted me but stopped, stupefied, as I sped by out the front door. I stumbled down the porch steps and onto the sidewalk.

Frank was already leaving. I watched his stiff, angry back as he moved away.

Annika, holding the door handle, watched him, fury in her eyes. When she turned, she caught my eye, and they flashed with anger.

"What do you want?"

I had no idea. I sputtered, "Annika…"

"Leave Dak alone. You, too."

"Annika, I saw you arguing with Frank."

She broke in. "He asks too many questions."

"About?"

"And so do you." She slipped into the car and slammed the door.

Chapter Ten

An hour later Clorinda phoned to invite me to that afternoon's five o'clock service at the Assembly of God. Tired, I hesitated, but the image of the furious Annika assailing Frank stayed with me, so I said yes. Perhaps I could understand Annika better if I talked to her…or to Dak. Especially to Dak, that young man who seemed at the heart of so much of the mystery I was witnessing.

Clorinda also implored George to accompany me, and though he grumbled that he feared my succumbing to my own personal Protestant Reformation—"You'll be nailing chapters of *Show Boat* to the walls of some rural church, and masses will follow you into the Mississippi River"—he cavalierly sat next to me as Alexander, Clorinda's driver, picked us up.

"I never see Tobias Tyler in town," I said to Alexander. "Clorinda, once, at the Five and Dime…"

The quiet man glanced over his shoulder. "Mr. Tyler does not *come* into town. Ever. He goes from his home to the temple. Back and forth—only. Sister Clorinda *rarely* comes into the Village. Miss Ilona does the errands. Mr. Tyler doesn't like the town."

"Why?"

Alexander shook his head. The conversation was over.

The Assembly of God temple looked like a dated art deco movie palace plopped into a field at the end of Springfield Avenue, a densely wooded area of town. With gold-plated spire, massive Corinthian white columns sweeping up the front of the building, and bulky marble statues of angels guarding the entrance, the temple struck me as a mishmash of architectural styles running the gamut from neoclassical through Baroque and even New England Colonial chapel. Stained-glass windows had been placed, almost willy nilly, into the façade, so random they seemed afterthoughts, with one, indeed, misaligned. Yet the overall effect of the large cavernous structure was one of over-the-top spiritual splendor married to gilded opulence. Deep pockets funded such a coliseum in these sad economic times. No Depression here.

Late afternoon, bright summer sunlight, and the cars streamed into the parking lot. Carloads of eager congregants, mostly women, I noticed, hundreds of them. Arms linked, heads covered, they surged toward the doorway. A line of green-painted old school buses shuttled hordes from God-knows-where. As Alexander drove by, circling around to the back, I could hear the excited babble of raised voices. A horn blared, and a pretty woman in a flowered Sunday-best dress waved to the driver. A woman munched on a White Castle burger and then stuffed the crumpled wrappings into her purse.

George and I sat in an anteroom where an old woman in a floor-length black dress, a sprig of real violets pinned to her dress, served us coffee and apple cake, telling us in hushed, reverential tones that Clorinda was meditating. "An ecstatic state of spiritual awakening."

"Much," George told me, *sotto voce*, "like the state you get into, Edna, when you put pen to paper."

I ignored him. "Are Dak and Annika around?"

Saying nothing, simply nodding, she bowed out, but in moments the door opened and Dak and Annika walked in.

"Annika," I began, "I must apologize for intruding this afternoon. I was out of line."

She glared at me and then glanced at Dak, who looked puzzled. "What happened, Miss Ferber?" he asked.

"I interrupted a conversation between Frank and Annika."

Dak's face froze. "Annika, what?"

She shrugged. "I told him to leave you alone. You told me that he bothers you."

George eyed me and mouthed a word: *troublemaker.*

Dak's voice was crisp. "I said that we *talk.*"

She glanced at the clock. "I have to go. I'm to begin." Another fierce glance at me. "The matter is over. Trivial. Forget it, Miss Ferber. You, too, Dakota."

We were left alone with Dak, who now looked uncomfortable.

"I told her how much I *like* Frank. But she doesn't like me working at the theater. You know, I'm *forbidden* to mention the theater at my mother's home."

"Annika doesn't like you out of her sight," I told him.

"She's afraid…" His voice trailed off.

"Of what, for God's sake?"

"That I might drift away again."

"To Hollywood?"

He shook his head. "No, never back there. Just"—he waved his hand around the room—"away from *here.*"

"One question I have, Dak." I rushed my words. "Why didn't you tell me you were once married to Nadine?"

A weak smile, his face flushed. "I don't know. Somehow I thought I was protecting *her.* Nadine. Nobody, especially my mother, was to know. I want to keep her away from all of *this.*" Again the cavalier hand swept the room.

"Be honest with me, Dak. You wanted her kept away from Annika."

"*And* your mother," George added, which surprised me. He nodded at me.

Dak stared from me to George. "Annika just knew there was a girl at the theater who talked to me. I never told Annika and my mother that…that Nadine from Hollywood was in town, but now everyone knows."

"Gus was the one who told me. And Nadine even suggested that her infidelity with Evan was ordered by your mother."

"Oh God, no. And Gus? You listen to him? That…that Nazi?" He swallowed. "And why would Nadine *say* that? That isn't true."

"Look, Dak. Gus was up to something with Evan. And Evan had Nadine's photograph in his desk drawer. I don't understand…"

Dak didn't answer, though his face had a worried look.

Finally, hurried, he reached into the leather satchel he carried and pulled out a rolled-up drawing, handing it to me. "This will be for you."

I took it from him. An exquisite drawing of some bucolic scene, a waterfall against black rocks, in the foreground a bush of bright red-and-white flowers. Pencil marks in the sky, faint and tentative. "It's beautiful, Dak." I breathed in. "But you're not answering my questions."

Pleading in his voice. "Because I don't *know* what's going on."

He took the drawing back from me. "It's unfinished. I need another night on it. It's for *you*. Special. I want it just right." He smiled that infectious smile. "And framed in a gilt frame I found at a thrift store in Newark. Perfect. For *you*."

"What am I?" George grumbled. "Chopped liver?"

Dak grinned. "Miss Ferber believes I'm innocent of murder."

"So do I," George said.

"But she'll *prove* it." A flat-out statement, bold and confident. I sucked in my breath and glanced at George. He was shaking his head.

"Dak," I began, "I have so many questions."

He stood. "If you want to hear my mother, we gotta hurry."

We followed him into the hallway.

"Are you attending the service?" I asked Dak as we hurried along.

He reflected a second. "I will be tonight. Because of the two of you. But Mother's sermons are so theatrical and exhausting that I find myself drifting…fatigued. Her congregants swoon and jump and soar. I'm a tad cynical, Miss Ferber."

"You're not a believer?"

"Oh, I believe in God all right."

George drew his lips into a thin line. "But not in your mother's God."

Silently, Dak led us into the vast auditorium, already packed with excited congregants, a rolling hum filling the space. Vast gossamer curtains hung from the ceiling, gigantic wall fans gently swirling them—like a breezy, cloudy sky—and the effect was that of a pasha's harem room, exotic and mysterious. We sat in the back, Dak on my left, as a curtain rose on a wide stage and a robed choir began singing. Hand-clapping, swaying, hands raised in the air as a man soloed on "Give Me That Old-Time Religion." Suddenly, slipping into a seat to the right of George, Tobias nodded at us, his face flushed. The chorus swelled, filled the room, and everyone got quiet. Then, clad in a rainbow-colored gown, veils trailing after her, a tiara in her hair, Annika appeared in a spotlight and, accompanied solely by an unseen piano, began singing "Amazing Grace." A high, reedy soprano, a little shaky on the upper ranges, but eerily sublime. Her face lost the hardness of her street look; instead, positioned under the brilliant spotlight, she looked…well, angelic, rapt, possessed. A handmaiden of the Lord, transported.

I glanced at Dak. At first I thought he wore the sliver of a smile, pleased, but then I realized that his look was one of embarrassment. It was as though he were witness to a sacrilege.

Then, the last notes fading away, Annika spoke, the gritty harshness back in her voice. She talked of tonight's topic, "Women in the Hands of a Demanding God." She pointed to anonymous women below her in the orchestra, all with upturned heads. "You and you and you and you, loyal women and girls, daughters of Mother Mary. Serving our Lord, Jesus Christ. Holy daughters. Holy daughters. Holy daughters."

The mantra grew, feverish, picked up by rows of swaying women, filling the room to the rafters.

Holy daughters holy daughters holy daughters.

Then, from a microphone offstage, though with a technical squeak painful to the ear, the thunderous words, "Holy daughters." And Clorinda appeared. "Holy daughters of Christ."

George whispered. "She's not talking to me, I guess."

I whispered back. "Not to me either, obviously."

Tobias glared at us and, shamefaced, George and I stared forward.

Clorinda swept around the stage in layers of filmy rainbow-colored chiffon that swirled and flowed around her. Isadora Duncan meets the Dance of the Seven Veils meets Salome—or, I thought irreverently, Little Egypt at a carnival. She looked luminous up there, moving, moving, undulating, her face magnificent under the soft overhead lights. She looked, bizarrely, a waif, some ethereal child, some forest denizen. But then, poised deliberately before the center-stage microphone, she began to sermonize, and her voice was whiskey-toned, honey-thick, soothing, awesome, even chilling. Not her speaking voice, to be sure, that mundane flat intonation, but now the cultivated speech of an actress. And actress she was—and I thought of her brief stay in Hollywood. Of—*silent* movies. No one back then heard those dulcet tones. Here she'd located her perfect milieu in her personal house of God.

She cast a spell on that crowd.

On me. On George. Only Dak, staring, seemed to be in his own world.

"'Women in the Hands of a Demanding God,'" she thundered. "A headline wrought with power. We are the daughters of Christ, and we have a job to do. Let the men build the railroads and the skyscrapers. Let the men climb mountains and ford rivers. We serve, as daughters. The woman as God's blessed emissary on the earth whose purpose is to insure the sanctity of heaven. Handmaidens of virtue." Like Annika, she pointed out the various women in the temple, scattered in the rows before her. "And you and you and you. The mother of Christ, Blessed Mary, an inspiration. The harlot Mary Magdalene, herself redeemed."

Slowly, methodically, she built her sermon, her voice rising and echoing off the gossamer-draped rafters. "To insure the sanctity of God's kingdom, we women must…must…must lift our heads in praise of the Almighty King Himself. If our men be wayward, He straightens the path. If our men be cruel, we apply the balm of peace. If our men be weak, we bolster their courage."

On and on, rousing and wild and chaotic.

Then her voice got incendiary, almost angry. "Look to the Bible. Look! Look! Therein lies the answer to our occupations. Not the feeble housewife in her kitchen. The typist behind her machine. The seamstress with her needle. No! As warriors, we conquer."

George leaned in, whispering in my ear. "I guess I'm obsolete now."

But Clorinda, in a trance, flowed from one subject to another. A half-hour flew by. She sang—for her spoken words seemed a melody—of Yael from the Book of Judges, the wife of Heber the Kenite, who saved Israel from the onslaught of King Jabin. "Deliverance!" Clorinda screamed. "It was a woman who saved the kingdom of Israel from the infidels with a dish of milk. The tyrant Sisera dead at her feet." Then Clorinda swayed and intoned:

Extolled above women be Yael
The wife of Heber the Kenite
Extolled above women in the tent
He asked for water and she gave him milk
Gave him milk
Gave him milk.

A woman in the congregation howled and collapsed. Hands were raised, swayed in the air. Isolated voices from the hall chanted: *gave him milk, gave him milk.*

"And in the Book of Judith the voice of God…again. Judith. Yehudit. The One Praised. A woman so beautiful she made men lose their breaths, but a woman who invaded the camp of the infidel, the unholy Holofernes, lured him, seduced him, until he lost his head. Israel is saved from the godless hordes. So, too, in America you women must save the country from the godless who are everywhere. Here and there—and even in here!" She paused, dramatically, and a moan swept through the crowd, swelled, broke, weeping in the aisles.

Then, totally spent, babbling, speaking in tongues, a mishmash of rambling phrases…"Nebuchadnezzar, Nineveh, Bagoas…*Mulier sancta*…into the hands of a woman…bare…fallen…grace…grace…Satan beaten down…decapitated…a strike in the eye…crushed the nonbeliever…the…sin…take you to…heaven…love."

She stopped. The stage went dark for a moment. When the lights came back on, Clorinda was gone. An empty stage. The crowd hummed.

I glanced at Tobias who was awash in tears, his body trembling. He struggled to compose himself, holding onto George's sleeve like a needy child. George looked at me, and, for once, seemed incapable of the cruel or even witty remark.

We didn't move. So pervasive was the contagious emotion in the hall that it seemed foolish to speak…to stand. It was, I realized, a wonderful display of utter belief. But as that thought came to me, I realized how removed Clorinda and her followers were from the real world. And that included the sobbing Tobias, a man who had given himself over to God, complete, entire. As I watched the rapturous crowd, I thought of Dak, still on my left, nodding his head. He had been told to join this inner sanctum of belief, and he hesitated. But thoughts of Dak immediately led me to Nadine and to Dak's past, his roving life. This was not Dak's world. I understood why Clorinda and Tobias feared for Dak now—the idea of murder had no place in a room filled with vaporized ether.

Clorinda built a kingdom for folks who led lives of unsurpassed dullness, whose hunger for wonder demanded release.

Frankly, I was in awe of the woman's power.

Tobias was in his own trance. With a large white handkerchief he mopped his brow and dabbed at his eyes.

"She is a gift from God, no?"

George and I nodded.

He leaned over, in front of us, and signaled to Dak. "Your mother is not of this Earth."

Dak bit his lip, but kept still.

The crowd began shuffling out, and I noticed there were ushers at the end of each row who cradled bushel baskets. As congregants left, coins and bills dropped into the baskets. Over and over each usher intoned, "Bless you, sister. Bless you, brother. Alms for the journey to heaven."

Suddenly Dak rose and tapped his leather satchel. "I'm headed home."

"Where's home?" I asked.

"I rent a room on Springfield."

"I'm surprised you don't live at your parents' home."

He didn't answer but waved a good-bye.

Tobias was talking, his wrinkled face inches from George's impassive one. "Clorinda is the incarnation of the great Billy Sunday." He paused. "That great Pentecostal revivalist. You know, like Clorinda, he was worldly in his youth, a baseball player with the White Stockings. But God had a different path for him"—he grinned widely—"even though he was a good base runner. God touched him on the shoulder and walked him to a tent where the spirit waited."

George and I stood, but Tobias was still talking. "I heard him preach once before he died. I can still remember his voice, horrible and compelling and seductive. He understood that we in America are in a holy war. A foolish nation, this one. No wonder the Depression has shut us down. We are drinking again—liquor in the bloodstream. Evil is afoot." A dark grin that showed stained teeth. "Billy Sunday told us, 'I have no interest in a God that does not smite.'"

Clorinda appeared in a day smock as though she'd just returned from buying groceries in the Village at Driscoll's Food Market. Her voice was back to her gravelly inflection. She stood in front of us, a little timid, and addressed me. "So what did you think?" The ingénue auditioning for her first role.

What to say: I simply nodded like a doll's head loosed from its bearings. The transformation in her was so radical, this shift from spiritual to worldly, that I was at a loss for words. Yes, the diamond earrings were in place, the only color on the unadorned face.

Clorinda insisted George and I accompany Tobias and her to their home for dinner. Though we begged off—George actually became mute and kept nudging me, so obvious a gesture I was surprised nothing was said—we finally agreed. "A short stay," I pleaded. "An early morning rehearsal. Right, George?"

He found his voice. "Edna needs special coaching."

I glared at him.

"It's settled. A feast awaits us."

I didn't know about that, but we followed both out to the town car where Alexander opened the doors for us. "We were hoping to see Dak and Annika again."

Clorinda tilted back her head and laughed. "Lovebirds, those two. Dakota wanted to go hide in his rooms, but I told Annika to waylay him for a short hop over to Newark. A weekly visit to an old folks home where, not surprisingly, my handsome son gets a few old ladies' hearts aflutter."

"A missionary," Tobias insisted.

Clorinda sighed. "If left to his own devices, Dakota would do nothing but hole up in solitude and draw, draw, draw."

Tobias muttered, "A dilettante, that boy."

I kept still.

At the grand home a supper was already spread, the house-keeper Hilda greeting us without humor and ushering us into the dining room. A buffet of cold dishes: an ice-cold Hungarian sour-cherry soup, aspic, sliced tongue, cold roast beef, various pickles and relishes. On the sideboard a monstrous Black Forest cake. Tempting, this confection, though I planned to pick at the other drab fare.

Tobias was still under the spell of his wife because he couldn't stay still, rocking back and forth on his heels, repeatedly touching Clorinda's elbow affectionately, nodding at her. Nothing short of utter delirium, I considered. She looked embarrassed by his fawning attention, but I caught her winking at him when George and I turned away.

"Before we eat, come." He pointed to a hallway that led to a study, the walls covered with floor-to-ceiling bookcases filled with—my cursory glance noticed—Biblical texts and scholarly studies. A concordance to the Scriptures lay open on a desk. On a library table a copy of *What Would Jesus Do?* as well as Bruce Barton's *The Man Nobody Knows*. Charles Sheldon's *In His Steps*. Popular fare, Biblical exempla glossily reduced for mass consumption. Best sellers all, hypnotic confections. Notes for Tobias' own book—what had he said it was?—the herbs and plants of the Bible?—lay in neat, careful piles. Dried herbs—or so I assumed—displayed in small, squat bottles, corked.

"There is something I want to show you."

He pointed to a small poster mounted under glass, a black-and-white placard for a silent moving picture. I peered closer: *The Way Back*, directed by Fred Fischbach, and starring Wallace Reid and Alice Blake. But Tobias indicated a line at the bottom, small print that identified some of the minor players. Included was: Clorrie House. He bowed toward Clorinda. "My beloved wife."

Clorinda was shaking her head. "He found that idiotic bit of my past in a Salvation Army store in Newark. Displayed in the front window with other best-forgotten junk. A past I *fled*." She looked at him. "Fled. My girlfriend Virginia got me the part. The two of us played sisters. Wide-eyed and innocent colleens. I had one real scene—We batted our eyes at Wallace Reid and followed him down the street."

"Then you found Sister Aimee," Tobias said.

"God directed me away from sin and perdition. Hollywood is nothing more than Satan's playground. A cesspool."

"But then you left Aimee Semple McPherson's church, no?" I said.

A deep sigh. "Ah, Sister Aimee—the temptations of the flesh. She was too enamored of Hollywood herself, with those radio broadcasts and onstage shows and the splendid sensationalism. She started small in a modest chapel, you know. A true believer. I loved her. But then she built the Angelus Temple in 1923. I started to suspect some great corruption there. The

International Church of the Foursquare Gospel. She was herself an advocate for women, but she was a bit of a fraud with her faith healing and the promised return of Christ. And of course look what happened to her—that fake kidnapping in 1926 at Venice Beach, that supposed adulterous tryst. Who knows the *real* story?" Clorinda shivered. "Horrible. I wanted a more rigid religion. Old-time religion."

"My religion," Tobias added.

"After my husband died, the world was different for me. A scary place for me."

Clorinda shooed us back into the dining room where, I discovered, Ilona was seated at the table. She was smiling, though it seemed an orchestrated smile, frozen in place. A long black dress, ruffles around the neck. She looked in mourning. "Hello again." We nodded as we sat down. "Did you enjoy Clorinda's sermonizing?" Again we nodded.

"I think they were…surprised," Clorinda confided. "I'm a different soul up there. When I am doing the work of the Lord."

"Very impressive," I croaked out.

"Wasn't it?" Tobias remarked. "It never fails to shatter me, this wife of mine."

I changed the subject. "I was hoping Dak would stay and talk with us."

A faint titter from Clorinda. "You know how youngsters are."

"Actually I don't. I've never married."

Ilona eyed me intently. "Nor have I, though I raised Dak as a son. The spinster mother, although our father"—she glared at Clorinda—"took special care of him, doting on him, favoring him, stupidly indulging, but nevertheless stern with a swift rod against the boy's bottom. The only grandson. I was sometimes…helpless."

"Yes, yes," Clorinda interrupted, nervous. "Miss Ferber heard you last time."

For a second Ilona wore a hurt look, mixed with some anger, but then her face looked resigned, the shuttled-about sister dependent on the largesse of Clorinda and her Johnny-come-lately rich husband.

"How long have you lived here?" I asked her.

The question surprised her. "Since our old home was sold." She glared at her sister.

"I came back to our old home," Clorinda added. "A comfort zone, that place. Those interminable tours on a broken-down bus—tiresome. When Dakota and I needed to refresh ourselves, we came home. But when I married Tobias, he wanted a grand place. This place. After Hollywood I just wanted to come home. Away from *there*." She looked around the room. "All the old furniture. Calm. Serenity. Tobias insisted we not change the old trappings. The table we're eating at was my grandfather's, brought from Vermont in the last century. This was to be a home for Dakota. A sanctuary. Someday he'll live here. With Annika."

"Where does Annika live now?" I asked.

"In a young ladies' lodge in Newark. A refined Christian home. She is happy there. She was an orphan who came into town for the Junior Christian Endeavor Society on Saturday nights. Then she found us."

"Of course." My words might have been too clipped. George shot me a look, which I ignored.

Then, out of nowhere, Tobias launched into an animated— and unnecessary—animadversion on the proper conduct of young folks, some screed I imagined Cotton Mather would deliver as an Election Day Sermon, filled with admonition and punishment and Biblical quotation. He went on too long, of course, and it got worse when Clorinda added her New Testament softening to his Old Testament harangue. A genial battle of damnation and redemption for a heaven neither George nor I was allowed to enter. Or, I supposed, most folks living after the Enlightenment. No matter; their spiritual and dogmatic banter was obviously some sort of marital foreplay, private and cozy and titillating, and the rest of us were idle spectators.

At one point during a particularly tiresome ramble about America as metaphor for Sodom and Gomorrah and the trials of a beleaguered Job—my mind wandered, lost as I was in my own irreverent reverie—I caught Ilona's eye: a bemused look that suggested she understood how bored I was—and a certain joy that I had now had insight into the horrible hell she was living in this grand mausoleum.

She actually winked, then looked away.

I noticed how pronounced the veins in her neck were, how tense her fingers were as they gripped a fork. She was wearing a shrill crimson lipstick, so out of place in the puritanical room and with her own pitch-black monastic outfit, as though she'd slapped on a blood-red mouth to garner attention. A scarlet letter for the untouched spinster. Now, unfortunately, the garish red had smeared onto her front teeth. She looked as though she'd gnawed into raw flesh.

George seemed to be nodding off, though I knew such feigned drowsiness was one of his preambles to a barrage of cruel comment. Sometimes unexpected dinner invitations were fodder for his satire. The people you dine with—especially invitations you were compelled to accept—were born to be mocked. That was his impish thinking. Elmer Rice once quipped that George said many "devastatingly witty things, but never a kind one." And George once dismissed me as a Confederate general, then added, "Remember, I'm from Pittsburgh." We'd been through this scenario before, and I was always the recipient of a headache. I sensed a volcano ready to erupt, so I caught his eye. No, George, I signaled, no.

Tobias shifted the conversation with a remark about saving Clorinda—and now Dakota—from the clutches of Hollywood's fiery maw and the satanic hold of life on the stage.

George looked up. "I know that there are people who see the theater as evil but"—a clownish grin on his face—"does anyone really want to know such people?"

Quiet in the room. Ilona snickered.

Tobias narrowed his eyes. "They *murder* each other, sir." Said with a finality that silenced us all.

Clorinda, fluttering, reached for the iced tea. "Annika is a calming influence on Dakota." Another throwaway line.

Tobias went on. "The only theater is a church hall."

"Clorinda," I began, "an idle question. Last time when I mentioned Nadine Chappelle, you were horrified. In fact, you ran out of the room. You didn't know Dak's ex-wife was in town…"

"Stop!" she yelled. Her fist pounded the table. "Did you hear what Tobias was saying? *She* is Hollywood. She tried to destroy my boy…that…that foolish marriage. I could not believe that she's come here. To Maplewood. She came back with one purpose. To seduce him back to Hollywood." She pounded the table again. "I won't allow it."

I'd had enough. "There was even the suggestion that you employed Evan to seduce Nadine as a way of getting Dak to agree to an annulment…"

I stopped, so raw was the look on her face.

"How dare you, Miss Ferber?"

"I have these questions. Believe me, Clorinda, I'm trying to save Dak from a murder charge."

"And you do it by accusing me of being a…a panderer?"

"I'm trying to clear…"

George was clearing his throat. "Edna."

Tobias stood, his small body shaking. All of us turned to look at him as he trembled, head bobbing, his skin an awful purple. He shook his fist at me. "How dare you? In my own house. How dare you?" He reached out toward Clorinda, his fingertips touching her extended hand. It reminded me of Adam and God in Michelangelo's famous ceiling fresco. Fingertips touching. The blessings of heaven on earth. The merest touch that suggested volumes. Tobias grabbed at his heart and bent forward. "How dare you? My wife is a saint."

Chapter Eleven

The desk clerk called to me as I headed into the breakfast room. "Miss Ferber, a package came for you this morning." He handed me a rectangular box wrapped in wrinkled brown paper and tied with white string. I joined George at the corner table and as the waiter poured me coffee—with the whipped hot milk I requested—I tore open the package. An exquisite drawing in a burnished gold Victorian frame, the fully realized landscape that Dak had promised me. Finished now, and beautifully done: the result of his sensitive, intimate touch. A luminous work that reminded me of the Durand landscape Dak had pointed out to me. A woodland scene in lush summer. I fairly lost my breath. An accompanying note said, briefly, "Miss Ferber, as promised. Fondly, Dak." The drawing was signed on the back: *Dakota Roberts for Edna Ferber, Orange Mountain in Summer.*

"I know where I'll hang this."

George smiled. "I'll sell you the one he made for me, Edna. Then you'll have a matching pair." A lengthy pause while he lifted a coffee cup. "Oh, that's right. I haven't received mine yet."

"I'm the one who believes in his innocence."

"As do I."

"I'm…looking into it."

"And I've been your tagalong jester, Sancho Panza lurching uphill while you tilt madly at windmills."

"Jealousy is an awful thing, George."

"Edna, eat your breakfast. You have a long day. You need to hide the painting so I can't steal it, attend a rehearsal under my direction, and catch a murderer. In that order."

"It's not funny, George. Evan is dead."

His voice got small but with an edge. "Oh, I know, Edna. And I'm worried that you'll blunder into something that will get you killed."

"Nonsense."

"I joke about everything, my dear, but I'm not joking about this."

I touched Dak's gift affectionately and tucked it back into the box.

"I have a busy day. I'll be rushing back to the city after rehearsals, George. I need to meet with Doubleday, and I'm having dinner with Aleck." Aleck Woollcott was a close friend who invited me to dinner after a brief business meeting with my publisher. Aleck Woollcott, bon vivant and critic, the inspiration for the popular drink, the brandy Alexander; and, unfortunately, the enormously rotund instigator of some of my most vitriolic and smoldering feuds. At the present time, however, we'd called a *pax manahatta*. The two of us were cut from the same piece of easily bruised cloth. Tonight's dinner—a prelude to Aleck's making the trek to Maplewood next week for my own final curtain—was to test the waters. Aleck could not wait to see a disaster. Or perhaps not. Lately, I'd practiced good behavior, cloyingly sweet with the café society legend, though sometimes it took all my strength to avoid the easy skirmish with the gloriously round Aleck.

"Are you going to behave yourself this time, Edna?" George grinned his ah-shucks Huck Finn grin.

"Why should I?" Then I smiled, too. "We're friends this summer, Aleck and I. I've decided to have peace in our time. I have nothing on Chamberlain selling out Czechoslovakia."

George stood. "Good. Time for rehearsal."

Which went smoothly, with George very pleased. Louis almost dropped me in a crucial staircase scene, but didn't. Panicking, he jostled me as if I were a burlap sack of old potatoes. His face turned scarlet as he whispered an apology. As the author of *The Royal Family*, I was treated with undue reverence, and Louis Calhern, a longtime star player and robust man, usually picked me up as though I were a fragile Ming vase. George, noting his tentative scooping up of the lovely authoress, had yelled, "Christ, Louis, imagine she's a clay pot from Woolworth's."

"Thank you, George," I answered back.

"Edna, that's not a line from the play I wrote."

Everyone laughed, and so did I. Louis, grinning, swooped me up as though I were a bale of hay and hurled me up the stairs.

Spontaneous applause, and Louis bowed. I tried to look ten pounds lighter.

After lunch, I caught the Lackawanna into Manhattan, a half-hour ride. Arriving at bustling Penn Station, for a moment disoriented by the ebb and flow of rushing crowds, I veered toward a taxi stand to head uptown. Queued up, hit by a blast of noxious bus fumes, I turned away, shielding my face. My eyes locked on a small kiosk where daily newspapers were suspended on a rack.

The *New York Post*, a subway tabloid usually considered by me as tawdry yellow journalism, caught my eye, an array of papers hanging left to right. The garish big-font headline:

NAZI NOSE DIVE!

Stunned, I handed over a nickel and scanned the front page, looking at the sheet-covered corpse positioned on a subway platform, alongside a steel post that identified the stop as Times Square.

"Lady." I looked up as the young man squiring folks into taxis called to me. "You going or not? I ain't got all day." Grumpy, yet oddly friendly, the paradoxical mix of New York City attitude. I nodded and slipped into the backseat and gave the address of Doubleday.

To this day I cannot say how I knew, what dark atavistic impulse told me, but I knew under that morbid sheet was the body of Gus Schnelling. No matter: sometimes my journalistic nose understood situations long before my intellect grappled with them. A nose for news, my father once called it.

The *Post* misspelled his name: Gus Shelling.

The article contained very little information. There had been a much-publicized Nazi rally at downtown Union Square, which drew upwards of fifty people, many of them carrying placards and banners displaying swastikas and the ferret-like visage of the German madman. Inside the *Post* there was a photo taken of the rally—arms raised in grotesque salute, straight-out, rigid, menacing. A fiery speaker lauded Hitler's economic rejuvenation of the Rhineland—and his rapid dominion over brutalized Europe. Photographs of families, too, with one man holding up a child whose simpering grin especially alarmed me. The father was a beefy lout, adenoidal looking, and a woman with stringy hair and pasty face clung to his arm. The starved, pinched faces of the Depression. Other men and women celebrated German ascendancy, German-American alliance, the awful Bund, a worship of the Führer, whose redundant picture dominated so many posters. Swastika armbands graced upper arms. Nowhere in the photo—I stared, eyes close to the grainy shot—could I see Gus Schnelling or Meaka Snow.

Yet, hours later, his body lay on a subway platform blocks north of Union Square.

The rally had been rowdy, the *Post* reported, the police ringing the crowd as anti-fascist protestors yelled catcalls at the Nazis. The boisterous rally was intended as a crowd-provoking preamble to a speech in a hall up in Yorkville at ten that night. But Gus never made it. After the rally, a dozen cohorts headed through the underground, planning to make a transfer at the Forty-second Street subway stop. Some vociferous protestors followed, monitored by the police. Both groups screamed at each other, and the police broke up fistfights. On the packed subway platform at Times Square, around nine o'clock, an hour after the rally ended, the jostling crowd shifted. While police restrained another aggressive protester who tried to assault a taunting Nazi, the train approached and, in a flash, one of the Nazis, standing on the edge, was pushed into the path of the speeding train.

Gus Shelling (their spelling), aged twenty-seven, of uncertain address, was pronounced dead moments later.

Witnesses said an old man, white-haired and wearing a baggy trench coat despite the awful heat down there, had deliberately pushed Gus. The sign Gus carried flew into the air, and in the ensuing panic, as cohorts tried to reach him before the train crushed him, the old man had fled up the stairs and into the street. In the confusion the police, alerted, rushed to rescue Gus, not realizing he'd been pushed. When others yelled about the old man, they gave chase—to no avail.

I read and reread the short piece. Horrible, such a death. A violent end to a life that celebrated violence. What mattered now was that a young man had been crushed to death. Awful, awful.

There was no mention of Meaka Snow. I wondered whether she'd been there, at his side, the loyal comrade in a frightening cause. Gus' convert who came to love his cause. The Nazi maiden with the electric hatred.

Gus Schnelling, dead. Evan Street dead, his crony. Or enemy? Gus who wanted to retrieve something from Evan's room. Something incriminating? Evidence? Had he killed Evan? Well, Constable Biggers need not monitor the swaggering Gus any longer.

Now his full attention would rest on Dak.

Dak.

Back in Maplewood, a short train ride away.

My business at my publisher's concluded successfully, I met Aleck Woollcott for an early dinner at Maxim's on East Sixtieth Street, a familiar if pedestrian watering hole and eatery for the ragtag remnants of the old Rose Room of the Algonquin Round Table, long gone now but nostalgically remembered. Aleck relished the French cuisine because the elegant dessert cart, wheeled past him a number of times in the course of our dinner, was calculated to get the obese man salivating and tongue-tied. I liked the place because they always remembered my name and gave me the table by the front window. The maitre d' had a wife who had memorized parts of *Show Boat*—the autographed copy I gave her insured copious sherry aperitifs and the coveted table. The spoils of fame, mocked by me in my fiction yet, sadly, savored by a woman who liked her fame and fortune.

"Edna," Aleck began, "we're all driving out on Saturday."

"All?"

"I'm gathering carloads of your enemies, but I fear such a caravan would clog the highways."

"What cattle car are you commandeering?"

He squinted. "Fat jokes, Edna? A week in New Jersey and you're already indulging in puerile humor."

"I seem to recall that you were born in New Jersey."

He shut up, peering at the menu. "Ah, sirloin with fried potatoes."

Aleck sat back, adjusting his eyeglasses. A huge man, round as a bowling ball, with an owl-like pink face and short, pudgy fingers, he looked the court eunuch in his rumpled white linen suit that was his one summer look. For a while he discussed recent croquet games played in Central Park and at the Swopes estate at Sands Point, Long Island—everyone's current passion, Aleck being particularly good at it. George despised sports—except for croquet. Aleck told me an anecdote of Harpo Marx trying to cheat, which I'd heard before. Noteworthy games went on for eight or nine hours, Aleck indefatigable at the obsession. "Really, Edna, no one can beat me."

Then, suddenly, as we were served our dinners, he looked me in the eye. "I hear you're involved in a murder in Maplewood."

"Evan Street, an understudy."

A smile. "Let me ask you this, dear Ferb. How are you going to get away with it?"

I cut into my steak and then held the knife toward him, menacingly. "Aleck, if I'm going to murder someone, I'd pick a more expansive target to shoot. Then I wouldn't need a good aim. Just fury."

"Nice, Edna. Did you rehearse that witticism?" He chuckled. "Tell me all about it."

So I did, and Aleck, a curious man with keen observation, listened closely as I chronicled Evan's death and the cast of characters in Maplewood.

He reflected, sipping his cocktail, "You know, Edna, I talked to Louis Calhern one night."

"Louis?"

"Yes, an old friend, but this was before the murder. He did mention an understudy that got on Frank's nerves, and he was a little peeved at Cheryl for bringing him into the mix. Frank's not one to abide nonsense. Evan, I assume. Too good-looking for his own good. Louis told me that this Evan seemed too... hungry. A cocksure lad, annoying as spit."

"Aptly put, Aleck, I grant you. A man who relied on his looks and glib tongue."

"Good looks. Hah! You have to feel alone in the world to develop a personality." He let me consider the words for a minute. "So you know Frank Resnick?"

"Everyone on Broadway knows Frank. Except you, of course, who only socialize with the very rich or the very poor. All the rest—that middle road of drab functionaries—you cavalierly ignore. Not colorful enough for you. The rich intrigue you with their corruption and secrets, and the poor intrigue you with their pettiness and secrets."

"Well, thank you. Wit and wisdom from the oracle of Carnegie Deli."

"Ah, my dear Ferb!"

"Tell me about Frank."

"An efficient stage manager, much in demand, though Louis and I both discussed why he is in exile with you in Maplewood. People *leave* New Jersey—they don't *go* there. Not willingly. Not without a judge's mandate. Once again, you're the exception. And Frank, too."

"I wondered the same thing. He's giving undue attention to a charming young man who is suspected of murdering Evan."

"My, my, Edna, a regular cesspool you inhabit in that sylvan glen."

"Tell me about him."

He sat back, his fingers drumming the dessert menu. "Frank has always been a quiet, quiet man, almost a hermit. No one is ever invited to his place on West End Avenue. He refuses most invitations to get-togethers, unless mandated—you know, the demands of staying alive on Broadway. He refuses to gossip and argue—though he knows a lot of scandal, let me assure you. And he has decided to avoid all facial expression lest an onlooker assume he cares."

"But he obviously does care these days. He's a different man in Maplewood, it seems. Nothing like what you describe. I can see it in his fury. His pointed—almost manic—defense of Dak. Why such a shift in character? He had a confrontation in the street with this…this Annika Tuttle, one of the zealots of the town."

His eyebrows rose. "Really? Frank engaging in a street scene? Are you sure? The Frank I know walks away from confrontation." He signaled to a passing waiter and ordered coffee—a pot, not a cup—and a strawberry soufflé and a Bavarian chocolate roll. "Anything for you, Edna?"

I shook my head. "No, Aleck. Go on, please."

"Frank led a wild younger life, if rumor is to be believed—and it usually is. I always believe the worst of people. That why I'm pleasantly surprised when I notice crumbs of decency in them later on. But Frank—where was I?—Oh yes, Frank spent or misspent his young manhood in Hollywood, supposedly as a budding actor. I gather he got caught up in a life of parties, drinking, drugs, mayhem, women who should know better, and sleepy-eyed mornings waking up in a sheriff's cell. Hubba hubba, dance the night away."

"Frank?"

"Amazing, no? But he went sober, cold turkey as some would term it—a horrible metaphor, the maligning of a very good Thanksgiving repast—and came back East. No talent for acting, he realized, and a decided talent for asceticism and monkhood and teetotaling. Edna, he's no fun anymore."

"But he stayed in the world of theater."

"It's in the blood, dear. You of all people should know that."

"Well, he's demonstrating signs of life in Maplewood."

"I insist that is an oxymoron."

"Really, Aleck, it's a quaint village." I smiled. "The heart of the town is actually called 'the Village,' capitalized."

"Where folks are murdering one another—and not just the lines of *The Royal Family*."

I shifted the subject. "I picked up the *Post* coming in. That young Nazi who was pushed onto the subway track was working on *The Royal Family* as an electrician."

Aleck whooped, drawing the attention of the other diners. "Another death? Really, Edna, what is going on there?" Aleck contemplated both desserts the waiter placed before him. He groaned at the confectionary sight.

"Hold on, Aleck. I think it had to do with his fascist politics. He handed out a vicious Hitlerite leaflet as George and I sat on the porch of the Jefferson Village Inn. He and his girlfriend are—were, at least one of them—rabid followers of Nazism. The rally yesterday in Union Square."

Aleck was shaking his head. "An ugly crowd, that. I read about it, of course. Good riddance, I say. Hitler Youth deserves no old age."

I sat back, closing my eyes for a second. "I'm alarmed at the course of the world—and America, Aleck. You know that. This Nazism…this Hitler…I know there can only be worldwide conflagration now. I feel it in my bones. And that men like Gus can walk the streets of a town like Maplewood where American flags dot the landscape…"

The small eyes in the fat, bilious face became gleaming marbles. "Let me tell you a story, dear Ferb. A while back I was walking with Moss Hart on Eighty-sixth Street where, for years, I buy sauerbraten, and this young man, dressed like a fugitive from a labor camp, accosted us and whispered 'Jew' in my ear. I nearly fainted."

"But you're not Jewish, Aleck. Yes, Moss is, but…"

He held up his hand. "In times like these everyone different is Jewish." He sighed. "And, therefore, everyone has to declare themselves Jewish."

I trembled. "I get scared, Aleck. I've seen the signs in Yorkville…the swastikas…"

"I'll show you something when we're through."

We finished dinner and Aleck, deadly serious now, hailed a cab that dropped us off in the Eighties, in Yorkville on the Upper East Side. Not too far from where I used to have my home. Dark out now, the street awash in neon and streetlight, the neighborhood looked like any other complacent, decent Manhattan block.

"There," Aleck pointed, and I saw nothing. But he moved me closer to a storefront, a German butcher shop, brightly lit, cascades of sausage hanging in the window. Through the glass I saw white-aproned fat men, blood splatter on those aprons, sweeping a sawdust-covered floor.

"What, Aleck?"

He pointed to a back wall that led to a dark corridor. A large portrait of Adolph Hitler hung in a simple brown-wood frame, suspended over the glass cases of pork chops and rump roasts. Though it wasn't, that portrait seemed lit by fire, the comet in the dark night sky that stops you in place, transfixes you.

Under the grotesque portrait there was a sign: *German-American Bund meeting tonight, 10 p.m.*

"The back room," Aleck whispered, "is where the meetings take place. Once, passing, I heard roaring cheers, the chilling Heil Hitlers, the thick beer-besotted laughter. It spilled out onto the sidewalk." He turned, ashen now. "A taxi, Edna. Let's get out of here."

"But it's New York," I pleaded, though I was shaking.

"Deutschland in Manhattan. Germany on the East River."

On the late train back to Maplewood, I sat alone, my face pressed against the window. Voices near me seemed far away, echoey, false. And though the car was steamy on the hot August night, I shook from the cold.

◇◇◇

At the rehearsal the next morning, I learned that Gus Schnelling had given notice two afternoons before, as the stage crew began working. He had grandly strutted around, a swastika plastered to his arm, handing out valedictory leaflets promoting the rally in Union Square. Away from the theater, George and I missed that last performance. That same afternoon we were at the Assembly of God and, later still, having dinner with Clorinda and Tobias. Meaka Snow, similarly swastika clad, accompanied him, a look in her eyes that defied interference. An unsettling scene, I gathered, or so Constable Biggers told everyone afterwards. Before he disappeared that afternoon, Gus tacked flyers to poles and trees, tucked them under windshield wipers. Constable Biggers and his deputies—with well-intended local citizens—hurriedly combed the Village, ripping down the inflammatory notices. Gus and Meaka obviously caught the train into Manhattan for the rally—or maybe drove there in that jalopy—where he met his death. The next morning, at rehearsal, no one spoke of the departed Nazi. The news of his death was unannounced until later that day.

Now, of course, everyone was buzzing about Gus and Evan, though, save for Nadine, no one really knew either. Cheryl was asked about Gus. "I don't remember him at all." Dak, I noticed, was nowhere around, though early mornings he usually would be at the Assembly, only joining the stage crew in the afternoon.

Constable Biggers lingered in the orchestra, pad in hand, unmoving, and I noticed Nadine stayed backstage, cloistered in a tiny room. During a break, the constable chatted with George and me and noted that he'd admonished Gus to stay in town during the investigation of Evan's murder. Gus had nodded, though with a sickly smirk, and Biggers sensed that the young man had plans to skip town. "It's him or that Dak. I feel it in my gut." Biggers wrestled a cigar out of a breast pocket and tucked it into the corner of his mouth. "One of them most likely a killer. Now it's down to one to look at."

"Of course, Gus could have killed Evan," I protested. "And now, because of his politics, he ended up murdered."

"Life don't work that way."

"And what way is that, sir?"

"Too convenient. Wraps things up too easy."

"But sometimes…"

"It ain't a novel, lady."

George was grinning. "Said to the lady novelist."

When we were alone, George confided, "Edna, I'm worried."

"You think the two killings are somehow connected?" I deliberated. "Well, it's a possibility. Although I won't admit it, I agree with the constable—life doesn't work that way."

He bit his lip. "What if they are?"

"Then there's a madman afoot."

"Exactly. And here you are, stepping lively through the quicksand. Think of it, my dear. Gus, Edna. On the subway tracks, Edna. Evan shot in the chest. What next? A piece of scenery crashes down on your head?"

My eyes scanned the stage. "Nothing is going to happen to me."

"Well," he concluded, "I've been a tad frivolous as you've gallivanted around playing Nancy Drew. But from this point on, we're in this together. Collaborators to the end. This play's the thing—in which we catch the conscience of the…killer. Thank you, Shakespeare. You won't stop, of course. So when you head off to do your cockeyed mischief, Edna, knock on my door. We're a team."

"A team," I echoed.

"Yeah, like Weber and Fields without the pratfalls."

Late in the afternoon, strolling back from the Full Moon Café where I'd daydreamed over blueberry pie and a lemon phosphate, I spotted Dak sitting with Frank on a sidewalk bench. They didn't seem to be talking, both staring vacantly out at the street, elbows resting on knees, heads slightly turned away from each other.

"Hello." I stopped before them, waited. Frank eyed me warily.

"Miss Ferber." Frank threw a sidelong glance at Dak, who seemed absorbed in his own thoughts.

"I wondered about your reactions to Gus' death."

Frank said nothing for a moment, picked at the scab on this thumb, and then stared over my shoulder, addressing someone in the distance. "Oh, that Nazi insanity. A sad end, yes, but, I mean, Hitler. You set sail with a madman and the waters are rough. Gus kept his mouth shut at work—until that last day, that is. Then those nasty flyers. Hitler as hero of the Aryan lineage and all that nonsense. Joe, one of the Great War veterans, threatened to beat him up. Folks had to intervene. Still and all…"

Dak looked at me, his voice fierce and hard, a tone I'd never heard from him before. "You know, I never trusted him."

"I know."

"Out in Hollywood he was sneaky, slinking around with Evan, the two of them always with their heads together. Talking about me. Or…or Nadine. Evan would look up when I walked by and tell Gus to shut up. But he did it so…so obviously. Like he was getting a thrill out of it. A game."

"And when he arrived in Maplewood?" I prompted.

"I felt he was in the last act of some great scheme."

"But about what?"

He shrugged his shoulders. "I don't know. I wish I did. But don't you think it's funny he was *here*? The Nazi strolling under the maple trees. That surprised me. I know it surprised Evan—he wasn't happy when Gus came to town. I'd spot Evan watching Gus, anger in his face."

"And Meaka Snow?"

"I didn't know her till she appeared by his side one day. Evan said they met in New York. A vicious, nasty woman, hard as glass, cruel. I'm surprised no one killed her." A shaky laugh, dreadful. "Maybe they will. Evan's gone. That bastard. Gus is gone. Another bastard."

Frank bristled. His hand shot out and touched Dak's shoulder. "Dak, enough. Be quiet. You talk too much. Do you know how that sounds—your words? They're dead men. Dead."

"I want to hear what he has to say," I insisted.

Frank's face closed up. "Dak, no."

"What does it matter?" He stared into Frank's face.

Frank touched his sleeve protectively. "They already think you murdered Evan. Do you want to be blamed for Gus' murder, too?"

Dak shook away Frank's hand. "Why would you say that?"

"Are both murders connected?" I spoke to Frank but was watching Dak.

Crazily, Frank stood, twisted around. I watched him closely. There were tears in his eyes. Then, as though ashamed, he rushed away.

Chapter Twelve

Meaka Snow stood in front of me, blocking my path on the sidewalk in front of the Jefferson Village Inn. For a second I caught my breath, alarmed by the anger in her face. Unblinking cold agate eyes, the broken head of an old porcelain doll I recalled from my childhood. Macabre, that look, the innocent play toy now transformed into nightmare.

"What?"

"They're going through Gus' things at the rooming house."

"What?"

"The local cop Biggers and some FBI, I think. They won't let me in."

"But I don't see how I can…"

"You're telling everyone Dak didn't kill Evan. Yes, he did. He got you fooled with that pitiful look he has. And I think he killed Gus."

I thought of stepping around her but stayed in place. "That's impossible. Dak was here." I took a step toward her, but she didn't budge, standing there with her thick arms folded over her chest.

"How do you know?"

That gave me pause. I didn't know—how *would* I know?

"What do you expect from me, Meaka?"

In that instant the wide face crumbled, raw emotion breaking through. "They didn't have to kill Gus." Her voice cracked at the end.

"Who?"

"They hate us. It ain't fair. It ain't. We had a life together—tomorrow. Gus and me."

She rocked back and forth, this small chubby girl, her blunt head quivering. So unlovely, this woman, so purposely unattractive, I thought, with the stolid peasant garb, ill-fitting and gray; with the abundant honey-wheat hair pulled up and back so that she resembled a disorderly hay field. A driven political child, like so many of the agitprop players in the Greenwich Village social melodramas Peg Pulitzer and Franklin P. Adams forced me to attend: the ideological fury borne out of the Great Depression. Left wing and right wing—it didn't matter. What did matter was the fire within. This dangerous Nazi *fraulein* with the pancake face and thrift-store smock, in thick shoes, her nails bitten to the quick, the swastika pin stuck on her chest like an unfashionable brooch.

I tried to move around her, but she stood there, a rock, solid.

"Well…" Dismissive, casual, trying to end this futile conversation. But then I thought: Does she know anything that might solve Evan's murder? Gus' murder—that was confusing, yes, and I was uncertain whether it somehow related to the Maplewood crowd. But perhaps this hapless woman, this fanatical young Nazi follower, harbored bits and pieces of information that, mixed in with the other jigsaw pieces, might provide me with direction. Staring at her, I had the gut feeling that the answer to one murder might solve the other.

Yet…there was that hateful swastika pin facing me—an affront, blatant and awful. A small but dark sun in the noontime sky. Inescapable. Foul. Cruel. Hideous. But…

"Meaka, let me buy you a coffee." I pointed to the Full Moon Café.

The invitation took her by surprise, wariness coloring her eyes. Here was a woman who trusted no one, who had subsumed her self-loathing personality into that of her aggressive lover, the *über*-Nazi lad himself, Gus the agitator.

She nodded quickly. "A minute. I want to get to Gus' room when the FBI leaves."

Mamie Trout raised her eyebrows when Meaka and I walked in, a tilting of her chin that suggested I had a questionable range of acquaintances. But she smiled as she seated us, giving me an affectionate tap on the shoulder. "Seen you over to the Assembly," she whispered pleasantly.

"The Assembly of God? You were there?"

"I won't miss it. That Clorinda Roberts Tyler is a gift. Best show in town. The other night she soared—took me with her— all that talk about us powerful women. Talking *to* me, felt it to my core." She winked. "Better'n that *School for Scandal*, which I seen at the Maplewood Theater."

Surprise in my voice. "Will you become a follower?"

She was shaking her head. "Nope. I'm a born and bred Baptist. Good enough for my parents, good enough for me."

"But then why…"

"Told you. Best show in town. Maplewood can get a tad dull." But she glanced at Meaka. "Though if folks find religion there and save their sorry souls, it's all right with me. Fact is, it's time some folks stepped lively to God's tune." She glowered at Meaka. She walked away.

Meaka, under her breath. "A hideous, dreadful woman."

"She makes a wonderful blueberry pie." I smiled disingenuously.

"I don't care. Pie served with a slice of her pocket Jesus."

"Meaka," I began, "why did you stop to talk to me?"

She drew in her breath, fiddled with the cheap bracelet on her wrist, and glanced toward the door. For a moment she looked the dumb animal in a pasture, stolid, languid, baffled by the sudden falling rain. Meaka Snow, I concluded, was a plodding young woman, easily shoved out of the way or into danger, the mindless ox, saddled with a kind of blind faith in anyone who whispered a kind or loving word to her. A sad woman, one lacking a moral reserve, this *lumpen* who must have been unloved all her life until Gus Schnelling, dashing in a Prussian-boot sort of way, took her by the hand and delivered lines for her to recite. Once learned, she became the most vocal and strident proselytizer.

For that reason she was a dangerous woman, one whose emotions and intellect were the playground for the sly and the cruel.

"They're going through Gus' stuff now." She looked at me with angry, bitter eyes.

"I know. You told me. So what? He was murdered. The police have to do their job."

"I don't trust them."

"Well, that's your particular failing, my dear."

Mamie Trout, still frowning, handed us menus. I ordered a sandwich and fries for both of us. Meaka scarcely looked up at Mamie.

"They'll make him out to be evil. He's the…victim here."

"Stop that, Meaka. I'm sorry but he *was* evil. He was a Nazi. I know you can't see that, but your faith in Hitler is evil. Evil." Flat out, perhaps cruel.

The flesh around her eyes bunched up. "I'm a proud Nazi."

"Are you really? Or did you take on Gus' coloration to please him?"

She slammed her palm down on the table. "I believe in what he taught me."

"Tell me, were you with him when he was killed?"

She huffed in small, jerky grunts. "I was at the other end of the platform. When someone screamed, I thought it was another fight. Those protesters who followed us down into the subway. Then I looked for Gus."

"So you didn't see who pushed him?"

I waited for a sudden burst of tears, but none came. Instead, her eyes darkened. "He'll pay."

"Who?" Startled.

"Dak."

"Meaka, I don't think…"

"I don't want to go to the police. No one would believe me."

I cringed. "You have an idea that Dak did something?"

She actually yelled out, her voice raw. "Yeah."

"Then tell me."

Meaka nervously lit a cigarette and blew smoke rings into the air. "I don't even know why I'm sitting with you."

"Because I'm Jewish? Is that why you won't trust me?"

"That's part of it."

"The other part?"

"I don't know. Look." She leaned back and picked up a canvas bag she'd dropped onto the floor. "I was carrying Gus' bag—I don't know why. He had, you know, the bigger sign." A snicker. "German Solidarity in New York.' I colored that one in."

"Nice touch."

"You're being sarcastic."

"I'm Jewish. We tend to get sarcastic when we're having coffee with Nazis."

A scowl. "Maybe you should be afraid."

"Of you?"

"Of Hitler."

My mind went blank. Then I said, "There'll always be Jews, despite what your Hitler believes. There just won't always be a Hitler."

I could see the direction of the conversation confused her, and she stared at the glowing tip of her cigarette. Finally she snubbed it out and zipped open the bag. "I'm only here with you to prove to you that Dak is the murderer. Maybe then you'll do something about it—and stop believing him. He's a fool who hated Evan and hated Gus. And me, too. Him and that bitch Annika with her holier-than-thou mouth."

"Show me."

But she paused. "Gus told me you and George Kaufman *know* who killed Evan. Like you got evidence. You know that it was Dak but you are protecting him."

"Why would he say that?"

She shrugged her shoulders. "He seen you with that…that crowd. Cozy and all."

"How does that translate into a belief he's a killer?"

A puzzled look on her face. "I dunno. That's what he told me."

"Meaka, I don't know who killed Evan. That's the truth."

"But you wanted to pin it on Gus." She seethed. "But Gus got murdered."

"Perhaps Gus' politics did him in."

She shook her head vigorously. "No, it ain't so."

"The New York police are on it."

"Like they care. Did you read the paper this morning?"

I hesitated. "No. Why?"

"It said the police believe Gus was singled out by someone. Witnesses testifying to that. Like someone pushed through that crowd, edged near him, waited till the train came, and then shoved."

"An old man, I read yesterday."

"Nonsense." She wore the look now of a smug, bratty girl who raised her hand to answer all the teacher's questions. "The article said some witness said it *looked* like an old man but the moustache and white hair was something out of a vaudeville show or something."

"Still…"

"And then this old, old man scooted up the steps like a fifteen-year-old boy, lickety-split. Do you hear what I'm saying, Miss Ferber? A disguise."

I reflected on her words. "So he *was* chosen from the crowd." The knowledge hit me full-force. It wasn't political, this death, not the fiery anger of an anti-fascist zealot. Gus was targeted. "Intriguing."

"Yes, ain't it?"

She tapped the canvas bag. "The only thing I regret is that Gus didn't tell me things. He had secrets. I know he cared for me—took care of me—but he thought I was stupid. He thought women was stupid." She grinned. "He thought *you* was stupid."

"Me?" An unnecessary shriek from me.

"Because you believed Dak. Gullible, he called you. 'A sex-starved lady whimpering about a handsome Valentino boy.' His words."

I fumed. "How dare he!" Then, sheepish, I told myself: Lord, the man is dead, Edna. Murdered. He's beyond your censorious tongue.

"But Gus told me he had a secret."

"But of what? Any idea?"

Again, the dumb-ox shrug. "Dunno."

"You must have some idea." I leaned forward, frustrated. This young woman, so hapless and bungling, held the key to something. I knew it to my marrow.

A sly grin appeared on her face. She reached into the canvas bag and grabbed a handful of papers. Releasing her clumsy grip—I noticed dark yellow cigarette stains on her fingertips—the papers spilled across the table. Those infernal leaflets she and Gus had handed out and tacked to poles: Nazi propaganda, warnings about the Jewish international banking elite, the sanctity of precious Aryan blood, the blotchily reprinted figurehead of Hitler, a grainy reproduction that highlighted those insane eyes and that musical-revue moustache. Involuntarily, my hand swept them away from me. Meaka grabbed some and shoved them back into the bag.

As she lifted a pile of them, a wad of elastic-bound cash rolled away and bounced onto the floor. Quickly, Meaka retrieved it, wrapped her fingers around it, and cradled it to her chest, her head tilted up, a beautiful smile on her lips. It reminded me, perversely, of some Renaissance Madonna and Child depiction, so ecstatic and lovely was her look. A woman cradling precious money, a curious distortion of a venerated icon. "What?"

"He didn't tell me he had all this money. I didn't know it was in there." Her fingers lovingly caressed the wad of cash.

"What's your point, Meaka?"

She tucked the money back into the bag, though she tapped it affectionately first. Then, her eyes scanning the table, she reached for a small white envelope. "This." She pushed it across the table at me. "This was hidden in an inside pocket."

Inside the envelope were two slips of paper, small, torn sheets, both folded over and crumpled.

The first was written in a sloppy penmanship, with splotchy ink: *Yeah, I know. I don't owe you, friend. We'll see about that.*

I looked up, confused.

She peered forward to see which note I was reading. "Evan wrote that."

"What does it mean?"

Her voice got low, mean. "The secret I couldn't know about."

I opened the other slip.

Leave Nadine alone, Evan. I mean it. I swear you're going to pay. I'll hurt you. I mean it. Leave Nadine alone. You better listen now. Dak.

Meaka was watching me, a triumphant look on her face. "You see, Miss Ferber. Dak killed Evan."

I turned the note over—nothing on the back. I pushed it across the table, and Meaka grabbed it. "How do you know he wrote it?"

"Of course, he did."

I thought of something. "Why would this note to Evan be in Gus' bag? Why would Evan give it to Gus?"

"Maybe Gus took it off him. Another secret."

"What was Gus going to do with it?"

"Dunno."

"Did Gus talk about trying to break into Evan's room—when he was stopped by Constable Biggers?"

She nodded. "Yeah."

"What was he after?"

"Maybe these." She pointed to the slips of paper.

I shook my head vigorously. "No, he was stopped before he got inside. I was there. Think about it, Meaka—wouldn't he *want* Constable Biggers to find Dak's note? It's incriminating."

"Maybe he went back."

And so did I, I mused. And this note was not there, so far as I knew. "I don't think so."

"It doesn't matter *how* it got in Gus' bag, Miss Ferber. It's just, you know, that it *got* there. And Gus had it. It's proof that Dak killed Evan."

"Because of Evan's attention to Nadine?"

"Those two are still in love."

"So what?"

"So Dak was real protective of Nadine. I mean, you've seen her—she's this…this wilting violet, bloodless, skin and bones. A weepy girl."

"Unlike you?"

She bit her lip. "I can take care of myself. No one can use *me*."

"Except for Gus."

She didn't like that. "That ain't fair."

"So be it, Meaka. It may be poor taste to speak ill of the dead, but I've done it before and never regretted it. And somehow Gus Schnelling needs to be spoken ill of, even after his horrific death. The day he signed on as a Nazi he forfeited his right to compassion from souls like me."

She looked baffled. "What are you talking about?"

"And that's the sad thing here, my dear. You *don't* understand."

"Well, anyway, Gus got a hold of the note. Somehow."

I waited a heartbeat. "Maybe he took it off Evan's body after he shot him."

She screamed so loudly that Mamie Trout came flying out from behind her counter.

"It's all right." I waved her away.

"How can you?" Meaka was trembling.

"It's a possibility, no?" Meaka had placed the notes on the table, but I reached over to take them back. "Gus was in a hurry to get into Evan's room. There was something there that might implicate him. Maybe"—I pointed to the first note—"this is a piece of evidence. He was blackmailing Evan."

Her head was swaying back and forth, a puppet's wooden head loosed from its strings. "No, no. no."

I turned over the note from Dak. Something bothered me about it, and then it hit me. "Meaka, Dak's note is yellowing, dark at the edges. It's an *old* note." I pointed to it, happy with my discovery. "I think this note may date back to Hollywood. A time when Evan was in both Nadine and Dak's lives. And Dak not happy. This is *not* recent. It was stored away, saved—as Evan did with so many pieces of his Hollywood past."

"You're wrong."

"I don't think I am." I watched her face now. She was considering what I just said. "But I do wonder why everyone came to Maplewood this summer." I smiled. "Not to see my debut as an actress, surely. Evan, Gus, even Nadine." Idly, I thought: even Frank. Why? "Was everyone looking for Dak? Evan, the pied piper from Hollywood?"

Meaka breathed in. "Miss Ferber, Gus was scared."

That stopped me cold. "What do you mean?"

"He'd never admit to it. That's not the way soldiers for Hitler are built. But I could see it in his eyes. He was *scared*."

"Of what?"

"That's part of the secret. He didn't tell me."

I sat back, eyes narrowed. "Why are you telling me all this, Meaka? You don't like me."

She bit the corner of a fingernail, a squirrel-like gnawing at her cuticle. "I gotta tell someone. I mean, you're…like a writer."

"So?"

"You are the only one who'll listen to me."

"So go to the police." I shook the papers. "With these."

"No. No police."

"What do you want from me?"

Suddenly her face caved in. "I don't know. I got no one here to talk to. Gus is dead."

A small part of me relented, as I softened my tone. "Go home, Meaka. Leave this…this Nazi stuff behind." I waved one of the vagrant propaganda sheets left on the table.

"I gotta do this for Gus now."

"Go home. Where do you live?"

"Newark."

"Go home."

"No." The obstinate look, stolid, dull. She touched the swastika pin on her dress.

The door opened and George walked in, stopping short when he saw me sitting with the Nazi maiden. "Edna, I've been looking for you." But he was looking at Meaka. "I just got through talking to Constable Biggers. The FBI just left Gus' room." He looked at Meaka. "Hello, *fraulein*." She refused to look up.

"Did they find anything in Gus' room?"

He pursed his lips. "Just stacks of dirty clothing on the floor. A Spartan room, he said. So little there—a stack of Nazi pamphlets and some swastika armbands." He leaned into Meaka. "Hello, *fraulein. Wie gehts?*" She turned away.

"How nice."

"Nothing else." He continued to look at Meaka as he slid into a chair opposite her. "They're looking for this young lady now."

Meaka jumped up and grabbed the two notes, stuffing them into the white envelope, and placing it into the bag. She started to zip it shut, but the zipper snagged, refused to move. She whimpered like a hurt kitten. Then, fumbling with the bag, she swiveled, knocking a chair over, and rushed out of the café.

"Meaka, wait," I yelled. I stood and followed her outside. The screen door slammed behind me. "The police…"

She was shaking her head wildly as she tottered away.

"Was it something I said?" George had followed me outside, the two of us on the sidewalk, watching Meaka try to run.

"Look at her, weaving in and out of traffic."

"Constable Biggers is waiting at the train station, where she seems to be headed."

As she ran, she waved her arms wildly. At one point she stopped, dipped into the canvas bag, and pulled out a stack of Nazi flyers. With one chaotic move, she hurled them into the air, and they scattered onto the street. The wind from passing cars spread them about. One flew by us—Hitler's sour face immediately trampled by the tires of a car. Meaka moved in a straight line now, determined, headed for the train. Paralyzed, we stood there, George and I, watching the approaching world war rushing away from us.

Chapter Thirteen

Clorinda Tyler phoned me late that afternoon, panic in her voice. Nothing of the melodic, sweeping lilt of her transcendent sermon now, but instead, a strident cry of an animal penned up.

"Clorinda, for God's sake, what is it?"

"Can we meet? I know I need to see Constable Biggers, but the man...well, the man slams me into silence, the way he stares, accusing, that dreadful pad in those claw-like fingers."

"A little melodramatic, no? He's simply doing his job."

"Really? I step out the front door of the Assembly of God, those times with Dak at my side, and there he is, a statue, never saying anything, just staring. My Lord, had we lived in Salem, we'd all be hanging from a noose, innocence be damned."

"What can't you tell him?"

"Could you please meet at the Marlborough Inn? Around seven? I dislike going into the Village—people *stare*. An early dinner. On me, of course. Ilona has errands in town, and will join us. I know she can be...Well, you've met her."

"Seven is fine." I breathed in. "I was scheduled to dine with George and..."

She interrupted. "Oh, please, Edna. Not this time. He can be so...irreverent. Funny, yes, and I do appreciate wit, sardonic remarks, that repartee you New Yorkers cultivate. But last time he offended Tobias with his smart-aleck comments. Oh no. Please."

"And I didn't? With my remarks? You seemed to be made furious by my bringing up Nadine's name."

A little sob, swallowed. "Please, Edna, not now. Not that woman, that home-wrecking ingénue with too much lipstick and too few brains. Well, you I forgive…you're a woman who understands agony. I can see that in your face. I mean…everything…"

I cut her off. "All right. Seven. By my lonesome." A heartbeat. "Should I bring a pad?"

A whoop of false laughter. "Droll, Edna, that's what you are. Seven."

She started to say something else, but I hung up the phone.

I looked for George, then jotting down notes backstage, his brow furrowed. He glared at me. "You know, Edna, Shaw said that theater should make folks feel, make them think, and make then suffer. But these days only directors like me seem to suffer…"

I cut him off, telling him about Clorinda's frantic phone call—and his omission from dinner.

"Well, so the gods favor me this evening. A first, I'd say. There's only so much heaven my bloodstream can absorb."

"Pity me then."

"Almost everyone does, Edna."

"Don't expect me to summarize what happens later tonight."

"Edna, Edna, a glass of merlot and you're a chatterbox."

"It's all too horrible for words," Clorinda slipped into a chair opposite me at the Marlborough Inn and whispered the words. I'd been seated for a few minutes, waiting, and Clorinda seemed to float in, a woman in layers of apricot taffeta, trailing a heady scent of lavender. Heads turned and she nodded at them, the star of the show, huzzahs and bouquets.

"What's horrible?"

She leaned in. "I had words with Dak. We *never* have words. We are a loving mother and son, always. Always. What we've been through—dreadful—our early days. I know I get on his nerves because I get infused with the spirit and he stares as one befuddled, but we *never* fight. Argue. *Ever.*" She stressed the word, stretching it out.

"Tell me." Impatient, I looked for a waiter.

She whispered again. "It's because of the note. Ever since we learned about that…that horrible Gus being pushed to his death, there seems to be a pall on everything. Dak is so grumpy with everyone, short with Annika. I mean, Annika can be a little severe—she hasn't learned the grace of God demands a lighter spirit—but he *ignores* her. Evan murdered, and now this Gus. We assumed all along that Gus murdered Evan. For whatever reason. None of our business, really. It was…well…convenient."

"Clorinda, really! Convenient?"

"Oh, you know what I mean. I'm not heartless, but he was an odd young man. All that sickening Nazi spewing. Unnerving, no? Of course, Evan was his own worst enemy. The boy with the mirror stuck to his own face. I remember telling Dak when I *rescued* him in California from that two-bit actress harlot that Evan was a man to be shunned. The way he *slid* into your presence, a viper, like nothing could happen in the world until he showed up." She was watching me too closely, I felt, her eyes wary. Suddenly I didn't trust her.

"And then Evan showed up in Maplewood."

A narrowing of the eyes. "And look what happened to him. The mills of God grind slowly but they grind exceedingly small."

"I don't know if that tired expression applies to a sudden gunshot to the heart. Or, for that matter, a shove off a subway platform."

She ignored me, twisting her head around to gaze at the other diners.

"Clorinda, back up a second. What note? You mentioned a note you and Dak argued over."

"Well, not argued—more debated…"

I held up my hand. "Stop, Clorinda. Tell me. Stop! You circle around like a sun-drenched butterfly."

"Dak found it. He has rooms at Mrs. Judson's home, you know. The old mother-in-law apartment she has. It was in a manila envelope, sealed, his name on the front. Block letters."

She reached into a purse and extracted the folded-over envelope. Her hand trembled as she handed it to me.

I withdrew the slip of paper and read the bold print: BEWARE! YOUR NEXT! TIMES 3. A FRIEND.

I read it again, out loud. Clorinda gasped, as though hearing it for the first time.

"Dak brought that to you?" I asked.

She nodded and looked on the verge of tears. "He was taking it to that…that…Constable Biggers, but I grabbed it from him."

"Not wise, Clorinda."

"It's just too terrible."

"Well," I remarked, "it may just be the work of a mischief-maker, some town scamp. Or, I suppose, it's real."

Again, the gasp. "Tell me what to do."

"We do what Dak started to do. Hand it over to Constable Biggers. He is the sheriff in this town."

"But he's so dedicated to arresting Dak for…*murder*."

"You don't know that."

"Who else is left?" A helpless wave of her hand. "I mean, he was watching Gus and Dak and…and Dak…"

She closed up as the waiter came to take our orders. Clorinda refused to look into his face, tucking her head into her chest, hands buried in her lap.

I breathed in. "Clorinda, you know I believe in Dak's innocence. That belief seems to have acquired some currency in town. Everyone, it seems, defines me as his advocate." I paused, a dreadful heartbeat. "But is it possible Dak killed Evan? Maybe Gus?"

A long silence, her face frozen. "Edna!"

"I mean, we have to consider…"

Her words were laced with bitterness. "You're doing it again, Edna. You turn words around, glibly, cruelly, and I feel…feel assailed by you."

"It's a question we have to ask. Others are asking it. I have no power, but others do."

She half-rose from her seat. "Then what do we do?"

"We follow Dak's advice immediately." I pointed to the note.

She was nodding furiously. "Annika is having trouble with all this."

"About what?"

"This murder, disruption, mayhem. This is not the life she *planned* on when she embraced my gospel. Dak's wallowing in self-pity, drifting around, ignoring her to the point where she looks positively *hurt.*"

"Clorinda, did you ever consider that Annika is a poor mate for your only son?"

She eyed some diners walking by. Her voice seethed. "That's ridiculous, Edna."

"Have you asked Dak what he wants?"

An edge to her voice, short breathing. "Well, we've talked."

"But have you listened to him?"

"Of course. Now you're being ridiculous. You know him, Edna. Not like I do, of course, but enough. He's charismatic, sensitive, a boy lost in his own romantic thoughts. *Spiritual* thoughts. The wild oats…"

I showed my impatience. "I know, I know. I've heard that before. The blessed boy, prodigal. Fatted calves. Blessed is the frail…do dah, do dah. All I'm saying is that Dak's confusion these days, his distractedness, is because he may want something different out of life. He doesn't want to *hurt* folks he cares about. In the process he hurts *everyone*—mainly himself."

Her words were clipped. "And not want Annika? I've *trained* Annika. She is devoted to the church and to Dak. To *me!*"

"But Dak may not be devoted to her."

She looked away, silent for a moment. "You don't understand, I'm afraid."

"I don't think I'm wrong."

Suddenly her eyes locked with mine. "Are you ever wrong, Edna?"

I smiled wistfully. "Never."

She harrumphed, very nineteenth century *Tempest and Sunshine* heroine, and lapsed into silence. She refused to look at me.

Ilona joined us minutes later and stared from me to her sister, registering the awful silence. "What happened?"

"Edna doesn't believe what I'm telling her."

Ilona chuckled. "A woman of exquisite common sense." Ilona turned to me. "Did Clorinda show you that note Dak received?"

I nodded. "It confuses me."

"Not me. I *know* who wrote it." She sat down and dropped her hands into her lap, a smile on her face—the good student ready to please the teacher.

Clorinda interrupted. "Please don't tell Edna that harebrained theory."

"Tell me."

Ilona sat up and rested her elbows on the table. A small woman like her sister, Ilona purposely effected a negative to her sister's glossy print: where Clorinda was sensuous with a body accented by flowing robes and scarves and laces—a rainbow of pastels that made her seem a dizzy fugitive from a Grimms' fairy tale—Ilona wore drab unstylish dresses or, for this dinner, a mannish brown suit, square-cut, with shoulder pads that blunted her upper arms. But she chose lipstick—Clorinda wore none—that made her mouth seem a bold smear of bright red. A ring on one finger had a black topaz mounted in a square setting. A rectangular rhinestone brooch. It was almost as though she mastered Clorinda's round and flowing look, then purposely, viciously, countered it so as to make Clorinda look a little foolish, the aged ingénue still flitting across her own stage. It was as cruel a mockery, I thought, as any I'd seen. And, as with my own sister Fannie, a woman always poised to remind me of my unwed state and my unlovely appearance, I'd weathered a lifetime of similar savage sabotage.

"Dak wrote the damn note." Ilona sat back, watching as Clorinda winced at the mild curse.

Clorinda shut her eyes. "Why would you say that?" Tears welled at the corners of her eyes.

"Because you know it's true."

"That's quite an accusation." I sat back, arms folded, fascinated by the dynamic of the two sisters.

"It's a way of getting attention, stupidly trying to take the heat off him."

Clorinda was sputtering. "Foolishness, Ilona. Your usual foolishness."

The waiter placed a dish in front of Clorinda, but she pushed it away. Ilona eyed it and picked up a fork. Lips pursed, Clorinda pushed the dish close to her and shot Ilona a look.

"The kind of stunt he'd pull when he was a boy—to get people to pay attention. 'Look at me! Look at me! I'm so cute.'"

"Well, perhaps if you'd treated him better."

Ilona again flared, "I gave up my young life for him. Wasn't that enough? I could've married…"

"He always loved you." She hissed the words.

"So you say."

I stepped in. "The two of you seem content to barter Dak's love…"

Ilona was cutting. "Edna, you don't understand what happened back then."

"Well, tell me then. Dak these days is threatened with arrest for murder. Serious business, really. And yet you two play out some fierce and bitter memory that cripples everyone. And somehow—I don't know how—that memory, Dak's boyhood, plays a part in the murder."

"Nonsense!" From Clorinda.

Ilona said nothing but wore a thin, ironic smile.

"Ilona is angry at Dak."

"But why?" I pleaded.

"I'm not angry at Dak. I'm angry at *you*." She shot a contemptuous look at her sister.

Clorinda let out a fake laugh. "Oh, really?"

Ilona addressed me, twisting her body so that she was turned away from her sister. "Edna, I once had a chance for happiness. I was engaged, believe it or not. I was—comely, even pursued, but shy. While Clorinda was chasing dreams in Hollywood—she was always the runaway spirit, uncontrollable, soaring above the trees—I sat at home with a cruel and nasty father. 'Yes, Father. No, Father.' The country doctor, loved by patients, fawned over by the ladies with their mineral salts and garden herbs, but a man who disliked his own daughters. You could see his dislike—not indifference, *dislike*—such a face when you spoke to him. Probably because they resembled a wife who conveniently died to get out of the house. And I had escaped, too. But the Great War and a bloody battlefield in France took care of that. My Charlie died. End of story. And I was appointed the spinster daughter to tend to that madman."

Clorinda lisped, "Father was a saint."

Ilona, sarcastic, "Clorinda imagines all kinds of saints around her. Father, Dakota, even—well, truly—herself."

"He *was*. You…"

She raised her voice. "And then, just as I settled into my virginal bed in the old homestead, sleeping on the bed I still sleep on, shriveling up year after year as we speak, Clorinda, the madcap screen non-legend, marries the handsome actor who then dies. Yet the career had to go on, and Father, a man who despised the stage and Hollywood and, well, fun, demanded she deliver little Dakota—he of the preposterous name—see what happens when you go West in America?—to a stable life away from the hullabaloo of California. Father had already failed raising two children, so he saw no problem adding a third. The ultimate parental hat trick. And there I was, appointed surrogate mother."

I held up my hand. "But it seems to me you would love a child like Dak. You seem to dislike him so."

"I did. I suppose I still do. A troublesome boy, always acting out. I didn't know what to do. But Father kept telling him—your real mother is coming home. Any day now, the prodigal mama. So Dak looked *beyond* me. And then Clorinda found Jesus under a palm tree. And she moved from Father's blacklist of fallen women to the Blessed Mother Herself, the itinerant Holy Roller on the broken-down bus. A life of poverty, but a life cuddling with God. And once Father died Dak was scooped up and taken on the road. When they stopped back home in Maplewood, Dak was cold, distant. He looked *beyond* me."

"He's a moody boy." Clorinda was looking at me. "A special boy."

A flash of anger. "You bad-mouthed me to him. Told him stories. He ignored me, looked at me as if I was—I don't know—a dangerous stranger. You smothered him, Clorinda. You fed him God and not love. God is no answer for ruining a child." A loud, raucous laugh. "You envisioned yourself some marked-down Madonna with a scrawny Jesus, bringing your message to the boondocks. Dak served as a prop for you. A theater prop. Him upon that stage singing his sloppy song. No wonder he fled to Hollywood. You made him vain and hollow. And you told him he could inherit the kingdom of heaven."

"I saw in him what God planted there."

"Bratty children must get on God's nerves, Clorinda. Why not? They get on everyone else's. You turned him against… himself. That sullenness…that distance. You wanted him all to yourself. You never shared him. Ever."

Clorinda's voice rose. "He is *my* child."

"He was *mine* for a while."

"You borrowed him."

"He wasn't furniture, Clorinda."

"That's cold."

"And he's not the savior of mankind now."

"Yes, he is. Tobias has plans."

Ilona chuckled. "For a spiritual lady, Clorinda, you do have a love of worldly trappings." She pointed to the diamond earrings Clorinda wore.

"Tobias has been blessed."

"Yes, by a rich, foolish mother. He was more *your* savior than anyone else." Ilona faced me, her face flushed. "When Tobias entered the picture, everything changed. Suddenly Clorinda had enough clout to sponsor God."

Clorinda *tsk*ed. "You are so irreverent. Perhaps if you *heard* one of my sermons."

"I'd have to take to my bed. A welcome migraine, surely."

Clorinda lapsed into silence, a faraway look in her eyes. One of her hands picked carelessly at a piece of bread, but she seemed dreamy, her lips trembling. "I fear it's all slipping away."

"What?"

"My church. All I've worked for—for Dak. For God!" She reached across the table and grasped my hand. Her grip was tight, fierce. "Scandal. Scandal, Edna. Ilona doesn't understand, but scandal eats at—corrodes—rots—until there is nothing left but empty pews. Dakota has been a foolish boy, allowing himself to be a part of *that* world. If he had stayed in the chapel…It's driven us to our first words. Our first tension." She was whispering now, the words choked out. "Tobias is losing faith in Dakota. Can you believe it?"

Ilona scoffed. "The son of God laid bare."

"Stop it, Ilona," Clorinda snapped.

Ilona caught my eye. "Tobias' utter infatuation with Clorinda is an umbrella that covers both me and Dakota. There may be a problem in paradise…"

"Ask Annika," Clorinda added. "Annika ignored Tobias the other day. Unforgivable. I have created that child in my image—you know she was a lonely orphaned child from an uncaring family of distant aunts in Newark—and now she is slipping away."

"Of course, she isn't." Ilona winked at me. "You have that girl under your spell. You managed to wipe out all traces of her own personality, filling in the cavity with Jesus Christ and the baubles you and Tobias toss her way." A hearty laugh. "You're angry because it didn't work that way with Dakota. Such a willful streak in so weak a boy. Imagine!"

Clorinda was shaking her head. "Tobias yelled at Annika for something. Tobias never yells at anyone."

"Maybe it's about time."

Tired of this sisterly bickering, I shifted the subject. "Dak dropped off the most exquisite drawing for me, a landscape…"

Clorinda grunted. "Oh Lord, all that doodling."

"He's talented," I insisted. "The hours spent on his art…well, I was touched."

"You mean he actually *finished* something? His rooms are crammed with half-done canvases and watercolors." Ilona smiled. "He loses interest…"

"Well, not this time. It's a charming landscape."

Clorinda was staring over my shoulder, her face contorted with a look that was both baffled and stunned. I started to say something in defense of Dak the artist, but that sudden transformation silenced me. The prophetess of unconditional love now looked ready to faint—or to scream. It startled, quite.

Ilona and I both turned to see Frank and Nadine walking into the restaurant.

Frank looked grim-faced, though Nadine, stepping in front of him, was laughing, looking back over her shoulder at the older man. He was shaking his head like a befuddled parent teased by his child. It was, I thought, a curious tableau, those two stage folks somehow connected to Dak. While we watched, silently, the maitre d' seated them at a table some twenty feet from us, handed them menus, and Frank took out reading glasses and positioned them on the edge of his nose. As he did so, he absently glanced around the room, and froze. He mouthed something to Nadine, and the smile disappeared from her face.

"Clorinda?" I thought I detected a little concern in Ilona's tone, which surprised.

Clorinda said nothing, yet she didn't avert her eyes. Her eyes flashed utter hatred now.

Nadine, I thought. Clorinda once again dealing with the sweet temptress wooing Dak away from God and empire. The wife who disappeared in a heartbeat. The waving of a magician's wand. Nadine, whose presence in Maplewood—through my indiscreet revelation—so shocked Clorinda. Nadine, considered so safely in Dak's Hollywood past, a frivolous and transitory wedding, playing home among picturesque California palm trees. Nadine, conveniently annulled out of mind. The marriage that never happened. Nadine, back again. Nadine, somehow the electric current that tied Dak to Evan—and now somehow to Frank.

Yes, I thought, Clorinda's unrelieved stare, malevolent and arctic, took in the inauspicious Nadine.

Then, in a hasty retreat, Frank and Nadine, withering under Clorinda's furious look, pushed back their chairs and shuffled out of the restaurant. The waiter began speaking but Frank's hand flew out—no, no. He was shaking his head.

But watching them leave, I realized something awful. Clorinda was not displaying her venom toward the hapless young girl. Rather, her eyes were locked on Frank.

Her breath came in short, frightful gasps. A gagging sound from deep in her throat. Then, barely audible, a word: "Frank."

She watched as he left the restaurant, but she never took her eyes off the entrance. Her hand gripped a fork so tightly her knuckles were white.

She looked as though she'd seen a ghost.

Chapter Fourteen

The rehearsal was over, though I'd simply gone through the motions, distressed as I was by last night's scene in the restaurant. When Frank was in the wings and I stepped off the stage, I called to him. He glanced over, tilted his head toward an imaginary caller, and disappeared.

George overheard me. "Edna, what are you up to?"

"A conversation, that's all."

"With Frank?"

"It seems his presence in leafy Maplewood was unknown to Clorinda—until last night. He absolutely shocked her into silence and, I'm afraid, into a numbing anger that is not appropriate for this…this ambassador of God."

"Edna, I knocked on your door last night, but you weren't in. I wanted to hear about the dinner with Clorinda and Ilona." He rolled his tongue into his cheek. "Obviously it was eventful."

"Not really. But at the end…"

"Edna, you keep disappearing and I expect another body to be found."

"Don't joke, George. There really *is* a danger."

His face got tight. "What do you know?" he stammered, nervous.

"There are a bunch of pieces coming together, but something is still missing. The *how* these people are connected. Everyone knows one part of the large picture, and I need to put it together.

I keep talking to everyone. You know, George, people talk and talk and eventually somebody will say something."

George rubbed his chin with a finger. "You're making me nervous."

"I make everyone nervous. I'm hoping I'm making the killer nervous."

"Edna, is that wise? We're a couple days away from opening night, and I don't want to go to the closing of your casket."

"Not funny, George."

"I'm not trying to be funny."

I was nodding rapidly. "Let's take a drive after lunch."

"What are you planning, Edna?"

I caught a glimpse of Frank moving behind some scenery, turning his body away. He stepped out onto the stage, caught my eye, and then darted out of sight. George caught me looking. "Edna, what part does Frank play in this?"

"I don't know."

"So Clorinda recognized him?" he asked.

"That was my impression—and she wasn't happy to see him. And it had nothing to do with Nadine."

George was looking in the direction of the disappeared Frank. "What you're saying suggests that she didn't know he was working here. Dak never mentioned his name at home, obviously. Well, he said he was forbidden to mention anything to do with the theater."

"Exactly."

"Remember when his name came up in Cheryl Crawford's apartment? We wondered why so accomplished a stage manager—already connected to a bona fide Broadway smash—welcomed a trivial summer job in Maplewood."

"Yes, I do. And I've been thinking about that since last night. Just how well does Frank know Clorinda?"

"I don't think he's one of her camp followers, tambourines clanging in an upraised hand at one of her revivals. That doesn't sound like the man I know."

My mind was racing. "Hollywood? Was he out there when she went to rescue Dak from the clutches of Nadine? Was he a part of that?"

He rubbed his chin. "Maybe. Frank is all over the place. A single man, he travels a lot. I know that. He has friends in Hollywood, of course. Friends who drift from New York out to the Coast."

"But what could he have to do with Dak's annulment? Is it possible he knew Dak and Nadine out there? Was he involved with Nadine? All along I was thinking his hiring of Dak here was by chance."

"Perhaps he was friends all along with Nadine. They seem very close now in town, dining together."

"Possibly," I speculated. "Maybe he was *her* advocate during the separation."

"But why keep it a secret?" George wondered.

I shrugged my shoulders. "Well, maybe it's only a secret to *us*." I paused. "But no—Dak would have mentioned Frank being out there. Unless he had a reason to keep it a secret, but that makes no sense. Maybe Gus would have mentioned it, too. No one talked about Frank."

George wasn't buying it. "You know, Edna, Dak isn't always forthcoming. He didn't exactly rush to tell you he was married to Nadine while he was shadowing her like a love-struck puppy. You had to learn it, I seem to recall, from our young Nazi friend."

"True, so Gus could have known Frank out in California."

"So we can assume he didn't." He was lost in thought for a moment. "And someone hired Gus as an electrician. Did Frank play a part in that?"

"A Nazi? Frank?"

"Who knows?"

We stood there, the two of us, neither speaking. Finally, I blurted out, "Unless Frank knows Clorinda from somewhere else. From her own days in Hollywood."

"But that was decades ago."

"So what? Obviously the sins of the past have come to haunt more than one generation of Hollywood hopefuls."

"I'll ask him," George said.

"Not just yet, George. I want to watch what happens."

He nodded. "Where are we going for a ride?"

◇◇◇

DeHart Park lay in a section of Maplewood I didn't know. When I asked the desk clerk for directions, he eyed me suspiciously. Visitors rarely left the Village—the world of the train station, the theater, and the shops like Foster's Drug Store and Leonard's Barbershop. A close-knit community, built along Maplewood Avenue. The Hills were north of the railroad tracks, streets where the rich lived. The poor part of town—the other side of Springfield Avenue—had tough neighborhoods. DeHart Park was there, I was told. A scruffy park, unpopular.

I commandeered a Buick from one of the stagehands—he hesitated but finally acquiesced—and George and I headed for the park. George never learned to drive, adamant about the horrors of getting behind the wheel of a car, and I did so reluctantly. A careful driver, somewhat plodding, I cruised short distances, marking the miles by the number of cigarettes I nervously snubbed out in the ashtray,

"Lord, Edna," George joked, "a throwback to your flapper days. In one hand a martini and in the other a cigarette as you lounged in a speakeasy on the arm of some sycophant."

"George, you're a woeful fabricator."

I pulled the car into a parking lot under some overgrown willow trees. On the hot August afternoon there was no one there, and the thick foliage wilted under the blazing sun. I recalled Dak's description of the murder scene, but also from the local newspaper, in particular, which specified where Evan parked his jazzy new car. Under the bank of willows just right of the walking path, across from the fountain. "Here." I stopped the car. "Evan parked here." I stepped out of the car, which I kept running, and moved past a bank of hedges, trailed by a reluctant George. "And here." I pointed to a clearing where there was a picnic table and a stone barbeque pit. "Here. His body was found next to this table. On his back. Shot at close range in the chest."

"What are we looking for, Edna?"

I looked back toward the parking lot. "This clearing is sheltered from the parking lot. We can't see our car. Remember—he left it running, with the driver's door left open."

"But it's close by. He didn't plan on staying."

"Precisely. A planned meeting with someone in a place secluded by trees. But a spot known to Evan—and the killer. An appointment, a quick one. One that Evan didn't expect to end in violence."

"Because he was cocky."

"Most likely. Sure of himself. But what for?" I was baffled. "There had to be a reason they chose this spot. The killer also couldn't afford to be seen by anyone. And yet Evan trusted him."

"Or trusted enough to walk into a hideaway copse."

"Why not turn off the car?" Something bothered me. "Dak confessed to driving into the park that afternoon and spotting Evan's car. He even told Frank that he'd been following Evan. For whatever reason. He spotted Evan crusing by."

"Well, what reason did he have to follow him? What if Evan had seen Dak following him? And yet Evan pulled over, opened that door."

"Dak says he saw the door open and then drove away. He thought Evan was having some sort of…assignation. Maybe."

"With the door open?"

"All right, that doesn't fly. He was getting something from someone and he wanted to get away fast." I stared at the empty picnic table, the barbeque, and the bank of sheltering trees.

"What?"

"Only one thing. Money."

"Of course," George agreed.

"Blackmail."

"Frank?" George voice sounded triumphant.

"Maybe." A heartbeat. "Maybe. A scene he wouldn't want at the theater."

"He wouldn't have been meeting Gus—or Dak. He saw them all the time. The rooming house. In town. It had to be someone he couldn't conveniently contact in town."

"Or be seen with."

Someone who'd just given him cash, I think. All that flashy money. But then—why meet that person *again*?"

"Maybe his greed."

"Or something else? Information?"

"True," I agreed. "And where was the second car? Did the killer walk here? Or hide a car? And no one found a gun, I gather."

"There's about a three-hour window that afternoon when Evan was out on the town, cruising around. Where was everyone? Frank? Gus, I suppose? Even Meaka? Nadine?"

"How are we to ever know?"

"Well," George was nodding "we know where Dak was."

I sighed. "Unfortunately." I looked round. "But why would he confess to being in the spot where a murder took place?" I clicked my tongue. "*Following* him here. And obviously he didn't see another car. Just Evan's car. That's it."

George smiled. "He confessed because that's Dak, no? He doesn't believe it could implicate him."

"An innocent."

"Ironically, then," George summarized, "his being at the murder site is a sign of his innocence."

George and I walked into the Full Moon Café where Annika and Dak huddled at one of the tables. They were arguing, I could tell—sputtered words, abrupt silence, looking down, purple faces. A vein in Annika's neck throbbed. Dak was sweating and kept mopping his face.

"A lover's quarrel?" George impolitely asked, though I was glad he did.

Both looked up, though only Annika appeared annoyed. His head tilted back, Dak wore a bemused look, a little sheepish perhaps, but with bright eyes. "We're making a scene in public. Tobias would be furious." A pause. "It should embarrass us, I suppose."

"He doesn't favor public scenes?" I asked. "If you're going to make a scene, it's best to do so in public. Otherwise—why bother?"

Glancing toward the kitchen, I noticed that Constable Biggers was seated at a back table, not looking at us, ostensibly absorbed in a newspaper that covered his face. His legs were stretched out in front of him, two ungainly stumps. That infernal pad he always displayed lay on the table, the stub of a pencil resting on it, untouched.

Annika kept glancing at him, and finally sneered, "Our watchdog followed us in."

Dak bit his lip and glanced toward the policeman. "He's always around me."

"What is he expecting you to do?" Annika was whining. "Stand up and confess to a murder you did not commit? In of all places—here?"

"He thinks I did it."

Her voice was loud, aimed at the shielded man. "Well, let the fat man waste his time." She yelled toward the man. "We all know Gus killed Evan."

"How do you know that?" I asked, my voice a whisper.

"Well, who else? The process of elimination." She threw back her shoulders defiantly.

"Then who killed Gus?"

That stopped her for a second. "I dunno. That was in New York. Things like that happen there. He's running around with Nazi signs and praising Hitler. It stands to reason someone would shove him in front of a train, no?"

Constable Biggers lowered the paper and glared. His fingers drummed the untouched pad. Portly, with that round head with a few strands of sparse hair, with those big ears, he seemed a small-town Falstaff, eating pie and waiting for revelation.

Annika grabbed her purse and tucked it into her lap. She glanced toward the door and nudged Dak. "We need to leave now."

"A second, Annika." Dak motioned for George and me to sit down, which I did, with alacrity. Annika fumed.

"Is everything all right?" I asked.

They looked at each other. Dak sighed. "Just squabbling. Annika believes I should quit working for the Maplewood Theater."

Annika's voice was arch. "He has enough to do at the Assembly of God. This fall we're adding a satellite church in a warehouse in downtown Newark. Across the street from Bamberger's Department Store." She grinned. "They have Toyland at Christmas there—well, we'll have Holyland. Tobias is funding renovations and he's ordered a steeple built, shipped from Switzerland…"

Dak twisted his lips. "I'm supposed to be in charge."

"We both are," Annika said firmly.

"Annika, what does it matter that Dak works part-time at the theater?" I wondered.

Again, the glance from one to the other. "Tobias and Clorinda think he's wasting time."

Dak spoke up. "Work isn't a waste of time. I'm with new people, with…"

"With lost souls."

George snorted. "Well, thank you, my dear."

"I don't mean you."

"Oh, only Edna?"

Annika fumbled. "You know what I mean."

I narrowed my eyes. "I gladly wear the banner of being a 'lost soul,' Annika."

Annika snickered. "You're welcome, then."

I cleared my throat. "Dak, I don't know whether I thanked you for the landscape. I'm forgetful. It was a pleasant surprise. A wonderful gift."

Dak looked embarrassed. "It was nothing."

"You finished it?" Annika asked. "The one with the waterfall on the mountain?"

He nodded. "I gave it to Miss Ferber."

"You have a real talent—as befitting a descendant of Asher Durand."

Annika raised her eyebrows. "He told you he's related to that artist? That cockamamie story?"

"Yes. A legitimate heir, I'd say." I glanced at George. "Dak has a real passion—yes, that's the word, truly—for art. It should be cultivated."

"A hobby," Annika insisted.

"I think people should follow their hearts."

Annika eyed me. "And I think people should follow their souls."

I locked eyes with her. "That can be the same thing, Annika."

"That's not what you're getting at, is it?" She tapped the purse in her lap. "You're not religious, are you, Miss Ferber?"

"I know what I believe in."

"You're avoiding the question," she said hotly.

"No, I believe I answered it."

"Perhaps you have to understand Jesus Christ."

"And, I suppose, you are his spokesman,"

"He has spoken to me."

Dak jumped up. "All right, all right. Enough."

George, sitting there open-mouthed, echoed, "All right, indeed. I came in for coffee and some of Mamie's pie and I'm in the middle of a theological skirmish. Edna's unholy war."

I laughed, but Annika didn't.

Quietly, Dak provided a coda. "I think art is spiritual."

"Amen." From George, without irony.

Annika relaxed. "Well, I'm glad Dak *finished* something. All those unfinished sketches in his rooms."

"I spent hours—in fact, till two in the morning. Obsessed."

"Possessed." Annika's word.

"I don't have time to paint." Dak sighed. "I have to do missionary work at night. Our visits to the old and sick. Me and Annika. But…well, I made a vow to finish that drawing. I wanted it for *you*."

Annika smiled. "Our nights are in service to God. But I do give him a night off now and then."

Red-faced, but with a puzzled look, Dak mumbled, "I didn't mean that, Annika."

"Of course you did."

"Dak," I began, "how long were you in California?"

He stammered, "Under two years." He fidgeted, uncomfortable.

I waited a second. "Did you meet Frank out there?"

He squinted. "No, of course not. Why would he be out there?"

I shrugged. "Just a thought."

"Frank's a trouble-maker," Annika added.

"And you were married to Nadine for how long?" I went on.

"Months." Said with some bitterness.

Annika was squirming, as I intended.

"It didn't work out?"

"No, it didn't." His eyes got dark and sad. "It wasn't *her* fault."

"He wasn't ready for marriage," Annika interrupted.

"And he is now?"

"Tell her, Dak."

But Dak got evasive. "Everyone wants me to speak ill of Nadine—and my years in Hollywood. I won't. My failings are my failings."

"And what are your failings?" George asked.

He took a long time to answer. "I mean…I don't know."

"I know one of his failings," I ventured.

"What is that?" From Annika.

"Listening to other people."

"Really, Miss Ferber. Sometimes you have to listen to others—ones who have answers. Obedience to God…"

"Dak." I touched his wrist. "Someone is always going to tell you how to live your life."

Annika stood and tapped Dak on the shoulder. "It's been lovely." The word caught in her throat.

"Oh, for God's sake, Annika. Be nice."

"I'm always nice."

With that she tugged at his sleeve, and the two left the restaurant.

"Interesting," I commented.

"What?" George asked.

"Sometimes people say too much."

◇◇◇

Back at the inn, the reception clerk reached behind him and withdrew a letter. "Miss Ferber." I stopped walking.

"Yes?"

"A letter for you. Someone put it in the wrong slot, I'm afraid. It's been sitting there since yesterday." He handed it to me. A plain white envelope, with just one word on it: "Ferber." With a lower-case "f." No date.

"Yesterday?" I asked.

"I guess someone left it at the counter. After my shift. So… last night sometime. The night clerk slipped it into another resident's cubbyhole." He looked over his shoulder. "Another guest named Felson. A simple mistake."

"I don't appreciate mistakes."

George confided in the clerk, his voice laced with laughter. "Miss Ferber doesn't make mistakes."

"This is bizarre." I ignored the two chuckling men.

I tore open the wrinkled, cheap envelope, the flap taped. A sheet of lined paper, as from a schoolboy's tablet.

I froze. I handed the sheet to George. "Look."

Block letters, in a child's wax crayon, bright red:
GO AWAY NOW. EVIL BRINGS MORE EVIL. DANGER.

Then, in a blotchy ink scrawl, almost illegible: "Trust me. Your being watched. This is the end. No more. No more. A friend of yours."

George wore a serious look as we both stared at the words, but he said, "Edna, the writer has your flare for melodrama." But I could see concern in his eyes.

"Dear George, what strikes me is the use of block letters. A cry for attention. It's more your style."

My heart was racing. Nervously, I scanned the lobby. No one but George and me and the reception clerk who had turned away. But I felt, to my soul, that I was being watched.

Chapter Fifteen

A restless night, those horrific words in the anonymous note floating around in my head. I was up at five, an obscene hour, the street quiet save for a milkman's delivery truck pulling up at the inn. The brakes squeaked, groaned, and I cringed, my nerves raw. Yet, perversely, that incendiary note did not convince. George had been overly solicitous last night, a little frantic, in fact, insisting I deliver it to Constable Biggers immediately, an idea I rejected. Though it alarmed, the note struck me as evidence that I was onto something. Still I didn't fear for my life—the message, I finally concluded, was executed out of someone's nervousness. That was all.

But perhaps I was being foolish.

Yet my instincts said: no, keep going.

Three days before opening night, and I scarcely thought about the play now. *The Royal Family*, that sardonic send-up of an Upper East Side theatrical family, seemed far removed from the nitty-gritty verisimilitude of Maplewood's tree-shrouded, though cruel, sidewalks. Like a well-oiled machine, it moved along—and I automatically moved with it, robotic, unthinking.

"You're scaring people," George concluded.

"That's the way I like it."

"Most times it's just me, but I don't threaten to kill you. Or, at least, not to your face."

At midmorning, in the middle of our first full dress rehearsal, with me slathered up in Fanny Cavendish's dowager costume and makeup, Frank signaled to George, who stepped away from the stage. A moment later, a baffled look on his face, he halted the rehearsal.

"A half-hour break," he told us, annoyed. "It seems we have a royal visitation. The *real* royal family of Maplewood."

The cast scattered, rushing for cigarettes and coffee and gossip, but he motioned to me. "Edna, a moment."

A bittersweet smile on his lips, the mischief-maker in a moment of anticipation.

"George, what?"

"The royal family, visiting."

He led me to the front of the house, where Alexander, Tobias' driver, stood, chauffeur's cap in hand, a slight twitch of his lips as he called my name.

"Miss Ferber, Mr. and Mrs. Tyler to see you."

"Where?"

"Outside."

I glared at George. He shrugged.

Outside, indeed! The long, black Lincoln town car had pulled up against the curb, and in the backseat, holding hands and dressed for some formal function, were Clorinda and Tobias.

George sighed. "Do what you have to do, Edna. We'll rehearse scenes you're not in." He nudged me. "Go."

Alexander whispered to me, awe in his voice. "Mr. Tyler *never* comes into the Village. Never!"

And yet he had, ceremoniously.

I knew that the reclusive man hid away in his mansion, venturing out only to services at the Assembly of God, and then back home promptly. The man gingerly stepped through his days, a man who imagined he floated on some ethereal cloud and not, lamentably, on wheels manufactured in Detroit. Dak had told me he was frightened of jostling people, of the gaping bystander, but not of the congregants who respected his silence as he sat in a rear pew. "Worshippers of Clorinda," Dak added, "move as though they are alone with God."

So this visit was auspicious—and troublesome.

Alexander opened the rear door, and Tobias leaned across Clorinda, who sat stone-faced, lips tight in a razor line. Despite the heat of the day, Tobias was dressed in his severe Cotton Mather broadloom suit, a somber purple ascot secured around his neck, a matching handkerchief in his breast pocket. The funeral director comes a-calling. His face was expressionless.

"Miss Ferber, I request a brief meeting."

"We're in the middle of a rehearsal." I pointed to my Fanny Cavendish garb. "I'm in makeup."

"No matter. I came myself because I sensed you would refuse dear Clorinda." He spoke in a squeaky voice that reminded me of rain beating down on a tin roof.

Clorinda turned her head away from me.

"Tobias…"

"It is urgent. The matter with our son Dakota has come to a head."

"Has something happened?" I asked quickly, panicked.

Clorinda spoke loudly, her words clipped, hostile. "Other than the fact that he argues with me constantly now and disappears for hours at a time."

Tobias, surprise in his voice. "He talked back to me, Miss Ferber."

Flat out, looking into his upturned face. "And I imagine no one dares do that?"

A thin, Uriah Heep smile, sickening. "No reason to. I'm a gentle man of God. God chooses others to execute his horrible wrath. Not I. Though I believe in the awesome might…" His voice trailed off when Clorinda placed a hand on his sleeve.

"Still and all." I looked back to the theater. George was standing in the doorway, watching, his hand over his eyes to shield the bright sunlight. Peculiarly, Frank was behind him, only partly visible behind a half-closed door. When I glanced back again, he was gone. Standing as sentry beside the open car door, Alexander was staring up at the marquee, which announced, in huge letters: EDNA FERBER in THE ROYAL FAMILY, Week of August 13.

Then he looked back at me, amusement in his eyes. It made no sense to me.

"Please," Tobias went on, "we know your heart is in the right place with regard to our boy."

Clorinda looked at me, her eyes dancing. "Tobias *never* visits the Village, Edna."

"I have my God and my Clorinda."

"I still don't understand…"

"A half-hour of your time. At my home. We'll have you back here soon enough."

I nodded: yes. Something was afoot here, though I sensed it had nothing to do with Evan's murder. Clorinda obviously read my assent because she slid closer to Tobias, and I climbed in. Alexander closed the door.

As the car pulled away from the curb, I could see George stepping out onto the sidewalk, looking after me. I raised my hand in the car, a wave to him, but I had no idea exactly what I was trying to communicate. Probably only my careless surrender to the enemy.

Silence as we moved along, my attempts at small talk met with cleared throats and a muttered observation about the day's horrible heat.

As we neared the circular driveway fronting the mansion, I spoke up, "I received the strangest note this morning."

A flicker of interest from Clorinda, but Tobias simply sat facing forward.

Neither said anything.

"It reminded me of that note Dak received. The death threat." I waited. "A warning."

Clorinda involuntarily grabbed at her throat, panicky, but still said nothing.

I quoted it from memory, stressing the "beware" and "stop" and other storybook warnings to be careful, adding my own melodramatic spin on the words.

Finally, as the car came to a stop, Clorinda turned to me. "Perhaps, then, you should heed the warning."

"You think so?"

"I mean, it sounds like nonsense some crew member with a macabre sense of humor. Theater folks like their…their dark games. But sometimes the most important messages appear in the most unlikely way or place." Yet her voice was flat, almost bored.

Tobias was making a gurgling sound from the back of his throat, which I interpreted as a reprimand to Clorinda. Her thin, nervous smile at him seemed an apology.

Inside we were met by Hilda, who seemed stunned by my lavish costume and heavy stage makeup. Her eyes blinked wildly. I felt like a circus clown. She led us to Tobias' office, that precious inner sanctum he'd earlier shared with George and me. A tea service was already in place, with chairs placed decorously around the small mahogany table. A plate of cookies. A place set for me. They'd been confident I'd journey back with them, an observation that annoyed me. I dislike it when others predict my behavior—and are right.

"Tell me," I began after we settled in and Hilda poured tea. "Does this have to do with clearing Dak's name in Evan's—maybe even Gus'—murder?"

"Gus?" Clorinda asked, as though she'd never considered him part of the Maplewood mystery.

"He *was* murdered."

She sipped tea. "A filthy Nazi, that one." Tobias narrowed his eyes at her, and she sat back. Suddenly, almost magically, the atmosphere in the room got chilly, the air heavy. It had to do, I realized, with the way Tobias and Clorinda looked at each other, and then, as one, back at me. I shivered in that hot room where all the windows were shut.

When Tobias addressed me, all the gentleness and tentativeness of his usual manner had disappeared. Rather, his words were cold steel now, laced with a fury I'd not anticipated—or, in fact, thought he was capable of revealing.

"Quite simply, we had nothing to do with that ill-considered note you received this morning, Miss Ferber, but our purpose this morning is to demand one thing from you—stay away from Dakota."

"But I thought you both wanted my help…if I remember from the dinner in this very house."

Clorinda's hand went up, palm out. "Tobias thinks the issue of the murder—that is, Dakota's being arrested—is simply preposterous. Otherwise, it would have been done."

Tobias added, "That fool Biggers is a decided ass. He has harassed Dakota, but clearly there is no evidence. I consider the matter over, so far as the Assembly of God is concerned."

"Still," I insisted, "the investigation is continuing. What makes you so—confident? I'm not privy to what evidence is being gathered, and I know the FBI secured Gus' room. I've seen the resident state trooper talking with Constable Biggers."

Again, the hand in my face. "Nonsense, all of it." Clorinda's voice dripped with venom, and I realized how thoroughly she disliked me now.

"If this has nothing to do with the murder, then what? Why was I kidnapped this morning?" I waved my hand around the palatial room. Here, a short time ago, Tobias had eagerly showed off this room, his leather-bound books, the Persian carpet, his extensive research notes—indeed, that framed poster of Clorinda's appearance in that forgotten silent movie. Yet now, sitting there, I felt unwelcome—in fact, a hated pariah. A woman invited solely to be talked down to, to be chastised.

"Kidnapped?" Clorinda chuckled without humor. "You do go on, Edna."

"It's very simple, Miss Ferber," Tobias stated. He intertwined his fingers and rested his chin on them, staring over the small fingers with eyes so icy I thought of ogres and menacing trolls from long-ago fairy tales. "You have launched a campaign to draw Dakota away from the church—from his future among us. That notion suddenly dawned on me. The true mission of the infidel sort. You are committed to seducing him back to the stage."

Clorinda's tone was bitter. "You betrayed our trust, Edna. You don't think we haven't heard of your coaxing Dakota to chart a life *away* from *this*." She reached for her teacup, and then thought better of it. "Annika reports—indeed, Dakota himself, loose-tongued now, and frivolous—your…your sabotage."

My mind reeled, though I lingered on his facile definition of me—the infidel sort. George, I knew, would relish that remark, and bandy it about. "Dak is a grown man, unsuccessfully defined by you as something he is not. His own freedom should be something you…you celebrate."

Tobias' eyebrows rose and the mouth twitched. "Celebrate? He has a calling before God."

I caught a glimpse of myself reflected in the glass of Clorinda's poster—shadowy, yes, but there I was: Fanny Cavendish, matriarch of the theater, imperious, haughty, smug—but also baffled by a changing world. A throwback to a genteel time when life seemed predictable, sure. So, touching my face with the thick stage makeup, I assumed the part, even using my stage voice. "Perhaps you and Clorinda—and maybe Annika—have such callings, but Dak sees the world differently. You've confused him tremendously, turned him around, set him adrift, so much so that he's been a…a robot at the altar you've set up."

Tobias actually gasped, rising from his chair. A small man, wiry and pinched, he seemed a frantic monkey now, a chattering, pesky animal.

"God comes first, always comes first, Miss Ferber."

"Would you have him arrested for the murders?"

Clorinda glanced at her husband, sharing a smug smile. "We've spoken to folks at the state capital. The lieutenant governor, in fact, whose wife is…well, never mind. Tobias is not without influence. Constable Biggers will be spoken to. The matter is finished."

Tobias was furious. "Clorinda, you talk too much. Like Dakota, you stumble about among strangers, disclosing this, revealing that."

Clorinda panicked. "Forgive me, Tobias dear." A quicksilver smile, desperate, as she leaned in to touch the gyrating man. "Please sit, dear." As she answered him, her brilliant diamond earrings caught the overhead light, and shone beautifully.

"Enough!" Tobias thundered. "Satan has cohorts at his side. Our enemies will be vanquished. A loving God is a God who will gladly and justly smite the heathen."

Fanny Cavendish gave back her own thunder. "And I'm that heathen?"

The infidel sort.

At that moment, I thought of my nemesis, Ethel Barrymore, that redoubtable actress, furious with Tallulah Bankhead's imitation of her at a party I was at—and Ethel's resounding slap across Tallulah's face. Tobias, gesturing wildly, looked ready to slap me, his hand trembling near my face.

"Enough! You will be gone in a week or so, as I understand it. Dak will not be returning to the theater so that…that Jezebel Nadine will not have him to tempt. Gone, all of you. I offered Nadine a huge settlement to leave town. The stupid girl refused. Gone, all of you. I've made myself clear."

With that, he turned and left the room, followed immediately by Clorinda. I was left sitting there, feeling a little foolish. Idly, I stared at the walls of books, at the cheap, framed poster of Clorinda. Idly, I debated my next move. But within seconds Alexander tiptoed into the room, nodding deferentially at me. "The car is ready to return you to the theater."

As I followed him out of the mansion, I looked for Tobias or Clorinda. No one was around. From the backseat of the town car, I glanced back at the house as Alexander turned out of the driveway. In a second-story window, a curtain shifted. For a moment I glimpsed a face, but I couldn't tell whether it was Tobias or Clorinda. Then I thought: no, perhaps it was Ilona.

◇◇◇

Late that afternoon, sitting by my window reflecting on that encounter with Tobias and Clorinda, I looked down into the street as Nadine strolled by. I thought of Tobias' offer of money, refused by her. She was with two stage crew members, and they were laughing at something. I watched her closely: so pretty, so fresh-looking, lighthearted, and yet I sensed she was part of something awful here, though perhaps not of her own doing. A young woman whose little-girl demeanor disguised some inner resolve. After all, she stood up to Tobias and his wealth. And, curiously, she'd journeyed to Maplewood with a purpose in mind. I assumed it was Dak. Or was it something else?

The three young women were enjoying themselves.

A car slid to a stop ahead of them, stopped sideways on the street, blocking them. Horrified, I watched Annika jump out of the driver's seat, the car left running and the door wide open. She rushed toward the startled young women and shouted something at Nadine. Her words drifted up through my open window. "You think I don't know what happened? What you are doing?"

Nadine and the others didn't move.

In a blind rage, Annika's hand flew out, slapping Nadine in the face. So raw a moment, so unexpected, that one of the other women screamed. The other, clutching a bottle of Coke, let it slip from her hand onto the pavement. Nadine stood there, silent now, her body bent at the waist, her hand rubbing her cheek.

Annika stepped back, head bobbing, and she began sputtering, "Oh, my God. I didn't mean that. Oh, my God. I'm so sorry. I'm…sorry…I…" She looked around, wildly flicking her head, and she rushed back to her car, jumping in and slamming the door. She sped up the street, driving on the wrong side of the line. For some reason she was leaning on her horn.

Ilona House joined me as I sat in the Full Moon Café. She didn't wait to be invited to sit, but pulled up a chair, placed her elbows on the table. "So Tobias and Clorinda have shunned you." Her own words delighted her because she laughed loudly, so hard she started to choke. "Shunned from God's glorious kingdom."

"It wasn't funny."

"Oh, but it is. From my point of view, Edna dear."

I sipped iced tea with mint. "Frankly, they did stun me." I managed a smile. "The infidel sort. Here I defined Tobias as a gentle, gnome-like little man, a little elf with deep pockets and a deeper love of God. A little maddened, yes. And Clorinda, fawning over me and giving that fiery Calvinist sermon that somehow still guaranteed salvation."

Ilona scoffed. "None of it's true—or partly true. I don't know. But Clorinda has taken on Tobias' weird coloration—she's appropriated that fire-and-brimstone belief, old New England, Puritan, predestination, stockades on the town green, the dunking of witches. Clorinda used to be the angel of forgiveness, all soft and fluffy. Under Tobias' tutelage she became the fiery sword of damnation."

"Harsh words, no?"

Her eyes pierced mine, riveted. "Didn't you see it firsthand today when they commanded your presence at their lair?"

"You heard?"

"I'm an eavesdropper, dear."

"Yes, I saw a different Tobias and Clorinda. But I don't understand—they've abandoned fear of Dak's being arrested. They're more afraid of Dak fleeing back into Nadine's obviously waiting arms."

"The problem with Dakota is that he's always been—malleable. A boy who's easy to like, but just as easy to hate."

I broke in. "You hate him."

"Speaking of using harsh words, well, I used to love him. That little boy I had *thrust* upon me by a father very similar to Tobias. An authoritative, vindictive man. I showered Dakota with love, I fairly smothered him, but he was foolishly indulged by a long-distance mother. And when Clorinda returned to take him back, she poisoned him against me. 'Aunt Ilona doesn't love you like I do, my sweetie.' I admit I turned nasty"—a smug smile—"because I'm not a nice person. That stays with a child. I didn't know how to be a mother. And, I suppose, I resented it thrust on me. But neither did Clorinda." She scoffed. "She *still* doesn't know how to be a mother."

"So what does Dak think of you now?"

"I don't think he likes me. I know he doesn't."

"Because of Clorinda?"

A long pause as she seemed to be fashioning an answer. Finally, with that same sly smile, she said, "Because I didn't *save* him *from* his mother."

"How sad!"

"Is it really? I don't really care."

"Clorinda and Tobias have tucked all their own dreams into Dak. That never works."

"And look where it's got them. Lord, Clorinda handpicked Annika from the fawning, dizzy worshippers, groomed her into a less attractive replica of herself. A soulless girl who does nothing but talk of her soul."

I mentioned the incident I witnessed that afternoon—Annika slapping Nadine on the sidewalk, followed by her stuttered apology. Ilona shook her head back and forth, amused. "I'd love to have seen that. Annika seldom slips out of the angelic mold fashioned for her."

"It wasn't pretty." A pause. "Annika sometimes strikes me as a taut wire ready to snap."

Ilona ignored that. "You know, of course, Clorinda is always afraid of Tobias."

"What?"

Ilona's eyes sparkled. "Think about it. Clorinda is carrying the weight of Tobias' impossible dreams. At first it was all right, both hallelujahing their spiritual chorus. Then, as the church became better known—as Clorinda became celebrated for her messianic oratory, her flamboyant flare—well, Tobias demanded more and more from her. I mean, she's invited to do revivals from upstate New York to Tampa, Florida. That's *one* year only. Sometimes I see her alone, tears welling in her eyes, and I wonder about the pressure. The...the loneliness. Those diamond earrings start to weigh too much, my dear. The price of a flawless stone can be deadly. Clorinda is like Tantalus pushing her three-carat diamonds up a hill. Somehow she never reaches that City on the

Hill. Will she fall apart like Aimee Semple McPherson—fake her own drowning off the Jersey shore? Take an obvious lover and be headlined in the tabloids? Be caught trysting in a bungalow on Boyden Avenue?"

"Let me ask you a question, Ilona. You don't care for Clorinda or Tobias. Or Annika. Possibly even Dak. Anyone, truly. Clearly. You don't buy into Clorinda's spiritual message. And yet you stay in that mansion—you serve them, you do the errands in the Village, you're…"

She ran her tongue over her red lips and absently fingered the butterfly brooch on her collar. Her voice got brittle. "I'm an unmarried woman. No money. No desire for work. My only enjoyment is the denigration of the people I live with. An old maid, the most pathetic woman of our pathetic culture. No? You and me, Edna, two fiftyish spinsters."

That rankled. "But there is a difference, Ilona."

"Which is?"

"I pay my own way through life."

A dark laugh. "And you think that I don't pay for what I have to endure. I pay, all right." She bit her lips, which trembled. "Oh, how I pay!"

"Do you think that Dak killed Evan?"

"I don't care. I met Evan once or twice. He deserved to die."

"Rather harsh."

"Most people I've met deserve to die." A thin smile. "You're not one of them. At least not yet." She leaned in. "Let me tell you a secret, Edna. Dak confessed to spotting Evan driving around, even pulling up behind his car in that park. He made it a *point* to follow him. Everybody knows that, even Biggers. But I was in town that afternoon and saw Dakota idling at the municipal building, just waiting. A half-hour later, done with my errands, I saw him still there. Waiting until Evan passed by, toot-tooting on that shiny horn. He waited a bit and then pulled behind, following him. He didn't accidentally spot him and stupidly follow, as he told everyone. He *stalked* him."

"Oh, dear! Then…"

"'Oh, dear' is right, my lovely Edna. Dakota may have con-fessed but not to everything he did that day."

"Did you tell Constable Biggers?"

"Of course not. I like to see people get away with murder."

"You don't really think Dakota…"

She grinned. "As I said, I don't really care."

I shifted the subject. "Clorinda was shocked to see Frank Resnick in town. Our stage manager. She didn't know, I guess…"

"Yes, I heard all about it. The price you pay for praying all day—things are happening around you, and you don't notice. The world outside your door. Perhaps if she'd bought a ticket to a show…"

"She knows Frank?"

"*Knew* Frank. Ages ago. In a fantasy land called Hollywood. What I know is that he was in love with her—this, mind you, is *her* version. A boy with mooncalf love-struck eyes, a minor Hollywood player when *she* dreamed of being the next Theda Bara or Pola Negri. Nazimova."

"Well, he can't still be in love with her."

"Of course not. Clorinda wears out fast. A bright and colorful balloon, soon pricked by a necessary pin. Not to Tobias who's terminally smitten, but then he's a fool. But Frank disappeared about the time my beloved sister chose to marry another man."

"But he's here in Maplewood."

She winced. "Yeah, that's troubling. Maybe a coincidence, but most likely not. Of course, I was surprised to see him in the Village—I met him years ago. Briefly. But Clorinda was really surprised. No one told her. Not me, obviously. Dakota told Clorinda he got a job at the theater, but he neglected that other piece of dangerous information. But why should it matter? Their fling was a second in time. Long ago. Far away from here. Over."

"But he wanted to come to Maplewood."

"Maybe he's up to no good."

"You have proof?"

"I don't need proof. I never have proof for any of my biases or opinions. Facts get in the way of irrational dislike."

I mused. "Mother and son both had brief moments in Hollywood. Turbulent, riotous, crazy. And then...nothing."

"Or maybe something."

"You know, Ilona, the more I think about it the more I believe the seeds of this murder—or murders, Gus included—can be traced to Dakota's days in Hollywood. It's the only answer. Nadine, Evan, Gus—Dak. A whirlpool of emotion and event. Perhaps that sojourn there led to—to murder here."

Ilona eyed me a long time. Then, cryptically, she smiled. "Maybe. Maybe not. But it seems to me that the seeds to the present are found in the world of a different Hollywood."

Chapter Sixteen

The world of a different Hollywood.

Ilona's words haunted me all night long.

Something was being told to me, though off-handedly, perhaps unintentionally. Yet it lay there, percolating, in the back of my mind.

When I left my rooms for breakfast, I spotted cardboard boxes stacked outside what was Evan's room. The meager remnants of a short and questionable life.

George, I knew, was already downstairs in the breakfast room. He'd rat-a-tat-tatted on my door as he passed earlier, yelling out "reveille" or some such inanity as he sauntered by, a little too spirited for the hour of the day. Of course, when we collaborated on a play, George told folks I worked from nine in the morning till ten past three in the afternoon, and he from three to nine that night, which left, he insisted, ten feeble minutes for actual writing together. Some folks believed him. But *The Royal Family* was written noon to midnight, for months. Some days we did nothing but argue while George jiggled curtain cords and flipped pencils into the air. He tied and retied his shoes. I sat at the typewriter pecking away with my three fingers while he paced the room.

But now I lingered by the overstuffed boxes, though I knew their contents. I flipped open a flap. Garret Smith, probably under the direction of Constable Biggers, had jammed in the magazine clippings, the new clothing, the toiletries. The one that held my attention was that of the magazines and clippings, of course, and I scrunched down, leafing through them. The clippings: they told me something, surely. You clip an item from a magazine for a reason. Yes, magazines fascinate, especially those from decades-old Hollywood and Broadway past, but clippings suggest selection, decision, purpose. But what?

Evan's clippings dealt with tawdry or bizarre scandal: unsolved murders, feckless suicides, drug overdoses, sexual peccadilloes, promiscuous flappers in the Roaring Twenties, untoward remarks blurted out when drunk, insane Prohibition binges with unadulterated grain alcohol hootch or spiked needle beer—all the claptrap fodder of gossip columnists. A ticker-tape blip of printed innuendo. Olive Thomas. Fatty Arbuckle. Thomas Ince's death on Hearst's yacht. The murder of Desmond Taylor. Sex-themed movies, banned. Attacks by the Catholic Church. It was all there, random and strange—yet, I felt, telling me something.

Hurriedly, I crammed the papers back into the box, resealed the flap. A resident, passing by to the landing, watched me closely. An old man in a powder-blue linen suit with a gold-tipped cane, a droopy walrus moustache on a ruddy face. He paused, contemplated my kneeling there, and commented, "The murdered boy? This is what's left of him." A melodramatic valedictory as he sauntered by, tapping his cane as he walked.

Hollywood! I thought. The answer to everything lay buried in the short, fitful lives these folks lived in the land of movie-lot palm trees, endless sun, and make believe. Hollywood!

The four young folks met out there: Dak, Evan, Gus, Nadine. Friends for a short time, though with differing personalities, at odds with one another, transitory friendships, followed by betrayal and dislike. Evan seducing Nadine, Dak's momentary wife. Why? And Gus, the young Nazi strolling the wide boulevards. Or was he a Nazi then? Hitler Youth—perhaps the creation of not-so-secret political cells on the East Coast, the impressionable boy seduced by bombastic rhetoric and German schnitzel in a Yorkville eatery? Who knew? And Nadine, the slight yet pretty ingénue, still in love with Dak—and he with her? All of the nonsense of those bright-lit Hollywood days transported now into serene Maplewood.

But—

The world of a different Hollywood.

A different Hollywood. Frank and Clorinda—and, I supposed, silent movies and Aimee Semple McPherson. Cecil B. DeMille. Theda Bara. Mary Pickford. Valentino. Other failed movie careers. All the sad boys and girls hopping buses to oblivion under incredible sunshine. A sad marriage for Clorinda. A dead husband. A skittish little boy sent back East from the Coast, and into Ilona's confused care.

Ilona's albatross: the world of a different Hollywood.

After the rehearsal, I hurried to leave, but a voice stopped me. "Miss Ferber, wait." Dak, climbing down from an overhead catwalk and jumping the last few steps, waved at me.

"Dak." I smiled at him. "You're here."

"Surprise." He was beaming.

"I thought…"

"I heard about the mandatory visitation to the family mansion." Though he smiled wistfully, his voice was weary, ragged. "I'm sorry about that."

"It wasn't your idea, Dak."

He sighed. "Yet I seem to be the source of all sorts of misery this summer."

I waved my hand around me. "But you're *here*."

He saluted. "Against orders."

"Tell me."

I walked toward the front of the theater, Dak leaning into my side, brushing against me as we moved.

"My mother and Tobias summarized the royal audience to me, expecting me to nod and thank them. Putting Miss Ferber in her place." He grinned.

"Lesser folks have tried to put me in my place—without success."

He laughed out loud. "I can imagine. You're a wonder, Miss Ferber."

"Doubtless one of seven in the world."

"I wouldn't be surprised!" A heartbeat. "But seriously, that conversation about you butting into my life made something… well, click in my head. I sat there, stupefied, and it was like I was slapped awake Like I'd been in a stupor, a coma, for years. You, Miss Ferber, you are responsible—and I don't mean to embarrass you. Something about your candor—your *faith*. A real faith."

"It's called nosiness in some quarters, my boy."

"So be it." He reached out and touched my sleeve, a gesture I would have found questionable in most circumstances but, done by the soft-spoken young man, it came off as pure affection. I was touched.

I stopped walking. "What happened?"

"I told them *this* job is important to me. Tobias sputtered and had to sit down. My mother screamed about me giving him a stroke. She clutched her heart. She kept fingering her diamond earrings like they would be taken away by a genie. I also told them I had some important thinking to do—about the Assembly of God, about…"

"About Nadine?"

A slight frown. "I suppose. Yes, to be truthful. And, of course, about Annika."

"Ah, yes, Annika, the evangelical debutante."

"That's not nice, Miss Ferber."

"It wasn't meant to be nice."

"Annika is not a bad person. She's too bendable. My mother can charm birds out of trees—and Annika, coming from a faithless childhood, unloved, was a vacuum ready to be filled."

"Nevertheless, she holds on to you as though you're feeble."

"I *was* feeble…of sorts."

I grinned. "So that's over?"

"Well, let me say the process has begun. By the way, Annika told me about her confrontation with Nadine in the street. I mean, she was horrified by her own behavior—the public scene.

That's not like her. She said she just lost control, she who prides herself on discipline and structure. She harbors this…this *fear* of Nadine—now that she knows Nadine and I once were married."

"It was a violent, unnerving scene."

"She's penitent."

"I think she needs to apologize to poor Nadine."

Dak looked over his shoulder. "I talked to Nadine this morning. She's all right with it."

"That's not the point."

"Annika made me promise not to tell Mother. Or, especially, Tobias."

"Will she be excommunicated?"

He *tsk*ed but said, "She's afraid of Tobias."

"Such a small, jittery man. He seems to wreak such fear in so many hearts. Even your mother."

Dak echoed my words. "Even my mother."

I pointed to a row of seats at the rear of the theater. "Dak, let's sit a moment."

"I only got a moment."

I sat down and he followed, though he kept looking back toward the stage.

"Do you love your mother?" I asked suddenly.

The question stunned him. "Of course." Too glib, I thought, but he pulled back. "Sometimes I think I don't. Sometimes I think she has no room in her life except for God and Tobias. I feel I don't *know* her."

"How sad!"

"Well, it's just the way it is."

"And Ilona?"

"You know, I *want* to love her, but she pushes me—everyone—away."

I laughed. "She's an angry woman."

He looked me in the eye. "Well, wouldn't you be? She's been in bondage all her life. A chance of love ruined by a battlefield in France. A servant to a puritanical father—I remember him as a humorless man, paddling me, slapping me, lecturing me on my bad behavior. He never said a warm or nice word to me, and yet he was proud of the *idea* of me—you know, a male, a lineage. I was a slot in a family tree. And then Ilona was in bondage to Clorinda and Tobias. A helpless woman, inconvenient in everyone's lives."

"A sad commentary."

"Well, an epitaph for a failed life."

"She could have left. She could have made a life for herself. A schoolteacher, something else. A woman *can* define herself."

His eyes got wide and bright. "You miss the point, Miss Ferber. That would have denied her the role of martyr, a role she wanted."

"Then it's been a successful life, no?" I ran my tongue over my lower lip. "She got what she wanted."

"That's always worse, no?"

I shifted the subject. "Is Constable Biggers still following you?"

"It's almost a joke now. We nod at each other. I expect we'll be having lunch shortly. I've become his life."

"Well, there *is* a murderer in town."

Dak froze, bit his lips. "I know, I know. It seems like it's suddenly on the back page of the newspaper now. Evan—and Gus. Two people connected to me."

"And with others, don't forget."

"But I'm the one who was on the outs with both."

"You know, Dak, it seems to me that the roots of the murders reach back to Hollywood. Something happened *there*."

He looked puzzled. "Why?"

"I sense it. Haven't you thought about it? You must have. You and Evan and Gus and Nadine, all there, your brief marriage, explosive, Nadine's sorry infidelity with Evan, Gus lurking on the sidelines. Anger, jealousy, resentment, piddling dreams—all simmering in the rarefied hot air of Hollywood. And then all of you appear in little Maplewood."

"Yes, of course I've thought about that. When Miss Crawford opened the theater, it became a…I don't know…a *reason* to be here. But I was here first. I was living here…"

"Then they came here because of *you*."

He tensed up. "Coincidence?"

"No." Emphatic, loud. "No. Something about *you* drew them here. Nadine is obvious. She wants reconciliation. She loves you." Dak grinned at that. "But Gus followed Evan here. That made Evan angry. Gus' Nazi sympathies may have distracted us from the truth—perhaps they have nothing to do with his murder. A political view that simply identified a character defect in the man. Evan, though—think about it. Why would he want a two- or three-week job here? Because *you* are here."

Dak lapsed into silence. Upfront, some technician was fiddling with the stops on the Wurlitzer organ, and the intermittent bursts of sound jarred, annoyed.

Dak sighed. "But you know everything about Hollywood, Miss Ferber. It was so…so short a time—a time I didn't deal well with. I *betrayed* Nadine, horribly. I know, I know. She slept with Evan. I don't care because I know what Evan was capable of doing. Nadine felt alone—deserted by me. I didn't stick up for her. I *abandoned* her. Nadine, for all the makeup and…and Hollywood worldliness…is real naïve." His head tilted backward. "That's why I like her."

"Love her, Dak. That's why you *love* her."

"I guess so."

"You don't love Annika."

Another long silence. His mouth trembled. "No, I don't. But I respect…"

I gripped his forearm tightly. "Stop it. You can't respect someone who always wants to tell you who you are. Stop it."

He checked his watch and jumped up. "I have to get back. Frank will be on my case."

"Just a minute, Dak. One more question. About Frank."

Dak stepped back but didn't sit down. "What?"

"Your mother was stunned to see Frank in town. I gather they knew each other back in Hollywood."

"I asked her about that. She said he…well, pursued her, relentless. And she was involved and shortly married to my father, who was his friend. A betrayal. She claims Frank was sneaking behind my father's back. They had a fight—I mean, my father and Frank, and Frank, she says, said some nasty things. Cruel things. So when she saw him with Nadine—and here in Maplewood, of all places—she was horrified. The last time she saw him was unpleasant. That was *before* I was born. A ghost from her past."

I waited a bit. "And you believe that story?"

He squinted and glanced off toward the stage. "I do."

"I don't."

He rolled his head, helpless. "But what else?"

"Does that sound like the Frank you know? Frank is taciturn, unobtrusive, a shadow."

"Ah, but remember that it was back decades. I don't know— 1916 or so. They were young and hot-blooded—and it was Hollywood…"

"And now here he is again. Because of your mother?"

He was shaking his head. "Then wouldn't he have contacted her? He's in town, working on *The Royal Family* and other plays. If he chose to come here for that reason, wouldn't he have called her? Or accidentally bumped into her in the Village? He'd find a way to reach her. And who waits a couple decades for a contact? Over twenty years."

"I don't know, but it seems to me everyone came to Maplewood for a reason that had nothing to do with my stunning debut as Fanny Cavendish."

He smiled warily, that broken smile that so charmed me. "Are you sure?" He did a little dance step. "I've been watching you act from the wings, and I'm loving it. You're…good."

"And you're being kind."

He bowed. "No, it's a pleasure."

"And Frank, I might add, has taken a shine to you, Dak. He's very protective. And of Nadine, I gather. Perhaps he's using *you* as a way to get to your mother. Perhaps not—just a thought."

"That's preposterous. He's never mentioned her at all."

"That doesn't mean he's not planning something."

He tapped on the back of a chair. "I like him."

"He strikes me as a harmless man, but who knows?"

A sudden lightning flash in his eyes. "Miss Ferber, you don't think Frank is the murderer, do you?"

"I don't know who the murderer is."

"You're not answering my question."

"Because I have no answer—yet."

That thin, infectious smile, the mouth crinkly. "But you will."

I thought about Ilona's remarks—the *other* Hollywood. "Maybe Frank's tempestuous sojourn in Hollywood, back when your mother was acting in the silents, is the genesis of murder in Maplewood."

"That seems impossible."

"Well, this is the summer of our discontent. The world is crumbling. Hitler walks under the Arc de Triomphe. The Battle of Britain begins. Gestapo troops march across farm fields. Bombs destroy cities. When the axis of the Earth shifts and all the players topple into Maplewood, then there's havoc on the land."

"You're a cheerful lady, Miss Ferber."

"Yes, everyone says that about me."

I skipped lunch, stopped back at the inn where a message was waiting for me. I'd called Loretta Dawson, a part-time researcher I sometimes employed. Loretta, a down-to-earth buxom woman with an intelligent, adventurous mind, had the uncanny capacity to ferret out arcane facts and anecdotes worth their weight in gold. Yes, her message informed me, she was free to meet me that afternoon at the New York Public Library on Forty-second Street. "I'll be in the reading room all afternoon. I'm intrigued by your request—but, Edna, all your requests intrigue me." I checked my wristwatch. I'd be able to grab a sandwich and catch the 2:11 into Manhattan. Loretta, I knew, would have stacks of reading materials assembled on a table, notepad at the ready.

By the time I arrived at the reading room, Loretta was already sequestered at a library table in a back corner, pasty-looking under two green-shade lamps, piles of books at her elbow. She looked up and smiled. "Quite the assignment, Edna. And I thought you'd have a peaceful, though challenging, respite acting in Maplewood. This is a whole different world." Loretta indicated the stacks of books, and smiled.

An efficient woman, thorough, her iron-gray hair pulled into a severe bun and her schoolmarm reading glasses tipped on the front of her nose, Loretta understood the dark recesses of any library—where exquisite treasures were hidden.

"What do you have for me?"

She started handing me bound volumes, slips of paper indicating pages. "Here." She pointed to a copy of *Variety*. "You asked about Nadine Chappelle."

While Loretta busied herself with other pursuits, I read the short article, a brief account of Nadine represented by the Caldwell Agency, scheduled to play the role of "sister" in *Rainy Summer*, a minor part, but pivotal, according to the notice. She'd taken courses in Los Angeles at the Leland Pouten School of Dramatic Arts, did some summer stock in Anaheim, and was signed to do a second movie titled *Chicago Moonlight*. Four or five lines of laudatory prose, with a picture of her. A promo squib, doubtless paid for by her agency. A studio shot, head tilted coyly, lips parted seductively.

Loretta looked over as I closed the volume. "And then she disappears from the trades. Another Hollywood almost-was. They never made *Chicago Moonlight*."

Another volume, tiny pulp print, flaky to the touch. A Los Angeles directory. I had no idea what I was looking at. Loretta cleared her throat. "It's a 1934-35 municipal guide. Sort of a Chamber of Commerce business and residence directory. Where people are." She indicated Nadine's address on Sepulveda, and then flipped one page. "Two blocks away, Dakota Roberts and Evan Street, obviously in the same rooming house—or even roommates. Maybe. Hard to tell." Another volume: 1935-36. "Nadine and Dakota married, new address. Evan Street in an apartment on the same street. Your Gus Schnelling"—she flipped another page—"across town." Then finally: "Dakota gone. Nadine alone. Evan and Gus gone from the records, but that doesn't mean they weren't in town."

"Dak's short marriage."

"Which leads to the best article of all." She reached for a volume of *Hollywood Beat*, some yellow-pulp tabloid with grainy pictures and bold-font headlines, a gossip sheet of intrigue and scandal. I thought of Evan's collection of sordid Hollywood stories.

The headline read: "Famed East Coast Preacher Squelches Nuptials." A revelation, this article. Given Clorinda's fame as spiritual leader—particularly her earlier association with Aimee Semple McPherson—it was not surprising her sudden descent in Hollywood garnered some yellow press. The article spoke of "newcomer Nadine Chappelle, a pretty ingénue" who was married to stagehand Dakota Roberts, son of famed evangelist Clorinda Roberts Tyler. "Mommy frowned on her boy's quickie marriage to the once-divorced young starlet whose first husband committed suicide in a prison cell." I gather Clorinda created a ruckus, involving the police, and Dak was cited for public nuisance—an explosive scene in a restaurant. What I also learned was that Clorinda made two visits to California—the first to try to extricate Dak diplomatically—and quietly—from his marriage, the second with a team of lawyers to complete the annulment.

"Interesting," I told Loretta. "A powerful woman. She got what she wanted."

Loretta looked up from her reading. "But they never win in the end, do they, Edna?"

"No, they don't."

The rest of the article caught my attention because it focused, with silly titillation and innuendo, on Clorinda's own brief Hollywood career, mentioning her brief acting in silent pictures during the Great War, an uneventful career that ended when she became a follower of Aimee Semple McPherson and her "Knock Out the Devil" crusade. "Screen siren goes angelic"— so read the sub-headline. The article mentioned the streetcar death of her husband Philip Roberts, who played the romantic sidekick in two or three Fatty Arbuckle two-reelers at Keystone Pictures, including *Fatty's Day Off* and *The Village Scandal*. The writer speculated that Clorinda—Clorrie House then—met Philip when she appeared in *She Did and She Didn't*, a movie being filmed on some back lot during the production of one of Arbuckle's movies. Clorinda had been roommates with two other starlets, and the three played "three young beautiful sisters" in *A Foolish Romance*. But Clorinda turned her back on Hollywood after finding God. The writer embellished the information, talking of Clorinda's Assembly of God "cathedral" in New Jersey, her "many thousands of worshippers. "The stink of Hollywood transformed her into the perfume of heaven." I cringed. And reviewers lamented *my* purple prose?

"Clorinda must have cringed when the article appeared," I said to Loretta. I pointed to the stack of volumes. "Anything of Frank Resnick?"

"Not much. A short time doing production work at Universal. A year or so. He worked on a movie that Philip Roberts was in, but I don't know if they knew each other."

"Supposedly they did. Friends, until Frank tried to move in on Clorinda and Philip, then an item."

"Yeah, sure." Loretta the cynic.

For the rest of the afternoon, absorbed, I read back issues of *Moving Picture World*, *Screenland*, *The Motion Picture News*, and *Variety*, even searching through bound L.A. newspapers. Dakota's life in Hollywood. Clorinda's life in Hollywood. Parallel disasters. Late in the afternoon I found a piece in the *Los Angeles Times* about the streetcar death of Philip Roberts, a "budding actor in Fatty Arbuckle's comedies and in one-reel westerns with William S. Hart." He was killed when a passing streetcar jumped the tracks. He died immediately. He left behind a wife who was expecting a child. A brief, sad coda to a short life. The obituary, though vague, spoke of his "presence" on the screen, and quoted Buster Keaton who praised him.

Then, in *Hollywood Scoop*, two years after Philip's death, a bizarre obituary: Maddy Olivia Roberts, once married to dead actor Philip Roberts, died of influenza, leaving behind a young daughter, Marcella.

Loretta and I talked about it. Had Philip been married earlier? To the mysterious Olivia? Possibly. Was Clorinda his second marriage? We backtracked our research, but found nothing. The tidbit fascinated, but did it mean anything?

Throughout the afternoon I became absorbed in Hollywood stories, particularly the scandals that so fascinated Evan Street. Fatty Arbuckle, the baby-faced slapstick comic with the bowler derby and bowtie and spats, the highest-paid actor in Hollywood, more popular than Chaplin, enmeshed in a drunken sex orgy in a San Francisco hotel on Labor Day, 1921, at which a minor-league starlet Virginia Rappé died. There were accusations of rape, cruelty, cover-up. The scandal encapsulated all the worst stories of Hollywood as suspected by the America out there in small towns and on farms: sexual romps, drunken sprees in the middle of Prohibition, drugs, booze, rampant disorder. And Fatty's illustrious career crashed down. The Prince of Whales, destroyed. Three trials, and he was finally found not guilty. But a career over.

As I read about Fatty Arbuckle's fall from celluloid grace, I wondered how much Philip Roberts had been a part of the riotous abandon. How well did he know Fatty? Mabel Normand of the pie-in-the-face fame? Yes, on the set—but in private life? Did Philip carouse with the wild revelers? Partying in Catalina, Tijuana, San Francisco? What about his young pregnant wife? The baby Dakota, born after the accident, sent back East for puritanical upbringing. Did Clorrie House join the revelers? Did she indulge in rotgut gin and cocaine? Had Philip's involvement in the dark side caused Clorinda to seek peace in the stained-glass reflection of Sister Aimee?

Who were these people?

Late that afternoon, exhausted, Loretta and I had an early dinner at Mannie's Deli on Second Avenue. Then she taxied to her studio apartment in Washington Heights while I caught a cab to Penn Station.

As the train chugged back to Maplewood I drifted off, a fitful nap. When I woke, disoriented, I realized what I'd been dreaming: a runaway streetcar ended the life of a mysterious young man. Philip Roberts, who never saw his son. What about his first wife? And the daughter, Marcella? Suddenly, like a blow to the head, I believed that the answer to murder could be found in the short, unhappy life of a long-forgotten, small-time Hollywood actor.

Chapter Seventeen

Dak's father.

Philip Roberts. Who was this man?

"What do you know about your father?" I asked Dak. He was walking past me during the end of a rehearsal, carrying a ladder, and my question, sprung out of the blue, caused him to twist his body around, the ladder clanging against a steel girder. He said nothing, but scrunched up his eyes, baffled.

"I'm sorry," I said, not really apologizing, "but I've tried to get your attention all morning."

His reply sounded disingenuous. "I had something on my mind."

"Can we talk about some things?"

He glanced around backstage. "Yes. This afternoon. But"—the smile more hesitant, disappearing—"I gotta meet with Annika at the Full Moon Café at two."

Now I was curious. "Something has happened?"

He put down the ladder. "Well, I won't go to see my mother, though she's demanded I show up. Tobias even sent Alexander to my rooms late last night. And Annika is frantic. She phoned last night. She was crying."

"Are you sure she's not an emissary *from* your mother?"

A vigorous shake of his head. "No—I mean, maybe a little." A mixture of confusion and suspicion in his look. "I just don't know. She's worried about me."

"Well, when can I…"

"Meet us there. I *want* you there."

I shook my head. "No. Annika won't like that."

He shrugged. "I'm getting a little tired of doing what makes other people happy."

I smiled and clapped twice. "It's about time." But I deliberated. "I'll arrive an hour later. You talk to her first—that's appropriate."

"My father?"

"I have some questions."

He started to walk away, forgetting to pick up the ladder. "I might not have any answers for you."

George walked by and hissed at me. "Opening night in two days, Edna, and you're disappearing. I knock on your door—silence. You got lost in New York yesterday."

"Research." I sighed. "I told you I was leaving."

"We've already written *The Royal Family*. No more research."

"George—the murder."

"A good title for a melodrama. *George—the Murder.*"

I bit my lip. "*George—the Murdered.*"

"Edna, be careful."

"I am."

"Edna, Edna. The liar. *Edna the Liar: A Cautionary Tale.*"

"That's what fiction writers do."

"Edna, Edna." With a tilt of his head and a nervous pushing at his eyeglasses, he turned away. "When you need me, call me."

Later, he walked with me toward the Full Moon Café. Pausing in front, peering through the front window—Mamie had taped a *de jour* menu left of the door, a hand-written sheet that highlighted her dessert list, with peach cobbler underlined twice, the best advertisement there was!—I could see Dak sitting with a stiff-backed Annika. George warned me off, saying, "Edna, into the lion's den...again."

I smiled. "At least I'll die with peach cobbler in my system." I peeked back through the window. "No one is armed, George."

He shook his head.

Both Dak and Annika appeared nervous at my approach, but I slid into a chair.

Dak's voice was low and rumbling. "Annika isn't happy I invited you. I seem to make everyone unhappy."

"Hello, Annika. I'm sorry, my dear, but I need to talk to Dak, too."

She kept silent, but I noticed her eyes were red-rimmed. Her chin trembled when she turned her head.

"I haven't been to see my mother," Dak told me. "That's what we've been talking about—for an hour. I won't—*yet*. I need time to think about things. When I go into that house, I...weaken."

Annika spoke for the first time, addressing me, her voice scratchy. "I'm worried about him. The silences. I don't like Dakota drifting away."

"Well," I began, "things are happening."

"What things?" From Dak.

"Well, I have questions, I should say."

Suddenly Annika was not paying attention to me, her eyes in her lap. She was talking to herself. "Clorinda is in a horrible state. Oddly, she blames *me*." A weak, unhappy smile, as she finally looked from Dak to me. "You, of course, Miss Ferber. You're the principal culprit in this drama. But she says *I* scared him away."

Annika had undergone a troublesome change. The severe young woman, driven and fierce, had been transformed into a shaky, troubled wreck. She fidgeted, elbows on the table, then elbows off. A bead of sweat trickled down her chin, and she ignored it. Those agate eyes—a zealot's determined stare—were cloudy and distant. When she spoke, her sentences trailed off into faint whimpers. Her "scared him away" remark was ragged and sputtering.

Dak looked concerned. "Annika, I'll get back home soon enough. You're taking this too hard."

She shook her head languidly, as though under water. "But I doubt that you're coming back to the church."

A long hard look. "No, I'm not."

She gasped and cried out, "Or to me."

He didn't answer.

"Annika," I started.

She held up her hand. Her nails were bitten to the quick: lines of dried blood.

"This is all wrong." Her head swung back and forth. "Wrong, wrong, wrong. Mistakes made." Then in a measured voice, "I must have prayed to the wrong God."

That made no sense. Dak looked helpless, his eyes catching mine, pleading. He didn't know what to do with her, so catastrophic the change in her.

"I thought I owed Annika this meeting," Dak said. "It isn't fair to her." He nodded at her. "I haven't been fair to you."

"I have to know," she pleaded. "I'm left in the dark, Dakota."

I looked at Dak. "Annika's right, Dak. And you know it. You have to be honest with her. Play fair."

That seemed to surprise Annika. Her eyes got moist. She mumbled, "Yes."

"I know, I know." Dak was breathing in short bursts.

"You know, I listen to Clorinda," Annika went on. "She's wise and God-like and…Dak's mother…and I *listen* to her. But now she's screaming and cold and bitter and—" she tapped the table furiously—"she tells *me* I should have listened *better*. I somehow missed the word of God."

"For heaven's sake, Annika." I touched her wrist gently. "You're too hard on yourself. You didn't do anything wrong."

For a second the old fierceness in her eyes. "Of course, I did. I *listened*."

She sat back, dropping her hands into her lap, resigned, her eyes closed. Her body swayed back and forth. "I'm guilty of leaving my old world behind, as bad as it was. The emptiness. But that emptiness wasn't filled with all *this*."

Dak and I both exchanged looks.

I cleared my throat. "Dak, would you mind answering that question I asked you earlier?"

He glanced at Annika, tucked into her shell, and nodded. "All right, Miss Ferber. But I don't know much about my father. Just what my mother told me. Why is it important?"

"I don't know if it is. But humor me."

"Well…" He scratched his head. "Let me see. An actor in Hollywood, he partied hard with my mother's crowd, had bit parts in some Fatty Arbuckle comedies, really loved to play in westerns with William S. Hart, which is why I got this strange name, and then a streetcar hit him. I guess he was around my age now. My mother says I look like him—dark, olive-skinned, slim reedy body, high cheekbones, the black hair, even the loping walk." He shrugged. "Devilishly handsome, as my mother says." But the last sentence was caustic, cold.

Annika looked up. Her voice echoed, "Handsome." Then she looked back at her hands.

"I get those things from him—plus my last name."

I waited a moment. Then the shocker: "Did you know he was married before he met your mother?"

Dak sat up. "What? No, really?" A puzzled look. "What?"

I filled him in on the tidbit unearthed from old Hollywood magazines. "And it seems you have a half-sister."

A crazy grin covered his face. "You're kidding." But immediately his eyes darkened. "A sister. That seems impossible."

"Why?"

He glanced at Annika. "I mean, of course, it's possible, but… but wouldn't my mother have known?"

"Maybe she does."

He yelped, slammed his palm on the table, then seemed embarrassed. "Maybe she does. But why not tell me?"

"Maybe she had her reasons."

He shook his head vigorously, a flash of anger. "A sister. This is…nice."

"Nice?" Annika's voice broke. Her eyes betrayed fear.

Dak's voice rose. "Hey, I just thought of something." He swallowed and reached over to touch Annika's arm. She jerked her hand back so quickly she nearly toppled a water glass. "My marriage. Nadine." His eyes on Annika, a pleading look. "One of the reasons she fought my marriage, so she said, was because Nadine had been divorced. That is forbidden, a stain, a curse. Unacceptable. Nadine was damaged goods—important for me,

the heir apparent to the Assembly of God kingdom. Divorce—
and her husband's suicide. Tobias despises—forbids—divorce.
A betrayal of the sacred marriage covenant." He bit his lip. "So
if my father was divorced, well, she'd want to keep that a secret."

"A divorce? Scandalous?"

He tapped his tongue with his finger. "Think of Tobias. The
church. Tobias often rails out against divorce. The decline of
Western civilization. The death of the family. Right, Annika?"

Annika lifted a trembling hand. "Your mother sermonizes
against divorce."

"Well," I said, "it wasn't Clorinda who got the divorce. Yes,
she married a divorced man, but..."

"It doesn't matter. That's why." Dak concluded, "So Nadine
and I were annulled...never married. But, you know, I'll tell you
something, Miss Ferber. As a little boy, I always *felt* something
was strange. I could never put my finger on it, but whenever
my mother talked of my father to me—this is after she returned
to take over my life and I drove her crazy with questions—she
always got a faraway look in her eyes, her voice hesitant, and
she'd stammer. She always said the same few lines—like a part
in a play. It always troubled me in the way unsaid things stay
with you, and she'd shift the conversation."

"A divorce that bothered her. And a little girl growing up
somewhere. Marcella Roberts."

"Somewhere," Dak echoed. He punched the air dramatically.
"I love the idea of a sister."

I thought of Loretta in New York, following up on that tidbit.
I'd asked her to locate that young woman, if possible. What
would that tell us? Philip's first wife. The divorce. A mystery.
Another Hollywood piece of the puzzle.

The news seemed to exaggerate Annika's depression. She
sagged deeper into the chair, shoulders slumped. Dak kept eyeing
her, concerned. Now, solicitous, he reached over and touched
her shoulder. "Annika, you all right?"

She shrugged him away. Then, quietly, "Why wasn't *I* told
about that? Clorinda told me everything. Why wasn't I told? I
had a right to know."

"Dak." I shifted the subject, drawing his eyes away from her. "Another problem I have."

Annika was speaking over my words: "I need to leave. I'm expected back. Your mother…"

"Did she send you?" I asked.

Quietly, "No. She wouldn't *allow* it, you know. But I had to know…to see Dakota."

"Good for you, Annika."

Surprise in her eyes as she looked at me, mixed with gratitude. "I've made a mistake, I know."

"Stop saying that." Dak's words came fast.

Silence, then I repeated what I'd said. "Something is bothering me, especially after this conversation. Two things, actually."

They waited, the two of them, Dak anxious, Annika the picture of a slapped-around child. Then Dak grunted. "Sometimes your words alarm me, Miss Ferber."

No humor in my voice. "They're meant to." A pause. "Ilona told me you lay in wait for Evan that day, idling in your car, waiting. You purposely stalked him."

Dak's face blanched and his mouth dropped open. "Why would she say that? Yes, as I've told Biggers, I spotted him, and followed. But I didn't *wait* for him. Why would she want to get me in trouble?"

I drew my tongue to the corner of my mouth. "Have you met your aunt?"

"She's wrong, Miss Ferber." He looked shell-shocked.

"Another thing. I've been thinking about that threatening note you received—the one that said you were next, presumably to be murdered, after Evan and Gus. And that strange note I received, telling me to back away."

Annika gasped out loud, then apologized.

Tense, Dak whispered, "What about it?"

"Ilona thought you wrote the first note to get attention. Which, of course, made little sense to me. Your mother was terrified but wanted to keep it away from Constable Biggers, though she knew he'd have to see it. Last night something dawned on me. Not so much the words, which were slapdash phrases from a dime novel perhaps, but the...the spelling."

Dak laughed nervously. "The spelling? Did you parse the grammar, Miss Ferber?"

"I remember clearly the word 'you're' as in 'you're next' was misspelled 'y-o-u-r'—a common enough misspelling, an indictment of the American school system."

"So?"

"So when you sent a note to Evan, the one that was found in Gus' satchel and shown me by Meaka, you used a similar construction but the correct spelling of 'you're' in your note. Simple as that. The realization came to me suddenly—always there, nagging, until last night."

Dak waited, pensive. Then he said, "I didn't think anyone thought that I wrote those stupid notes."

Annika spoke up. "Ilona shouldn't have said that. Of course, Dak wouldn't write such a foolish letter to himself. Or the note to you, Miss Ferber."

Dak was nodding.

"It was an attempt to steer the police—however bumbling Constable Biggers might be perceived—away from Dak."

Dak was watching me closely. "What are you saying, Miss Ferber?" An edge to his voice.

"I think you know where I'm going with this. Someone is obsessed with your innocence—and the need to provide cover. At first I thought it might be Annika here"—Annika made a gurgling sound, unattractive, then covered her mouth—"because of her devotion to the Cult of Dakota, newly established, Maplewood branch."

"You're mocking me, Miss Ferber." He smiled.

"A little. It comes in handy as a tool."

Annika rushed her words, "No, not me."

"No," I agreed, "not you, foolish though your behavior has been. But only one other person comes to mind, perhaps."

An echoey voice. Dak looked over my shoulder. "Who?"

"Your mother."

"No." Emphatic, strong.

"Your mother seems to have little concern with the murder nowadays—or the apprehension of the killer. It's as though all this horror hasn't happened. What only concerns her is—you, Dak. She might not lie or cheat—good disciple of God that she is—but she'll…well, dissemble. That note, including the one sent to me as well, had her handwriting all over it."

Dak didn't like the tenor of my words. "No, she couldn't. I mean, my mother's dictatorial, vain even, over the top, God-maddened, if there's such a word—but such a note is dangerous. The police would not look too kindly on it…" A deep breath. "I did it, Miss Ferber." An astounding statement, so abrupt that Annika cried out.

"Dakota, stop. You know you didn't…"

"I did it. I was tired of Constable Biggers trailing me."

"Stop it, Dak. You're being childish and foolish. Of course, you love your mother, but her foolish act—perhaps a mother's misguided stab at misdirection—shouldn't be cause for your foolish act."

He sat back, sheepish. "I'm sorry. I'm not sure what…"

Annika broke in. "Clorinda did it."

The words hung in the air, frozen, stark. "Annika?"

"She told me she did. She *had* to, she said. 'My Dakota is in trouble.'"

"And you didn't tell me?" Dak said to her.

Annika looked helpless, trembling, "How could I? Your mother is God's daughter. She knows best."

Dak frowned. "Oh, Christ!"

But Annika looked confused. "But she never mentioned any note to Miss Ferber. I don't think that she did that she would have told me…."

"It makes a certain sense," I went on. "Three friends—of sorts. Two murdered. Evan and Gus, dead. Dak is left, and he was not fond of the two dead men. Evan, obviously. Gus, probably."

"Why do you include Gus?" A question, his eyes wary.

"Well, I'm convinced now his murder is somehow connected to Evan's. I didn't think so at first, but now it's clear to me."

Dak looked perplexed. "But, well, Annika and I talked about it. A lot. I mean, Gus had got real involved, more and more each day, with that Nazi crap. Out in California, I remember, he started buying these books and yammering on about Aryan this, Aryan that. Master race this or that. We made fun of it, thinking it was nonsense. But then, like overnight, he got deadly serious. That's when he disappeared. One time Evan mocked him and Gus stormed away, purple in the face. Then we knew he really was caught by it. 'Hitler?' I said to him once, mocking, but he yelled. 'A great man! A leader!' And he swelled up with pride."

"He had no problems being friends with you two?"

A deliberate pause. "We weren't *friends*. Not really, I mean, he and Evan seemed closer. But I could never understand their friendship. They didn't *like* each other. I know they bumped into each other back in New York—that's how Gus learned about Maplewood. To Evan's horror! I was the oddball out there—even here. I was surprised when Gus appeared in Maplewood, but he claimed he needed work real bad. He couldn't find a job in New York, he said. He couldn't hold a job. Somewhere along the line he'd met Meaka Snow, and she was eager to listen to his nonsense, and she got more fanatical than him, pushed back at him, and they both went over the edge. I mean, he created her, and then she scared him, so fanatical she was. The two of them started wearing swastikas and pasting flyers on walls and poles. When he died, I—we"—he looked at Annika—"just thought, well, you reap what you sow."

Annika was nodding her head. "Reap what you sow. A Biblical judgment."

I drew my lips into a thin line. "No Biblical judgment here, I'm afraid. Just out-and-out murder. A convenient subway train and a mob scene. Calculated. Gus had advertised his plan to be at that Union Square rally that afternoon."

Annika squinted. "A Nazi hater, the paper said."

"No," I insisted. "Why was he chosen from all those congregated on that platform to be shoved in front of that oncoming train? An old feeble man, whiskered, who became amazingly fleet of foot the minute the deed was done."

Annika sneered, "You're not saying people think Dakota did that, are you? It's pretty far-fetched."

"How so?" I glared at her, which made her squirm.

"Miss Ferber, do you really see Dak doing such a deed?"

"Of course not. But that's not to say others might see it differently. Clorinda obviously feared Dak would be blamed for the second murder, too."

Annika suddenly looked scared and grasped at Dak's elbow. He gave her a puzzled look.

"Dak couldn't have killed Gus," she declared with such force that Dak leaned forward and stared into her impassioned face. Annika was rolling back and forth in her seat, a dervish, and her face was ashen, drawn. A wreck of a woman, I thought, someone whose mechanical spirituality had masked what was really there: a real concern for Dak. That concern was coupled with another awful thought: she knew she'd somehow lost him. So she sat there, a shattered woman, confused yet ready to do battle. "I have proof that Dak couldn't have done it."

"Whoa," Dak burst out.

"And what is that?"

"He was with me that night. I remember we heard about it the next day. You'd had dinner with Clorinda and Tobias, and Dak and I spent the evening doing missionary work."

Dak was fidgeting, his foot nervously tapping the floor. "Annika, for God's sake. No, I wasn't. I spent that night finishing Miss Ferber's drawing for her. You *know* that."

She furrowed her brow. "Are you sure?" Then, "No, you didn't. We were together. I remember."

Baffled, he looked at her. "You don't need to lie to protect me, Annika."

"I'm not. We were together. You couldn't be two places at one time."

Suddenly Annika looked baffled, as though she'd missed something. As Dak babbled about the evening spent in his rooms, drawing for hours, she struggled with her words. Almost under her breath, she begged, "Are you sure?"

"Yes," he insisted.

But the look on her worn face was hard to interpret.

She looked ready to faint. "Are you sure?" she whispered.

Chapter Eighteen

Ilona House was leaving Simpson's Bakery as I headed back to the inn. Distracted, I nearly collided with her, but she'd spotted me first and tried to step behind three chattering women. Avoiding them myself, I looked into her face. What I spotted was a mixture of dread and curiosity. She was holding a white box tried with string, cradling it against her chest.

"Ilona!"

Nervously, she swung around, as though ready for flight. Finally, her back against the plate-glass window, she acknowledged me. "You seem to be everywhere, Edna." For a moment her tongue stuck out, ran over her upper lip. "Like certain strains of bacteria."

"Unfortunately some folks are immune to my contagion."

"Ha!" A vaudeville laugh, artificial and arch.

"A moment of your time, Ilona?"

She breathed in. "That doesn't auger well for my mental health. I'm on strict orders to avoid talking to you."

"From Clorinda?"

"From Tobias. Well, really both."

"And since when do you listen to either one?"

She leaned into me. "I may detest both and feel free to mock them—at least Clorinda, not Holy Tobias—but I know which side my bread is buttered on."

"Maplewood has turned out to be a buttered-side-down kind of town."

"Now you're speaking in tongues."

"I just saw Dak and Annika."

That surprised her. "Annika? She's betraying Clorinda's strict orders? My, my, a rebel in the family." Then she thought better of her words. "That gal is a wreck. Dak's self-banishment is temporary. He'll come home wagging his tail shortly. He always does. But Annika surprises me—she's lost her energy, looks like a specter, and seems headed for a breakdown."

"She knows now Dak'll never marry her."

"Which is why she's cracking up. The awareness has settled in. Like a fatal and disfiguring disease. That beautiful phantom Nadine has the upper hand. A wanton Jezebel, I hear." She took a step away. "Well, it's been a pleasure…"

"Wait a second." My most acrid tone, a leveler of the best of them—and she was not of that ilk. "Just a moment. I wanted to ask you about Clorinda's husband, about Dak's father."

"Philip?"

"Yes. Dak only knows the mythology Clorinda shared with him. What do you remember?"

"Well, hardly anything. A wild Hollywood romance, not talked about because of Father, who was suitably horrified. Clorinda wrote brief gushy letters and sent a few snapshots. Philip was a good-looking man, although I remember little of it. He was wearing a New Year's Eve party hat in one shot. Stupid grin on his face. Nice moustache, very villainous. I never met him. Clorinda got pregnant and gushed about *that*. I suspect they had to get married, if you know what I mean. She didn't plan *that*—her career, you know. But that's a taboo subject, let me tell you. Then the sad accident, accompanied by the clipping from the newspaper. The untimely death of a young unknown actor. When Dakota was born, Father insisted I raise him under his severe tutelage. You've heard that story. She went a little wild for a few years, then found Aimee Semple McPherson, the evangelist of all evangelists. The holiest of the holy. And the seeds of a new empire—heaven on earth—were sown." She took another step. "End of story." A cynical wave.

"Did you know he was married before? He divorced his wife and left behind a little girl—Dak's half-sister."

It was as though I slapped her in the face.

She choked on her words. "What did you say?"

"So you didn't know?" I waited, watched her breathing in short, audible gasps.

"Clorinda never mentioned…" But she recovered immediately, her jaw set, her eyes unblinking. "Goddamn it! That Clorinda. I always *knew* she had a secret."

"Why keep it a secret?"

"Hah! A divorce, a child." Her grip on the pastry box tightened. "You know, one time a young girl came to services. She stayed afterwards and wanted to meet Clorinda. She approached me, told me her name. She had the same last name as Dakota. She was wondering about family connections, she said, because Clorinda uses her first married name—Roberts Tyler. Let's hope she never marries again. She'd string another name after 'Tyler.' I wish I could remember. She was…Linda Roberts or Martha or something. I can't recall. She didn't claim to be related—after all, it's not an uncommon last name—she just thought it… wonderful. Another ecstatic acolyte, I guess. But when I spoke to Clorinda she went white. 'Tell her I'm busy,' she insisted. Of course, hundreds want to *meet* the messenger of God. Now, well, I wonder." A maniacal laugh. "So that was the deep dark secret she kept from Tobias." She raised her voice. "I love it. Divorce, Hollywood-style. Miss Holier-than-Thou got herself a secret. And Dakota's got a sister."

"Dak seemed happy with the idea."

"He's a simple boy, that Dakota. He's happy with a smile and a candy bar."

I bristled. "Such dislike, Ilona."

"How many times do I have to tell you that, Edna? I don't like most people."

"I don't trust you," I blurted out.

"Good judgment on your part."

"I don't know what you really think about people and things."

"And that's the way I like it."

Now, deliberately, she elbowed her way past me, purposely brushing my arm.

But she looked back over her shoulder. "Just this morning, Clorinda, out of Tobias' earshot, told me how much she despised me. It was a beautiful moment. Truly a sisterly spat that got raw and almost poetic. Shakespearean. 'I hate you.' To which I replied, 'I hate you.' 'You're a liar,' she screamed. And I laughed. 'I may be a lot of things, but a liar I'm not. Didn't I just tell you that I hate you?' She sputtered and said what she always falls back upon. Her malevolent God, that vindictive Being whose sport it is to toy with us, watch us grovel like silly ants. She yelled, 'God smites the unbeliever!' Very Spanish Inquisition. I loved it."

"Good Lord."

Ilona was so fiery, thrusting out the pastry box, stamping her feet. Passerby lingered a second, then fled.

Ilona spoke to her absent sister, "Oh, you're wrong, dear sister of the diamond mines. Our lady of the three-carat ring. I'm indeed a believer. It's just that I don't believe in what you believe."

With that, Ilona thrust her head back, a grande dame affectation, and sailed away. She stopped at the corner a block away and leaned against the plate-glass window of Perkin's Stationery Store. From where I stood, still staring after her, I could hear the nasty ripple of her hysterical laughter.

George was waiting for me in the inn's lounge, nursing a cup of coffee and reading the *New York Times*. Reluctantly, my eyes searched the headline. Something about a British bomber shot down. So many souls butchered. America was sending four thousand tanks to Britain. In London sirens pierced the dark nights. I looked up because George was saying something. "Do you ever come home to roost, dear Edna?"

"I just had a bizarre encounter with Ilona House. And one with Dak and Annika. And…"

"Edna, Frank says it's time he spoke with you. He knows you're in pursuit of a murderer. He also knows you think he's part of the mix because he's spotted you staring after him, watching, watching, judging. Your evil eye. Such scrutiny can make a man go mad. It's a wonder that I, your collaborator on *The Royal Family* and *Stage Door* and *Dinner at Eight*—masterpieces all—gold mines, to be sure—have a modicum of sanity left. You do eviscerate a man, dear Edna."

I groaned. "Someone has to do it, dear George." A pause. "Your wife has other men on her mind."

"Right for the jugular, Edna?" He bowed.

"Thank you. Now what about Frank?"

"I've invited him to dinner with us. He has something to tell you."

"I hope it's a confession."

"Maybe, but I doubt it. He refused to give me a clue. You, I gather, are the choice for shared confidences. Perhaps my kindness and all-around decency scare folks away."

An hour later Frank picked us up in his car, a creaky old Ford, missing a fender and a hubcap, rusted doors, smelly seats. Like me, George had a fear of germs, so he tried to sit with his bottom elevated and his hands cradling his chest. The car also had an erratic horn that blared whenever Frank took a right turn. He kept apologizing, wending his way to a small restaurant in nearby South Orange, driving maneuvers that involved a series of out-of-the-way left turns, a route that was starting to drive George balmy. George despises automobiles, dreads bumpy rides, and gets nauseated when a driver exceeds a speed limit greater than that of a mildly trotting horse. I recalled—with a smile—George's ashen face after Evan's madcap spin with us in the backseat. By the time we arrived at Balboa's, a rustic steak and chops eatery nestled under hemlocks and crisscrossing power lines, George was positively bilious. He spoke not a word for the short-circuit journey. A green pallor did not coordinate with his salmon-colored shirt and the bright red bow tie and white linen jacket. He looked like lime sherbet with a cherry garnish. I'd have to remind him of it during one of our future skirmishes.

Walking into the restaurant, George found his scratchy voice, out of Frank's earshot as Frank struggled to lock a car that had a window that wouldn't shut. "He's probably going to kill us, you know."

"He's made a good start with that rodeo ride over here."

"He bought the car off a farm boy going into the service. He confessed that he doesn't have a driver's license."

"Wouldn't you say that was obvious?"

But inside the knotty-pine paneled room, dimly lit with chianti bottles stuck with dripping red candles, Frank assumed a sober expression. "Miss Ferber, Dak has told me your concerns. And I admit I kept my distance from you on purpose. You're probing a murder and…and I'm not sure I knew why you were doing that."

George broke in. "She likes to tempt death."

"But," he went on, "I was afraid to get involved. You see, I came to Maplewood—well, to be a stage manager, yes—but, truthfully, I had other reasons." He sucked in his breath and scratched his head. A heartbeat. "The murder of Evan Street got in the way of my reasons for being here. A distraction. I know that sounds callous and cold, but it kept me from…from…well, I feared it might make me look like a killer."

"You're doing a good job of making yourself suspect now, Frank," George offered.

"Why? Really? Oh God, I didn't think that. I'm a man of few words. I like the shadows. I do my job, behave."

"Frank," I interrupted, "your discussion of your taciturn character is welcome, I'm sure, though not to me, yet it doesn't explain why I'm sitting here looking at unswept floors and unwashed tables. The food, I'd hazard a guess…"

"I didn't want people to see us together."

"What's going on, Frank?" George asked quietly.

Frank withdrew a small envelope from his breast pocket. "This arrived late this afternoon when I wasn't at the theater." He pushed it across the table. George opened it, took out a tiny piece of paper, and clicked his tongue.

"What, George?"

He handed it to me. It was a note from Dak to Frank, scribbled as though in a fury, with blotchy ink and cross-outs. A couple lines in which Dak told Frank he wouldn't be at work that afternoon. "Constable Biggers and the state police demand that I visit them in Newark. I believe I'm going to be taken in for murder." Signed, dramatically, "Dak the Accused."

Frank was shaking. "He came to see me but I wasn't there."

I looked at Frank. A palpable fear in his eyes, he reached out to take back the note, returning it to the envelope as though it were precious, an ancient scroll, coveted.

"They're questioning him again." My voice was flat, deadened. "I was afraid of this. Biggers seems dead-set on naming Dak the murderer because there's no one else. It's a horrible way to do business, that."

George was watching Frank. "This really bothers you, Frank. You know, I've known you for years, though we are not very close, and you've struck me as a man who…hides away, and avoids getting close to folks…and yet…" His shoulders shrugged.

I finished for him. "And yet you've taken undue notice of Dak. A real concern. Dak—and Nadine, as well. And you're making scenes on Maplewood Avenue."

He smiled wistfully. "I've taken a liking to Nadine. She's young and a little foolish as she stumbles into situations, but she's good-hearted, decent. I know she looks like a…a vamp with that makeup—a little too Betty Boop for my taste—but I'm a old codger, and young folks, you know…"

I broke in. "Did you know she was Dak's wife in California?"

"Not at first. But she told me early on. When he came looking for a job, I know it pleased her that I hired him."

"He came to you for a job?" I asked.

A few hesitant syllables, then a sigh. "I'm lying. I saw him in town, so I struck up a conversation and offered him work. I confess—I followed him, purposely. I'd had dinner with Nadine, and she'd pointed him out. And he was eager to do anything to get away from the Assembly of God."

"There's something you're not telling us." I looked into his eyes, demanding the truth.

But George was speaking over my words. "Tell us about Evan Street."

"I hated him. A blustery, arrogant ass, so taken with his own looks, strutting around, a peacock, sidling up to Nadine and whispering something so that she'd run away. I never would have hired him. I knew he got the job because of your wife"—he glared at George—"who had a college friend whose wayward son needed help…all right, all right. That's the way it is sometimes in this business, hand washing hand—dirty though it might be, but then he showed up."

"No one liked him?"

"How could you?"

"How did he act with Dak?"

"Well, Dak wasn't around much during rehearsal time, only afternoons. And Evan was only there for a few days, really. But Dak would watch for Nadine, anxious, and, oddly, if Evan approached Nadine any time, Dak would suddenly appear, almost out of the bushes, so to speak, and step into the scene."

I looked at George. "That's not good for our side."

"Evan kept insisting he was friends with Dak—and with this Gus fellow, a squirrelly guy who should never have been hired. I spoke to the head of the crew. It seems an electrician had just quit—and there was Gus. Convenient. I saw Evan brush off Gus one time, and Gus wasn't happy. This sullen Nazi with his toolbox. Well, Dak would go off with the two of them, you know, having drinks in the lounge, driving around, that sort of thing. But he never looked happy. Like he *had* to do it. Like he was trying to get to the bottom of some question he had."

"They had fights. I saw one shoving match."

"Evan taunted Dak all the time. Dak's a little weak, insecure—Christ, look at the horrible life he's had. Raised by Ilona House, who once told me she hated children. She even told *him* that one day: 'I never wanted a child, and here you are in my care.' Imagine telling that to a little boy, already taken from his mother. A tyrant of a grandfather, brutal and cold. And when his mother got him back, Ilona played victim, like he was a precious gem taken from her. Clorinda and Ilona pulled at him."

"Then the years on the road with Clorinda."

"Yes, horrible, those years. Clorinda in a broken-down bus, gaining fame, yes, but living in flea-bitten flophouses, going to bed hungry."

I was shaking my head. "Dak never found a home until he married Nadine."

"And look where that got him. Clorinda swoops in and huffs and puffs and blows the house down."

"But he came back to Maplewood," George said.

"Where else could he go? Well, of course, that's not true. *Anywhere* would have been better. I think he was looking for… for footing. Traction. Find out what went wrong and then move on. You know, when he was around fourteen or fifteen, he got a little famous as a boy preacher. Crowds loved him, and he got a little intoxicated with it. That's why he went to Hollywood, I think. He had a certain charm up there, Clorinda's angelic, pretty boy, mouthing all these words about salvation and damnation and warriors for Jesus. But after he came back, lost, Clorinda put him into the arms of Annika, the store-bought bride."

George was shaking his head. "And then everyone shows up here. Act two."

Frank's eyes got bright. "No, last act here. Maplewood. The final curtain. Evan, the dark protagonist of the tragedy."

"But that's where we hit a roadblock," I announced.

"Evan was playing a game. Let me tell you something that still bothers me. Ilona and Evan."

George and I exploded at the same moment. "What?"

"I don't like Ilona. She's a hard shell of a woman."

"But you don't really know her, do you?" I asked.

"Back up," George insisted. "Evan and Ilona?"

"Hold on." Frank held up his hand.

"Tell me," I insisted.

"No, I don't know her, but I met her briefly three or four years ago. I was hired to stage an Easter pageant in Princeton— a favor to a friend, some rich donor. No matter. It was a brief task, uneventful. But Ilona had been 'volunteered' by Tobias, I guess, to work with some church committee. Because of her last name—House—we all knew she was connected with the famous evangelist Clorinda Roberts Tyler at the Assembly of God. She was known as Clorinda House Roberts before she married Tobias. And, of course, we were told how important her contribution was. I mean Ilona was a terror, spiteful, nasty. Lord, she was so mean she fought with the young fella playing Christ, and, during a performance, he broke down in dreadful sobbing—which, sad to say, caused a ripple through the audience that made the performance memorable to this day. Christ weeping on the cross. Ironically, Ilona's bitchiness probably brought many more souls back to Christ than Clorinda's sermonizing." He chuckled at that.

"And your point in this?" I demanded.

"I had to deal with her. She unloaded her anger at Clorinda and Tobias, and even at Dak, who was then still on the West Coast. I heard it all. Actually I *wanted* to hear it. It was news to me, this Assembly of God phenomenon, and…and I was curious."

"You're not telling us something."

He fidgeted. "Anyway, Ilona struck me as someone not to be trusted. When I got this job here this summer, I saw her in town, but we didn't speak. She looked at me, and there was recognition—or at least I *think* there was—but she purposely drew back, turning away."

"What about her and Evan?"

"Well, that's the strange part. One day I saw her passing by in her car and in the passenger seat was Evan, chatting up a storm. She'd thrown back her head and was laughing at something he said. You never saw Ilona laugh. Ever. She'd do that false *ha ha ha* noise that's more cackle than humor. But she seemed to be enjoying herself."

The news bothered me. "Why? What connection? What did he want from her?"

"That's what I wondered. I remember asking Dak about it at work. 'Your aunt Ilona was driving Evan around,' I said. But he looked stunned and walked away. Evan had to be up to something. Perhaps he thought he'd melt the ice lady, charm her, but for what reason?"

"Money?" From George.

"She doesn't have any. Maybe a few bucks." Frank waited a heartbeat. "But maybe she does. I don't know."

"Dak." My voice was hoarse. "Dak. This had to do with Dak."

"I dunno. Maybe. But what?" Frank rubbed his chin.

"He wanted information on Dak."

Frank's voice dropped. "I saw them a second time. Evan was standing on the sidewalk by the train station and Ilona drove by, pulling up alongside him. She was yelling something, but he simply smiled, made an obscene gesture, and actually turned his back on her. She waited a bit—I mean, I didn't move, frozen there—and then she gunned the engine, sped off, pebbles flying, dirt clouds in the air. As she passed me, I saw her face—fury there. Cold, hard fury."

"A woman jilted?" George pondered. "But Ilona? Seems impossible."

Frank fidgeted. Sweat on his brow, he kept wiping it with the back of his wrist. "I gotta tell you something. Otherwise I'll go crazy."

"Oh Lord," George whispered. "Confession in New Jersey usually leads to bodies in murky swamps."

"Quiet, George." I turned to Frank. "Confess."

In a ragged, halting voice Frank began. "Evan did know something about Dak. Or he suspected something. Now and then I'd hear him taunting poor Dak about his dead father. He'd slip next to Dak, who was busy shifting a backdrop or something, and lisp menacingly, 'It's a wise father who knows his son.' Something like that. 'If a streetcar is traveling at five miles per hour and a man is walking at two miles per hour...'"

Or: 'Maybe father doesn't know best.' 'Some boys are raised by old maids.' I could see it confused Dak no end, but he tried to shrug it off. What was he getting at? I knew Evan was into scandal and Hollywood rigmarole, but what? It's like he had something to hold over Dak. When I tried to talk to Dak about it, he just walked away."

"And yet it bothered you." I watched him closely. Something was not being said here. "Tell me."

He nodded. "You see, I took this job in Maplewood for a reason."

"You've told us that." I was getting frustrated. We waited, George and I, pensive.

Frank closed his eyes for a moment, as though choosing his words carefully.

"And?" A prompt from George.

"I believe Dak is my son."

Silence in the room, the ticking of a clock, a waitress moving through the swinging doors out of the kitchen. Trays of greasy spaghetti unloaded onto tables. The sound of an automobile backfiring in the street. The grainy rattle of a jukebox tune from the bar.

"Tell us," I demanded.

"I knew Clorinda in Hollywood back in 1916. I was there for a short time."

I interrupted. "Less than a year." Loretta's research at the New York Public Library.

He raised his eyebrows. "You do your homework." He smiled. "But, yes. I hated it out on the Coast—hated silent movies, hated the climate, the people. Hollywood is new, crazy, insane. I met Clorinda at a party after the release of one picture I worked on. She was wild then, she and her roommates. The fa-la-la triplets, we called them. Dancing the night away. Drinking, drugs, you name it. I got caught up in it, too. Suddenly we were having a wild affair, and I really fell for her. Madly. An affair through that summer and into the fall. But I could tell she didn't care for me. It was just, you know, sex. Her roommate Ginny was worse, let me tell you. She'd just had an abortion, I knew. And not the first. Then, like that, it ended. Just before Thanksgiving. Clorrie got cold and distant. I figured she'd found someone else."

"Philip Roberts?" George asked.

"Maybe. I didn't know him, although he'd acted in one movie I worked on. I never said a word to him. But he was a party boy, too. She probably met him around then. Anyway, I was dismissed and, depressed, left Hollywood. Some time later I heard through the grapevine she'd married. Out of the blue. Then, later, I bumped into a friend in Manhattan who mentioned Philip had been killed. I learned there was a little boy named Dakota. Born that March. Bits and pieces of information. The timing was all wrong for *them*. But not for me. I'd learned Dak's age when I met Ilona, who told me about raising him. His birthday. His age, the month. March. My time with Clorinda the previous summer. My affair. Not Philip's. Or maybe not. She could have been seeing him on the side, but I don't think so. I'd have known. Someone would have said something. In June and July we were going…heavy. Exclusive. But I pumped Ilona for information. And I started to believe Dak *had* to be my son."

"My God," I exclaimed. "This is a new wrinkle."

"Tell me about it. That's why I came here. To Maplewood. I kept asking around, you know. Ilona told me Dak was in Hollywood. But I found out later he was back here. But when Cheryl Crawford opened the Maplewood Theater, I thought it was my chance to *see* him."

"And here he was."

"And here he was. I maneuvered him into this job, I hovered over him. Edna, he looks like me. I mean, the olive skin, the cheekbones, the way he tilts his head when surprised, the long, tapered fingers, the walk…I know it."

"Do you think Evan knew?" I asked breathlessly.

"That's the curious thing. No, he didn't. He made remarks about Philip Roberts, Some scandal about Roberts, I thought. But there was no way he could suspect me as Dak's father. I would know. Evan played every card he had. He was looking at the story from a different viewpoint."

"I wonder," George offered.

"Then where does this lead us?" I wondered out loud.

"Evan was playing a different game."

Frank's words shook me. At that moment, in a blare of awful light, I believed I knew the answer. Suddenly I stood in Evan's menacing shadow—and I knew why he had to be murdered.

Chapter Nineteen

Dak asked everyone to go to his mother's home the next afternoon, an invitation that made me wonder what he was up to—not a good feeling, indeed. "To clear the air," he told me that morning at rehearsal. "After my little session in Newark with the impassive Constable Biggers and a very militaristic state police captain named Caruthers, I need to curb some rumors. Rumors of my hanging are premature."

"Is this a good idea?" I asked him. "Your mother has deemed me the town leper. I don't think she'll welcome…"

He broke in. "I haven't been back there. She wants me back. There are conditions, Miss Ferber. I *want* to do this."

George grunted, but finally agreed. Tomorrow was opening night, and George, given his meticulous, if overbearing, directorial style, had fashioned a tight, seamless production of *The Royal Family*, our mother lode progeny. One last dress rehearsal in the morning, with full makeup and costume, and by one o'clock we all sat in our dressing rooms, pleased, comfortable. So it begins, my acting debut.

Something else was beginning—and ending, I realized. Because, quite frankly, the pieces of the other drama I was experiencing had suddenly fallen into place, and the final act was blocked out. At least to my satisfaction—though a couple scenes had loose ends, dark holes, blank pages where appropriate dialogue needed to be inserted.

Last night, given my epiphany, I'd phoned Loretta in New York, fired off a list of questions and puzzles demanding her immediate research acumen, and, in her inimitable rapid-pace style, she'd phoned me at the inn after I'd returned from lunch. Now I had a couple more scenes fleshed out, polished, and, I hoped, ready to play well with the audience I'd encounter at four that afternoon. The audience as cast, and vice versa.

"Catch a ride with Frank," Dak had told me, and that surprised me.

"Frank will be there?"

I wondered whether Dak had any inkling of Frank's belief that he was Dak's father.

"Frank's a big part of this. And Nadine, too. She doesn't want to venture into the lion's den, but she's part of my announcement."

As George and I waited outside the inn for Frank, I told him what I needed from him—should I send him a signal—and he looked perplexed, but nodded again. Quietly, methodically, I filled George in on my suspicions—no, my absolute conclusion about this summer's mystery. And, though he wrinkled his brow and fretted—"Edna, didn't I tell you to stay out of it? Now look what you're planning!"—he understood what had to happen. We'd always worked well as a team on our hit plays, me at the typewriter, George pacing the room, the two of us creating dialogue, scenes, and then playing the parts. Somehow, despite different temperaments—my imperiousness, hard-fought, and his what-the-hell cynicism—we fashioned Broadway magic. We'd see now how our talents would translate in tree-shrouded Maplewood.

So the four of us crowded into Frank's brush-with-death jalopy and headed to Tobias Tyler's mansion. No one spoke the whole time, though Frank gripped the steering wheel tightly and Nadine nervously kept checking her lipstick in a small compact that she held in her hand the whole time. As we stepped from the car into the driveway of the mansion, with Frank and Nadine holding back, apprehensive, their shoulders touching, I whispered to George, "Follow my lead, George dear. This will be our best dramatic collaboration yet, though it'll never preview in New Haven."

George whispered back. "I still get to crack the funny lines."

My face tightened. "There'll be no humor at this matinee."

Hilda opened the door, and she looked frightened. What had Clorinda told her? She led us into the vast living room. Just the four of us, no one else.

"Is this a trap?" George quipped.

But then Tobias, Clorinda, and Ilona walked in, single file, regimented, and sat down. "Well," Clorinda began, "this is awkward."

"Where's Dak?"

"Late, as usual." Ilona glanced toward the window. "The boy was never on time. He's the one who called this—inquisition." She stressed the last word, booming it out. Clorinda shot her a look.

We sat there, all of us, uncomfortable. A tea service and a tray of cookies rested on a coffee table, but no one invited us to partake. I assumed everything was laced with strychnine or tannin or arsenic. I knew how dangerous people died in British melodramas, their murderers wreathed in chilly smiles.

Clorinda didn't take her eyes off me. Her cold, wary stare in those scrunched-up eyes told me how unwelcome I was. The interloper in town, the woman who helped her son exile himself out of paradise—Adam leaving the garden of earthly delights. And forgetting to take Eve with him. Edna the scaly serpent, slithering, whispering illicit enticements. Earthly delights, indeed: Clorinda sat there blazing in her diamond earrings and necklace, but today she'd embellished the outfit with a garish brooch, so ostentatious it seemed a midnight sun in the dim room, as well as tinkling bracelets and a hint of some exquisite gem in her hair. Dressed in a rainbow-colored sweeping dress, with a chiffon scarf draped over her head, she looked the part from a once-upon-a-time world. She was obviously telling me—and the world—something. Don't mess with me, my loves. I got God and cash in my corner.

Tobias sat still, his face contorted with fury.

So Clorinda glared, and once or twice she shared that dark glance with Frank and Nadine. Hatred, palpable and raw, in that cursory look. A fleeting look, then a cavalier dismissal. A hand raised so that the bracelets jangled. Frank and Nadine weren't worthy of her venom. That poison was reserved for me.

Ilona sat in a side chair, positioned back a bit, as though she were a spectator and not part of the proceedings. She'd donned a severe black dress that ended well beneath the knee, pulled in with a large leather belt. Thick, heavy-soled shoes. The dour chaperone at an Edwardian cotillion. The prison matron *sans* whip and club.

Dak suddenly rushed in, out of breath, paused in the archway, and frowned. "Where's Annika?"

No one answered.

He looked at me. I shrugged. "Dak, could we please do this? Everyone here is uncomfortable."

Tobias cleared his throat. A jack-o-lantern smile for a brief second, absolutely macabre. "I'm perfectly fine, Miss Ferber. I live here. Perhaps your sins fill you with guilt."

George started to laugh, but stopped, and tried to transform his chuckle into a sudden cough.

"I've never committed a sin in my life," I announced, haughtily. "I've done a number of evil things—all on purpose, I might add, with considerable joy—but they weren't sinful."

Tobias seemed to be reaching for some homiletic tracts on a side table, probably ready to do missionary work with one more Manhattan heathen, but Dak's voice broke the moment. "I think we all got enough sin to go around." He glanced toward the door. "I wanted Annika here. She needs to hear me out. It's only fair…to her."

"I think she knows the level of your abandonment—and cruelty." Clorinda's voice startled me: arctic, venomous, lethal. Even Tobias seemed alarmed by it, furrowing his brow and pointing at her.

"Anyway," Dak began, "I'm going to be arrested for the murders of Evan and Gus."

Clorinda let out a scream, and Tobias reached out to grasp her hand.

"There, there," he soothed. "We'll take care of it."

Nadine started sobbing. Frank put his arms around her shoulders.

"What? Dak?" I asked.

Dak shrugged his shoulders and grinned vacantly. "Who else is there to blame? I confessed to *following* him. I wanted to talk to him, but when I saw him stop in the park, I kept going. I swear I did. He seemed on a mission. But I gather some old lady walking her dog has stepped up to say she saw a young man running down a path and out of the park—uncertain of the time, but definitely that afternoon. In the vicinity of the murder. Her description of the runner fits me. I guess I'm the only young man in Maplewood. But I didn't kill him."

"Of course not!" Clorinda spoke through clenched teeth.

"Hardly concrete evidence." From George.

"But enough to warrant a grand jury probe, it seems."

"When?" I asked.

Again, the shrug. "The state police want me to turn myself in, accompanied by a lawyer, who'll arrange it all. By next week."

Clorinda was seething. "A miscarriage of justice, this…this…"

"Of course, it is," Tobias agreed.

I locked eyes with Clorinda. I saw confusion there, fright.

"Well, that may not happen," I announced.

To which George added, "Final act, scene one."

Ilona grunted. "Can we go now?"

"Wait." Dak stood and walked to Nadine who, I noticed, had sunk into her chair, so tiny, as though she wished to disappear into the cushions. "Wait."

Nadine looked at him, her eyes moist.

"Mother, I've done some thinking about Nadine and me and…"

Someone sneezed in the hallway. The sound of shuffling, hesitant feet. Annika drifted into the room, looking down and mumbling an apology for being late. She was looking at her feet as she slid into a chair positioned by the fireplace, a chair turned away from all of ours, so that we saw only the back of her head.

Her appearance alarmed me. Annika, when first met, had been iron-rod stiff, a martinet with a voice that was as confident as a struck gong, a woman in full possession and unconditional in her fundamentalism. A daughter of Clorinda's puritanical revival. No nonsense, this young girl, a believer defined by rules and a future written in the heavens. Now, lamentably, she'd undergone a dreadful sea change, understandably brought about by Dak's desertion of the church—and of her. Her firm moorings loosened, she had only chaos and waste. You saw a young woman who was hunched over, ashy-faced, twitching, frantic, unsure, a woman whose body movements were spastic and sudden. She looked as though any minute she'd topple in a faint.

We watched her, all of us, and Dak wore a sad look on his face. Slowly, barely audible, he said her name. "Annika." She glanced back at him and wistfully smiled. "I'm sorry, Annika." But, again, she faced away from us.

Clorinda fumed. "You see what you've done to her? Annika, you don't have to stay here. In fact, please go rest upstairs." She turned to her sister. "Ilona, take her to one of the bedrooms."

Ilona's voice was rich with humor. "Why would she want to miss the show?"

Dak eyed his aunt. "Ilona, c'mon. Behave."

"I don't know how."

Dak glanced at Annika but went on. "What I started to say was that I've given a lot of thought to…to what I had with Nadine." Again, he looked over at Annika, who still faced the fireplace. On the mantel, I noticed, there were two photographs: Clorinda and a boyish Dak, standing next to a bus with a painted-on slogan: *God Knows Your Sins But He Forgives You. Sister Clorinda.* Dak looked goofy, with cowlick hair and a toothy smile. And another photograph: Tobias and Clorinda on their wedding day, Tobias in a black tuxedo and Clorinda in white satin. Dak was nowhere in sight.

Dak softened his words. "In short, we're gonna try to make it work."

"No," Clorinda thundered.

Dak's voice rose. "Stop it, Mother. Enough of your meddling. I listened to you once—that was enough!" Pleading in his voice. "Don't you want to see me happy?"

"You don't know what happiness is."

Tobias spoke over her. "God gives you happiness."

"Well, God is late."

Tobias got red in the face. "How dare you blaspheme in my house?"

I held up my hand. "I have something to say."

Clorinda, out of the side of her mouth. "Big surprise, Edna."

I broke in. "I want to talk about the murder."

My words silenced Clorinda's sputtering.

Dak's eyes got wide. "You know *who*?"

"Yes." A pause. "Well, a suspicion."

Clorinda got out of her seat and pointed at Nadine. "There's your murderer. She came to Maplewood to destroy Dak and… and…me and…"

"Sit down, Mother. Miss Ferber is saying something."

"I repeat," George said, "final act, scene one."

I smiled at him. "An editorial comment first. A prologue, as it were."

"My pardon." George bowed. A working partnership, this.

I sat forward in my chair. "A murder always benefits someone."

"A planned murder," George qualified. "A deliberate murder."

"True, I suppose, although…well, never mind. But who in this room gained from the murders?"

Frank's voice was strained. "You're saying the murderer is in this room?"

"Yes, I am."

Ilona folded her arms over her chest and made a harrumph sound. When we all glanced toward her, her expression dared us to say anything. "Fat chance you'll prove anything."

"Let me at least share my thinking." I swallowed. "Again I ask: Who gained by Evan's being shot to death?"

George moved his chair closer to mine. My dedicated collaborator, at the ready. Opening night, curtain up. He fiddled with the band of his wristwatch. "That seems to include everyone in this room right now. The suspects." His glance took in everyone. So dramatic a declaration, I thought, and so interesting the reaction: Dak seemed amused, Nadine puzzled, Frank ashen, Tobias irritated, Clorinda steely, Ilona curious. Annika's head was turned away from us, still facing the fireplace, her head dipped into her neck. An array of responses, indeed. "The seven deadly sins," George added. "Is it possible?—sloth, envy, greed, lust, pride, and wrath. What am I leaving out?"

"Gluttony, George."

He nodded. "Well, there goes that theory." A pause. "Well, maybe not."

"I think King Solomon's seven are more apt, especially as we sit among holy people."

Tobias looked at me and mumbled, almost to himself, "The Book of Proverbs."

I nodded. "A dishonest witness who lies, a prideful look, a lying tongue, feet that run toward mischief, a heart that plans wickedness, a man who sows discord among others, and, of course, hands that shed innocent blood."

Tobias was smiling. "Very good, Miss Ferber."

I didn't look at him. "And every one done by someone in this room." I waited a second. "Evan's death," I continued. "Late afternoon. Shot pointblank in the heart at DeHart Park, doubtless during some sort of assignation. He knew his killer. His death was satisfying for whom? For Dak, the end of badgering and fights—and the avenging of an act that destroyed his marriage. For Nadine, the death of a cruel seducer and taunter. For Frank, the death of a disliked man who seemed a menace to both Nadine and Dak's lives. Of course, there could be more to his story—if Frank is correct about Dak's paternity."

I watched Clorinda's eyebrows rise—and she cast a fiery look toward Frank.

"How dare you!" she yelled at me.

"Oh, I dare. And then there's Ilona. What was her relationship with Evan? Spotted cruising around town with him, at least once, she seemed unnaturally buoyant, laughing at something Evan said, this woman who is notoriously bitter. And then, the negative of that print, an angry encounter, Evan obviously ignoring her. Could it be that Evan, the eternal womanizer and glib romancer, momentarily worked his charms on the ice woman, thawing her—only to shunt her aside?"

"Preposterous!" Ilona said in a low, whiskey voice that told me I was right.

"Evan came looking for information and probably believed Ilona had some to offer. So he wheedled his way briefly into her cold heart—and then, sated, dropped her. A reason to murder, no? A crime of passion. Or, shall I say, *lack* of passion."

Ilona stood, tottered a step, ready to lunge at me. George raised a hand, traffic cop style. "Sit. The curtain is still up, lady."

"And then, of course, we have the three members of the Assembly of God. Annika seems least likely, mostly unknown to Evan and he to her, though she wanted to protect Dak at all costs. But her killing him strikes me as extreme." Annika did not move as I said this, though I noticed her listening, the muscles in her neck taut.

"And finally Tobias and Clorinda, guardians of spiritual earth, the children of God. Evan was an impediment, a possible scandal. After all, he was privy to dangerous information: Dak's failed marriage. Nadine's divorce, her husband's suicide. Drug use. Tobias viewed his church as an old-guard temple, and divorce is anathema. Hence Dak's annulment—a marriage that never was. But Evan could besmirch the purity of Dak's ride to the throne. Perhaps he had to be removed."

"Hardly sensational." Clorinda spat out the words. "After all, the marriage was *voided*."

"Clorinda was frantic that Dak would be accused of Evan's murder, even trying to throw suspicion off her son, penning a stupid note about his being the next victim."

"I never."

"Of course, you did."

George added, "Your grammatical lapse, egregious in of itself, was telling. Dak's literacy is more…"

"Oh, Lord, do I have to hear this? Yes, I did it, as Annika confessed she told you everything. A misguided mother, foolish, foolish."

Tobias cleared his throat. "A little foolish, Miss Ferber, this theory. Killing Evan because he might introduce scandal? The committing of an unpardonable sin to cover a venal one?"

"True, it is a stretch."

Clorinda scoffed. "So we are left with seven possible murderers, and none with a reason monumental enough to commit murder."

"True. But the Assembly of God is hardly a peaceable kingdom. It strikes me as a rich man's folly—well intended, perhaps, for Tobias is a devout man, if narrow and doctrinaire, and Clorinda a charismatic spokesman—but it's also a kingdom founded on hard cash. And plenty of it. Tobias' Park Avenue inheritance became a kind of insulation from the world for him but also a tool for suppression, silencing."

"My money is God's gift."

"And yet money seems to have motivated all of Evan's behavior, no?"

"What are you saying, Miss Ferber?" Dak now looked anxious.

"Well, nothing yet. But let me say this. All of you had a reason—though in some cases very minor league—to kill Evan, but the murder of Gus Schnelling in New York was most baffling. Yes, some think it was the work of a fervent anti-fascist lunatic, but no: Gus' murder is part of the Maplewood tragedy. So the question presents itself…" A pause.

George, on cue: "Who benefits from Gus' murder?"

"And the answer to that will tell us the murderer of both young men."

"And now: Act two."

"But let me play historian here for a bit. My novels are called saga chronicles, generations after generations interplay, building, whole biographies predicated on what went before."

Ilona spoke in a rough gravelly voice. "So tell us what went on before."

"Generations. All along I thought the secret to Evan's murder had to do with the newest generation, the gadabout, restless crowd of Dak, Nadine, Evan, and Gus. Even Meaka Snow, now disappeared." I winced. "Probably as a Brown Shirt polishing her accent on *achtung*. Her goose step. *Deutschland über alles.*"

"Really, Miss Ferber." From Frank. "You sound like Fanny Cavendish in a traveling show."

"Wait till tomorrow night," George said.

I waved them off. "But I was wrong. Nadine's lapses—indeed, Dak's lapses—in Hollywood pale beside the real back story." I deliberated. "Ah, where to begin?" A stage pause, as George stood, excused himself, and left the room. I went on. "Clorinda's marriage to Philip Roberts bothered me—Dak's father, and that poor man's death in front of a streetcar. Let's think about Clorinda in Hollywood—those madcap, wild years of the silent pictures, a time of war in Europe and America on the brink of joining in, when there were few boundaries and endless money and scandal and frivolity. One long party. Drunk with rotgut gin. Clorinda, with her roommates, was a part of it—until she married Philip. But did she? The obituary mentioned that Philip left a wife, then pregnant. Later, another article mentioned his former wife dying of influenza, leaving a little girl named Marcella. I first thought that Philip had been previously married and divorced. But my research assistant reported this afternoon that Philip's daughter—she lives in Massachusetts now—was born the same week as—as Dakota. So I suggest that Clorinda found herself pregnant, unmarried, and simply invented a convenient marriage—and appropriated a real death—in her letters back home. Dak, the illegitimate child, given a last name not rightfully his. The time coincides with Frank's brief sojourn and affair with Clorinda…and Frank's belief that he might be Dak's father."

A low moan from Dak. We all looked, and he shared a bittersweet smile with us. He was looking at Frank.

A screech. "Stop this now!" Clorinda rose, flailing her arms, and seemed ready to charge at me. "Lies, all lies. Tobias, don't listen to this. This woman is nonsense. I was *married*. Philip was killed…"

"No, you weren't. I'm pretty sure of it. But all right. So what? Things happen. So far from home, an unwed mother, a little dissembling. No big deal. Dak had a father on paper. A grandfather on the East Coast was content."

Tobias grunted. "No big deal?" The man was standing now and wobbling, the little monkey-like man reeling. "Clorinda, this is perfidy."

"A lie," she whispered, and then hissed at me. "You stop this now."

"Her moral turpitude aside, the question still presents itself: Why is this important? But…more of the history. Evan Street, a scavenger of Hollywood scandal, a bottom-feeder of slime, obviously was in Hollywood when Clorinda sailed in to annul Dak's marriage—and there was that piece in the press—which he probably cut out. The story of Clorinda's actions in Dak's life, publicized because of her fame. Clorinda's transformation from vamp to evangelist. Some reporter found that history important enough to write about. And Evan relished it. Hence his questions about Dak's paternity. One taunt especially—*raised by an old maid*—got me thinking—not Ilona, as first thought, but Clorinda. The unmarried woman posing as a widow. Evan obviously did some searching around in Hollywood, found some answers. Maybe even about Philip's real marriage, real daughter. Who knows? All I know is that he felt armed with information and headed to Maplewood. That explains his pursuit of Ilona—what did she know?"

"I knew nothing."

"That was clear to me when I mentioned Philip's first marriage. But there had to be something else, something more earth-shattering. Evan traveled far in his quest for vast and quick money, his mercenary mind tabulating the sins of the past in terms of crisp dollar bills. The silent era again, as documented by *Moving Picture World* and *Screenland*—and Evan's mass of clippings. Because the article about Dak's annulment—written up because of Clorinda's celebrity—clued him into something else: a real scandal. You see, it mentioned Clorinda's film career, meager though it was. She was known as Clorrie House, a sultry temptress in the Pola Negri mold. This Philip Roberts connection was dangerous—some might remember whom he married and the daughter. But Clorinda knew Philip. She felt sure of herself. The East Coast was worlds away—there would be nothing in the local press about the real Philip Roberts' family. Philip was a small-time actor. But Evan was intrigued by Clorrie's past."

George reentered the room. He'd taken down the framed poster that Tobias had hanging in his office, the one that mentioned, in small letters, Clorinda House's bit part in *The Way Back*. George stood there with this wonderful prop, and I, like a hectoring schoolmarm, walked over and placed an index finger on her name—and then slid my finger to another name: Virginia Rappé.

"Virginia Rappé." I repeated it. "Virginia Rappé. Clorinda's roommate and the loose woman who notoriously died after the San Francisco orgy that Fatty Arbuckle supposedly orchestrated. There were allegations that the rotund Fatty raped her, abused her, and ignored her cries for help. Virginia most likely died from the complications of a botched abortion, one of many she had in her short life. A lover of gin and orange juice—the so-called orange blossom. After a few of those she often doffed her clothing…Anyway, accusations against the poor comic doomed his career, though a final jury cleared his name and believed his protestations that he had been railroaded. An innocent man, his life in Hollywood was over. A man shunned, beaten to the core, destroyed, dead in his sleep seven years ago of a heart attack. Largely because of a tapestry of calculated lies."

"Miss Ferber," Dak broke in, "I don't think…"

"Let me finish. The prosecuting attorney in San Francisco, probably unscrupulous, took statements from Virginia's fellow partiers, all sensational in content, but the extreme testimony of Bambina Maude Delmont, a chronic liar, was most damning. A woman arrested for bigamy, extortion, racketeering, the list goes on. But it turns out, according to the first press reports, before Bambina's story became center stage, all the drunken, drug-crazy guests gave their own damning statements."

A whimper from Clorinda. "Dear God."

"Indeed, dear God. Clorinda's third roommate, Zey Prevon, lied, then waffled. But another statement, a bold-faced lie, shortly discredited, was from Clorrie House, a young woman who was at the party. One mention in the San Francisco *Examiner*."

Tobias was sputtering. "This has to be false. This has to… be…"

"A wild time, and a horrible time. A man's life shattered. Clorrie House"—I pointed to the poster that George held before him—"disappeared from the accounts, never testified in court, but the harm was done. The evil Bambina was center stage, a practiced liar who tried to extort money from Fatty. Back in Hollywood, a stalled career, forgotten, alone, her baby Dakota—his name taken from a Philip Roberts western—was shuttled back to New Jersey, and Clorinda had a moment of reckoning, a flash of crystallization during which she rued her behavior, the life she lived. At that moment she found Aimee Semple McPherson. Beloved Sister Aimee."

In a faraway voice Clorinda echoed, "Beloved Sister Aimee."

"And the path of redemption, Jesus, salvation, and her traveling evangelical bus came into being. She buried the past. And then she met Tobias, the most rigid, unforgiving Christian on the planet, and he showered her with God and gifts. Clorinda had tired of life on the road—of poverty. The blessings of untold wealth. The wealth of untold religion. A new life—and a good life."

Clorinda roared. "I've done good deeds."

But Tobias was shaking his head. "Is any of this true, my dear?"

"Crazy lady," Clorinda muttered. A sob. "Crazy."

Squirming in her seat, Ilona was making a gurgling sound.

"Possibly true, but what I'm saying is true. Evan Street, an unscrupulous man, assembled a file of Hollywood tabloid scandal, particularly the lamented Fatty Arbuckle story, and once he discovered Clorinda's dark secret, he came East. Dak had led him, by chance, to his mother's explosive story. And what a story it was! The possibility of a big payoff. Suddenly the poor boy in the shiny suit and the cardboard-lined shoes was sporting a new car, flashing new clothing, and a residence at the pricy Jefferson Village Inn. How did he get his money? Well, we have to assume blackmail. After all, Clorinda had a lot to lose—Tobias, the Assembly of God, the money, the diamonds, this magnificent house, a life she coveted, her colossal fame. Worse, the future with Dak was threatened—his taking over the church, the perpetuity of the church. And she knew that Tobias would not abide such a past, especially one lied about. Lord, look at his reaction to Nadine's earlier divorce. The suicide of her ex-husband. A moral prig, the man could never forgive Clorinda for any of this."

Clorinda, standing, arms folded over her chest, gave a false cackle. "You have all the answers, but one. You have no proof. Why would I, an emissary of God, *murder* anyone? Impossible. Yes, I paid Evan cash, lots of it, dragged out of Tobias' parsimonious pocket, but I was silencing him. He promised me. Murder? A little far-fetched…"

George nodded at me. "Which leads us to the murder of Gus Schnelling, everyone's most disliked Nazi."

"My initial comment: Everyone here has a reason, though feeble, to want Evan dead. But who gained from Gus' death? That's crucial. Not Ilona, Dak, Frank, Annika. Only Tobias and Clorinda. Because, based on notes left by him, he'd somehow discovered Evan's pernicious plan and wanted in on it. Either

Evan babbled something in a drunken conversation—or Gus ferreted out the scheme. Clearly he was a Johnny-come-lately to the blackmail, but, once aware of it, he harassed Evan. He demanded his share. Why else come to Maplewood? After all, the pot was big enough. So Gus had to die. Perhaps Gus made a phone call after Evan died. Pick up where Evan left off. Perhaps Evan indicated he had backup—Gus. He may have used Gus as a type of false security so he'd be safe. Who knows? The last blackmailer who probably never got a chance to blackmail…"

"Ha!" Clorinda took a step toward me. "You seem to forget something, Edna."

"And what is that?"

"On the night Gus was pushed to his death in New York, if I can believe the news accounts, I was dining with you and Tobias in this very house. Obviously a mistake on my part, such hospitality to a foolish woman, but, oddly, a blessing now. We were laughing heartily as dear, misguided Gus was toppling onto those tracks." A dramatic sweep of her hands, that hypnotic voice covering the room now—the evangelist actress playing her last wonderful trump card.

George stared at me, waiting, but there was twinkling in his eyes, a twitching of his lips, and, relishing the moment—he mouthed the words *Last act*—he bowed to me. "And?"

A heartbeat. Silence, awful but deliberate. I had no proof, to be sure, but I'd anticipated a fierce coda to the question. So I waited patiently, while everyone watched.

"I did it."

A squeaky, exhausted voice from across the room. We watched as Annika Tuttle swiveled in her chair, facing us for the first time. A haggard face, spent. A woman ravaged by a guilt that had plagued her for days, the sad young girl most likely manipulated by a voice that could not be ignored.

I caught George's eye. The same surprise there, though tinged with a trace of melancholy. We'd wondered if this moment would actually happen. It gave me mixed joy that it did because the sight of the doomed girl was overwhelmingly disquieting.

"Annika," Clorinda seethed. "Shut up."

Annika stood, though she gripped the armrest. "I did it." A slight laugh, hollow. "On orders from a vindictive God." She pointed to Clorinda. "She told me to. I believed her when she said God's empire was crumbling, that Dak would be cursed, that Tobias was a sadistic tyrant, that she—only she—had God's words whispered in her ear. I did her bidding, driving frantically to the city after Dak disappeared into his art, stalking the rally in Union Square, following Gus in the subway. Dressed in a homeless man's coat and scraggly vaudeville beard and sloppy slough cap. I was one of God's angels. I already knew what had happened to Evan. 'Evan has to be taken care of,' Clorinda told me. She paid him off, but he'd demanded more money. More and more. And right away. Afterwards I took the gun she handed me—wrapped in rainbow chiffon—and tossed it into Pierson's Pond." She smiled. "Where in winter Dak and I went skating. Where in the fall, at Pierson's Mill, we bought apples together." She stopped, shook her head wildly. "The gun smelled of death in her hands. God smites the unforgiven, the unclean. It's the way of the Bible. Sodom and Gomorrah. Clorinda talked of Yael and Judith, Old Testament women who murdered justly—to save God's kingdom. Israel. The wrath of a fearful God. Evan had to go. And so did Gus." She fell back into her seat. "I did it." A whisper. "For a God that doesn't exist anymore."

Dak could barely speak, but he looked at her with sorrow. "You seemed happy when I said I'd planned to spend the night on Miss Ferber's drawing. Be by myself."

"We did it for you."

Restless, Dak stood and paced the room. "Mother, no. Tell me—no."

But Clorinda said nothing. Tobias, his face purple with rage and wonder, waved a gnarled finger at her, and then, letting out a raw plaintive sound from deep in his chest, slunk out of the room. He bumped into George, and the framed poster he held crashed to the floor, the glass shattering. From the hallway his cries echoed, a sobbing man, lost.

Annika was looking at Clorinda. "You promised me God and Dak."

George rolled his tongue in his cheek. "God has other plans for the two of you."

"I had too much to lose," Clorinda said with a surprising fire to her voice. "I had all *this* to lose. I couldn't. You don't know Tobias. He'd take all *this* away from me. My fame, my church." Suddenly she threw back her head, the jaw set, and fierceness came into her voice. I imagined Satan at the moment he understood that he would now reign in Hell. "They were sinners, those two. They had to die. The wrath of God on the infidel." Suddenly she laughed so menacingly that Nadine burst out crying. "Evan laughed at me—said he expected monthly payments." She laughed again. "His face when he saw the gun—'You're a preacher,' he yelled. So the cynical man actually believed in *something*. And Gus, demanding money. Remember the Old Testament God, my friends. He abided no weakness, no disbelief. He didn't forgive—he destroyed." Her voice shook with fury as she raised a fist to the ceiling.

George said the words from Billy Sunday that Tobias had once intoned: "I do not believe in a God who does not smite."

Clorinda looked at him, eyes blazing. She repeated that line. "I do not believe in a God who does not smite."

"But you're not God." My voice was even, cool.

Still defiant, her eyes maddened, her voice rich with pride, "I work for Him."

"Not anymore."

George looked at me. "And the curtain comes down."

Chapter Twenty

Opening night, the following night. The musical prelude began with selections from *Show Boat*—to honor me. The beginning of a weeklong production of *The Royal Family*. It was as though the murders of Gus and Evan never happened—as desired, the headlines in the morning press didn't mention George or me. Constable Biggers and the state police swooped in, and I noticed that Constable Biggers, stoic to a fault, stood with his pad at the ready—with nothing written on it. He did have the grace to nod at Dak, and Dak swears he muttered something about not trusting religious zealots. He knew it all along.

Opening night, and Louis Calhern, distracted, dropped me for real this time as he carried me up the staircase. An unlady-like grunt from me, sputtering from him, and a whole lot of uncontrollable laughter from the audience, which, sad to say, was filled with many of my friends—and a few enemies—from Manhattan. I swear Dorothy Parker, sitting third row center, could not contain herself, because I recognized her high brittle laugh. Across the way Tallulah Bankhead rose and left the theater. Her distinct bourbon rumble drifted back from the lobby. "God-damn!" The word punctuated the middle of one of my lines.

Worse, given my best-seller fame, the important New York newspapers sent their top reviewers to opening night. The *New York Times* and the *Herald Tribune*, among them. They prepared their tongue-in-cheek reviews. Doubtless, for some, venturing beyond the sanctified borders of the Hudson and East rivers and into plebian hinterlands caused them to sharpen their pencils (or claws) or, at least, generate an undue reserve of bile; for one or two reviews dismissed me as "adequate" and not "very embarrassing." A "workmanlike performance"—the kiss of death. Worse yet, the august *New York Times* saw fit to feature my name in bold relief—above those of the stalwart real actors, Louis Calhern and Irene Purcell—but, in a typographical mishap with wry results, misspelled my name as ENDA FERBER.

Well, "enda" it certainly was, so far as my acting adventure was.

My long cherished childhood dream of performing onstage was finally realized, and thus sated forevermore. For years I described myself in news biographies and interviews as a "blighted Bernhardt." I'd best stick to writing my novels and short stories. Sometimes you have to have something placed squarely in your grasp before you realize you don't really need it at all.

Opening night, and my New York friends visited *before* the show—not afterward, as custom demanded. *Before* the show— ostensibly to wish that I break a leg. But, in truth, they feared, this body of cowardly souls, that my acting would be so dreadful, so humiliating, that it were best to *avoid* me when the curtain came down. I viewed this all with appropriate jaundiced eye and accepted their well wishes and premature huzzahs in good sport. What choice did I have? George's wife Bea trooped in with Aleck Woollcott, who commented that my stage makeup as Fanny Cavendish suggested how I'd look someday in a velvet-lined coffin because my face seemed a Halloween specter. To which I shot back, "Dear Aleck, my garish face can be scrubbed off with a hot face cloth. That's one advantage I have over you." He fussed and chortled, and I sensed one of our chronic and public feuds in the offing. Bea sighed and said flatly, "New Jersey seems to make you two talk like you're on a grammar school playground."

Telegrams in my dressing room: "Love and Kisses to the Connecticut Duse"—from Alisa and Russell Crouse. "Gaylord Ravelstein Wishes Fanny Cavendish Great Success"—from Moss Hart.

Yet that first night—and the following week—the dust of the previous days lingered, collected around the corners of my long hours. The deaths of Evan and Gus threw dark shadows into the Maplewood Theater. *The Royal Family* is a sprightly, sophisticated account of a venerable Broadway family—not, I insist again, the Barrymores—and the audiences roared and clapped and stood on their feet. Yet there I was, delivering lines George and I had written, waiting for the necessary laugh…and yet behind me, like some elusive specter, Evan and Gus haunted. Men of questionable virtue, perhaps, but nevertheless men who did not deserve their moments of dying chosen for them. No, indeed! I really didn't know them, but of course I did: we meet them every day of our lives.

So the week went on, and I discovered I was colossally bored by acting. What nagged was the awful routine—arrival at the theater, enduring the makeup, spouting the same lines night after night (and two matinees). Tedious, I learned, and numbing. I welcomed the end of the run. Those poor souls who act a part for a year or more, night after night, oblivion, the absolute abyss of boredom. Not for me, though I looked at the actors who recited my lines with new appreciation and wonder. When the week ended and I made my final bow, my final curtain, I could have wept for joy.

That week, and the month to follow, summer passed into fall, the rest of the story unfolded—sad, but, in a way, bittersweet.

Clorinda and Annika were taken away in a blaze of headlines and newsreels. Such is the price of fame and fortune that when you fall…well, the descent is long and spectacular. Icarus topples down and down into the blue waters. Yet Clorinda, perhaps a little maddened now, remained defiant and strident, not giving a modicum of remorse, her behavior somehow justified in the eyes of the God she created for the hopeful. In court she stood wild-eyed, arms flailing, and spouted Old Testament maxims, a steady flow of them that ignored the judge's straightforward questions. She held one hand up and toward the high-placed windows in the chambers, and she announced that the coming world war was God's punishment for what we had all done to her. "God doesn't like to see His angels in chains."

Tobias disappeared. There was a front-page photograph of him in the *Newark Press* as he stepped out the front entrance of the Assembly of God, his driver Alexander padlocking the edifice behind him. He looked small and wizened, his face sagging under the weight of his loss. For Tobias truly believed in his God as he believed in his beloved Clorinda as the emissary of that vengeful God. Smitten with her, the old crusty bachelor, he lavished diamonds and other baubles on her, believing that a decorated Clorinda would also dazzle the worshippers. Like a medieval European Papist cathedral, resplendent in stained glass and marble frieze and carved-wood altar, plopped down in the middle of an impoverished world. So, too, Clorinda, flying across a stage in swirling rainbow chiffon and diamonds that caught the celestial light, was a beacon for the hungry believer. The only problem was that those cathedrals continue to dazzle. Human fragility and woe pass.

So Tobias was shattered and abandoned his bride to the harsh judicial Fates. The Assembly of God was no more, the luxurious manicured grounds allowed to go to seed, birds nesting in the spire, feral dogs driving off the curious Sunday drivers who parked out front. And Tobias vanished with his millions, hiding away from reporters. One rumor said he retreated into a Park Avenue apartment, but who knows?

Reporters noted that he did not return to the homestead out on Burnett Terrace. Hidden out in the bushes, their cameras ready, they saw nothing. Or, rather, they glimpsed Ilona now and then, though her biting condemnation drove them back. At night, I was told, the vast mansion was buried in darkness, save for one light at the back of the house, one light in a back bedroom, Ilona's sanctuary. It stayed on all night long.

On my last afternoon in Maplewood, the set taken down, Cheryl Crawford at the Jefferson Village Inn sitting with Paul Robeson as they discussed the next production, *The Emperor Jones*, the brief moment of *The Royal Family* was over. Louis

Calhern and Irene Purcell ran for the train back to New York, luggage overhead.

George and I sat in the Full Moon Café, a valedictory lunch with Frank, Dak, and Nadine. Dak's invitation to us, which surprised. After the arrest of his mother and Annika, he became sullen, moody, almost angry. We left him alone, George and I, watching the sad young man grapple with yet another abandonment in his short life. During the week's run of *The Royal Family*, he stayed away from the theater, and Frank simply shook his head when I asked about Dak. "Time." One word from Frank. "Time."

So as George and I prepared to leave, Dak called us to the Full Moon Café where Mamie Trout, once a visitor to Clorinda's puritanical religion, seemed a little distant. Yet she was graceful. George swooned over her apple crumble—the man who was indifferent to food—and she brightened and offered him another slice.

"I visited Annika," Dak began.

We waited. I watched Dak get teary-eyed, turning his head away. He rubbed his eyes with the back of his wrist. Nadine reached over and touched his arm.

"A sad, sad young girl." My benediction.

George spoke softly. "And how is she?"

Dak forced a wistful smile. "She wouldn't see me, so I came away."

At the time of Annika's arrest, she'd pulled herself into the oversized chair, hugging her knees up against her chest, her head dipped out of sight. I thought of a beaten pet, cowering, closing itself off, retreating. Annika, that bright young zealot so passionately devoted to Clorinda, had revealed the cracks in that world. The cloudiness in her eyes. But in the last days, as she realized what she'd done—and the wrongness of it—those cracks widened, ate into her, until she was without focus. Shattered, ruined. The awful deed she'd perpetrated ate into her. Taken away like a hesitant lamb, she sobbed quietly. My heart went out to her, of course, this lovely girl.

A day later, in a screaming jag, she had a terrible breakdown, attempted to take her own life, and was sent to the asylum in Newark. There, numbed by whatever medication given her, she stared at the cement wall.

"I wanted to see her," Dak went on.

"This is not your fault." I looked into Dak's eyes.

"Some part of me says it is."

"No," I stormed. "This story has lots of victims, and you're one of them. Annika, weak and hungry, listened to a powerful voice that made her kill. She was looking for a mother but found a…a dictator."

"Still…"

I held up my hand. "You have a chance to create a happy life now, Dak. Do it."

He smiled. "We will." He looked at Nadine. "That powerful voice made me leave Nadine. It won't happen again."

Nadine was nodding at him. "We're going to be married again."

"In the Congregational Church I attended as a boy. Before the loving God I remember from my early childhood."

George pointed a finger at Frank. "And maybe you've found a father, Dak."

Dak grinned like a little boy. "Of course, I have."

Frank had a catch in his throat. "Well, we don't know for certain."

Dak stopped him. "I do. That's all that matters."

That night I was back in my Connecticut house atop that tree-covered hill in Easton, my refuge from the world. Early evening, I sat alone on the stone terrace and watched night fall on the rolling hills. Lush and deep green, the garden lay before me. My housekeeper had prepared a succulent salad with the overripe tomatoes and leaf lettuce from my own garden. I had a bowl of sweet peaches in cream, the luscious fruit bought at the market near the train station. Satisfied, a night I'd longed for. Not the clamor and shriek of Manhattan that I'd given up last year, the

Final Curtain 273

spurt of buses and the noxious fumes of squealing taxis. No, here was a night so quiet with only the hum of insects in the bushes, fireflies lighting on the hedges, the sporadic click-click of the persistent crickets. The heat of the August day gone now, a cool breeze like a zephyr swooping down from the massive oak trees on the hills that surrounded me.

But I couldn't rest. Idly, through my solitary supper, I'd leafed through the day's *New York Times.* Again, the horror of Europe slapped me in the face. Hitler's marauding troops. Capitulation. Despair. Death. All that grief before me. The horror of the last decade as I watched that madman assume power—the moustached dictator—until, at last, the invasion of Poland. The end of Czechoslovakia. The Third Reich. The Battle of Britain. The end of it all.

On the front page of the *Times* was an article about another Nazi rally in Union Square, and there, forefront, was a grainy but recognizable snapshot of Meaka Snow. The camera caught her facing off a protester, her hateful sign slung back over her shoulder. The photographer caught the blankness of her stare. I'd dropped the newspaper to the ground, dismayed. The message on her placard was hard to decipher but one word was evident: *Jew.*

Tonight in Yorkville the German-American Bund was marching. *Juden.*

Tanks plodded through the stark fields of France.

A catastrophic war was coming, unavoidable. My body ached with the horror of it. But my mind kept circling back to the murders in Maplewood. Annika's woeful face haunted me as she was led away: the devout believer, the humble follower, betrayed. The faces of Evan Street and Gus Schnelling came to me. So, finally, justice prevailed. The failed Nazi and the amoral gigolo. The soulless and the cruel. Yet perhaps a moment of grace for the two young lovers and the hopeful father. A sweet ending, there. But a story of a woman who strutted her moment on a stage and then was seen there no more. Justice won, though horribly. The price of freedom. America covers us all, and safeguards. Wrongs righted. An American story.

That story would have to save the world now.

A light rain began to fall. I sat on the terrace. The breezes picked up. Somewhere an owl hooted, and the trees shivered under the rush of rain. I looked up at the wet dark sky and felt a wave of peace move through me. But I waited, my eyes moist, for the world to fall apart.

To receive a free catalog of Poisoned Pen Press titles, please contact us in one of the following ways:

Phone: 1-800-421-3976
Facsimile: 1-480-949-1707
Email: info@poisonedpenpress.com
Website: www.poisonedpenpress.com

Poisoned Pen Press
6962 E. First Ave. Ste 103
Scottsdale, AZ 85251